TREE MAIL

D1301143

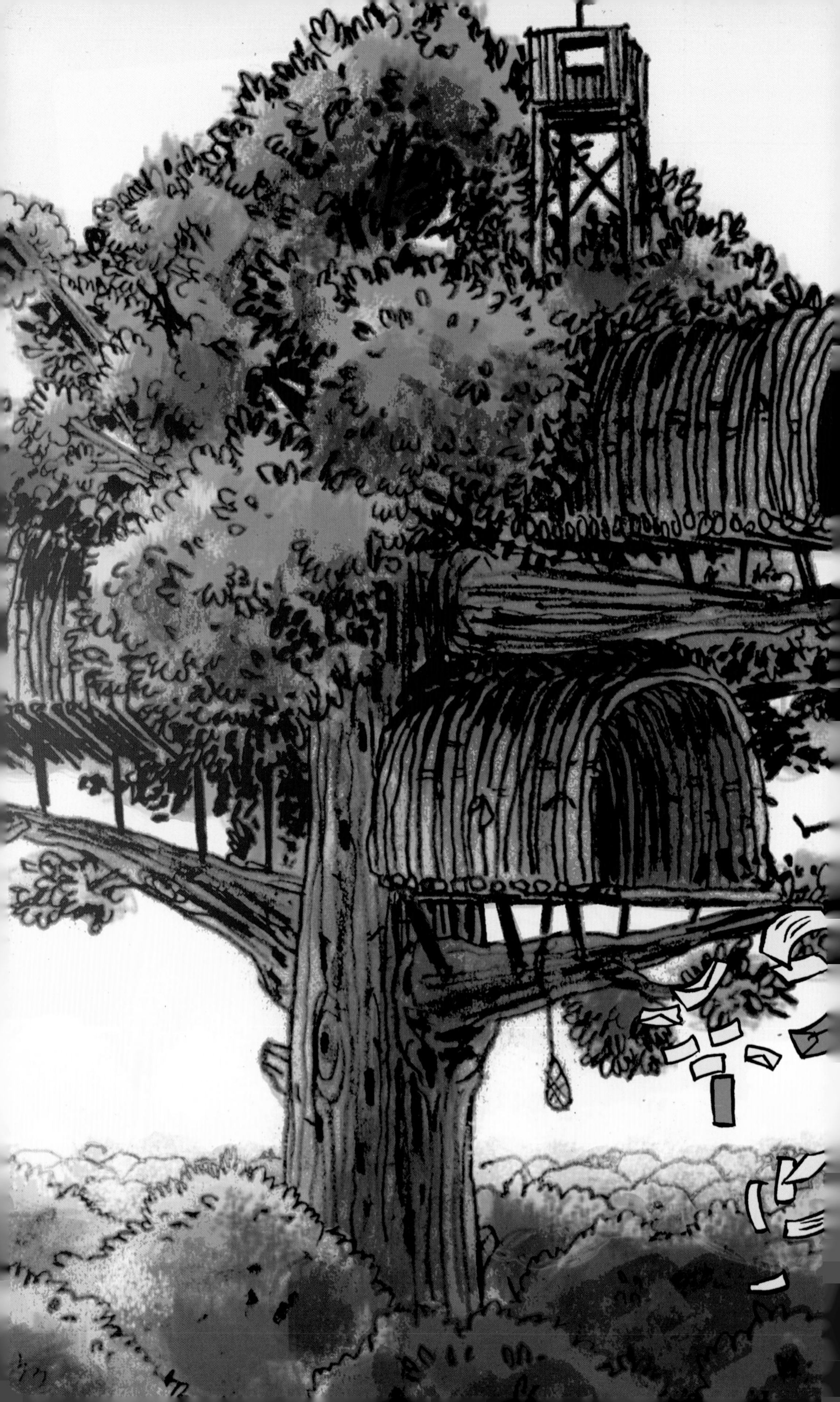

TREE MAIL ™

CREATED AND WRITTEN BY
Brian Smith and Mike Raicht

ART AND COLORS BY
Brian Smith

LETTERING BY
Sarah Smith

SPECIAL THANKS TO
Austin Harrison and Zach Howard at Noble Transmission Group, LLC

DARK HORSE BOOKS

PUBLISHER
Mike Richardson

EDITOR
Philip R. Simon

DESIGNER
Ethan Kimberling

DIGITAL ART TECHNICIAN
Melissa Martin

TREE MAIL

Tree Mail ™ © 2016 Brian Smith and Noble Transmission Group, LLC. All rights reserved. Dark Horse Books® and the Dark Horse logo are registered trademarks of Dark Horse Comics, Inc. All rights reserved. No portion of this publication may be reproduced or transmitted, in any form or by any means, without the express written permission of Dark Horse Comics, Inc. Names, characters, places, and incidents featured in this publication either are the product of the author's imagination or are used fictitiously. Any resemblance to actual persons (living or dead), events, institutions, or locales, without satiric intent, is coincidental.

Published by
Dark Horse Books
A division of Dark Horse Comics, Inc.
10956 SE Main Street
Milwaukie, OR 97222

DarkHorse.com | NobleTransmission.com

Tree Mail has been developed and funded in collaboration with Noble Transmission, a comic book entertainment company for the digital age co-founded with the mission to deliver engaging content and "characters with character" that inspire.

To find a comics shop in your area, call the Comic Shop Locator Service toll-free at 1-888-266-4226

First edition: November 2016
ISBN 978-1-50670-096-0

1 3 5 7 9 10 8 6 4 2

Printed in China

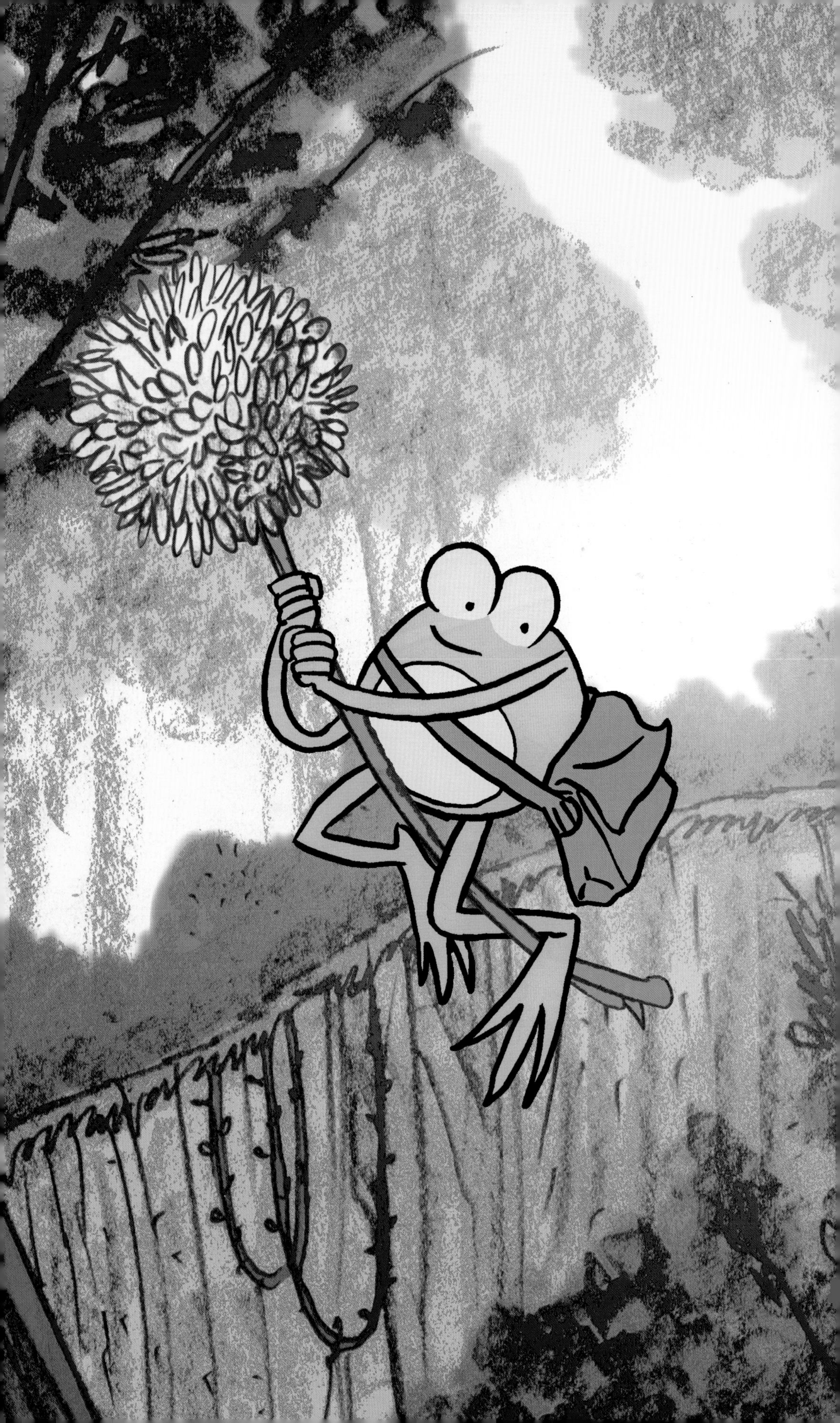

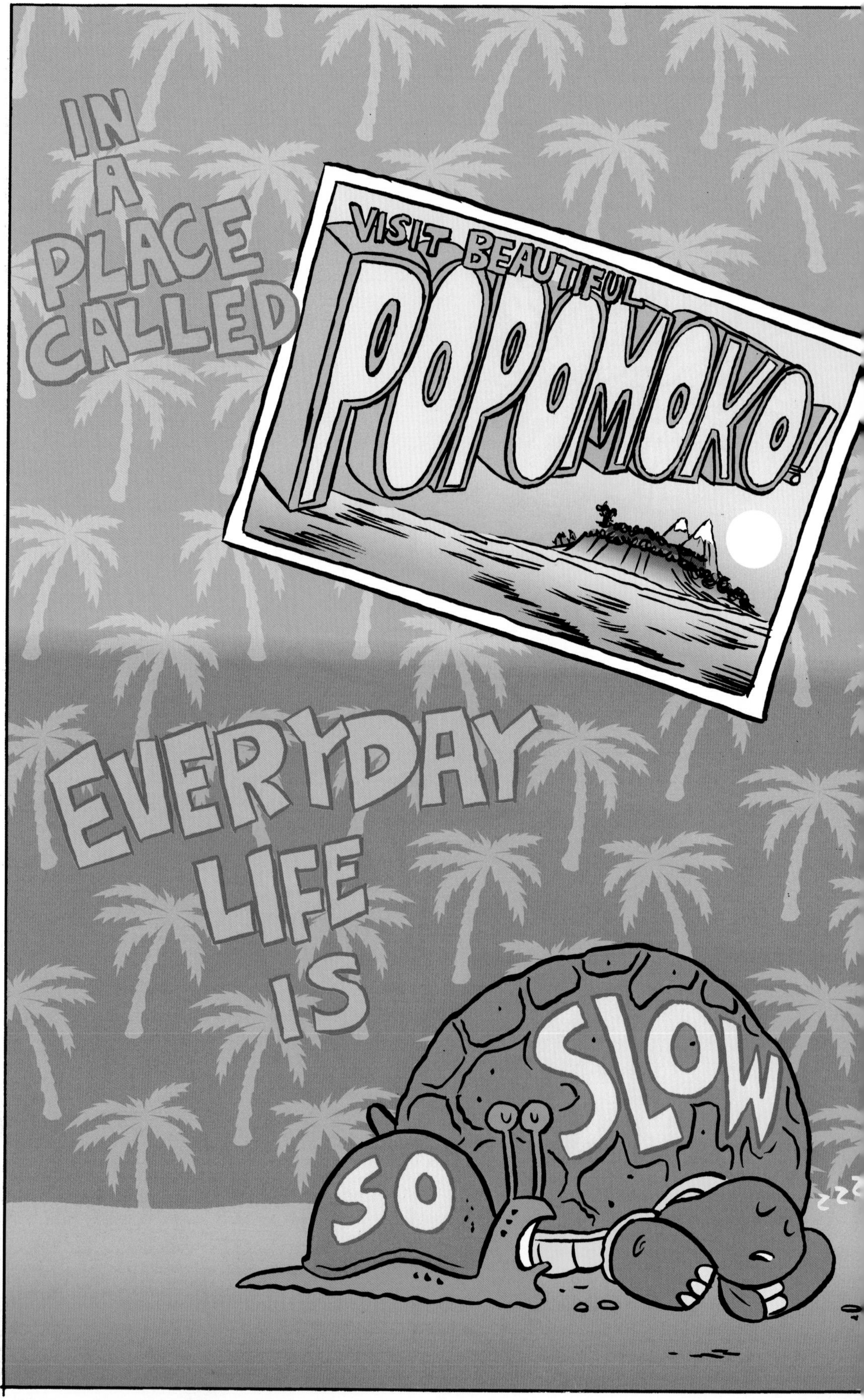
IN A PLACE CALLED
VISIT BEAUTIFUL
POPOMOKO!
EVERYDAY LIFE IS
SO SLOW

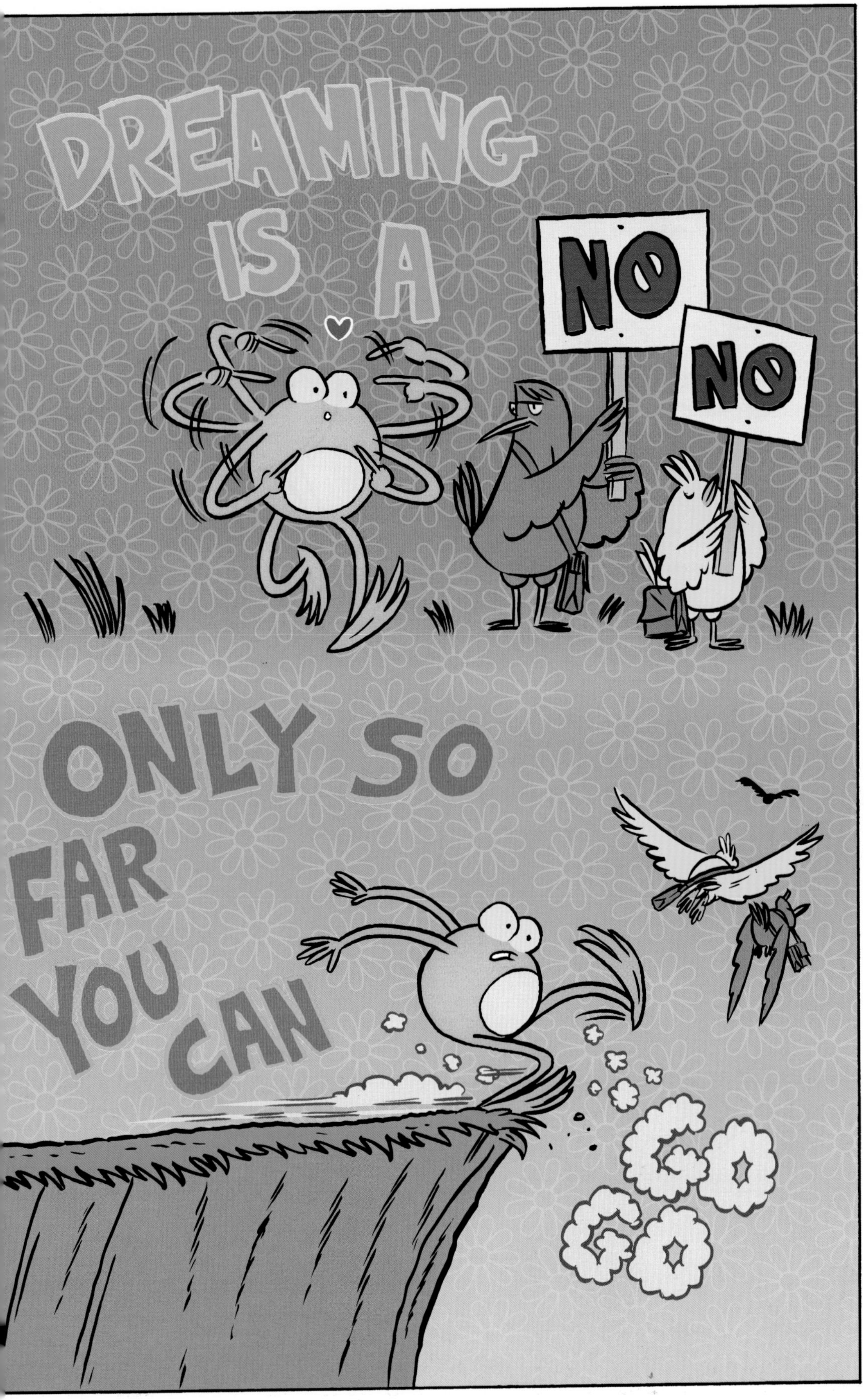
DREAMING IS A
NO
NO
ONLY SO FAR YOU CAN
GO GO

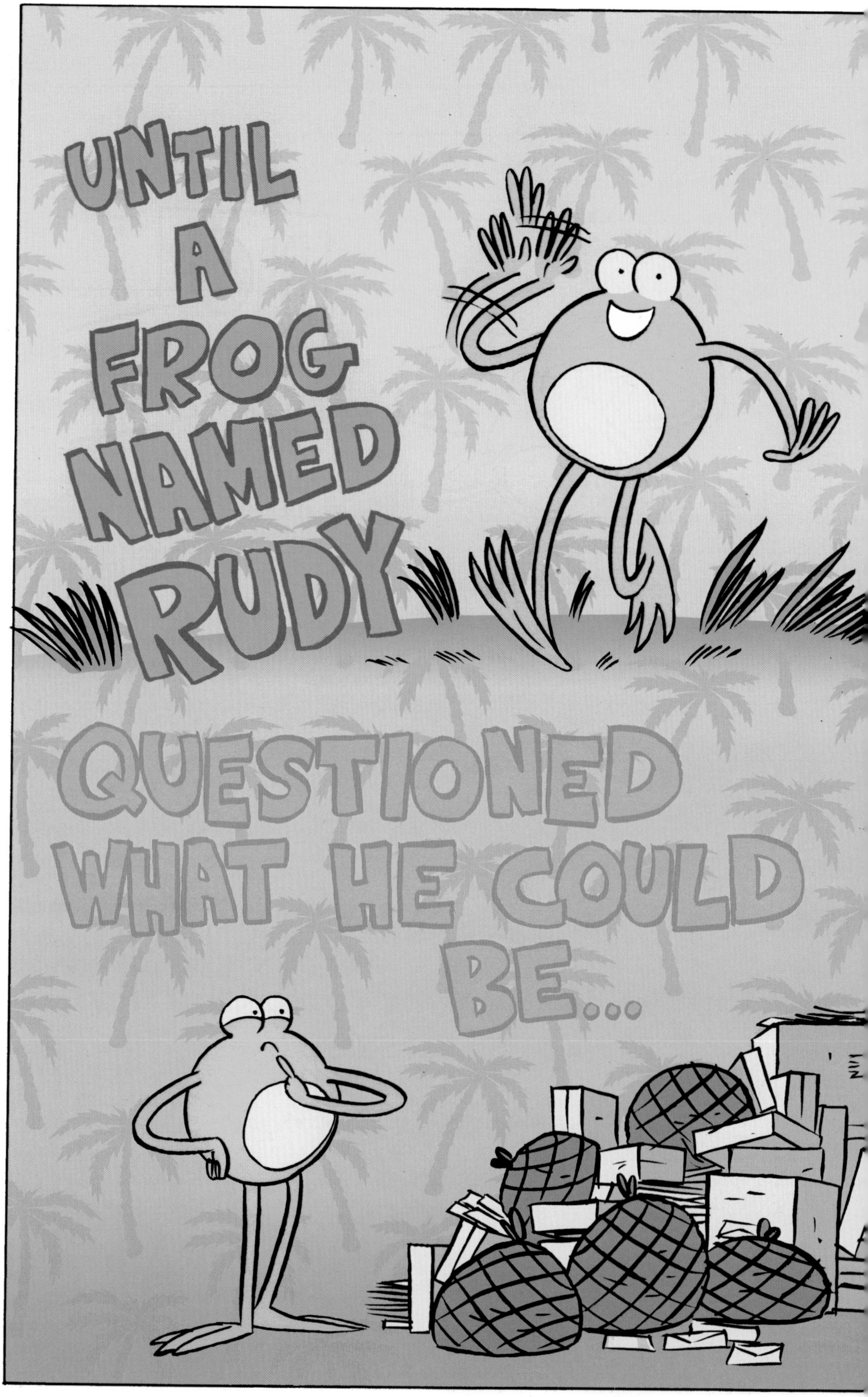
UNTIL A FROG NAMED RUDY
QUESTIONED WHAT HE COULD BE...

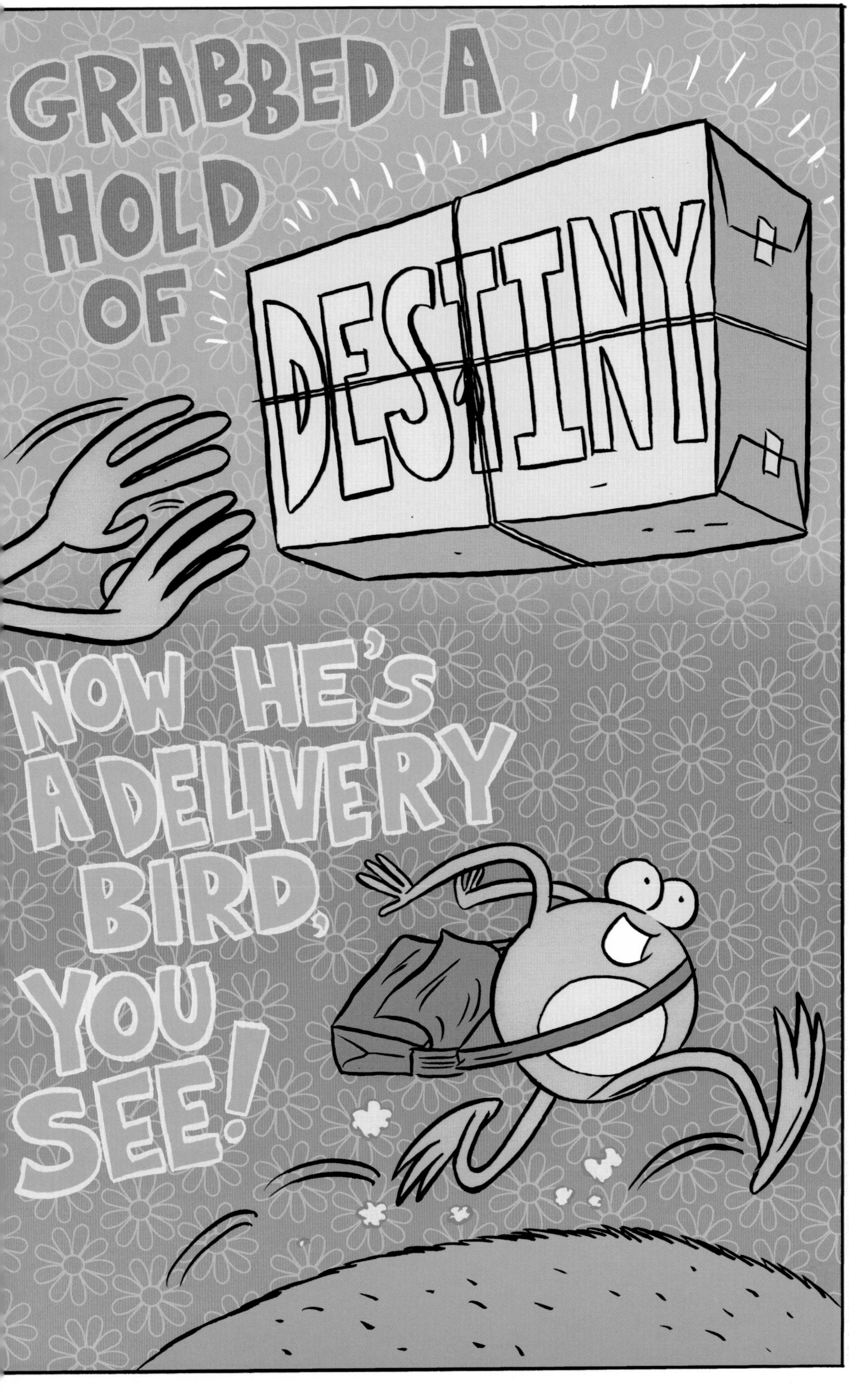
GRABBED A HOLD OF
DESTINY
NOW HE'S A DELIVERY BIRD, YOU SEE!

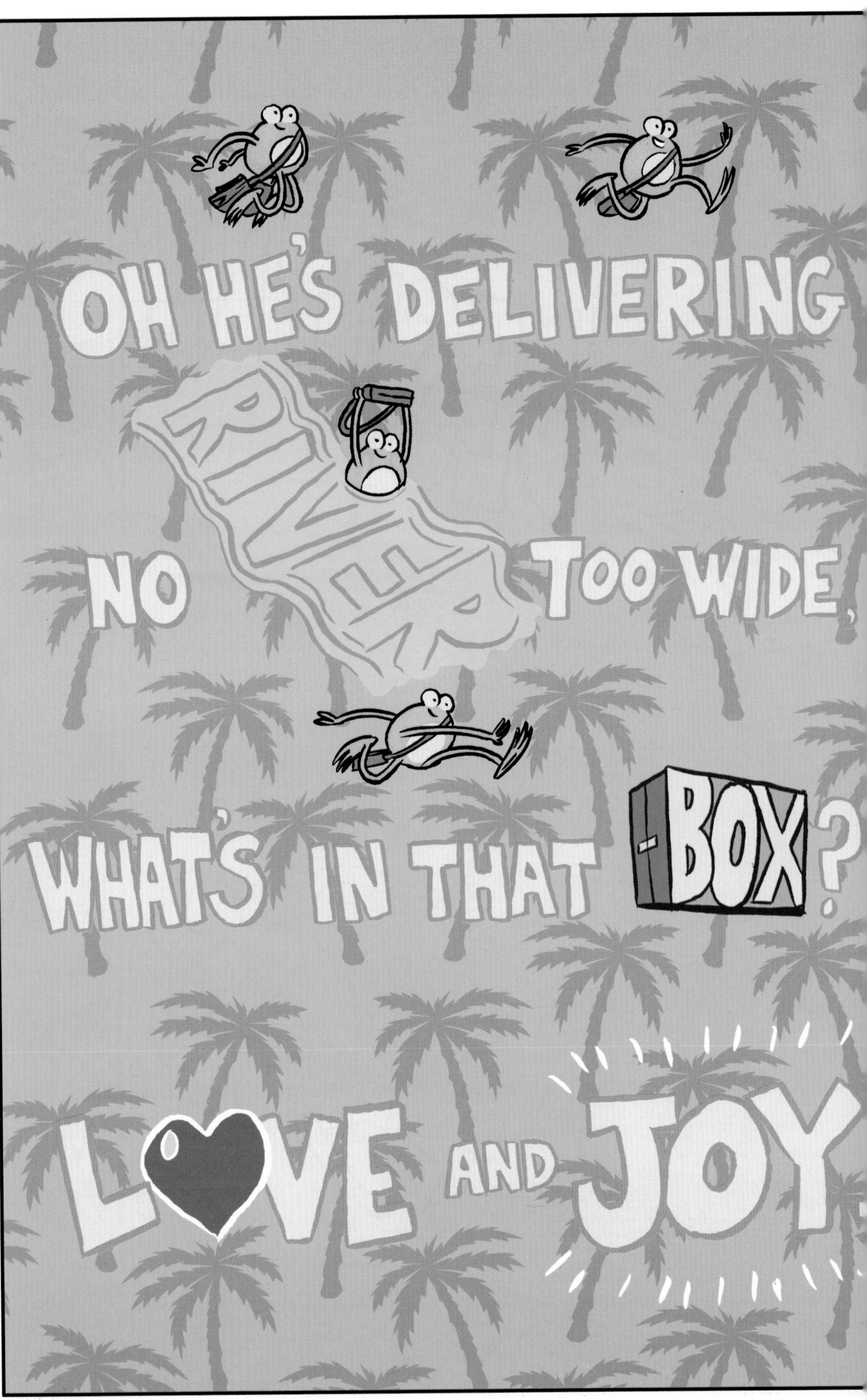
OH HE'S DELIVERING
NO RIVER TOO WIDE,
WHAT'S IN THAT BOX?
LOVE AND JOY

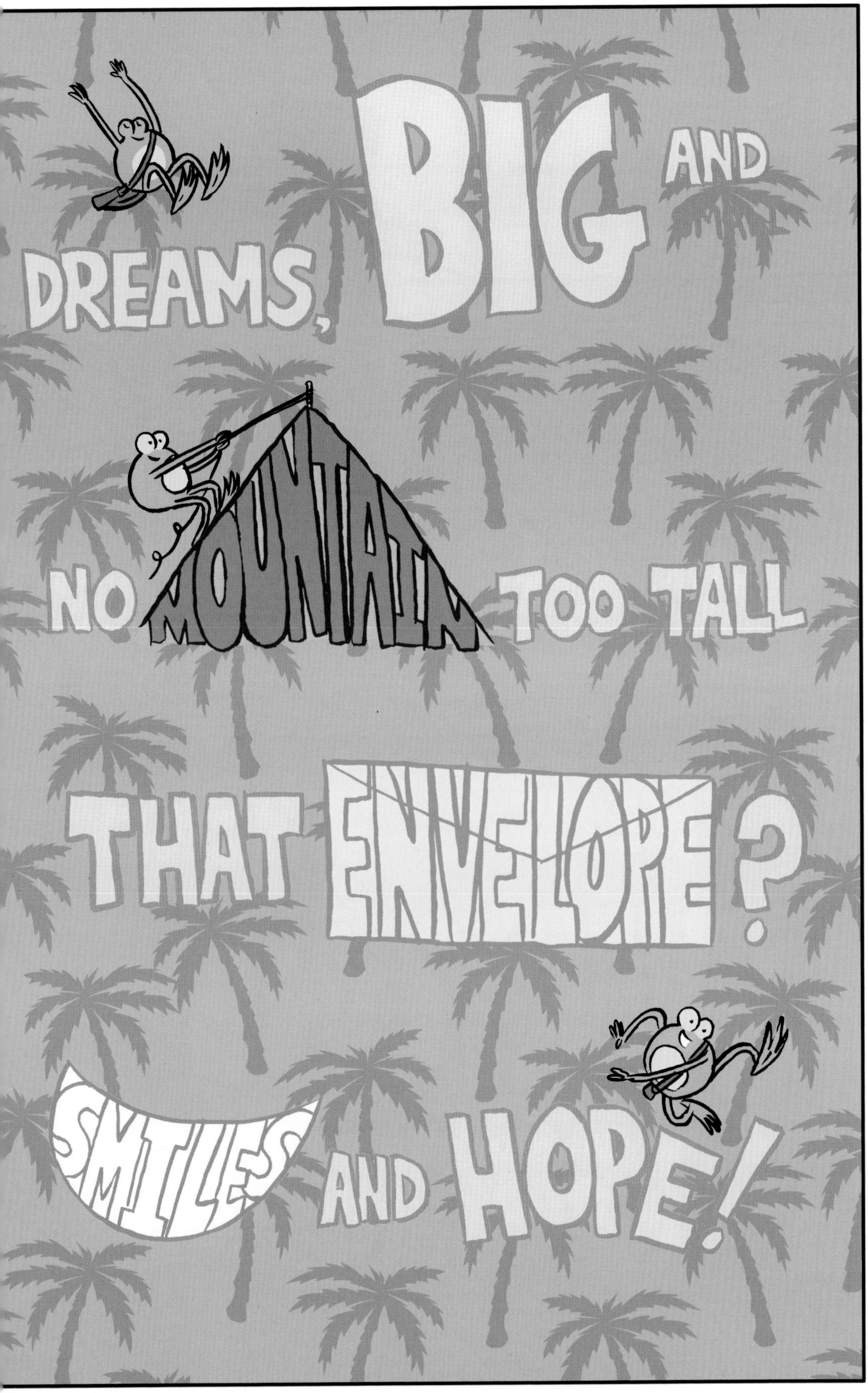
BIG DREAMS, AND
NO MOUNTAIN TOO TALL
THAT ENVELOPE?
SMILES AND HOPE!

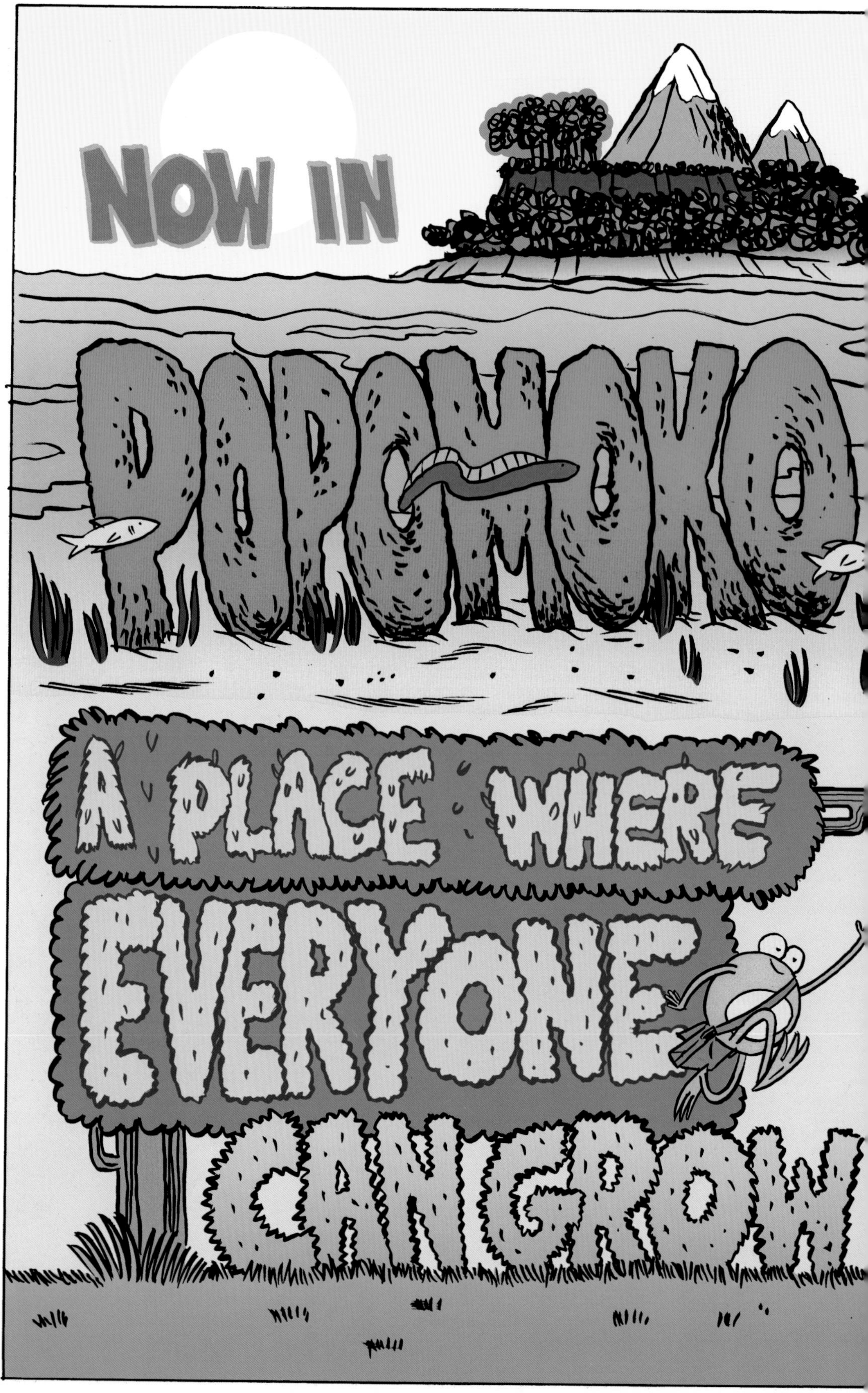
NOW IN
POPCMOKO
A PLACE WHERE
EVERYONE
CAN GROW

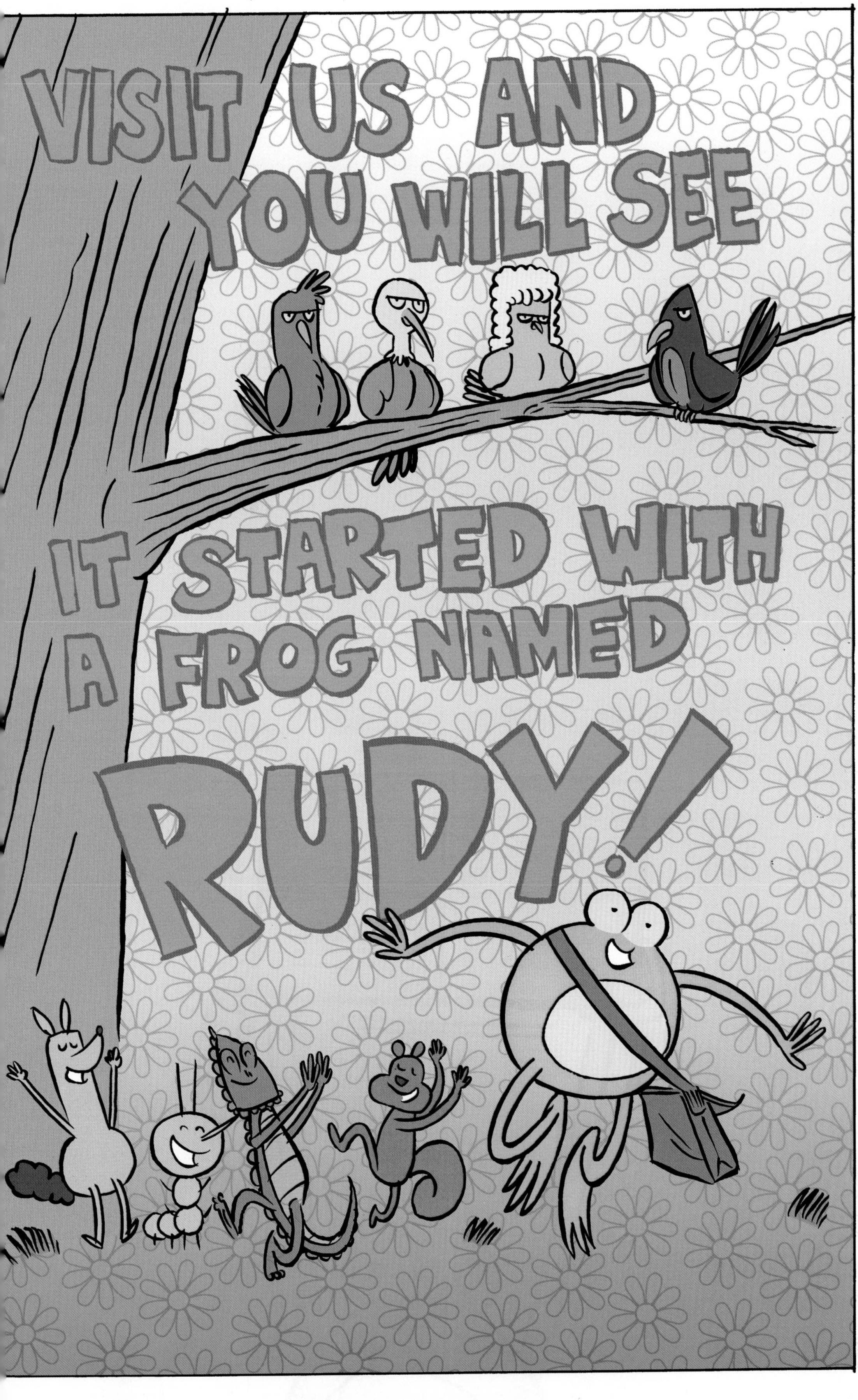
VISIT US AND YOU WILL SEE
IT STARTED WITH A FROG NAMED
RUDY!

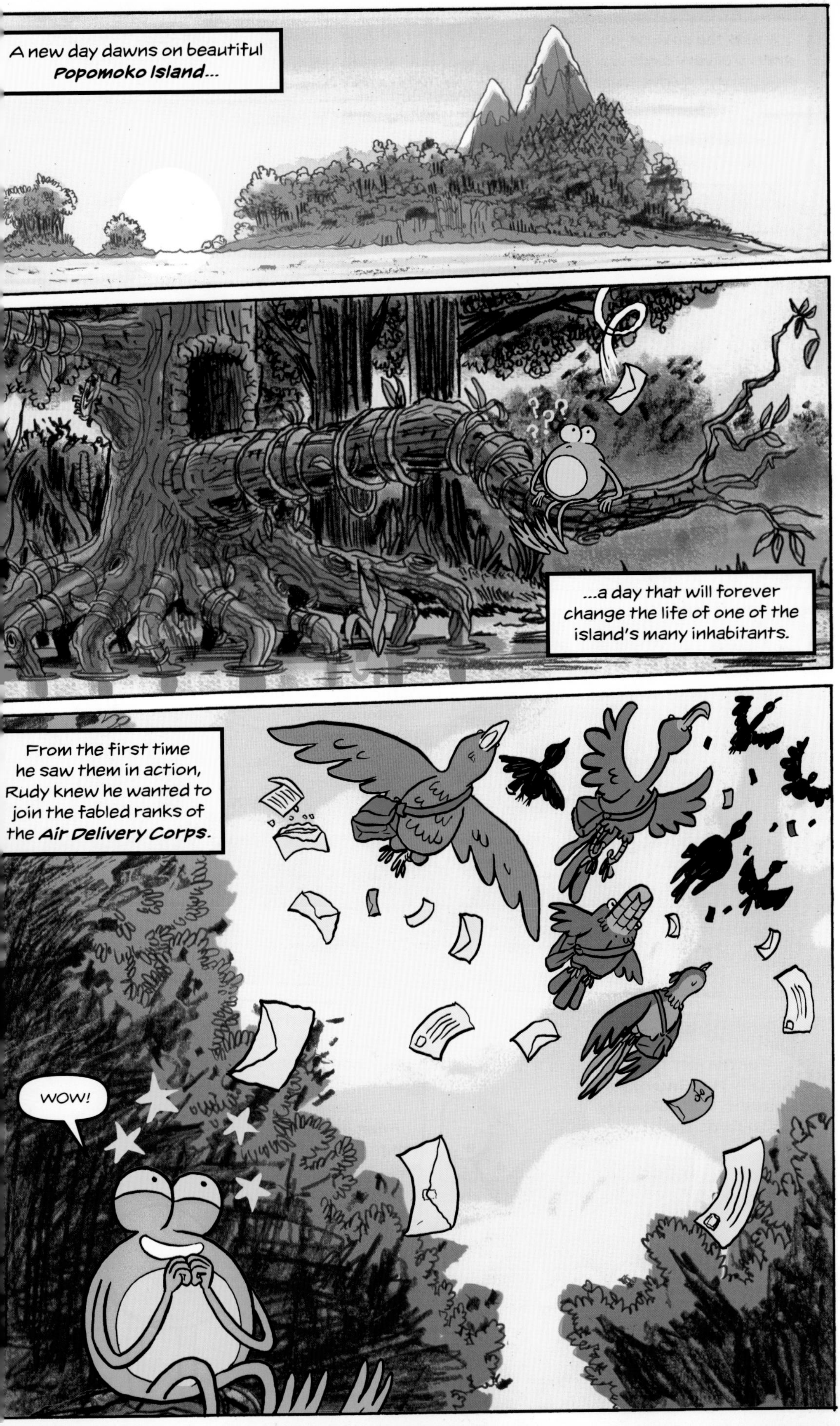

A new day dawns on beautiful *Popomoko Island*...
...a day that will forever change the life of one of the island's many inhabitants.
From the first time he saw them in action, Rudy knew he wanted to join the fabled ranks of the *Air Delivery Corps*.
WOW!

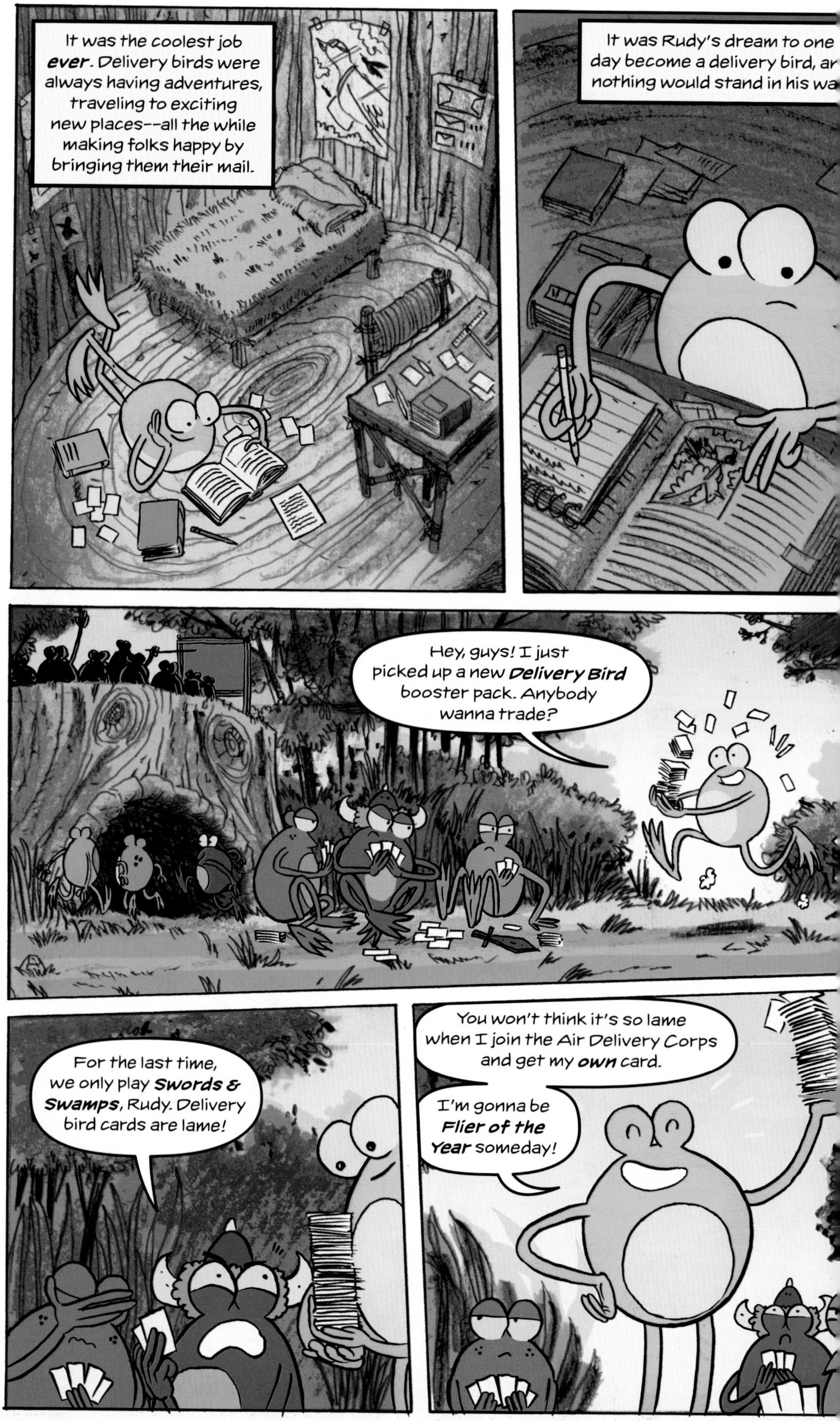
It was the coolest job **ever**. Delivery birds were always having adventures, traveling to exciting new places--all the while making folks happy by bringing them their mail.
It was Rudy's dream to one day become a delivery bird, ar nothing would stand in his wa
Hey, guys! I just picked up a new **Delivery Bird** booster pack. Anybody wanna trade?
For the last time, we only play **Swords & Swamps**, Rudy. Delivery bird cards are lame!
You won't think it's so lame when I join the Air Delivery Corps and get my **own** card.
I'm gonna be **Flier of the Year** someday!

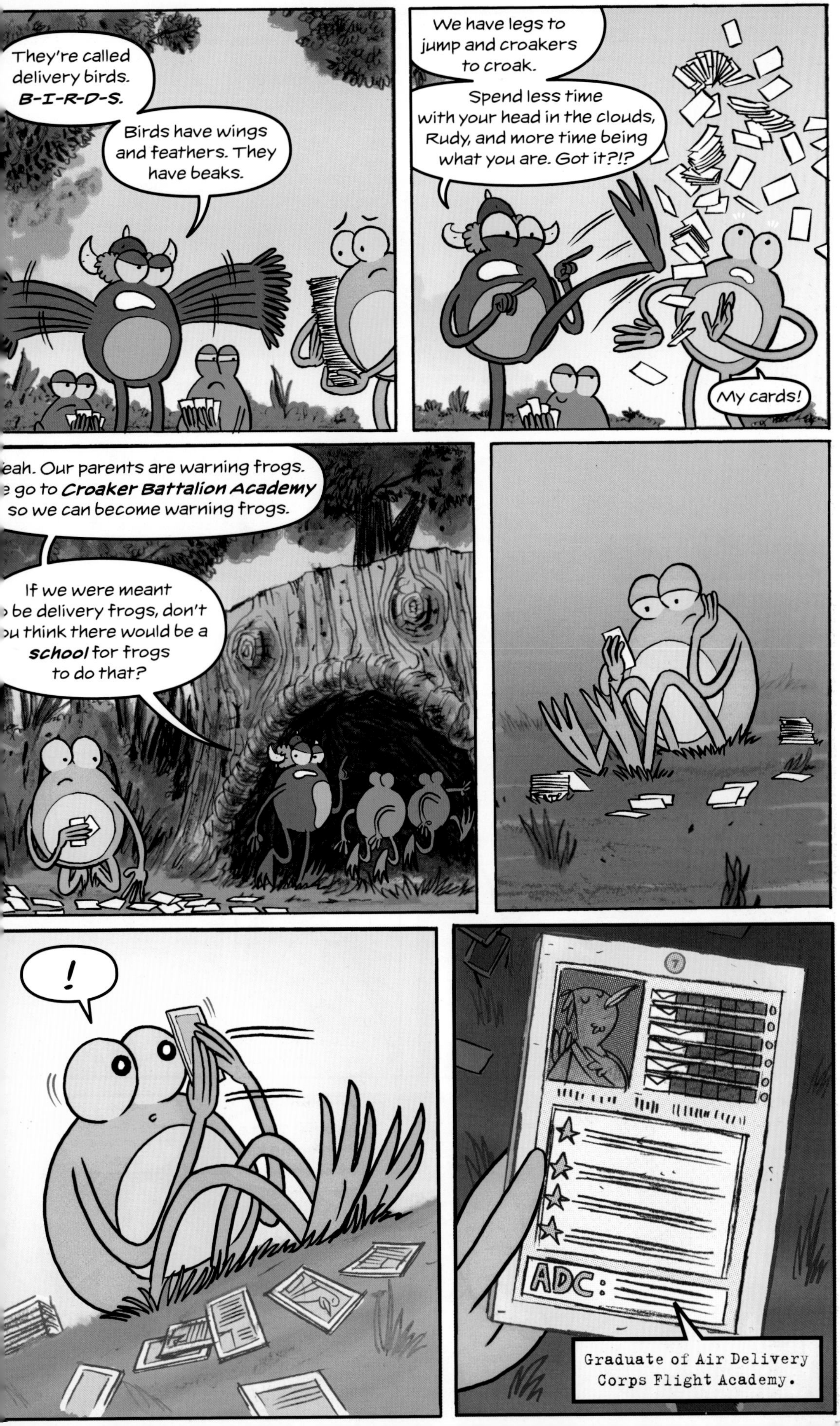
They're called delivery birds. B-I-R-D-S.
Birds have wings and feathers. They have beaks.
We have legs to jump and croakers to croak.
Spend less time with your head in the clouds, Rudy, and more time being what you are. Got it?!?
My cards!
eah. Our parents are warning frogs. e go to Croaker Battalion Academy so we can become warning frogs.
If we were meant be delivery frogs, don't u think there would be a school for frogs to do that?
!
ADC:
Graduate of Air Delivery Corps Flight Academy.

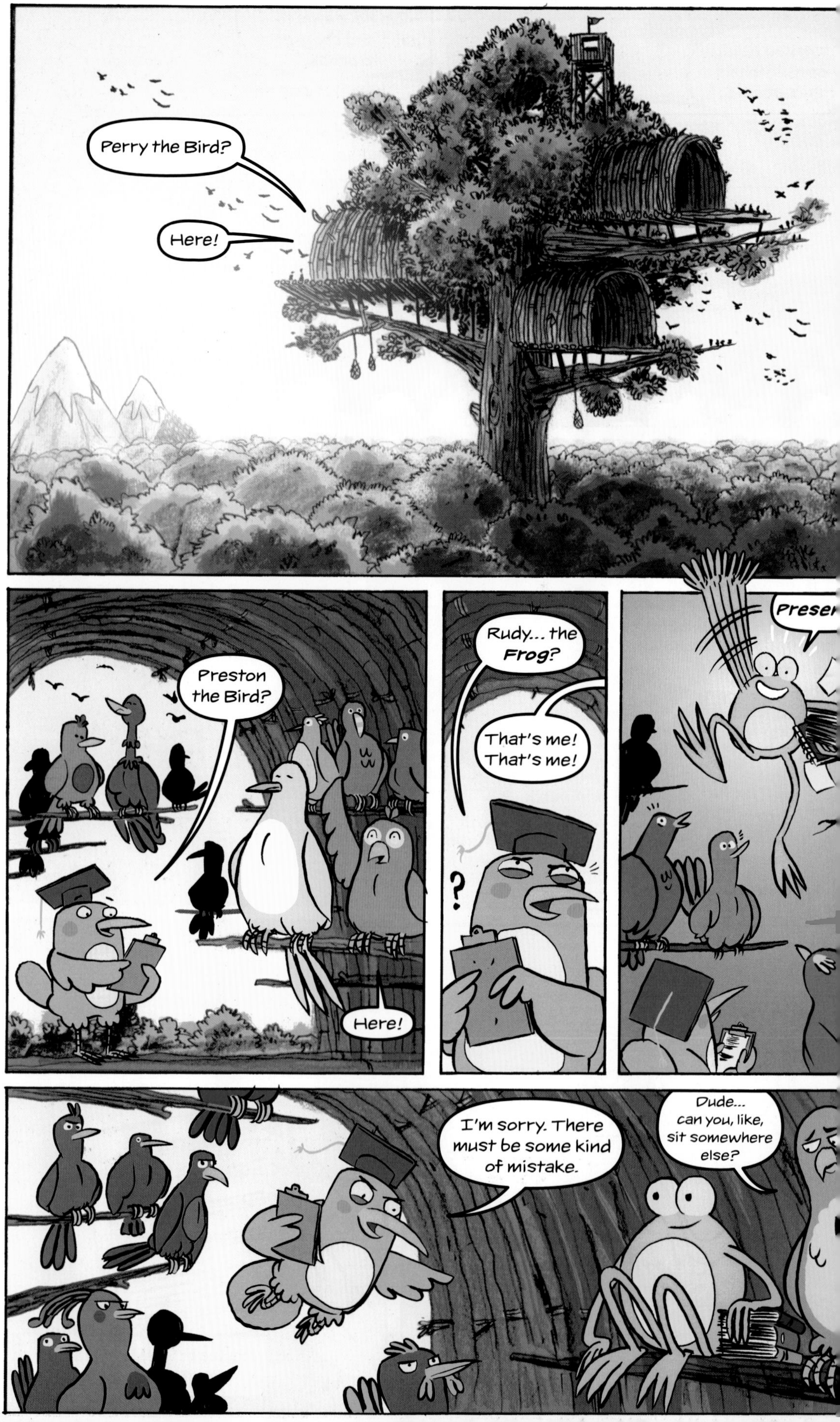
Perry the Bird?
Here!
Preston the Bird?
Here!
Rudy... the Frog?
That's me! That's me!
I'm sorry. There must be some kind of mistake.
Dude... can you, like, sit somewhere else?

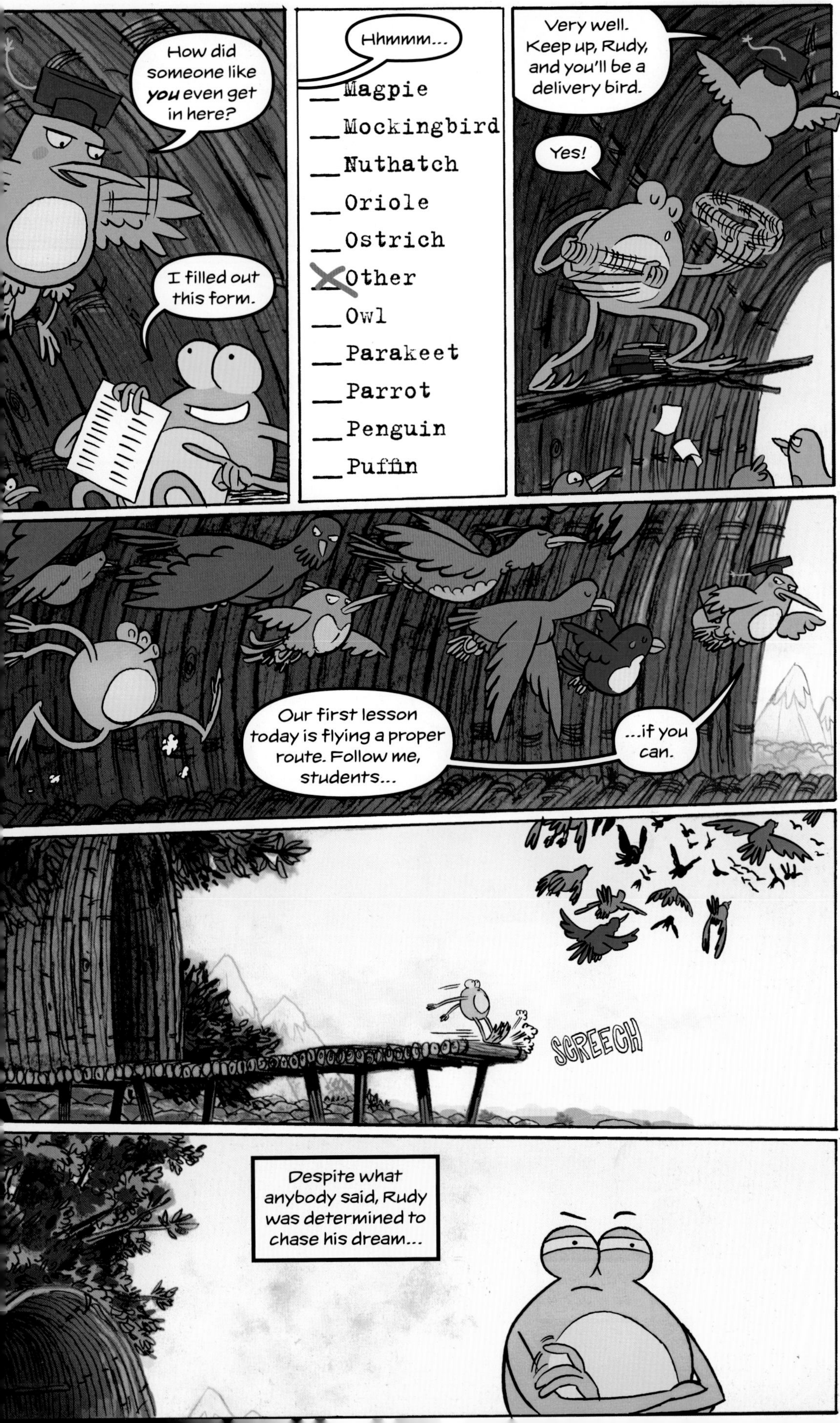
How did someone like *you* even get in here?
I filled out this form.
Hhmmm...
__Magpie
__Mockingbird
__Nuthatch
__Oriole
__Ostrich
X Other
__Owl
__Parakeet
__Parrot
__Penguin
__Puffin
Very well. Keep up, Rudy, and you'll be a delivery bird.
Yes!
Our first lesson today is flying a proper route. Follow me, students...
...if you can.
SCREECH
Despite what anybody said, Rudy was determined to chase his dream...

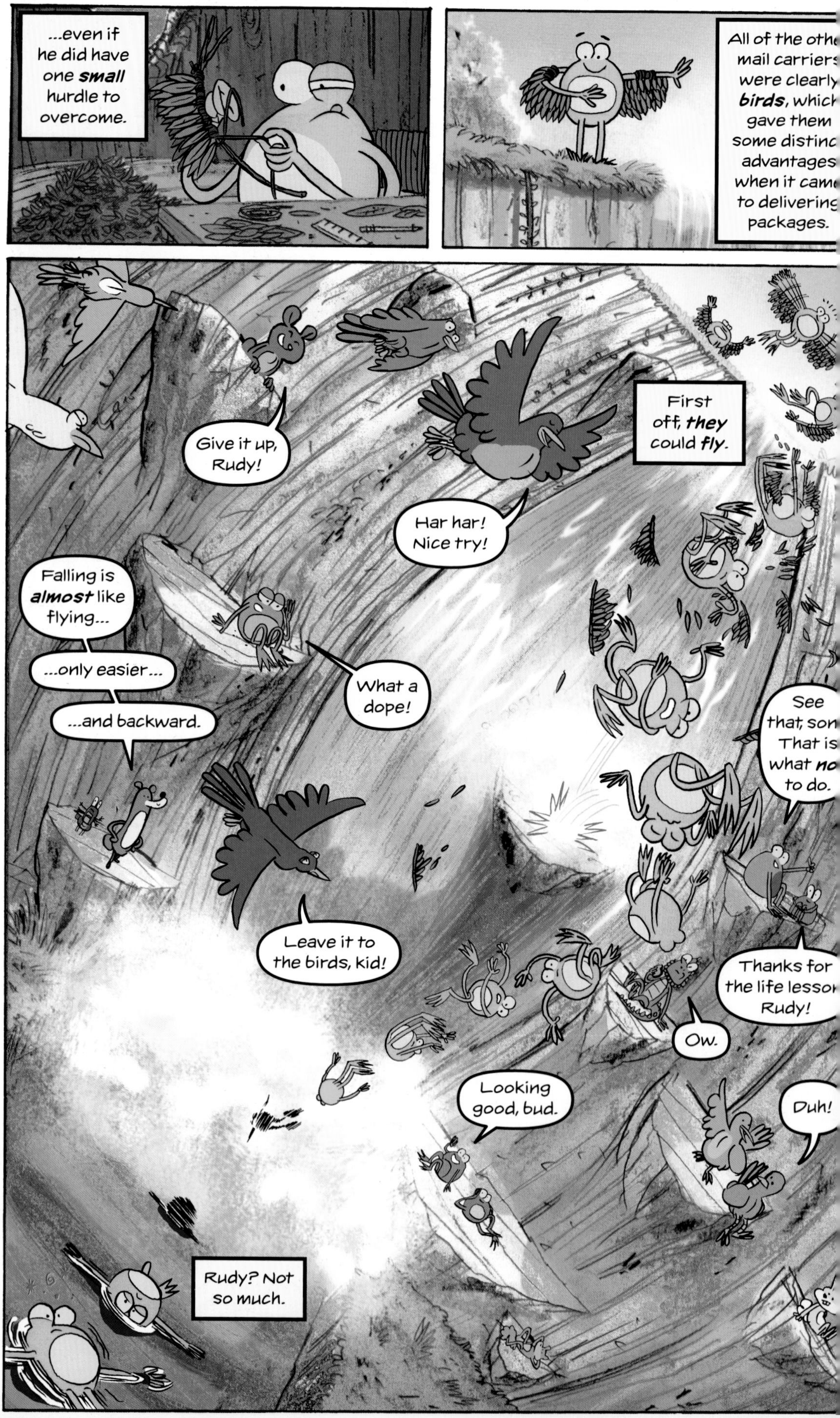
...even if he did have one ***small*** hurdle to overcome.
All of the othe mail carriers were clearly ***birds***, whic gave them some distinc advantages when it cam to delivering packages.
Give it up, Rudy!
First off, ***they*** could ***fly***.
Har har! Nice try!
Falling is ***almost*** like flying...
...only easier...
...and backward.
What a dope!
See that, son That is what ***no*** to do.
Leave it to the birds, kid!
Thanks for the life lesso Rudy!
Ow.
Looking good, bud.
Duh!
Rudy? Not so much.

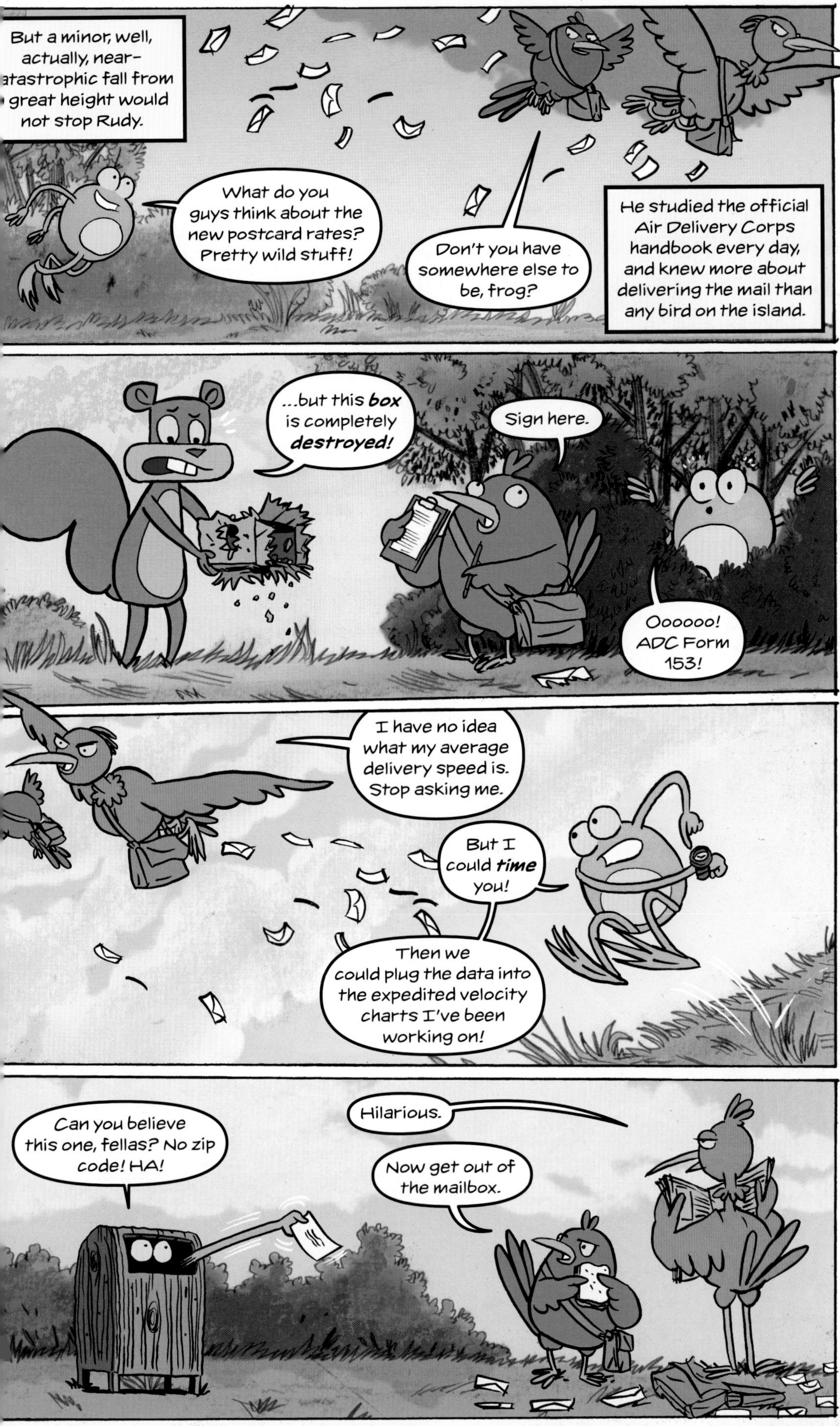
But a minor, well, actually, near-catastrophic fall from a great height would not stop Rudy.
What do you guys think about the new postcard rates? Pretty wild stuff!
Don't you have somewhere else to be, frog?
He studied the official Air Delivery Corps handbook every day, and knew more about delivering the mail than any bird on the island.
...but this **box** is completely ***destroyed!***
Sign here.
Oooooo! ADC Form 153!
I have no idea what my average delivery speed is. Stop asking me.
But I could ***time*** you!
Then we could plug the data into the expedited velocity charts I've been working on!
Can you believe this one, fellas? No zip code! HA!
Hilarious.
Now get out of the mailbox.

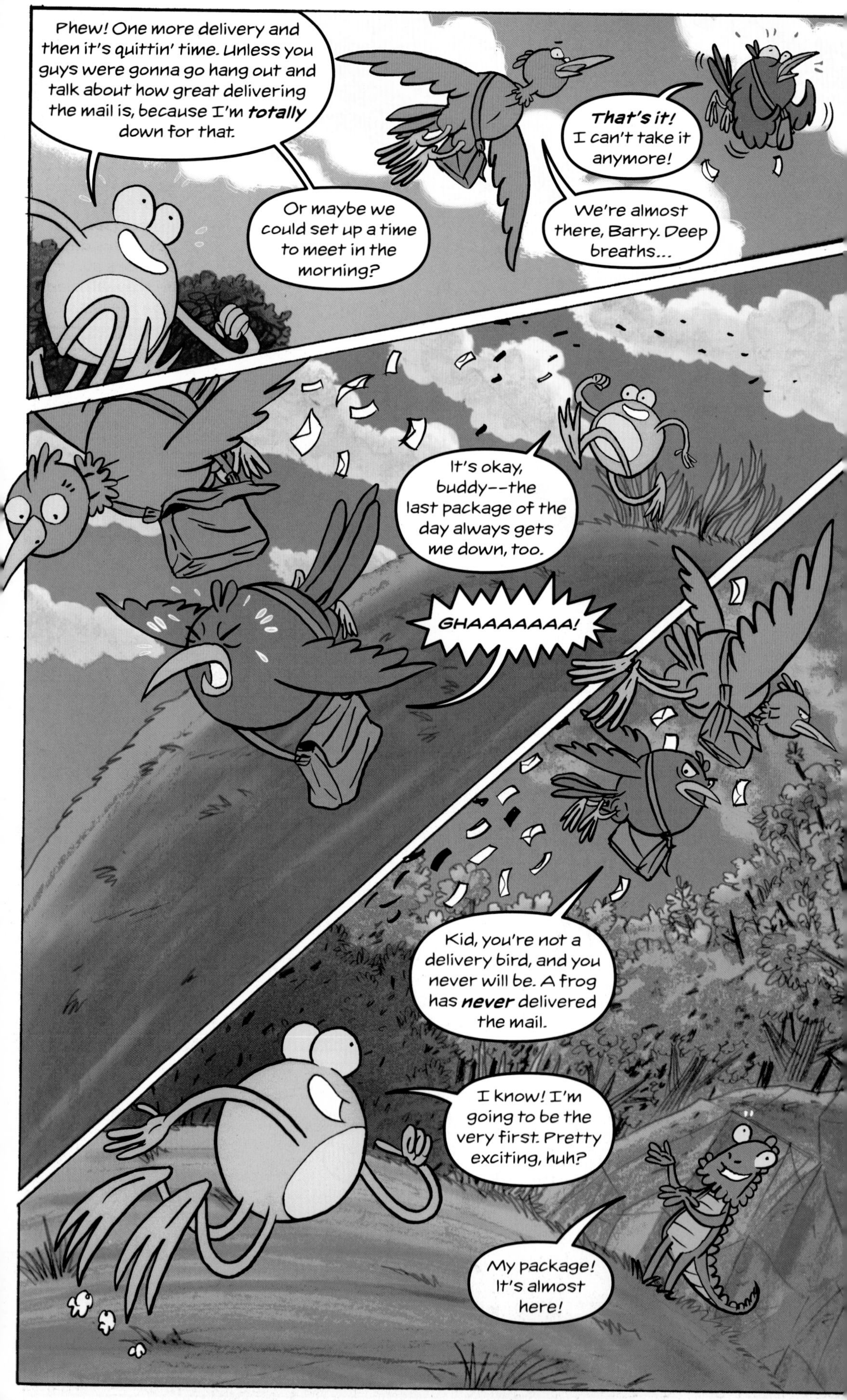
Phew! One more delivery and then it's quittin' time. Unless you guys were gonna go hang out and talk about how great delivering the mail is, because I'm **totally** down for that.
Or maybe we could set up a time to meet in the morning?
That's it! I can't take it anymore!
We're almost there, Barry. Deep breaths...
It's okay, buddy--the last package of the day always gets me down, too.
GHAAAAAAA!
Kid, you're not a delivery bird, and you never will be. A frog has **never** delivered the mail.
I know! I'm going to be the very first. Pretty exciting, huh?
My package! It's almost here!

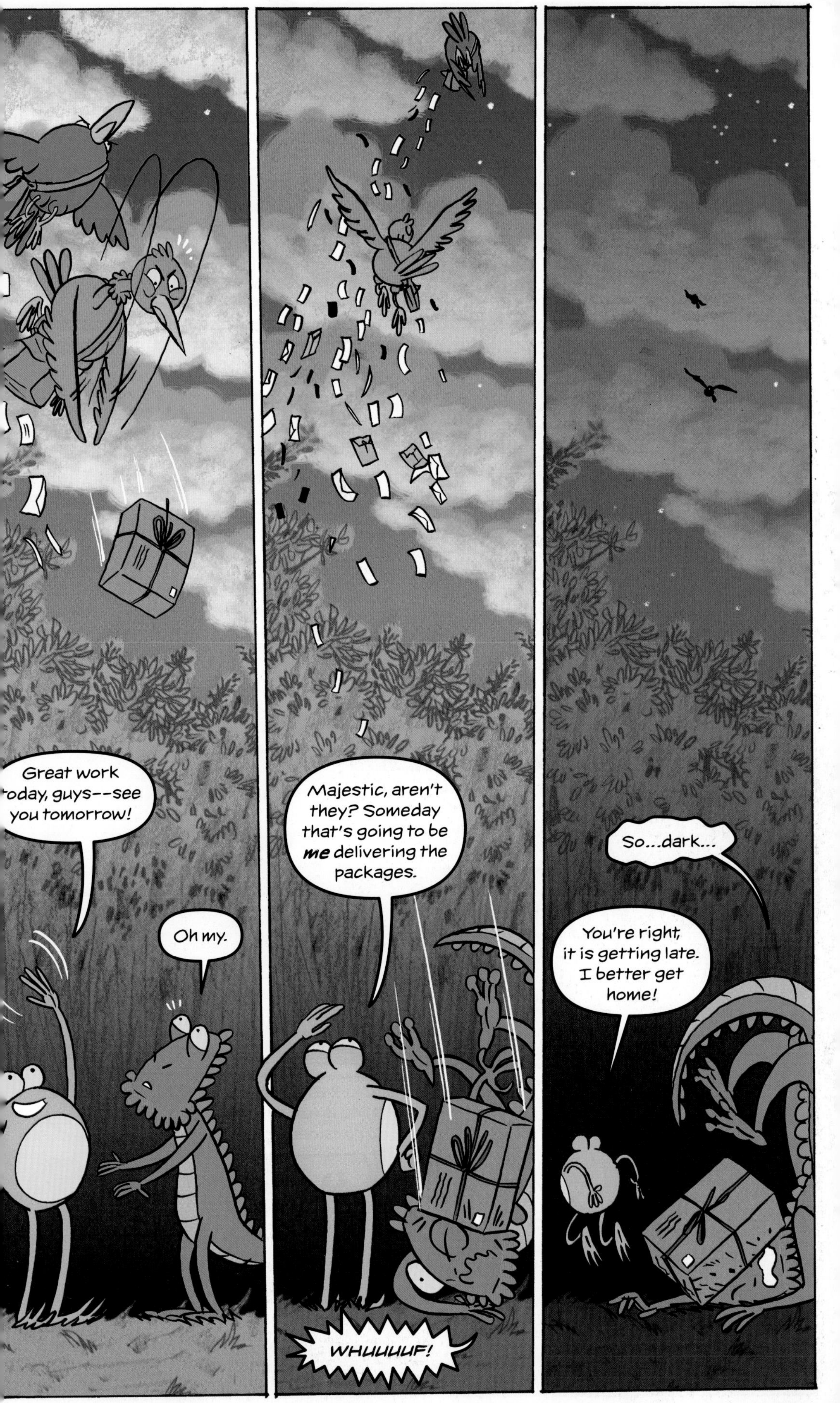
Great work
today, guys--see
you tomorrow!
Oh my.
Majestic, aren't they? Someday that's going to be *me* delivering the packages.
WHUUUUF!
So...dark...
You're right, it is getting late. I better get home!

Sweet papaya! That's it!

Rudy awoke the next morning with a brilliant idea hopping around in his head.

He had spent hours observing the birds in action on their routes, but in all that time Rudy had never *received* a package.

FWAP

TO: RUDY

If he sent package to himself, the delivery bird would have talk to him

Rudy could ask them a the question he wanted. Especially i he made it package he had to sign f on delivery

Rudy could barely contain his excitement as he approached the Air Delivery Corps office.

Ohboyohboy! Is this the line for deliveries? It's our lucky day, huh?

Lucky? Eight hours in this line is not something I consider lucky.

Now, please keep it down.

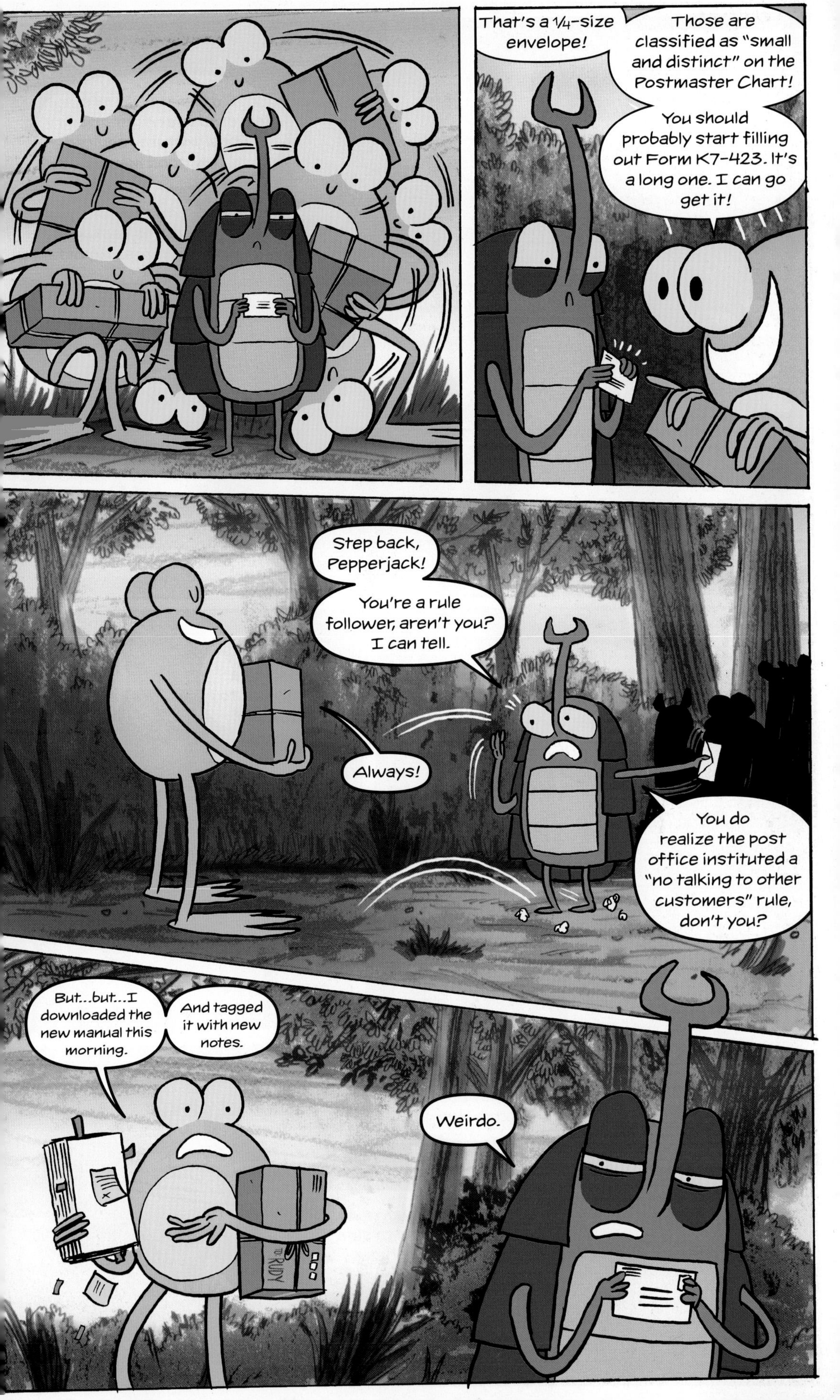
That's a 1/4-size envelope!
Those are classified as "small and distinct" on the Postmaster Chart!
You should probably start filling out Form K7-423. It's a long one. I can go get it!
Step back, Pepperjack!
You're a rule follower, aren't you? I can tell.
Always!
You do realize the post office instituted a "no talking to other customers" rule, don't you?
But...but...I downloaded the new manual this morning.
And tagged it with new notes.
Weirdo.
TO RUDY

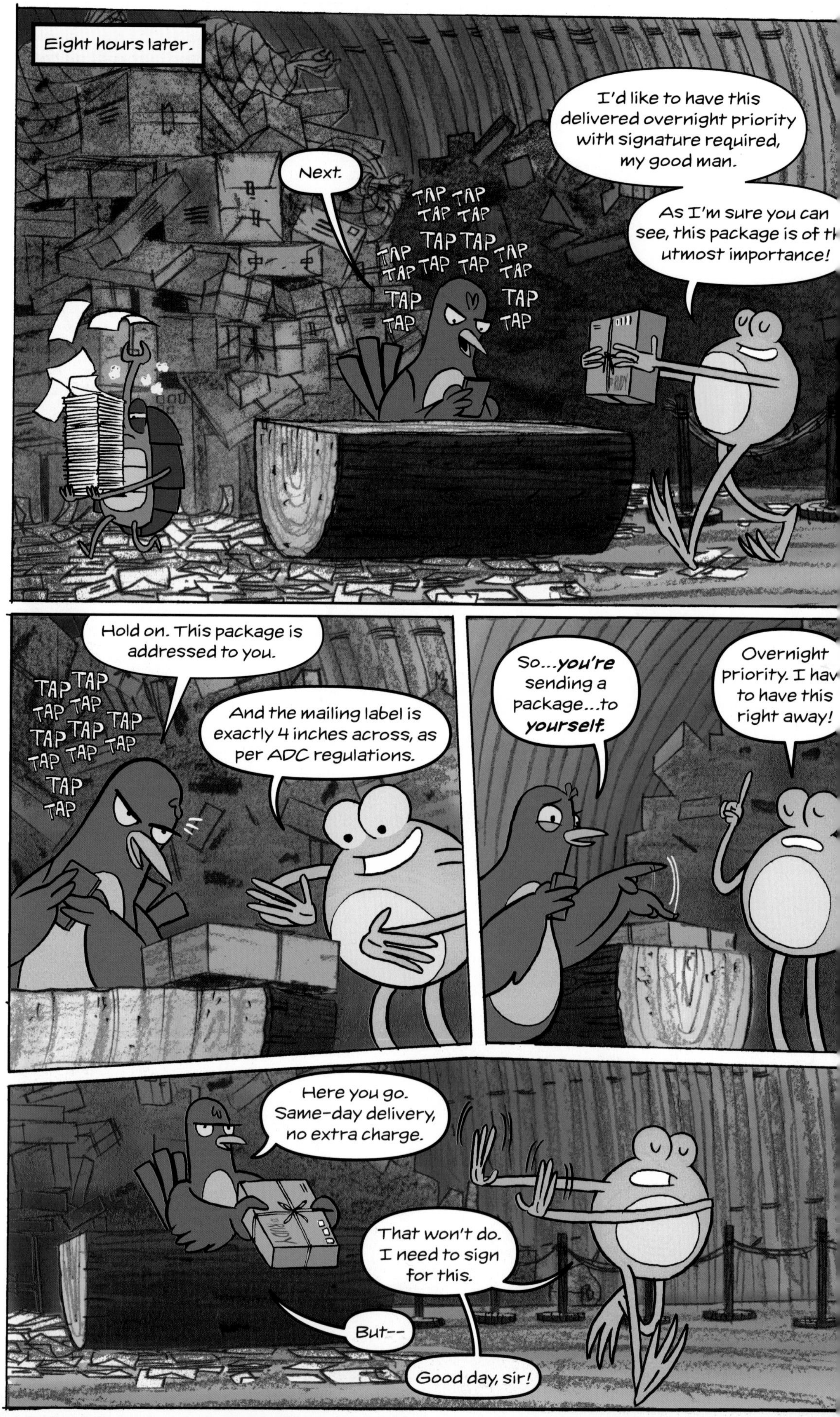
Eight hours later.
Next.
TAP TAP TAP TAP TAP TAP TAP TAP TAP TAP TAP TAP TAP TAP TAP TAP
I'd like to have this delivered overnight priority with signature required, my good man.
As I'm sure you can see, this package is of th utmost importance!
Hold on. This package is addressed to you.
TAP TAP TAP TAP TAP TAP TAP TAP TAP TAP TAP TAP
And the mailing label is exactly 4 inches across, as per ADC regulations.
So...*you're* sending a package...to *yourself.*
Overnight priority. I hav to have this right away!
Here you go. Same-day delivery, no extra charge.
That won't do. I need to sign for this.
But--
Good day, sir!

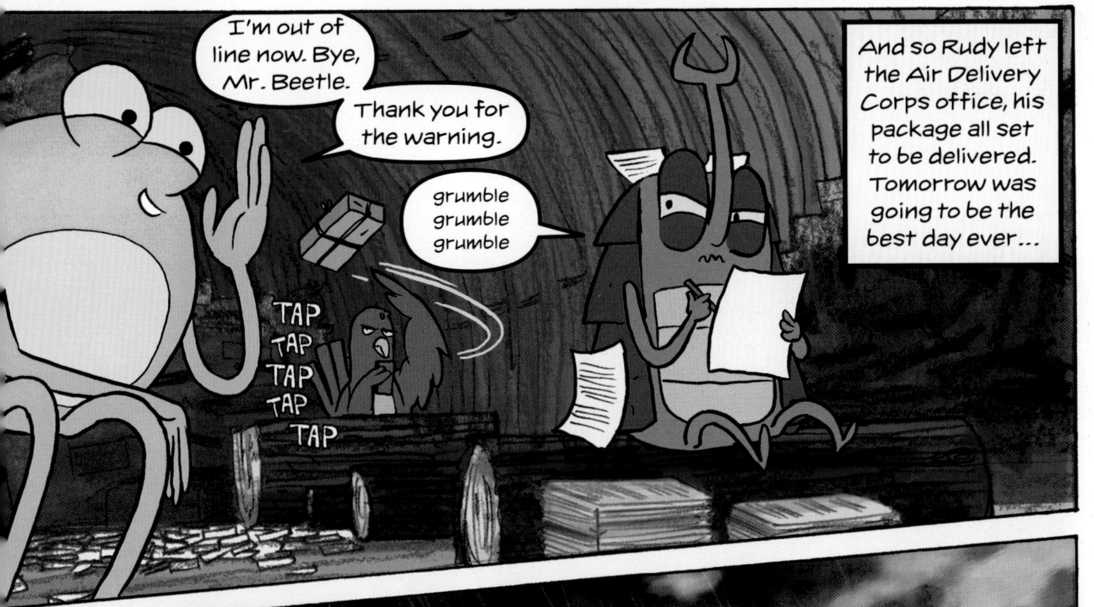
I'm out of line now. Bye, Mr. Beetle.
Thank you for the warning.
And so Rudy left the Air Delivery Corps office, his package all set to be delivered. Tomorrow was going to be the best day ever...
grumble grumble grumble
TAP TAP TAP TAP TAP

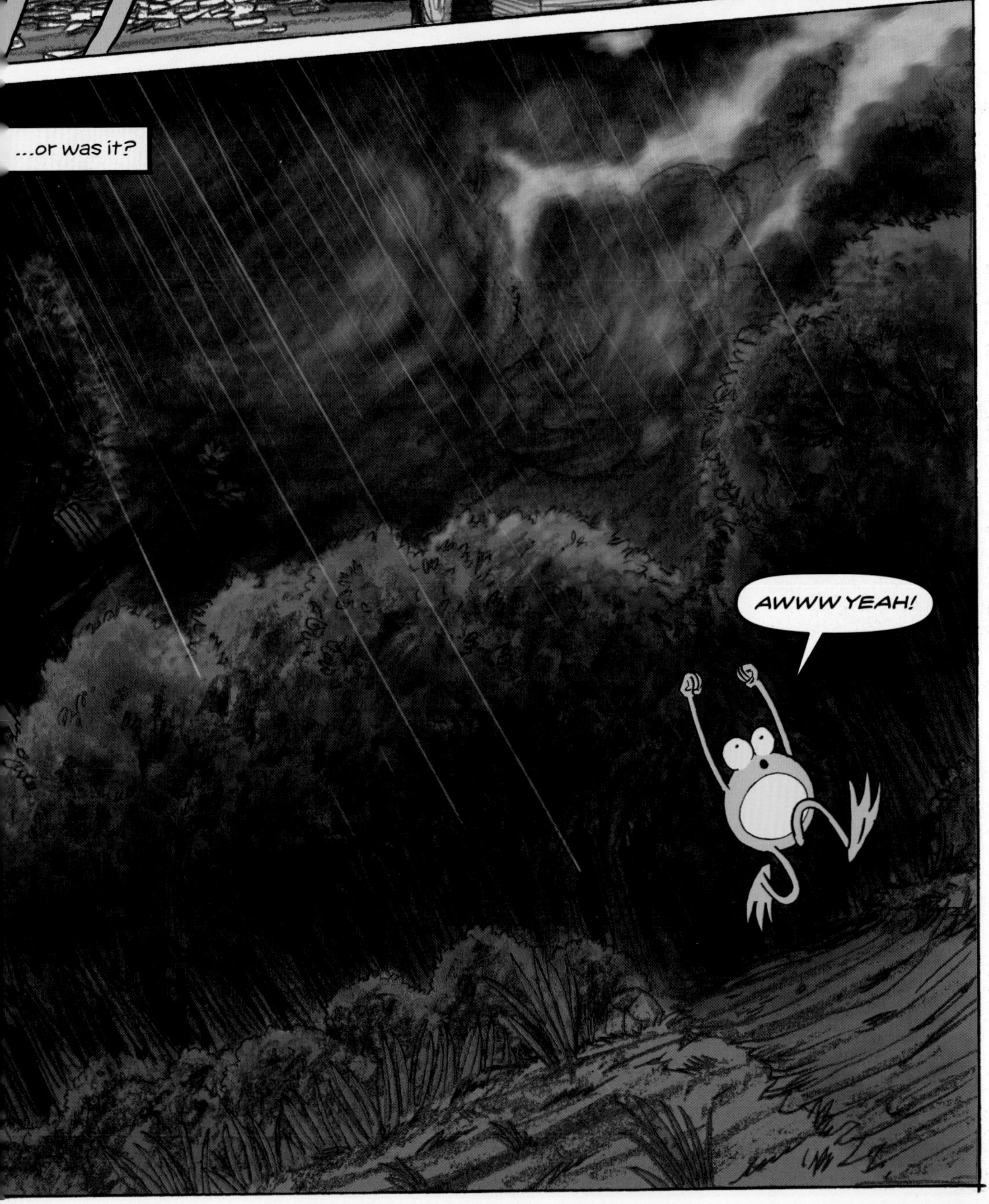
...or was it?
AWWW YEAH!

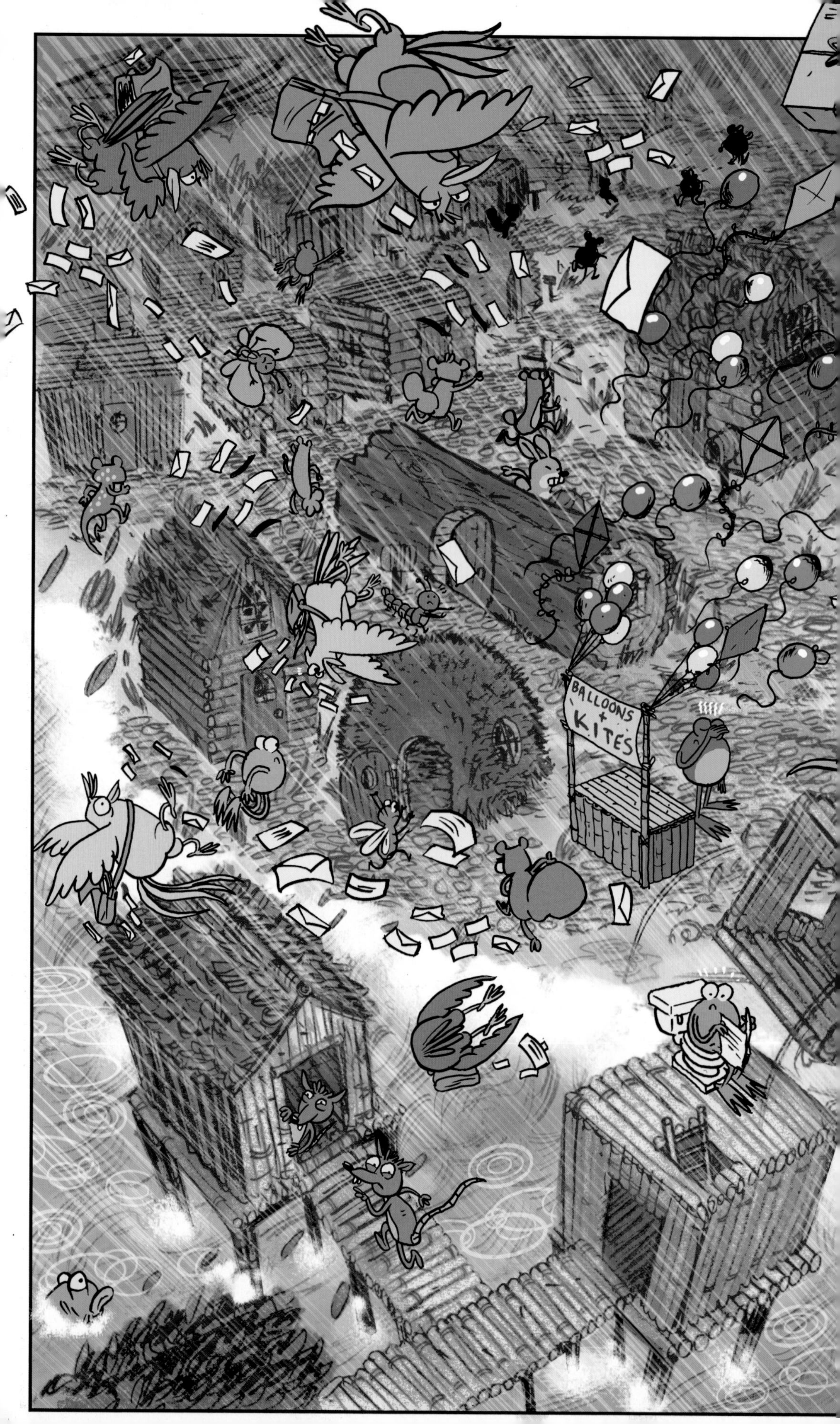
BALLOONS + KITES

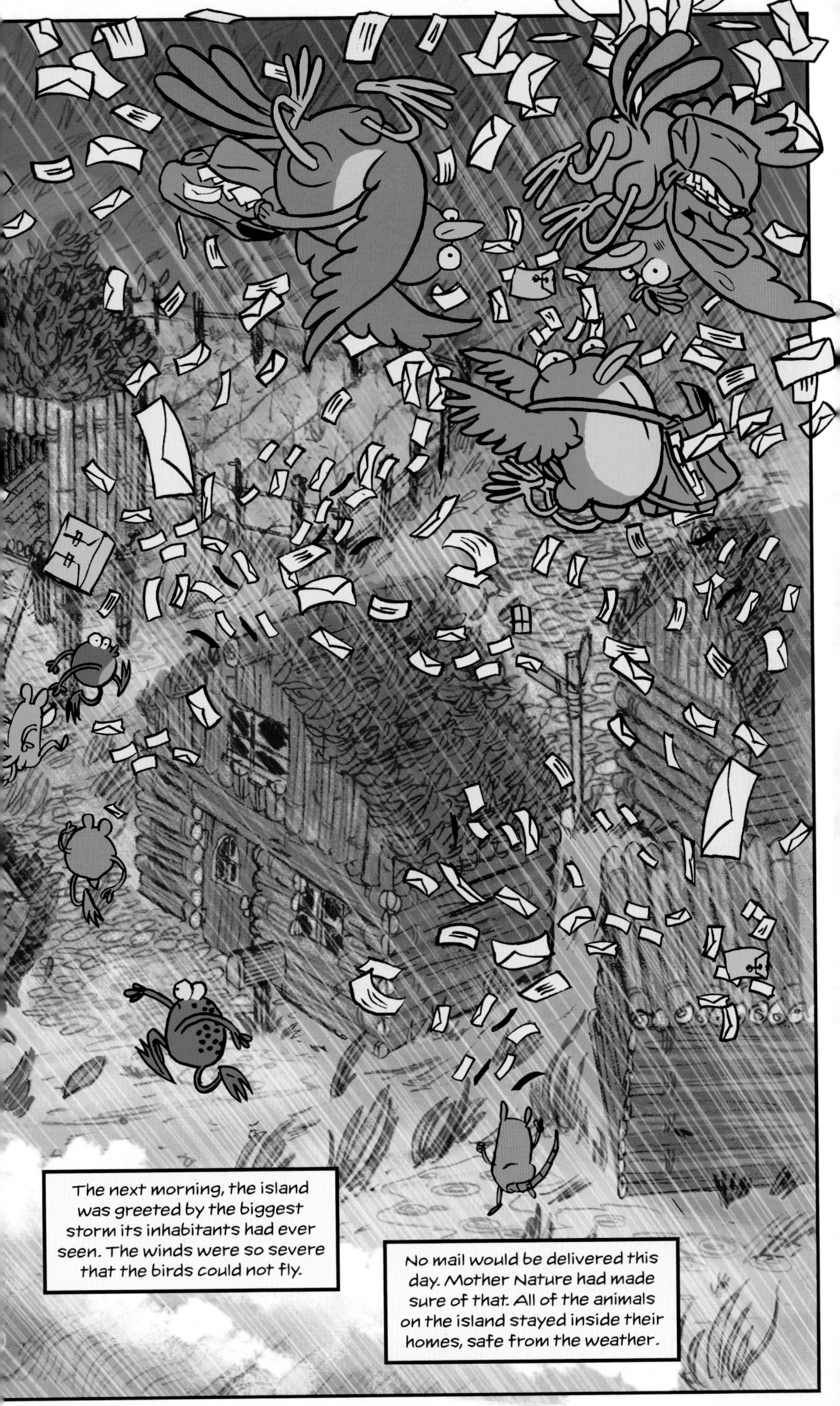
The next morning, the island was greeted by the biggest storm its inhabitants had ever seen. The winds were so severe that the birds could not fly.
No mail would be delivered this day. Mother Nature had made sure of that. All of the animals on the island stayed inside their homes, safe from the weather.

All save one.

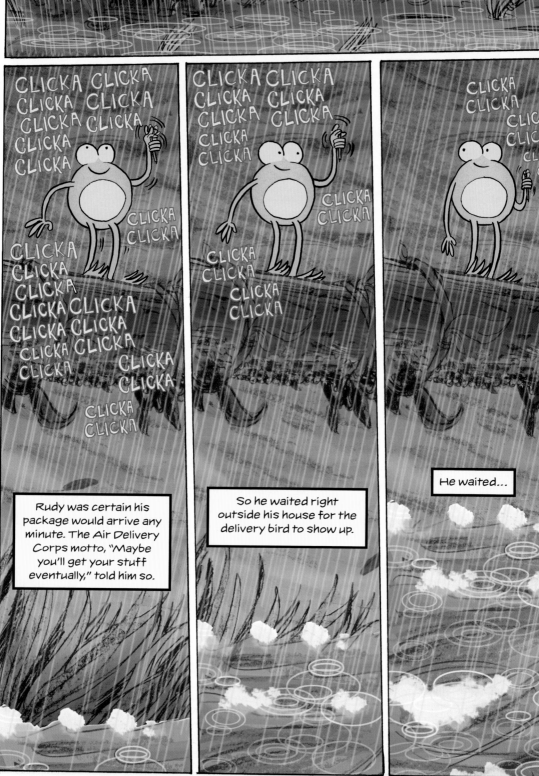

CLICKA CLICKA CLICKA CLICKA CLICKA CLICKA CLICKA CLICKA CLICKA

CLICKA CLICKA

CLICKA CLICKA CLICKA CLICKA CLICKA CLICKA CLICKA CLICKA CLICKA CLICKA CLICKA CLICKA CLICKA

Rudy was certain his package would arrive any minute. The Air Delivery Corps motto, "Maybe you'll get your stuff eventually," told him so.

CLICKA CLICKA CLICKA CLICKA CLICKA

CLICKA CLICKA

CLICKA CLICKA CLICKA CLICKA

So he waited right outside his house for the delivery bird to show up.

CLICKA CLICKA CLICK CLICK CLI

He waited...

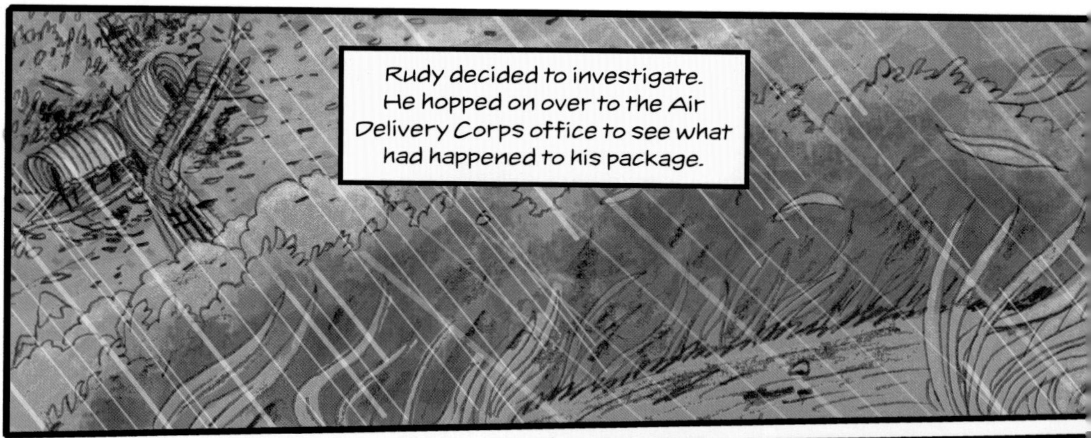
Rudy decided to investigate. He hopped on over to the Air Delivery Corps office to see what had happened to his package.

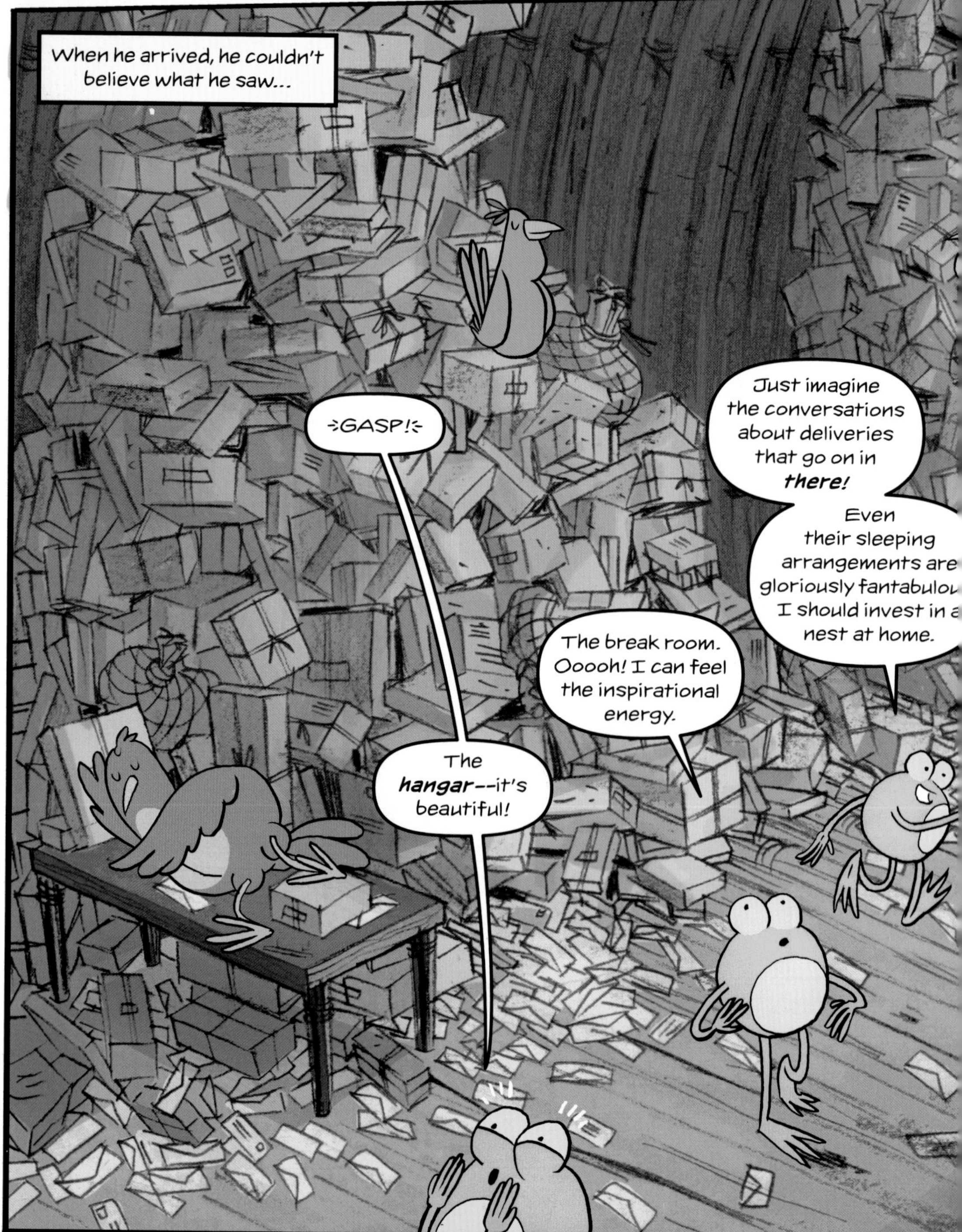
When he arrived, he couldn't believe what he saw...
GASP!
The hangar--it's beautiful!
The break room. Ooooh! I can feel the inspirational energy.
Just imagine the conversations about deliveries that go on in there!
Even their sleeping arrangements are gloriously fantabulou I should invest in a nest at home.

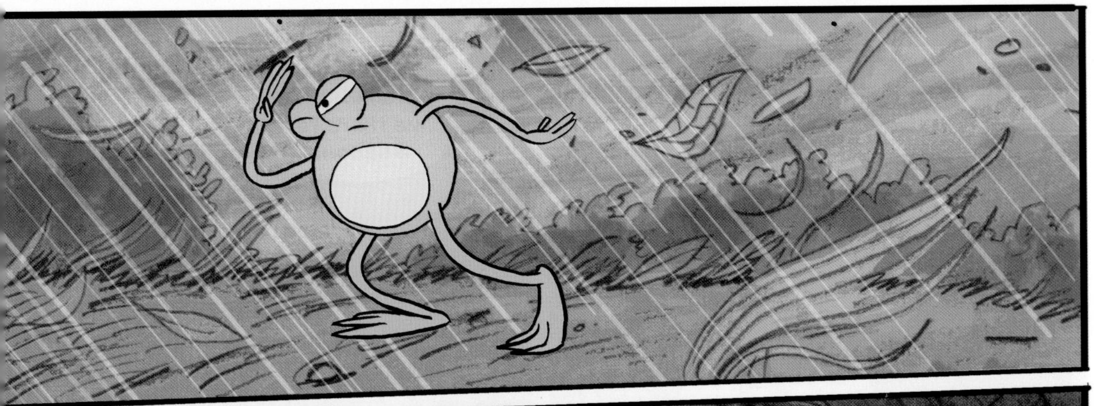

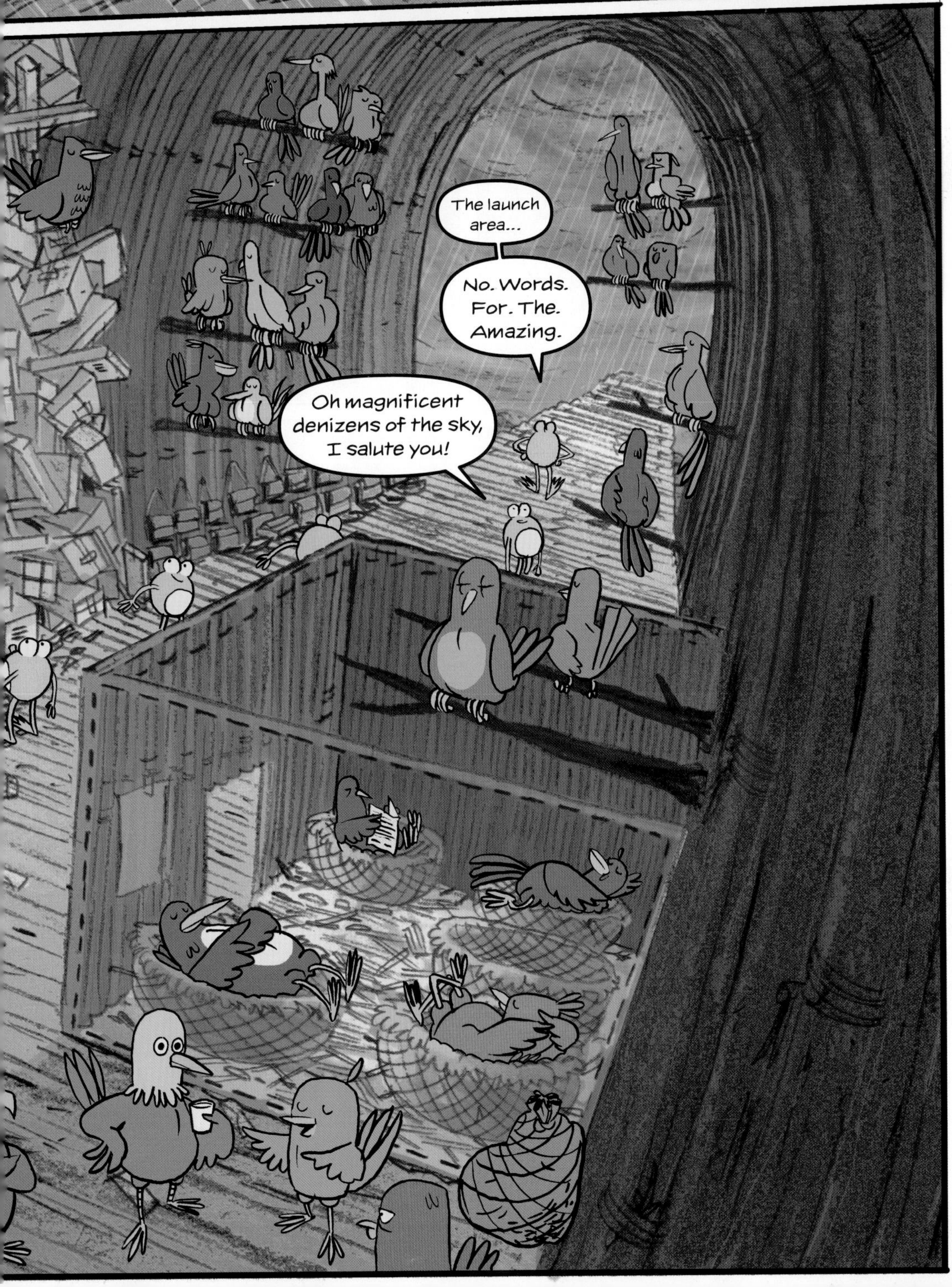
The launch area...
No. Words. For. The. Amazing.
Oh magnificent denizens of the sky, I salute you!

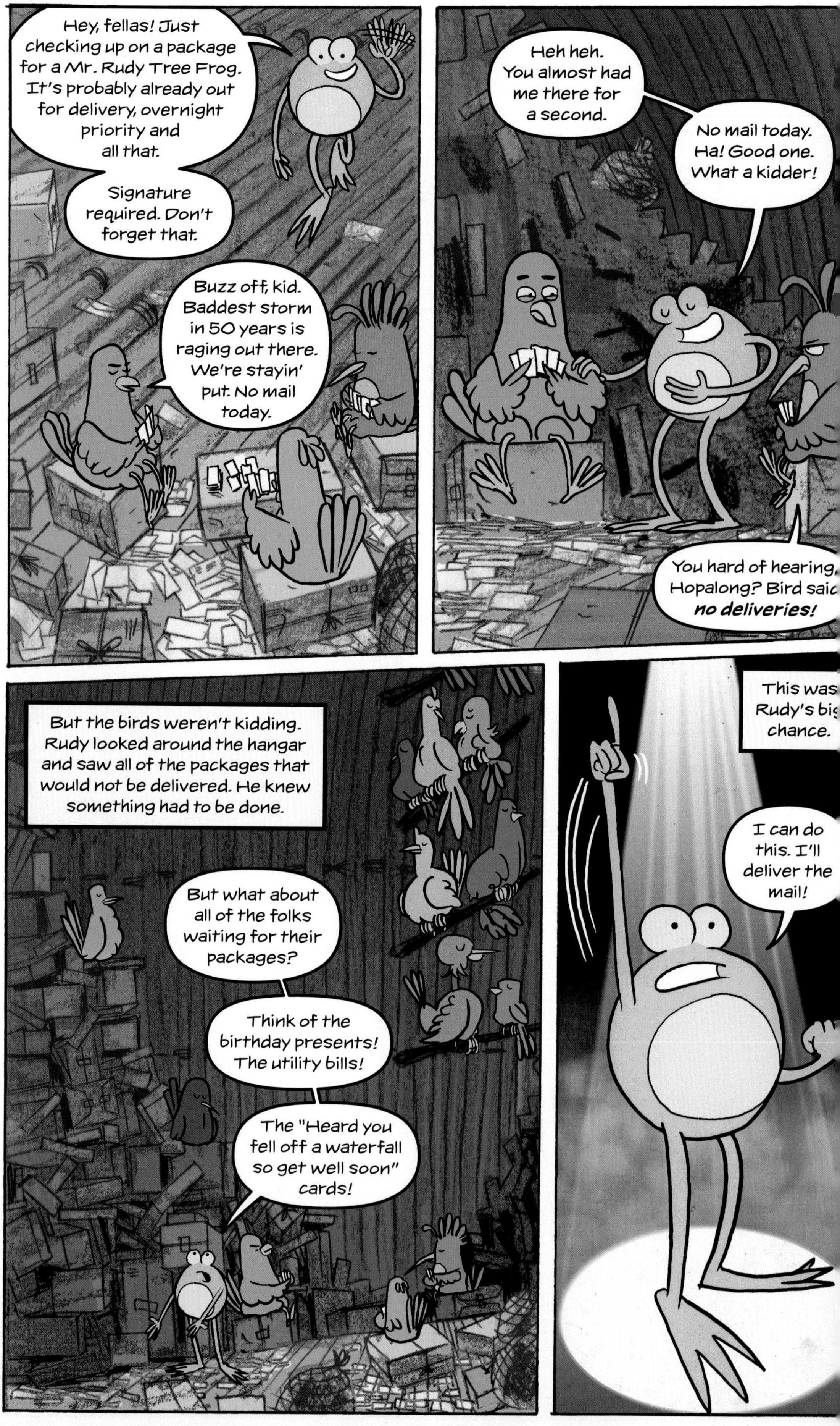
Hey, fellas! Just checking up on a package for a Mr. Rudy Tree Frog. It's probably already out for delivery, overnight priority and all that.
Signature required. Don't forget that.
Buzz off, kid. Baddest storm in 50 years is raging out there. We're stayin' put. No mail today.
Heh heh. You almost had me there for a second.
No mail today. Ha! Good one. What a kidder!
You hard of hearing, Hopalong? Bird said no deliveries!
But the birds weren't kidding. Rudy looked around the hangar and saw all of the packages that would not be delivered. He knew something had to be done.
But what about all of the folks waiting for their packages?
Think of the birthday presents! The utility bills!
The "Heard you fell off a waterfall so get well soon" cards!
This was Rudy's big chance.
I can do this. I'll deliver the mail!

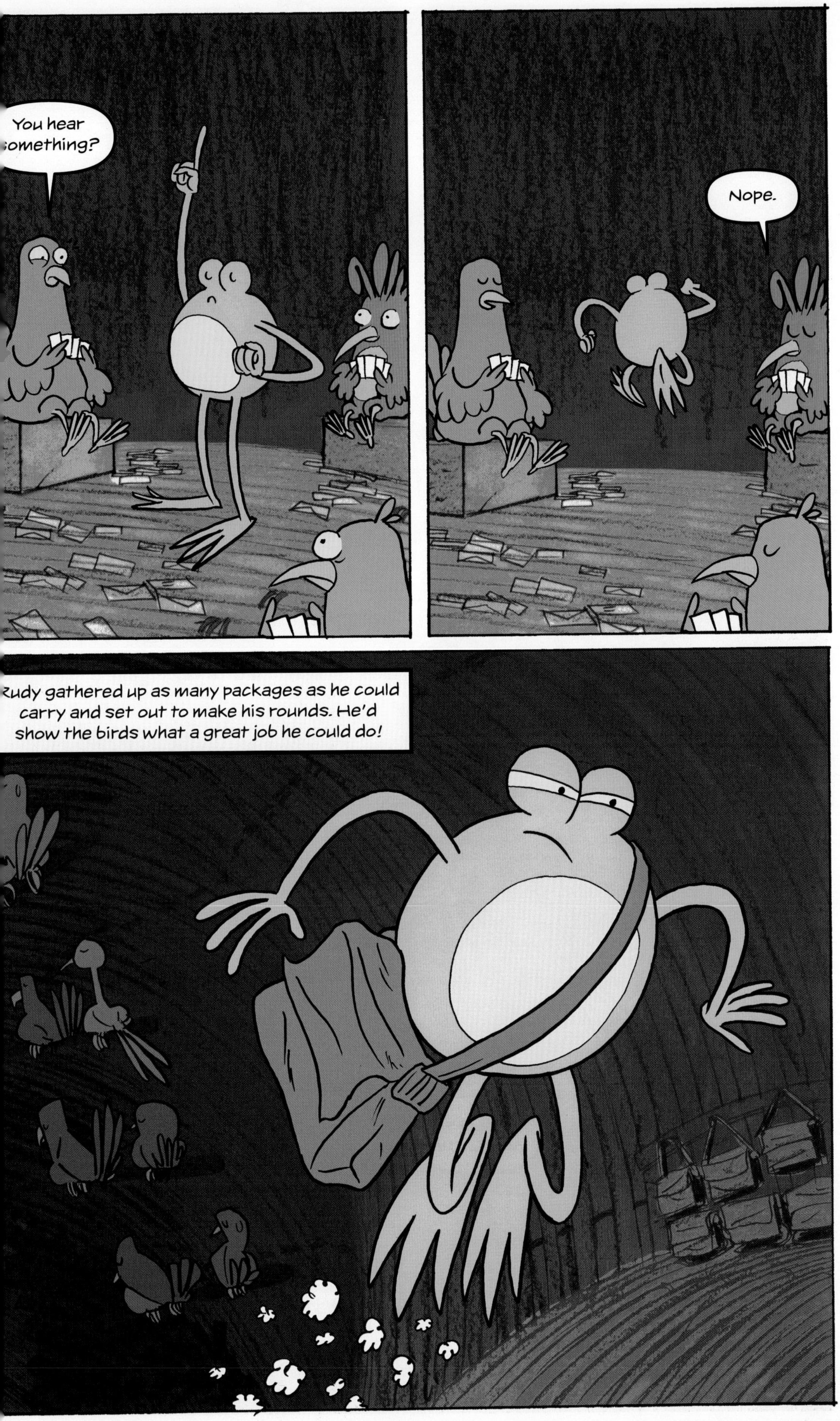

You hear something?
Nope.
Rudy gathered up as many packages as he could carry and set out to make his rounds. He'd show the birds what a great job he could do!

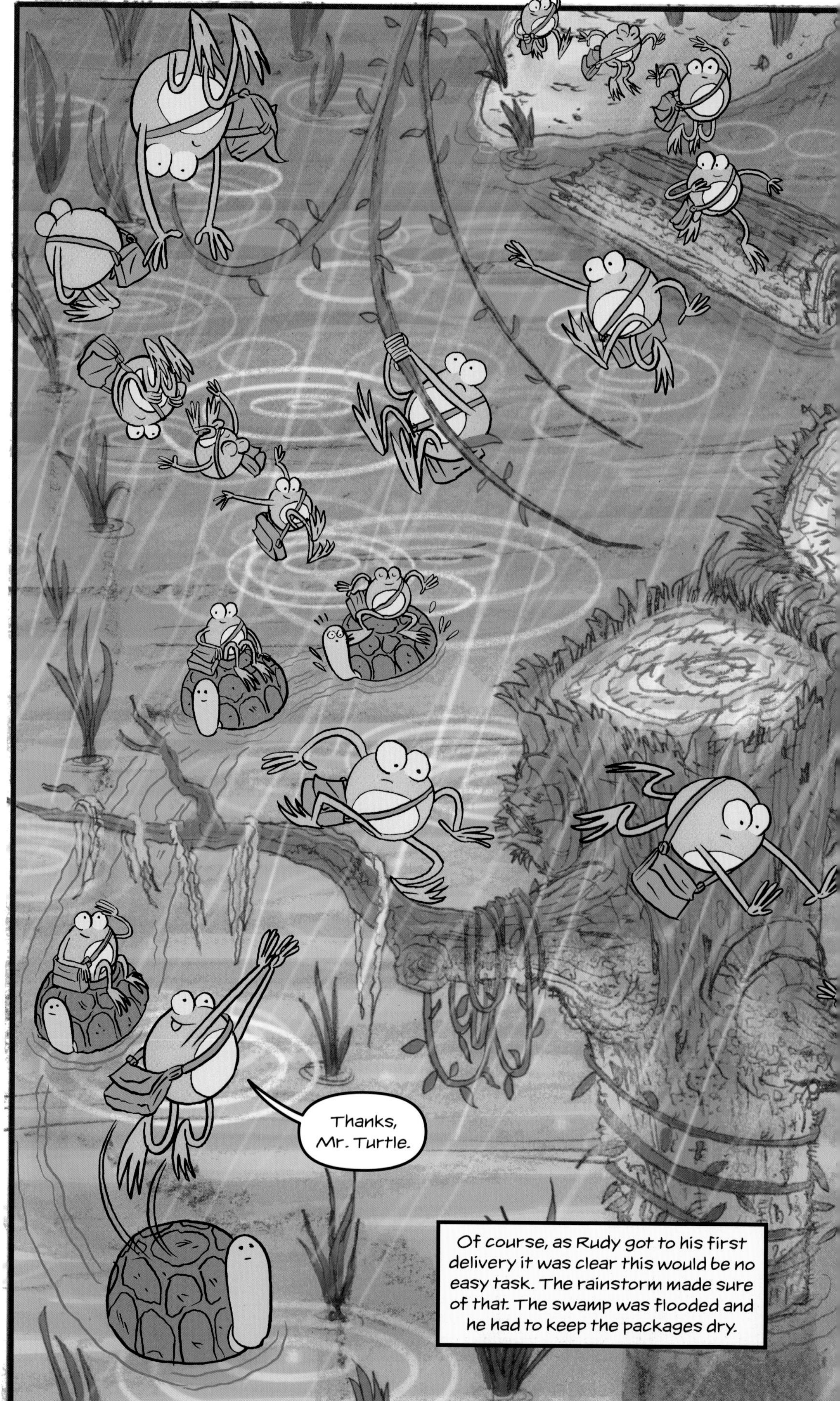
Thanks, Mr. Turtle.
Of course, as Rudy got to his first delivery it was clear this would be no easy task. The rainstorm made sure of that. The swamp was flooded and he had to keep the packages dry.

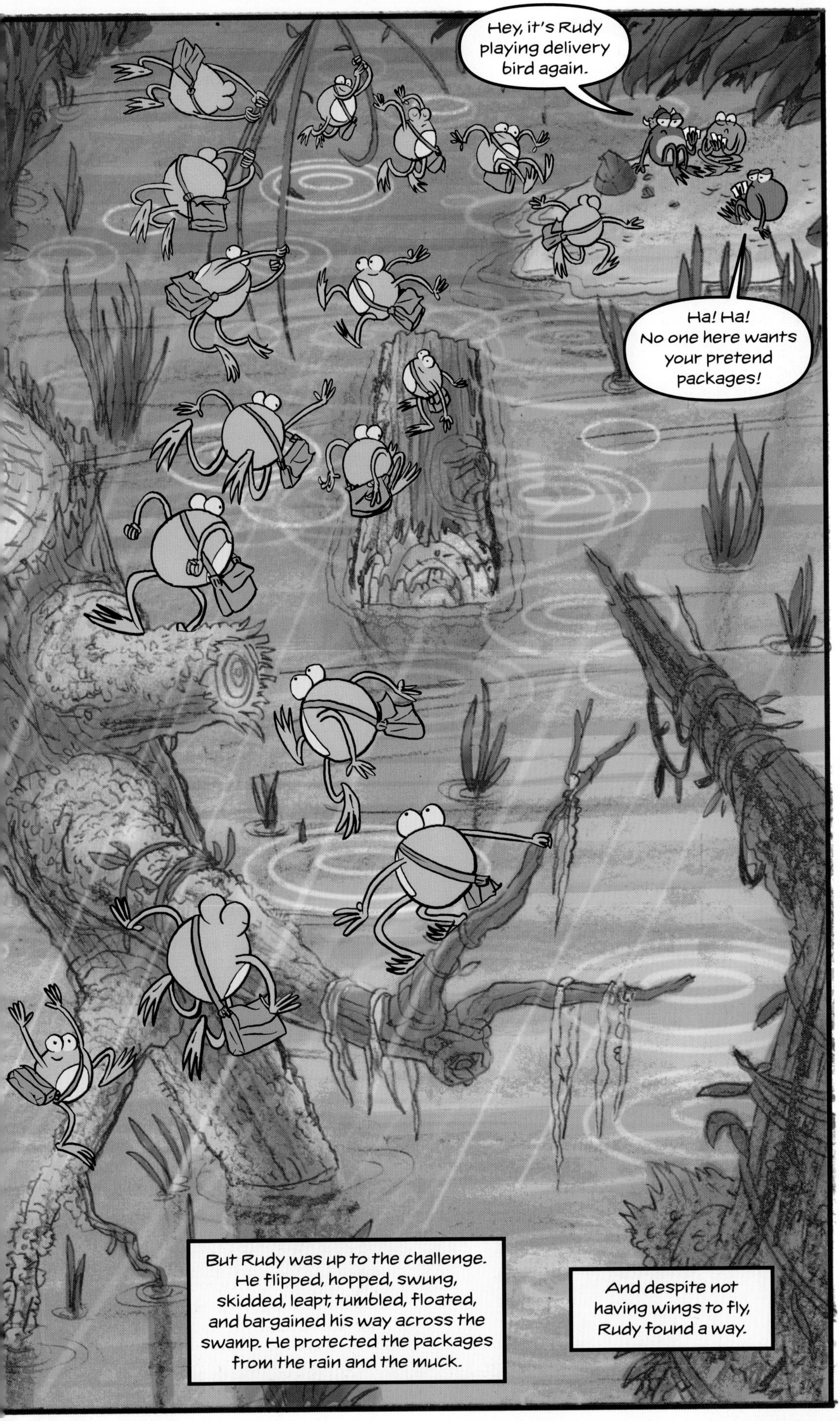
Hey, it's Rudy playing delivery bird again.
Ha! Ha! No one here wants your pretend packages!
But Rudy was up to the challenge. He flipped, hopped, swung, skidded, leapt, tumbled, floated, and bargained his way across the swamp. He protected the packages from the rain and the muck.
And despite not having wings to fly, Rudy found a way.

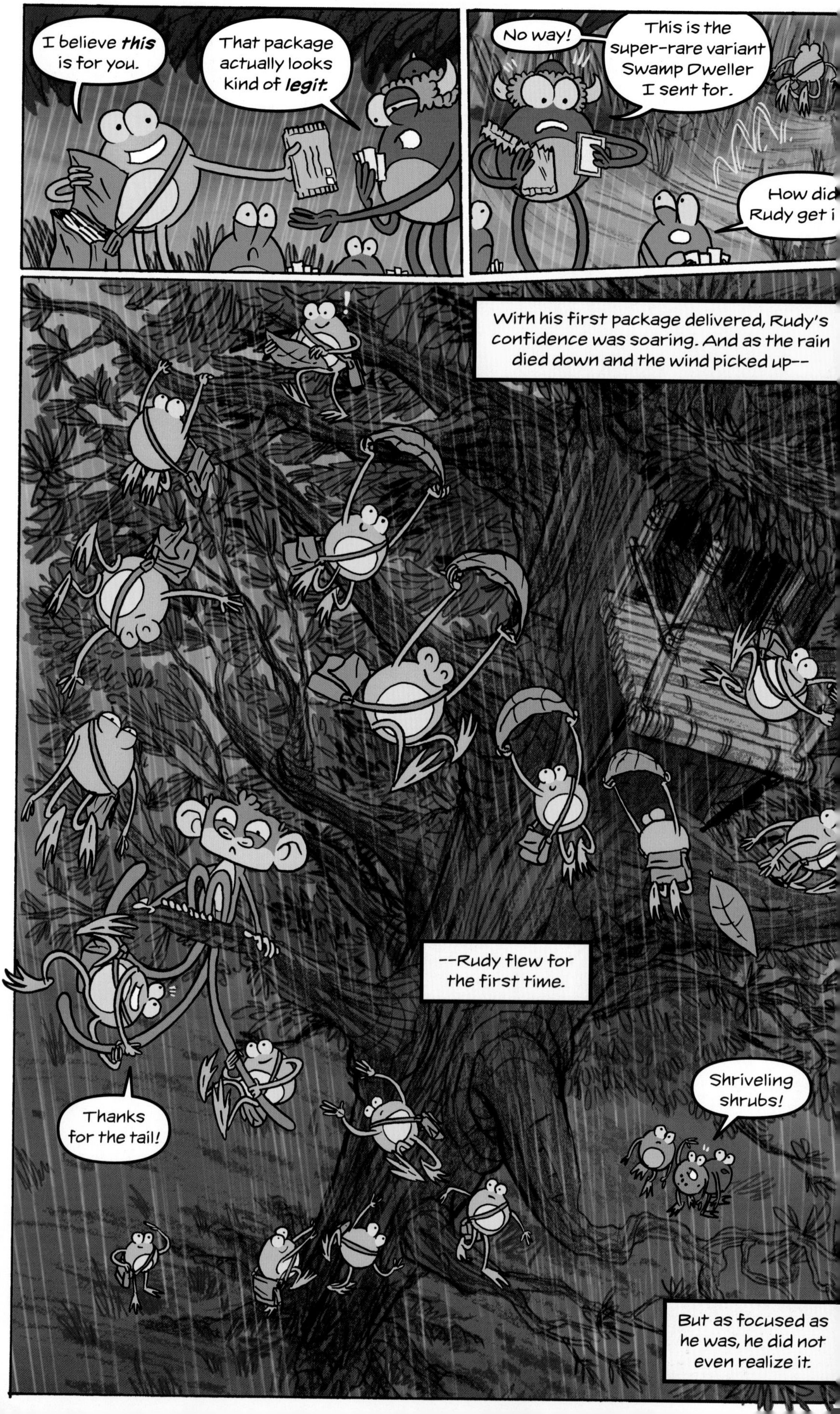

I believe **this** is for you.
That package actually looks kind of **legit**.
No way!
This is the super-rare variant Swamp Dweller I sent for.
How did Rudy get i
With his first package delivered, Rudy's confidence was soaring. And as the rain died down and the wind picked up--
!
--Rudy flew for the first time.
Thanks for the tail!
Shriveling shrubs!
But as focused as he was, he did not even realize it.

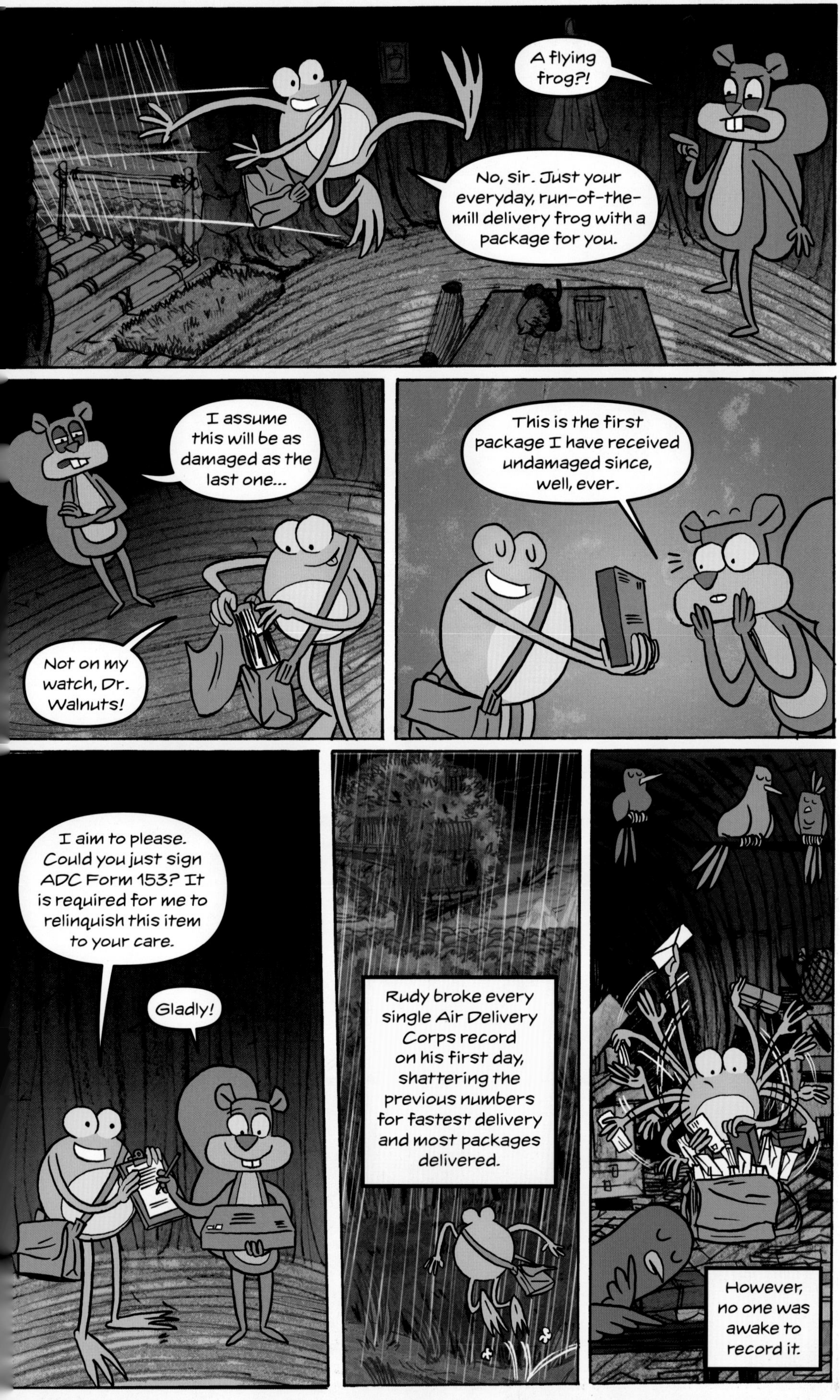
A flying frog?!
No, sir. Just your everyday, run-of-the-mill delivery frog with a package for you.
I assume this will be as damaged as the last one...
Not on my watch, Dr. Walnuts!
This is the first package I have received undamaged since, well, ever.
I aim to please. Could you just sign ADC Form 153? It is required for me to relinquish this item to your care.
Gladly!
Rudy broke every single Air Delivery Corps record on his first day, shattering the previous numbers for fastest delivery and most packages delivered.
However, no one was awake to record it.

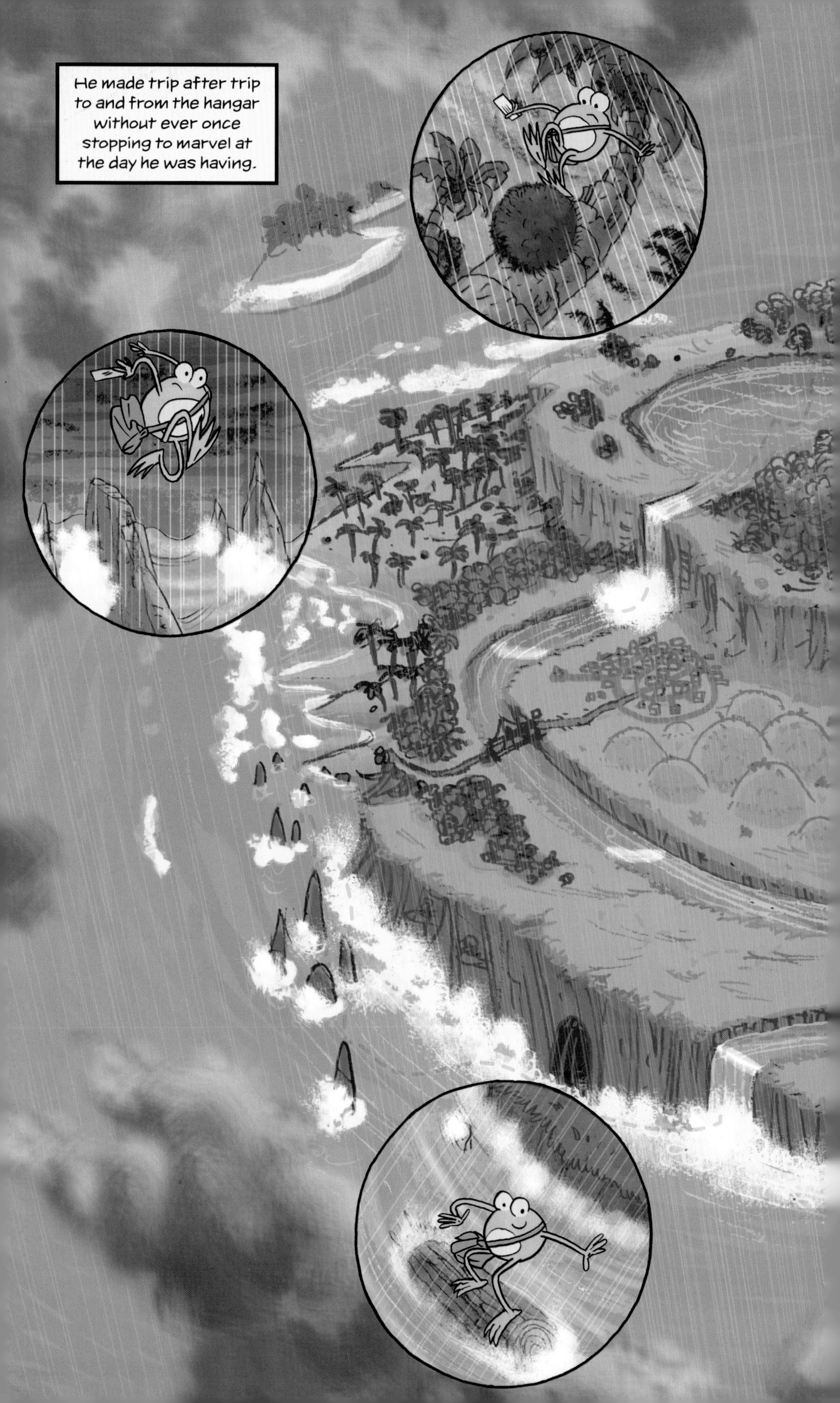
He made trip after trip to and from the hangar without ever once stopping to marvel at the day he was having.

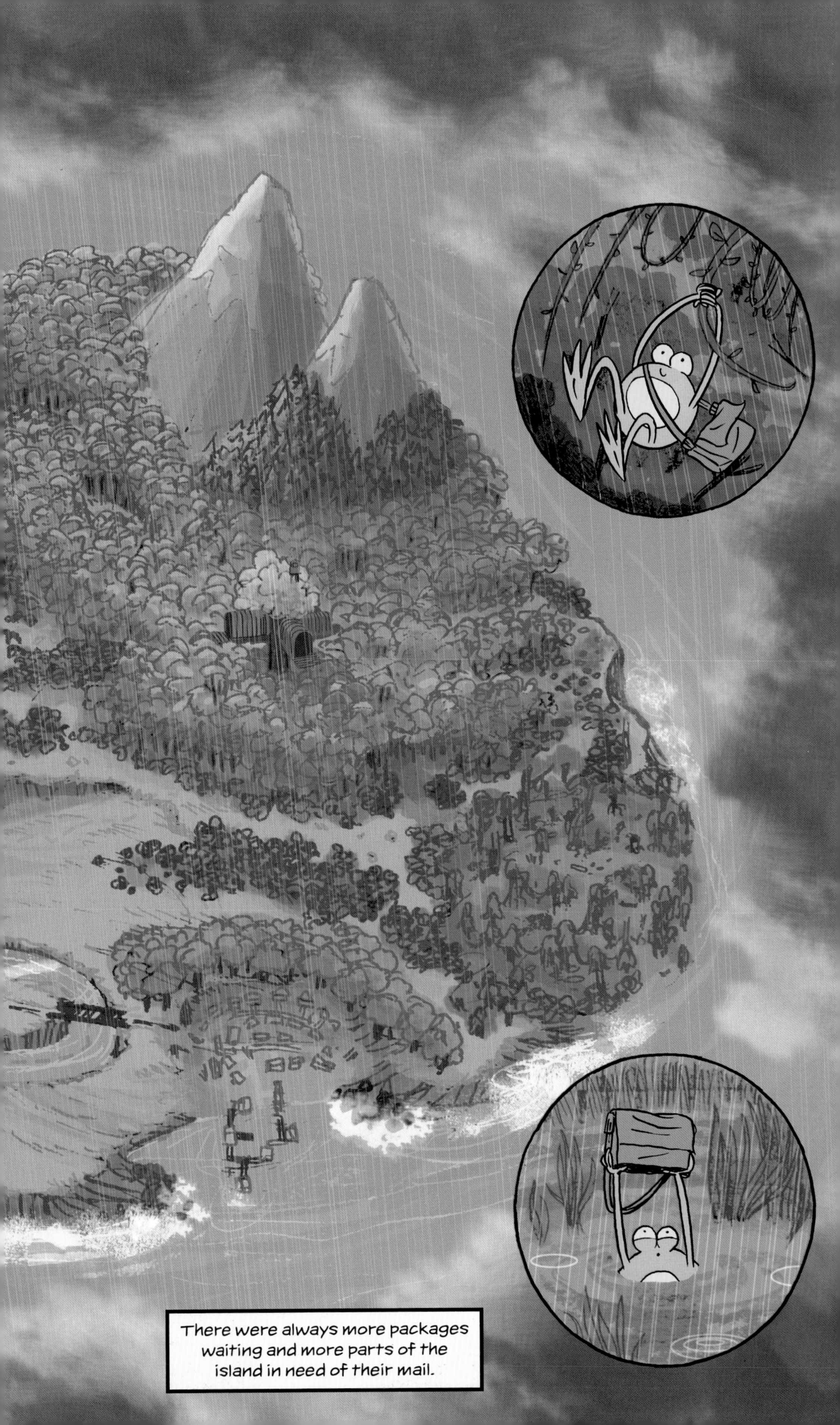
There were always more packages waiting and more parts of the island in need of their mail.

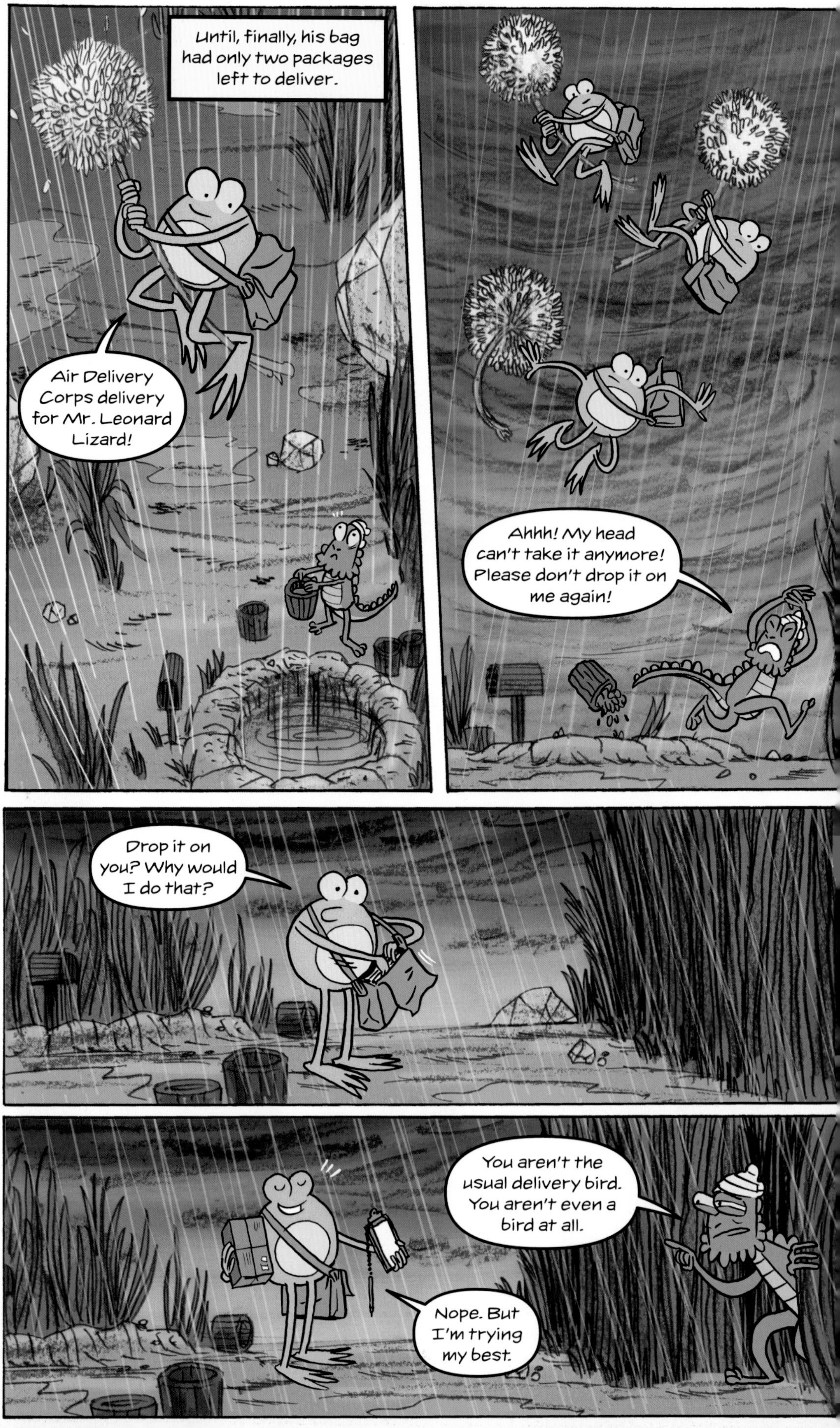
Until, finally, his bag had only two packages left to deliver.
Air Delivery Corps delivery for Mr. Leonard Lizard!
Ahhh! My head can't take it anymore! Please don't drop it on me again!
Drop it on you? Why would I do that?
You aren't the usual delivery bird. You aren't even a bird at all.
Nope. But I'm trying my best.

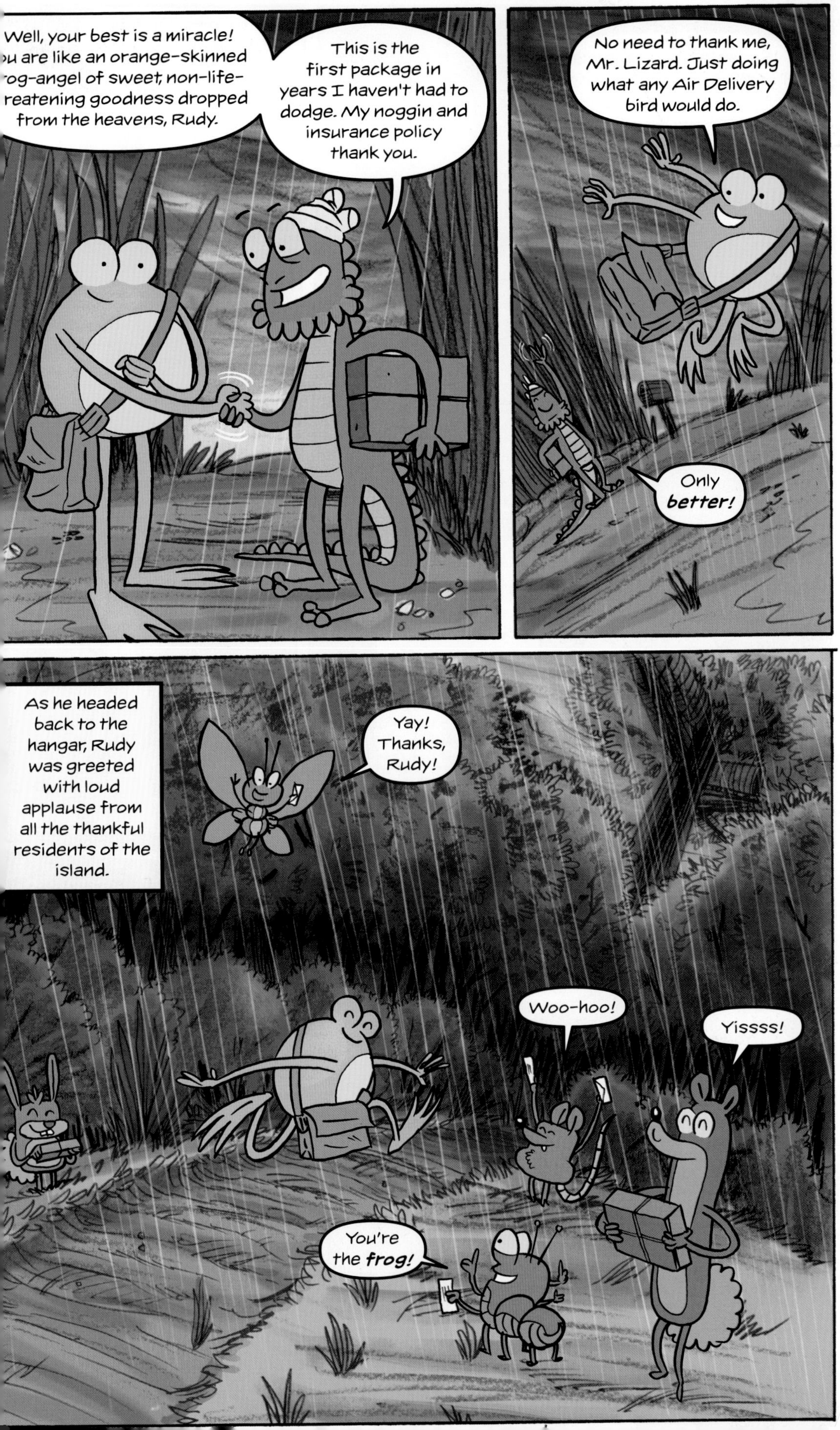

Well, your best is a miracle! u are like an orange-skinned og-angel of sweet, non-life- reatening goodness dropped from the heavens, Rudy.
This is the first package in years I haven't had to dodge. My noggin and insurance policy thank you.
No need to thank me, Mr. Lizard. Just doing what any Air Delivery bird would do.
Only *better!*
As he headed back to the hangar, Rudy was greeted with loud applause from all the thankful residents of the island.
Yay! Thanks, Rudy!
Woo-hoo!
Yissss!
You're the *frog!*

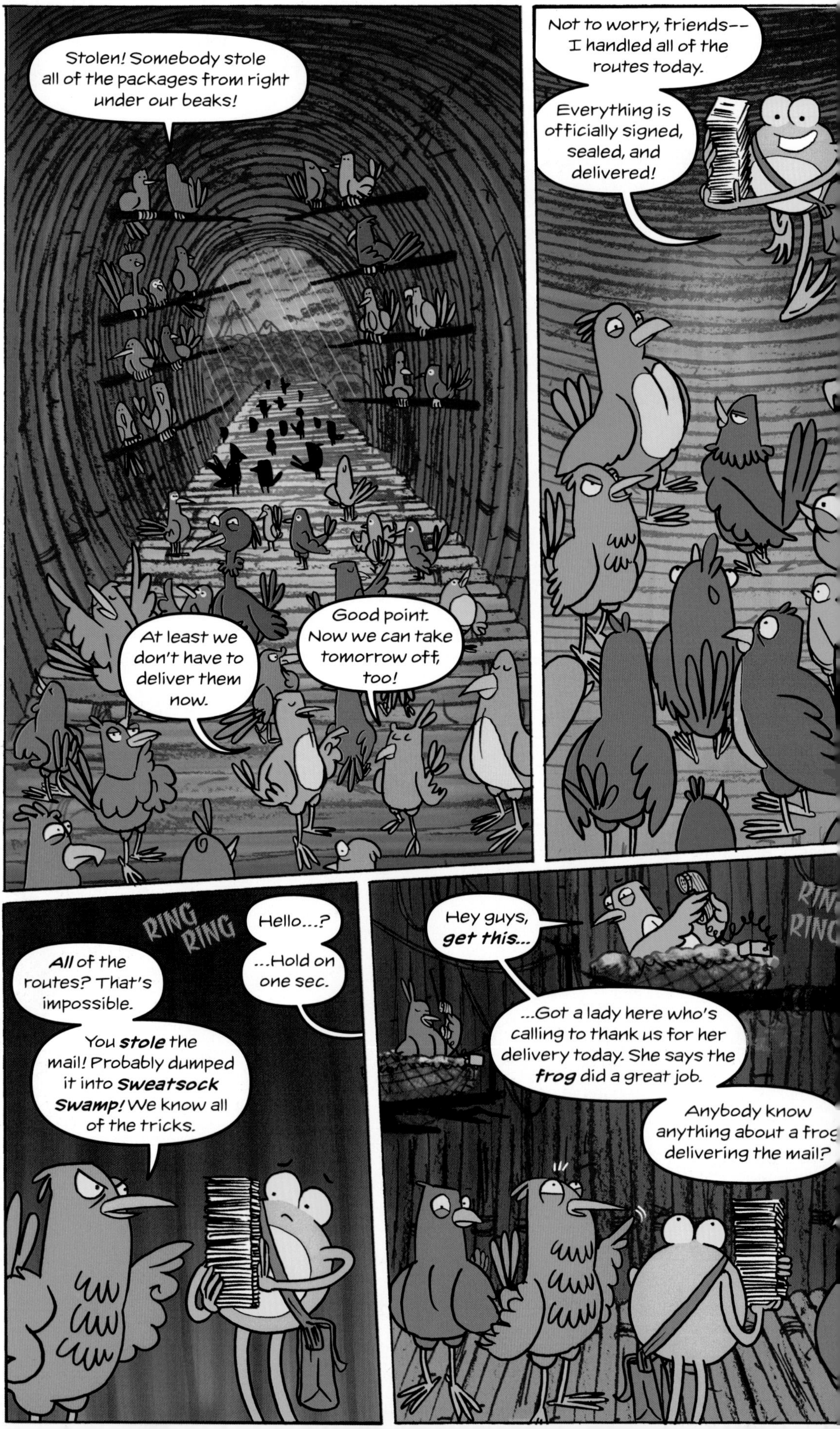

Stolen! Somebody stole all of the packages from right under our beaks!
At least we don't have to deliver them now.
Good point. Now we can take tomorrow off, too!
Not to worry, friends-- I handled all of the routes today.
Everything is officially signed, sealed, and delivered!
RING RING
Hello...?
...Hold on one sec.
All of the routes? That's impossible.
You stole the mail! Probably dumped it into Sweatsock Swamp! We know all of the tricks.
Hey guys, get this...
...Got a lady here who's calling to thank us for her delivery today. She says the frog did a great job.
Anybody know anything about a frog delivering the mail?

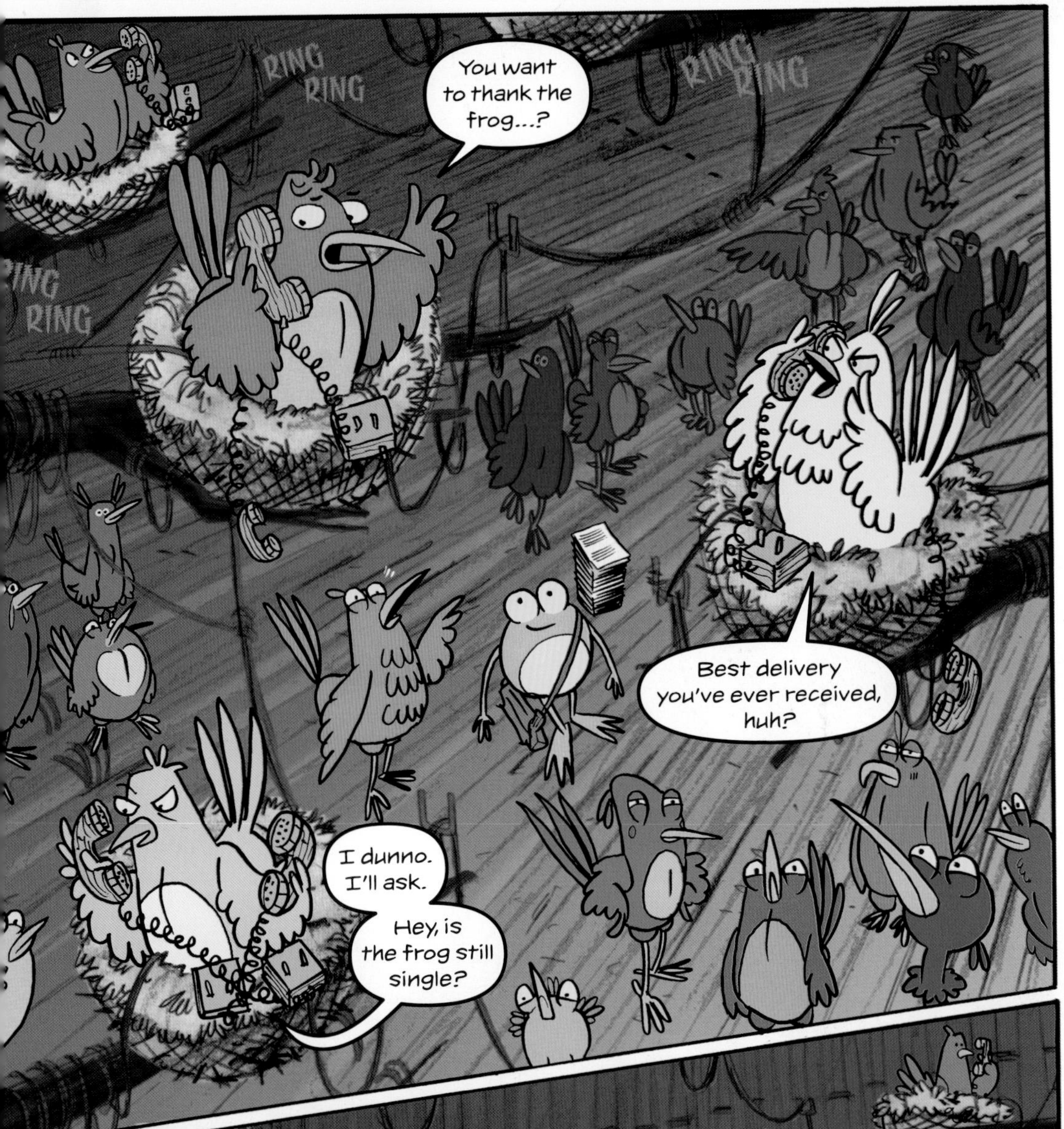
RING RING
You want to thank the frog...?
RING RING
RING RING
Best delivery you've ever received, huh?
I dunno. I'll ask.
Hey, is the frog still single?
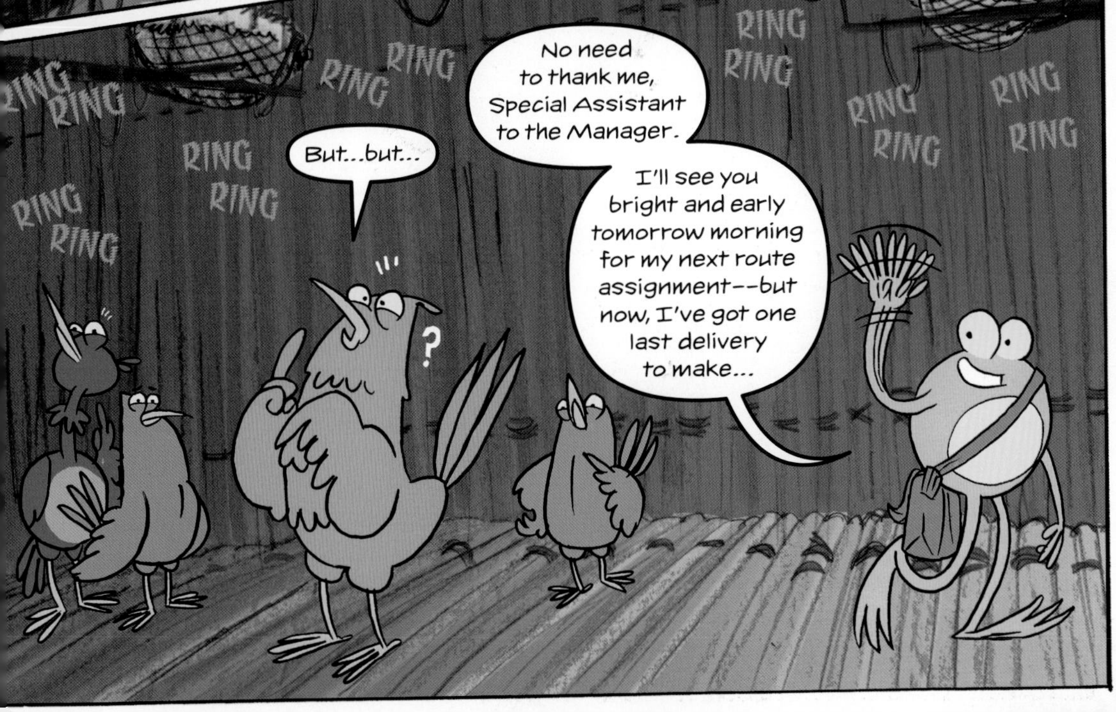
RING RING
RING RING
No need to thank me, Special Assistant to the Manager.
RING RING
RING RING
RING RING
RING RING
But...but...
RING RING
I'll see you bright and early tomorrow morning for my next route assignment--but now, I've got one last delivery to make...

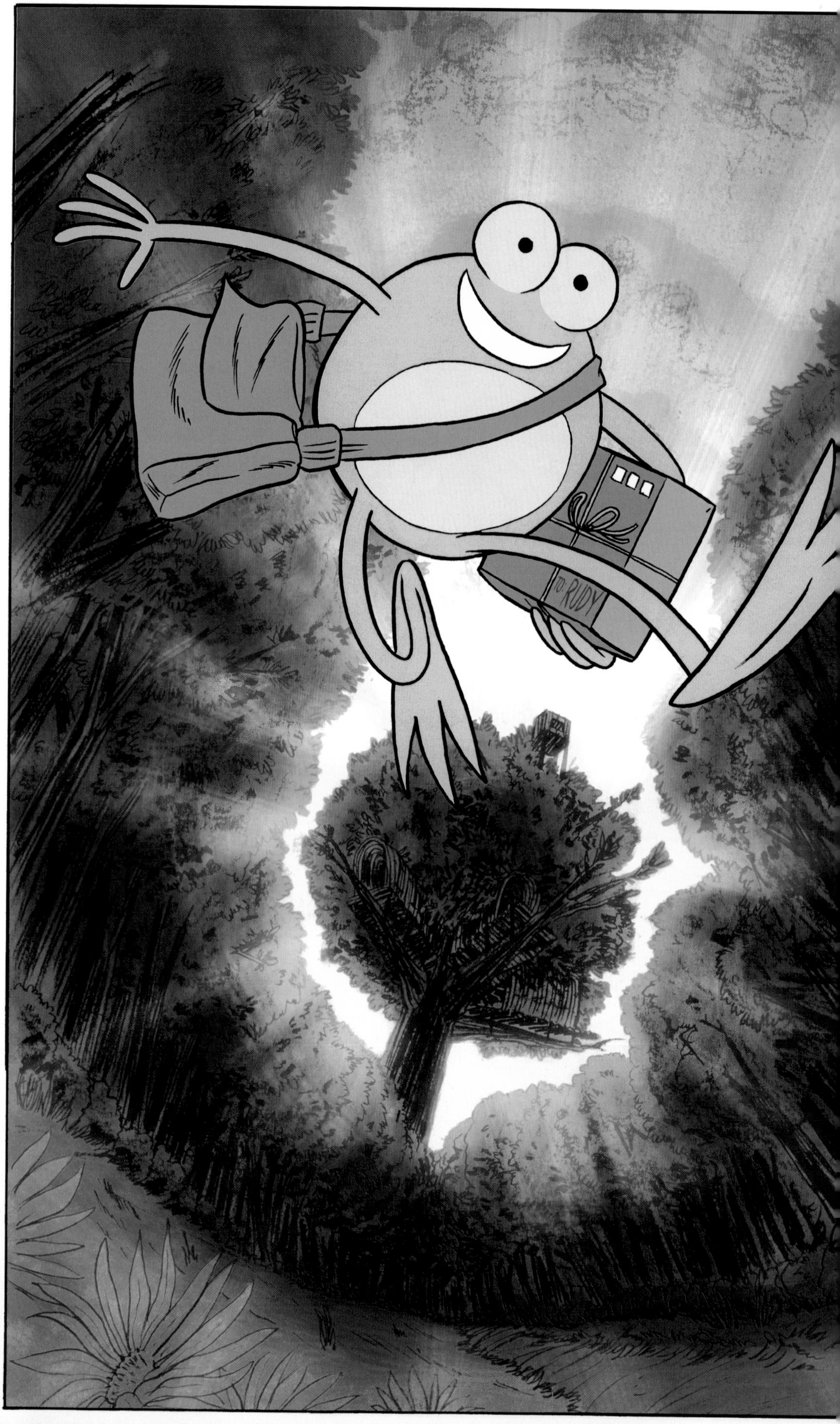
TO: RUDY

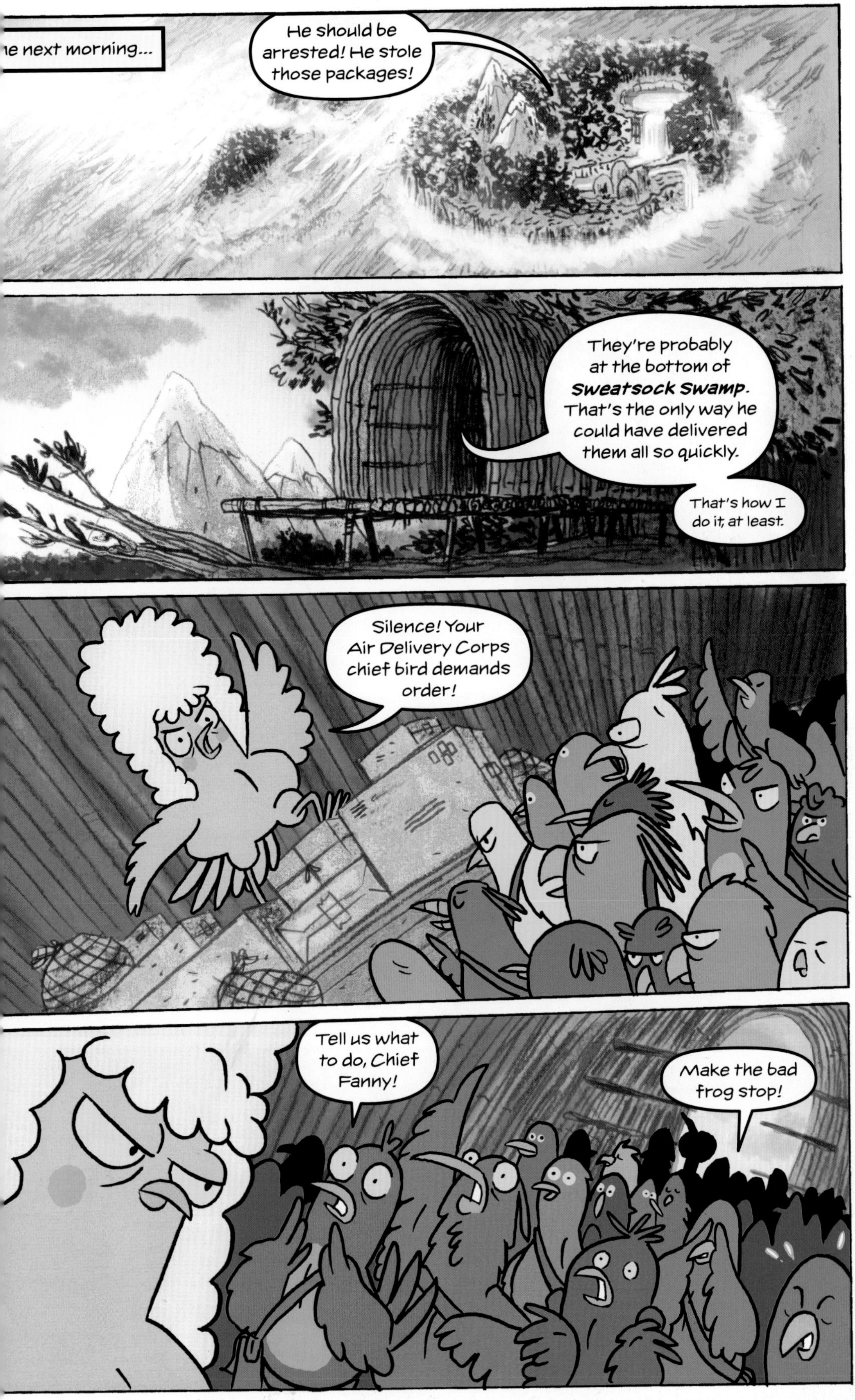

e next morning...
He should be arrested! He stole those packages!
They're probably at the bottom of **Sweatsock Swamp**. That's the only way he could have delivered them all so quickly.
That's how I do it, at least.
Silence! Your Air Delivery Corps chief bird demands order!
Tell us what to do, Chief Fanny!
Make the bad frog stop!

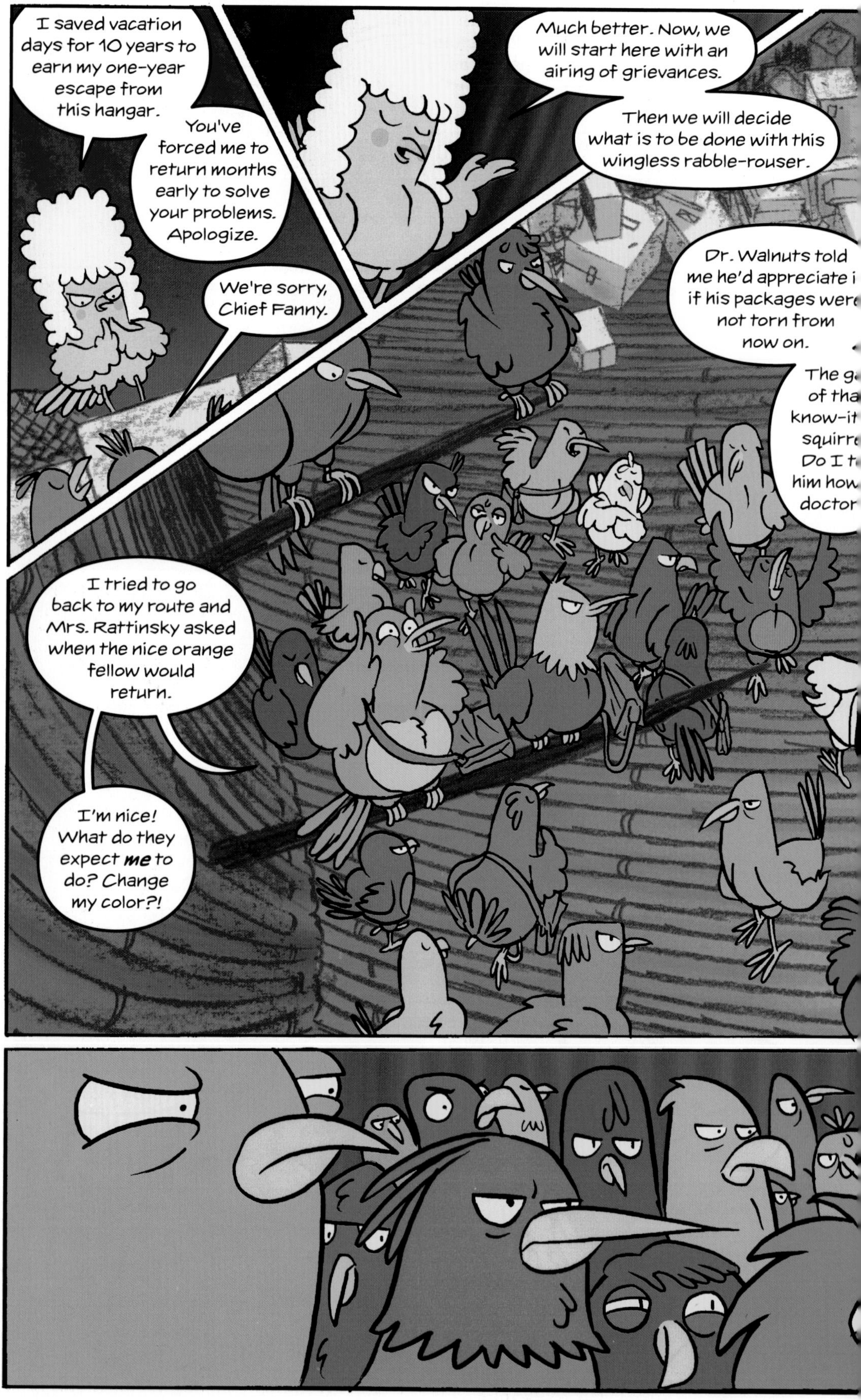

I saved vacation days for 10 years to earn my one-year escape from this hangar.
You've forced me to return months early to solve your problems. Apologize.
We're sorry, Chief Fanny.
Much better. Now, we will start here with an airing of grievances.
Then we will decide what is to be done with this wingless rabble-rouser.
Dr. Walnuts told me he'd appreciate i if his packages were not torn from now on.
The ga of tha know-it squirre Do I t him how doctor
I tried to go back to my route and Mrs. Rattinsky asked when the nice orange fellow would return.
I'm nice! What do they expect **me** to do? Change my color?!

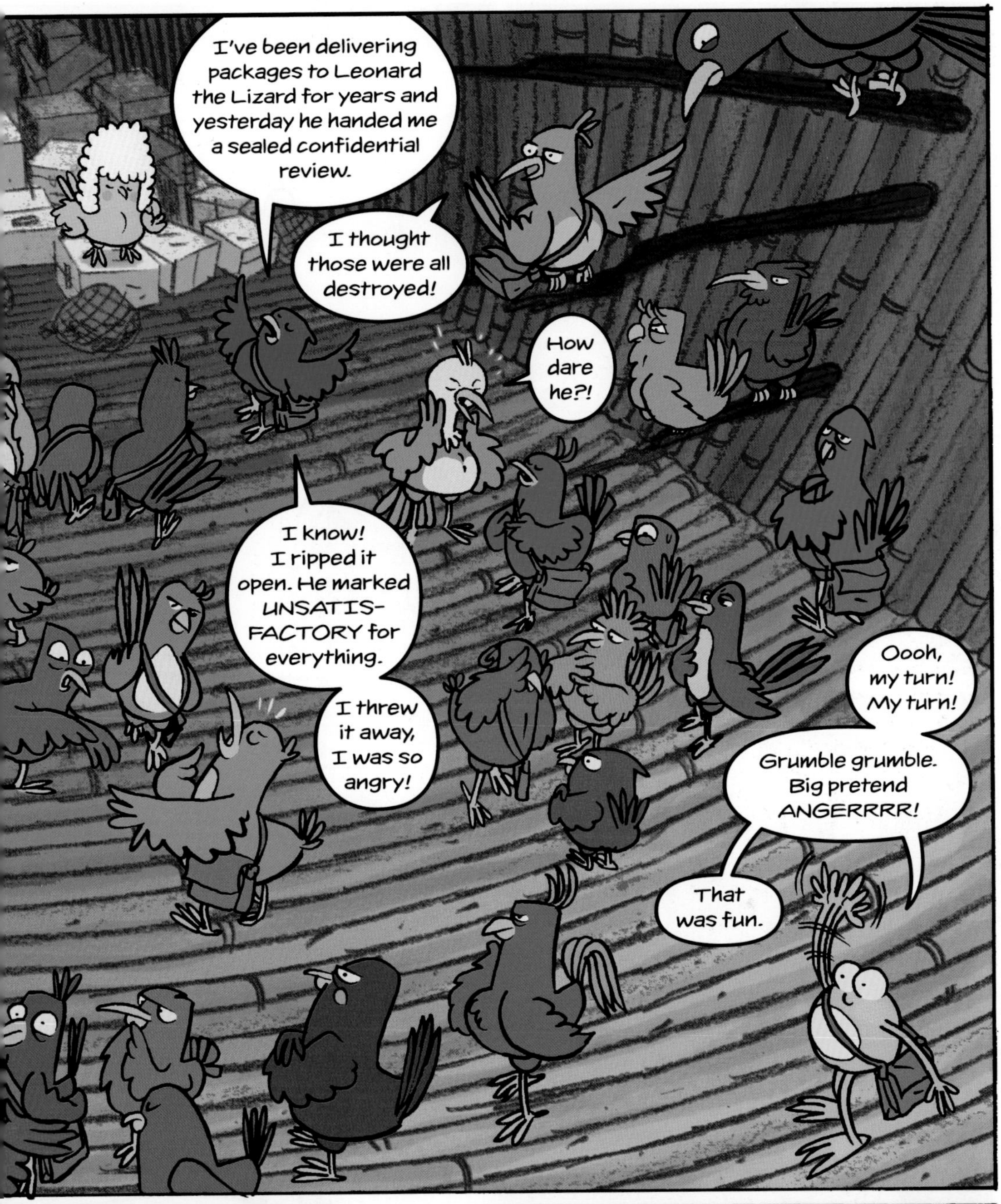
I've been delivering packages to Leonard the Lizard for years and yesterday he handed me a sealed confidential review.
I thought those were all destroyed!
How dare he?!
I know! I ripped it open. He marked UNSATIS-FACTORY for everything.
I threw it away, I was so angry!
Oooh, my turn! My turn!
Grumble grumble. Big pretend ANGERRRR!
That was fun.

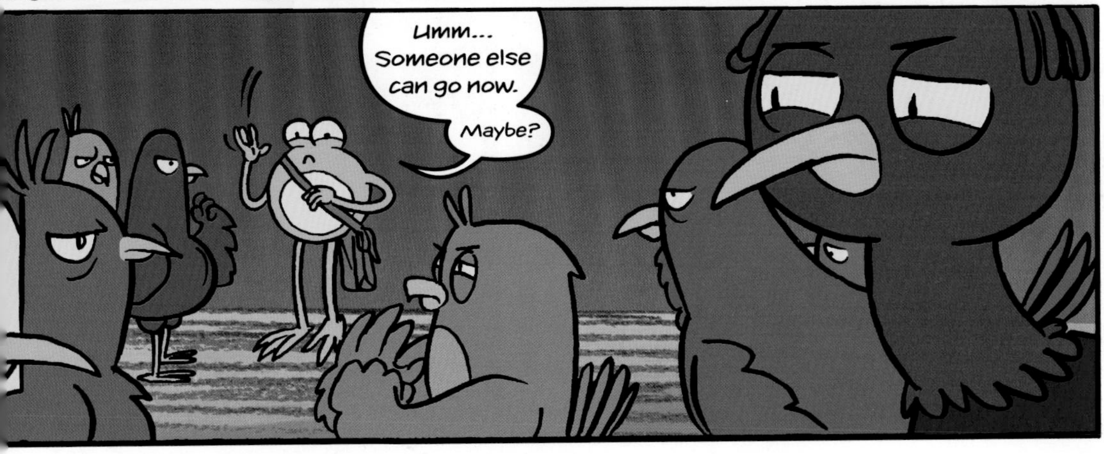
Umm... Someone else can go now.
Maybe?

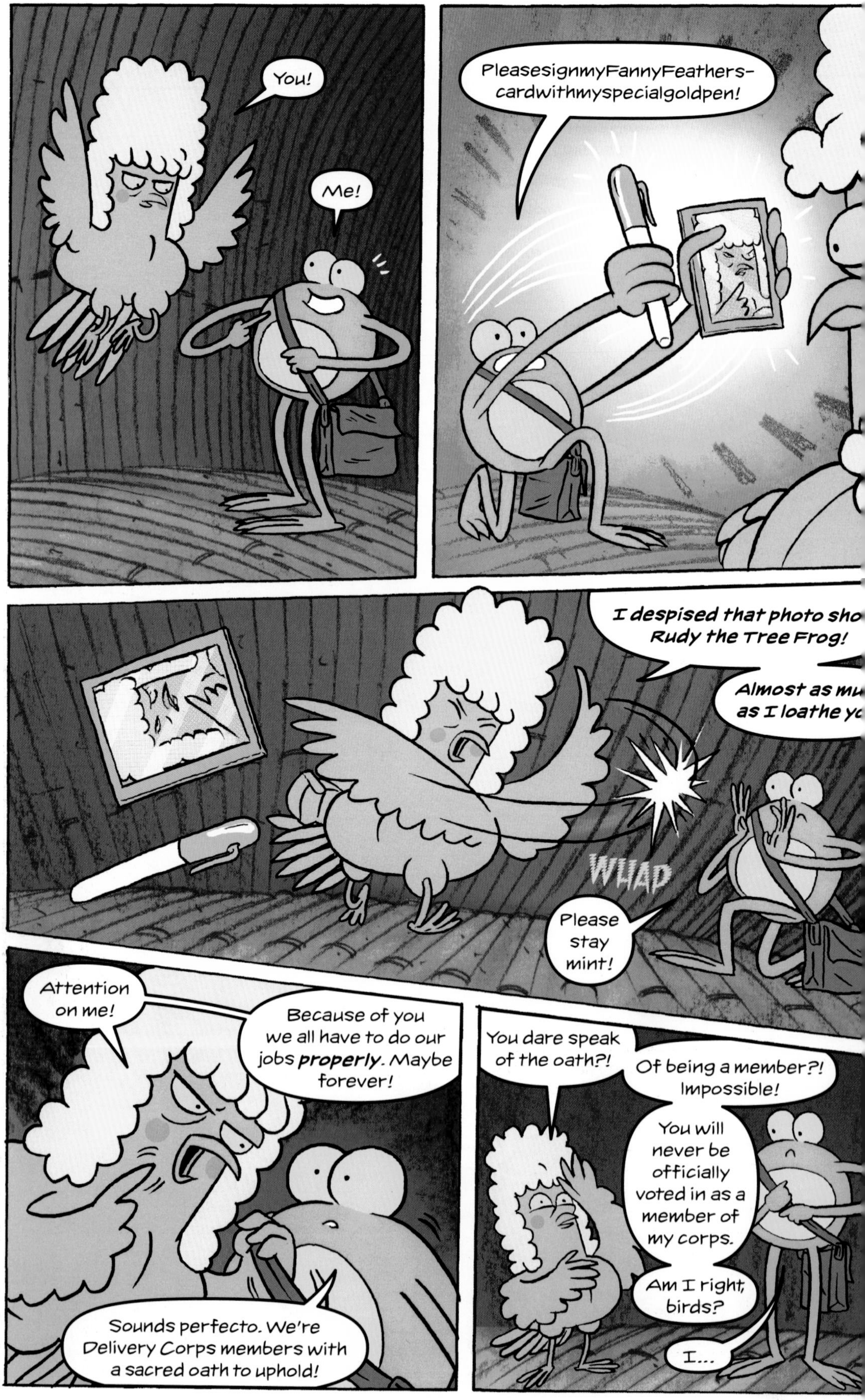
You!
Me!
PleasesignmyFannyFeathers-cardwithmyspecialgoldpen!
I despised that photo sho
Rudy the Tree Frog!
Almost as mu
as I loathe yo
WHAP
Please stay mint!
Attention on me!
Because of you we all have to do our jobs properly. Maybe forever!
Sounds perfecto. We're Delivery Corps members with a sacred oath to uphold!
You dare speak of the oath?!
Of being a member?! Impossible!
You will never be officially voted in as a member of my corps.
Am I right, birds?
I...

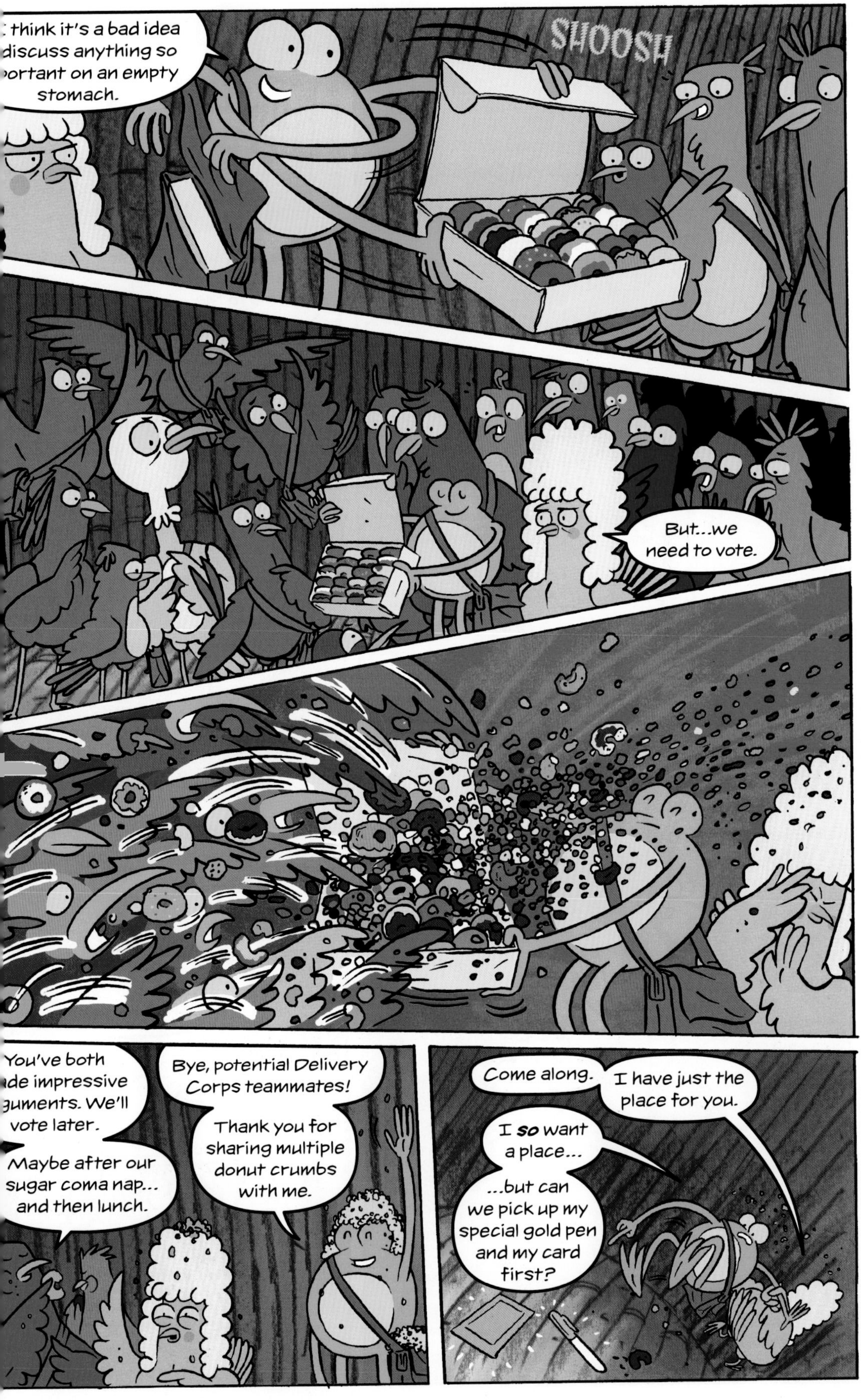
I think it's a bad idea
discuss anything so
portant on an empty
stomach.
SHOOSH
But...we
need to vote.
You've both
ade impressive
guments. We'll
vote later.
Maybe after our
sugar coma nap...
and then lunch.
Bye, potential Delivery
Corps teammates!
Thank you for
sharing multiple
donut crumbs
with me.
Come along.
I have just the
place for you.
I so want
a place...
...but can
we pick up my
special gold pen
and my card
first?

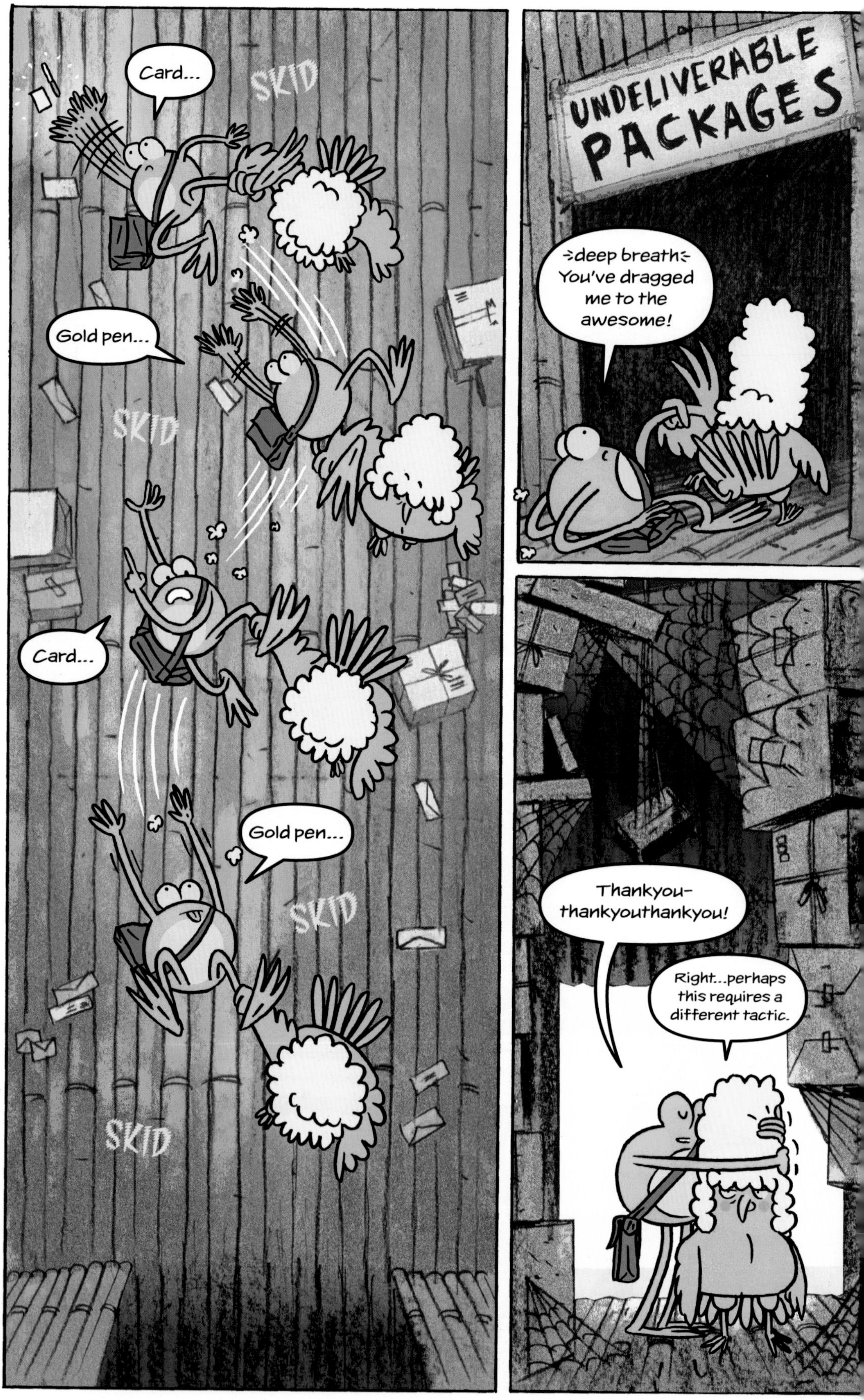
Card...
SKID
Gold pen...
SKID
Card...
Gold pen...
SKID
SKID
UNDELIVERABLE PACKAGES
≈deep breath≈ You've dragged me to the awesome!
Thankyou-thankyouthankyou!
Right...perhaps this requires a different tactic.

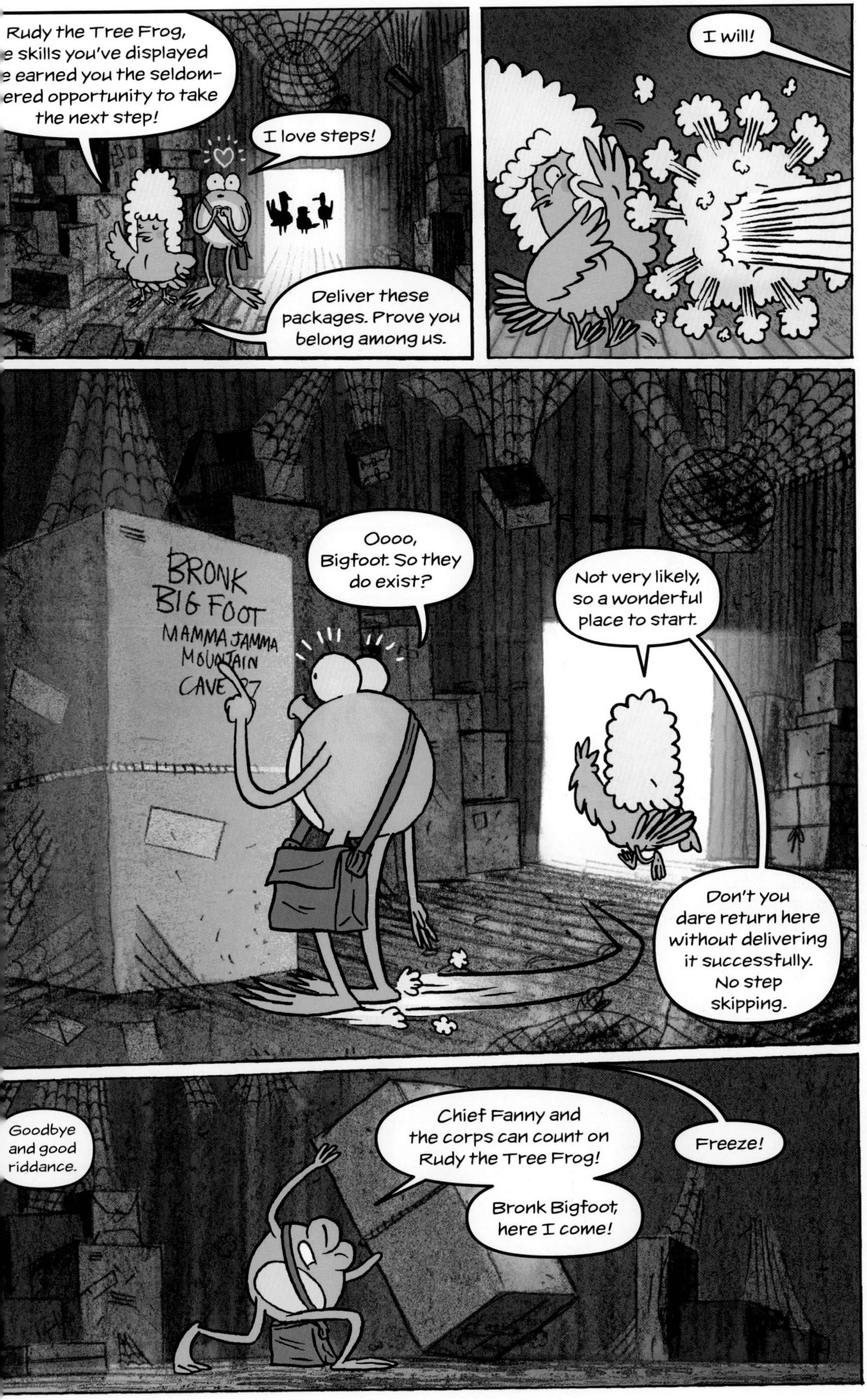
Rudy the Tree Frog, e skills you've displayed e earned you the seldom- ered opportunity to take the next step!
I love steps!
Deliver these packages. Prove you belong among us.
I will!
BRONK BIG FOOT MAMMA JAMMA MOUNTAIN CAVE
Oooo, Bigfoot. So they do exist?
Not very likely, so a wonderful place to start.
Don't you dare return here without delivering it successfully. No step skipping.
Goodbye and good riddance.
Chief Fanny and the corps can count on Rudy the Tree Frog!
Bronk Bigfoot, here I come!
Freeze!

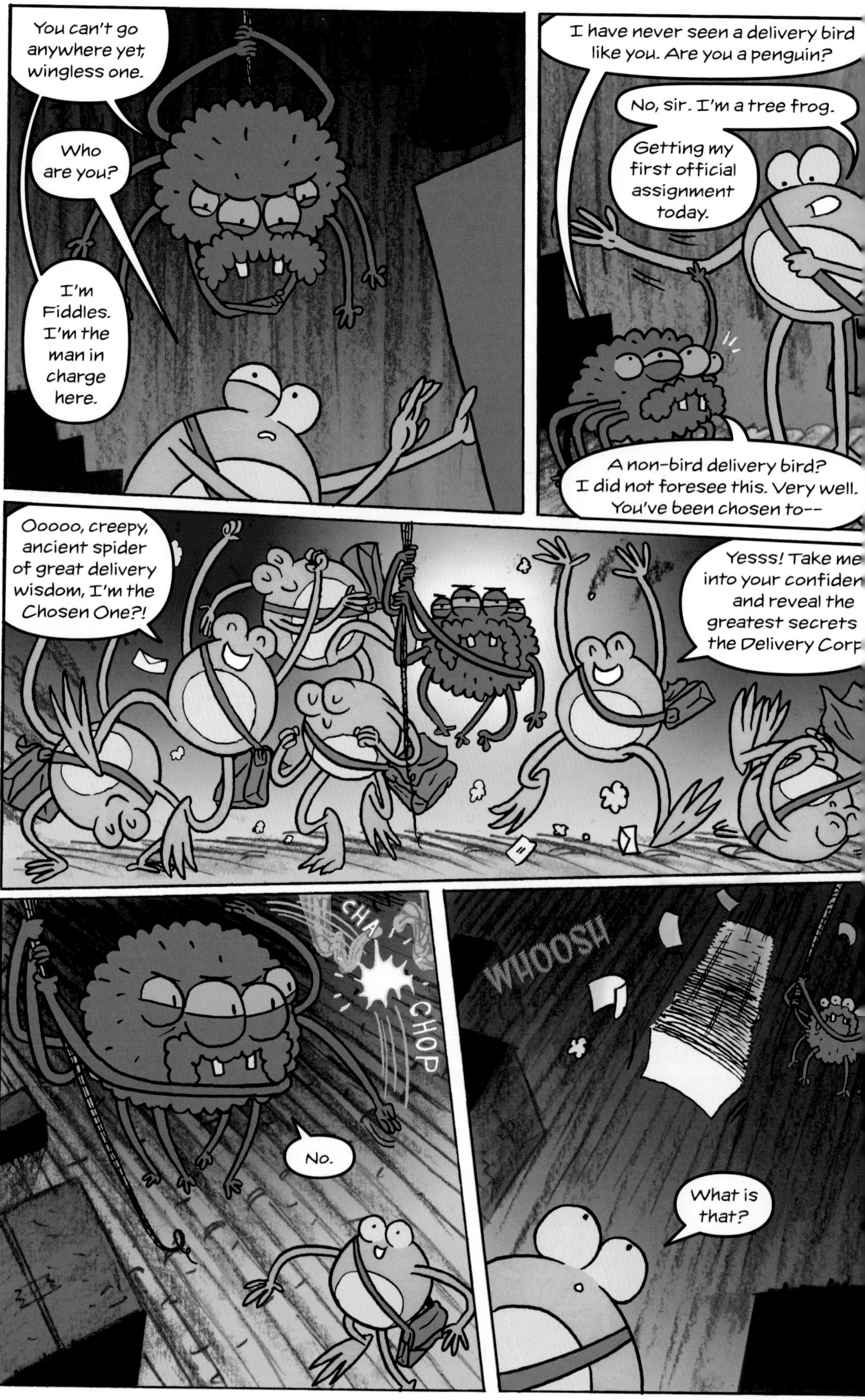
You can't go anywhere yet, wingless one.
Who are you?
I'm Fiddles. I'm the man in charge here.
I have never seen a delivery bird like you. Are you a penguin?
No, sir. I'm a tree frog.
Getting my first official assignment today.
A non-bird delivery bird? I did not foresee this. Very well. You've been chosen to--
Ooooo, creepy, ancient spider of great delivery wisdom, I'm the Chosen One?!
Yesss! Take me into your confiden and reveal the greatest secrets the Delivery Corp
CHA
CHOP
No.
WHOOSH
What is that?

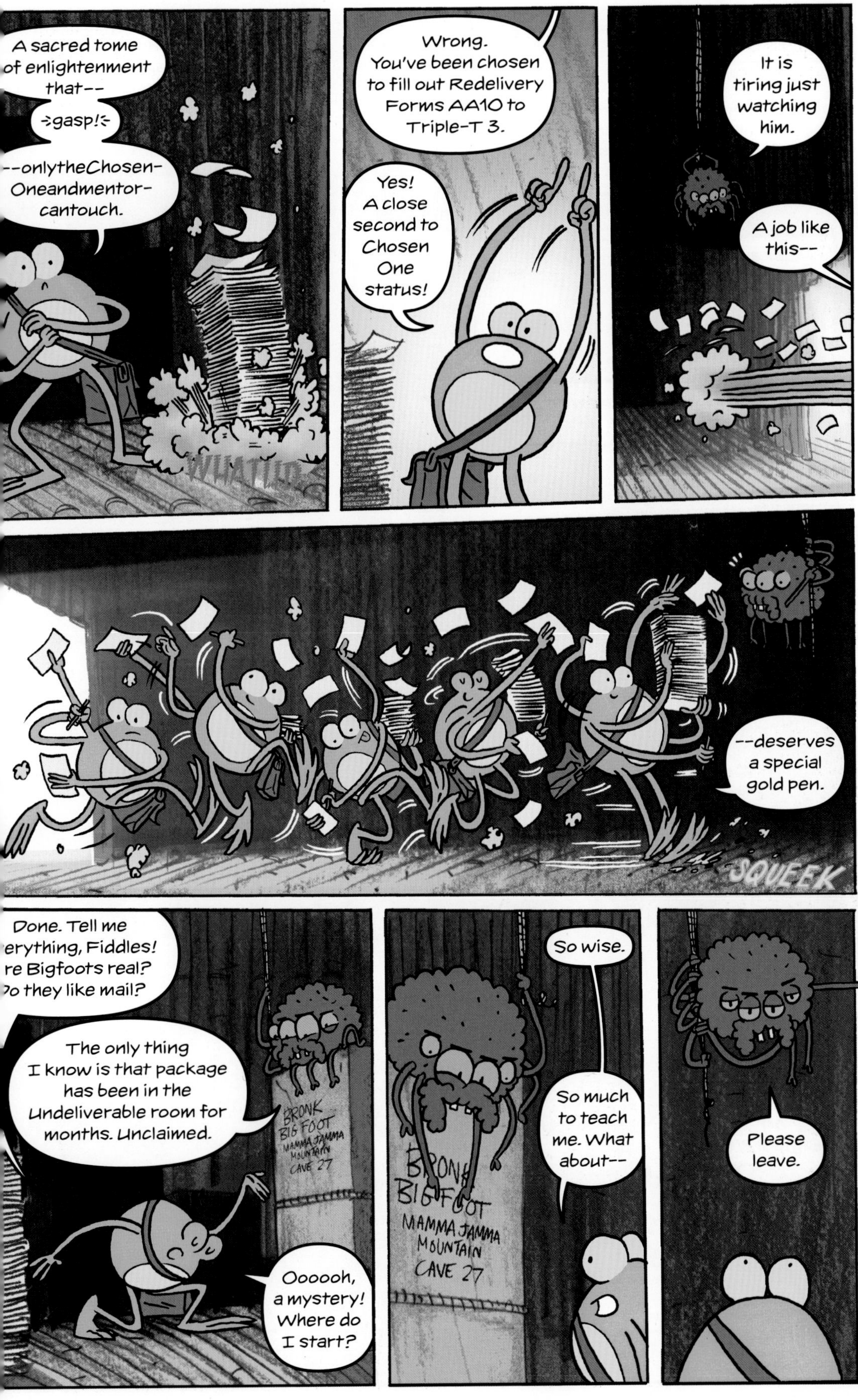
A sacred tome of enlightenment that--
gasp!
--onlytheChosen-Oneandmentor-cantouch.
WHATUD
Wrong. You've been chosen to fill out Redelivery Forms AA10 to Triple-T 3.
Yes! A close second to Chosen One status!
It is tiring just watching him.
A job like this--
--deserves a special gold pen.
SQUEEK
Done. Tell me erything, Fiddles! re Bigfoots real? o they like mail?
The only thing I know is that package has been in the Undeliverable room for months. Unclaimed.
BRONK BIG FOOT MAMMA JAMMA MOUNTAIN CAVE 27
Oooooh, a mystery! Where do I start?
So wise.
BRONK BIGFOOT MAMMA JAMMA MOUNTAIN CAVE 27
So much to teach me. What about--
Please leave.

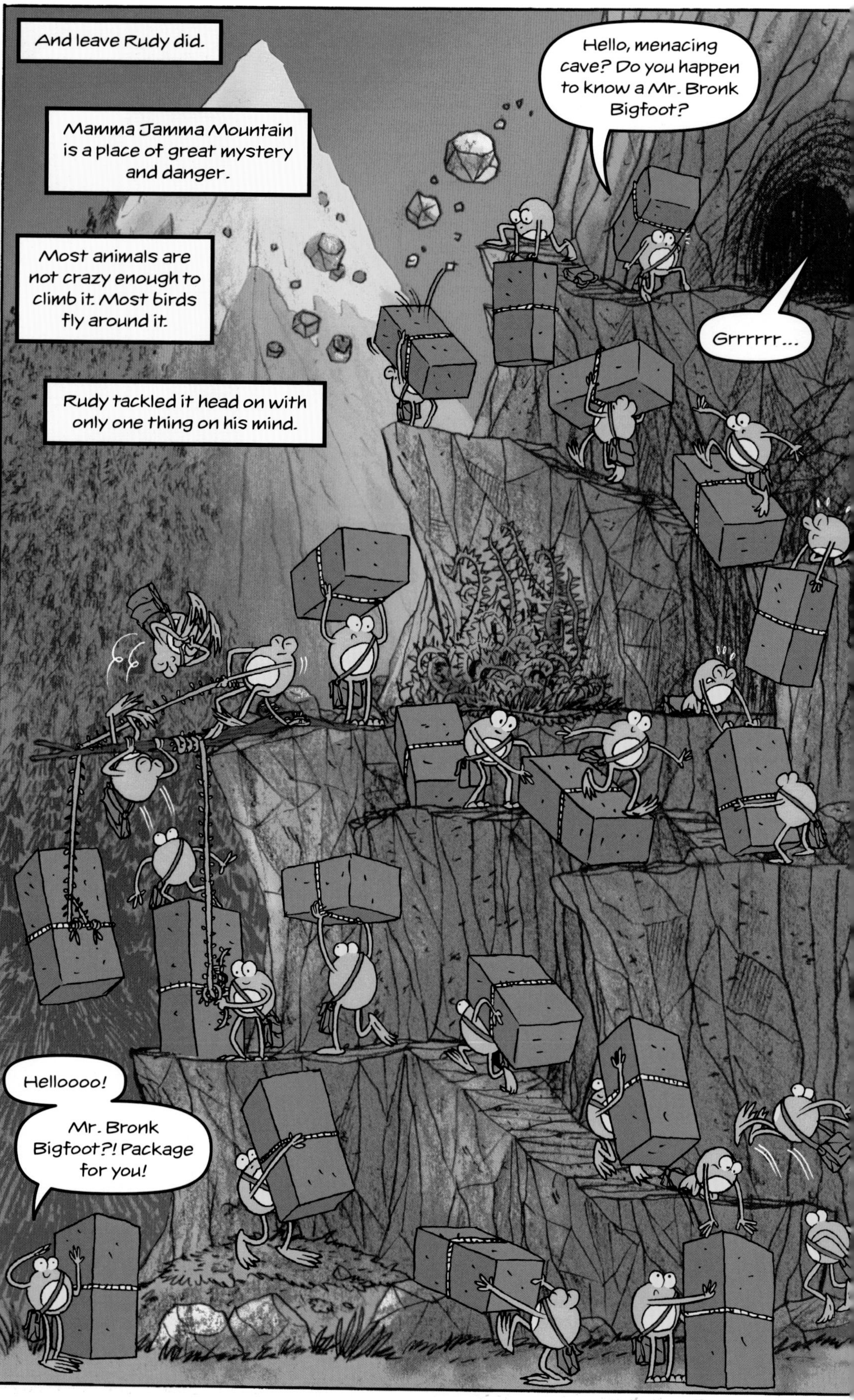
And leave Rudy did.
Mamma Jamma Mountain is a place of great mystery and danger.
Most animals are not crazy enough to climb it. Most birds fly around it.
Rudy tackled it head on with only one thing on his mind.
Hellooooo!
Mr. Bronk Bigfoot?! Package for you!
Hello, menacing cave? Do you happen to know a Mr. Bronk Bigfoot?
Grrrrrr...

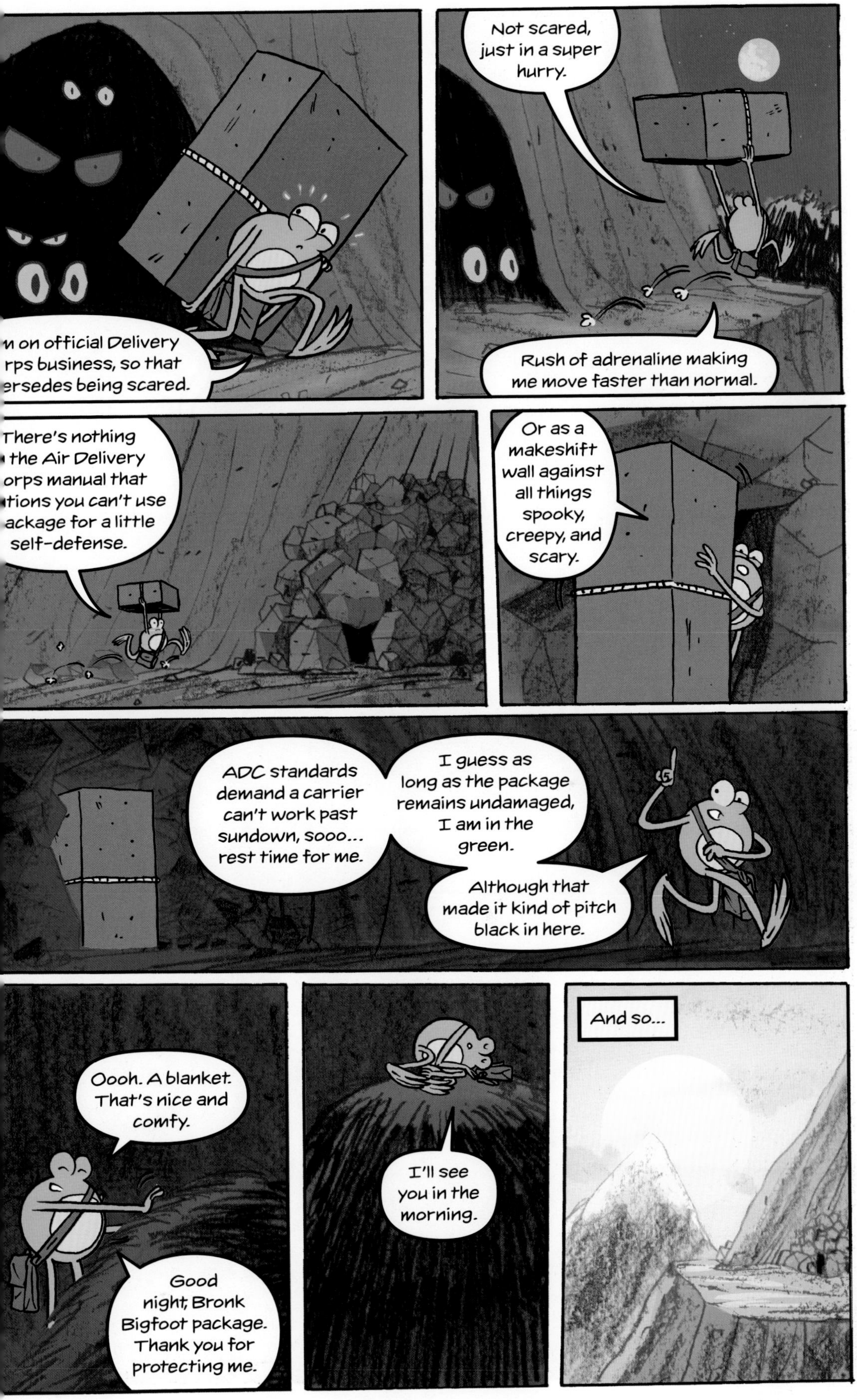
n on official Delivery
rps business, so that
ersedes being scared.
Not scared, just in a super hurry.
Rush of adrenaline making me move faster than normal.
There's nothing
the Air Delivery
orps manual that
tions you can't use
ackage for a little
self-defense.
Or as a makeshift wall against all things spooky, creepy, and scary.
ADC standards demand a carrier can't work past sundown, sooo... rest time for me.
I guess as long as the package remains undamaged, I am in the green.
Although that made it kind of pitch black in here.
Oooh. A blanket. That's nice and comfy.
Good night, Bronk Bigfoot package. Thank you for protecting me.
I'll see you in the morning.
And so...

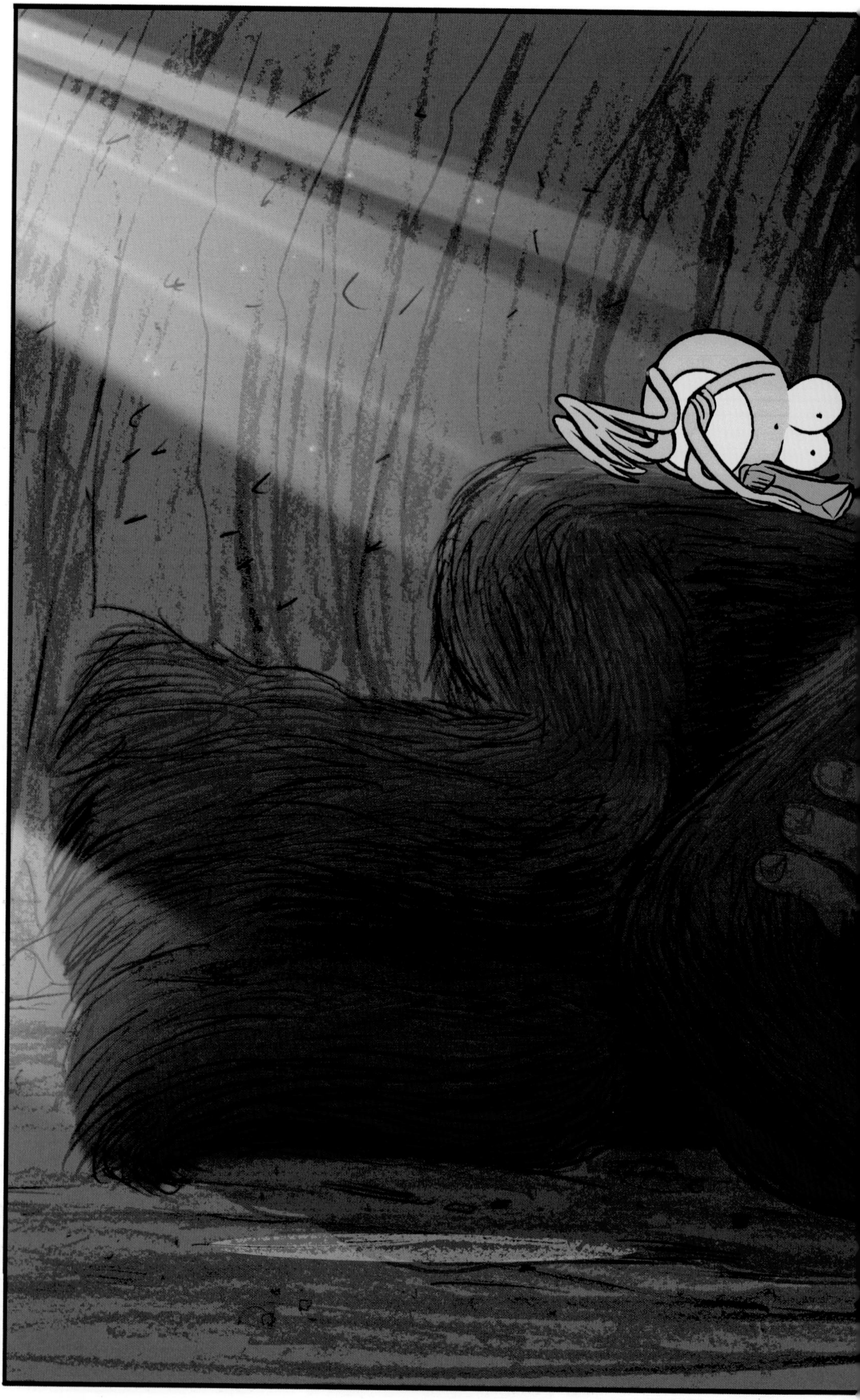

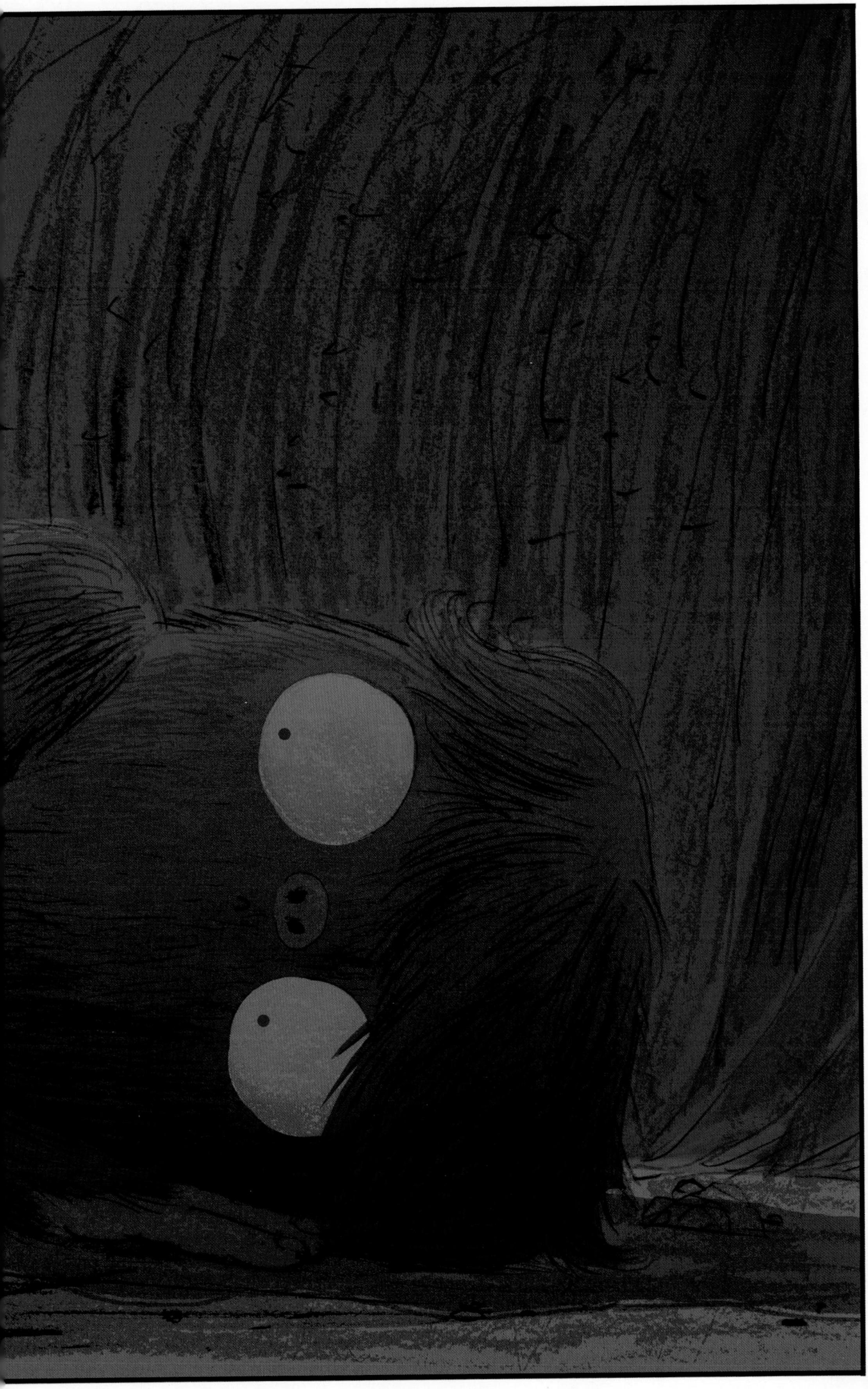

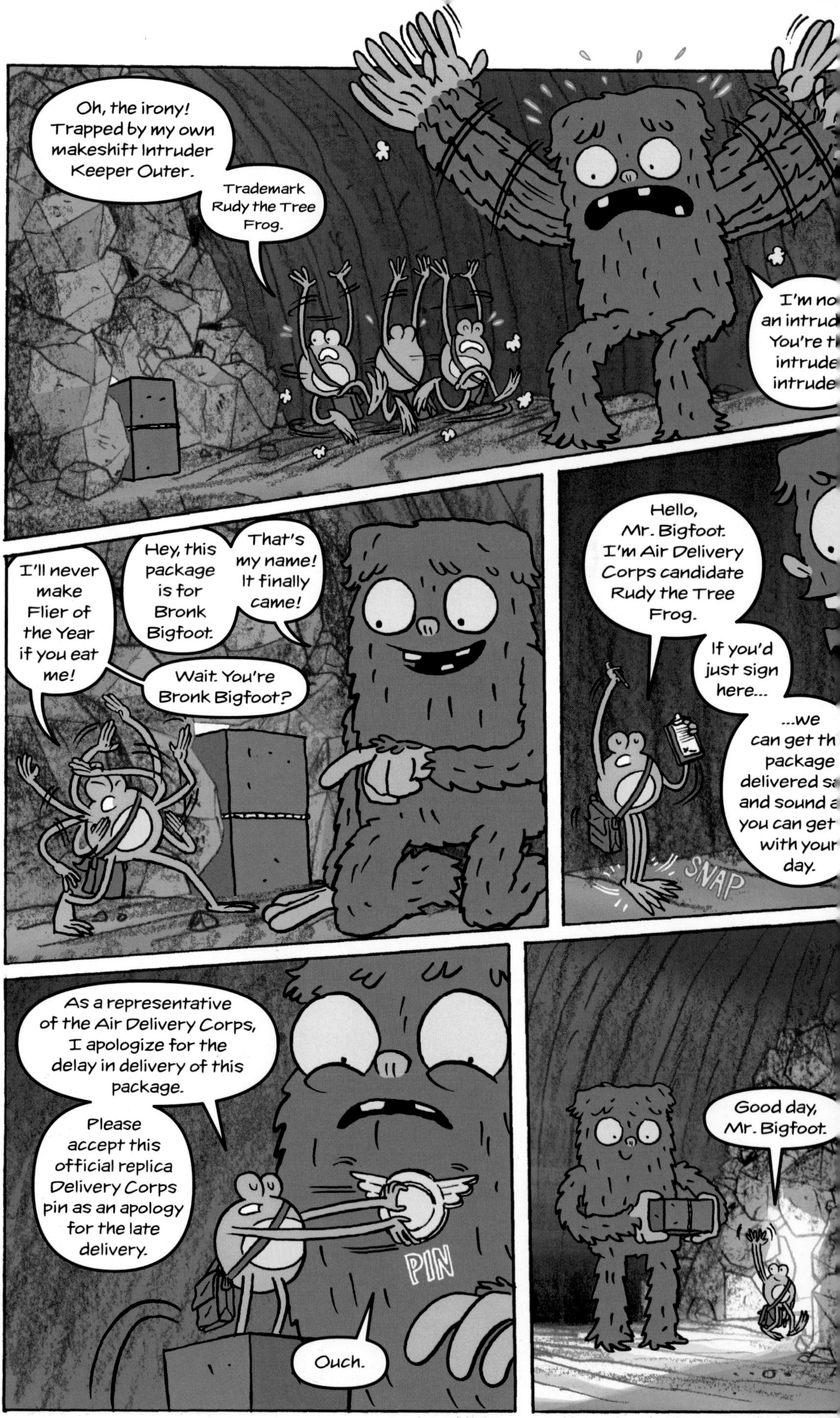

Oh, the irony! Trapped by my own makeshift Intruder Keeper Outer.
Trademark Rudy the Tree Frog.
I'm no
an intrud
You're t
intrude
intrude
I'll never make Flier of the Year if you eat me!
Hey, this package is for Bronk Bigfoot.
That's my name! It finally came!
Wait. You're Bronk Bigfoot?
Hello, Mr. Bigfoot. I'm Air Delivery Corps candidate Rudy the Tree Frog.
If you'd just sign here...
...we can get th package delivered sa and sound a you can get with your day.
SNAP
As a representative of the Air Delivery Corps, I apologize for the delay in delivery of this package.
Please accept this official replica Delivery Corps pin as an apology for the late delivery.
PIN
Ouch.
Good day, Mr. Bigfoot.

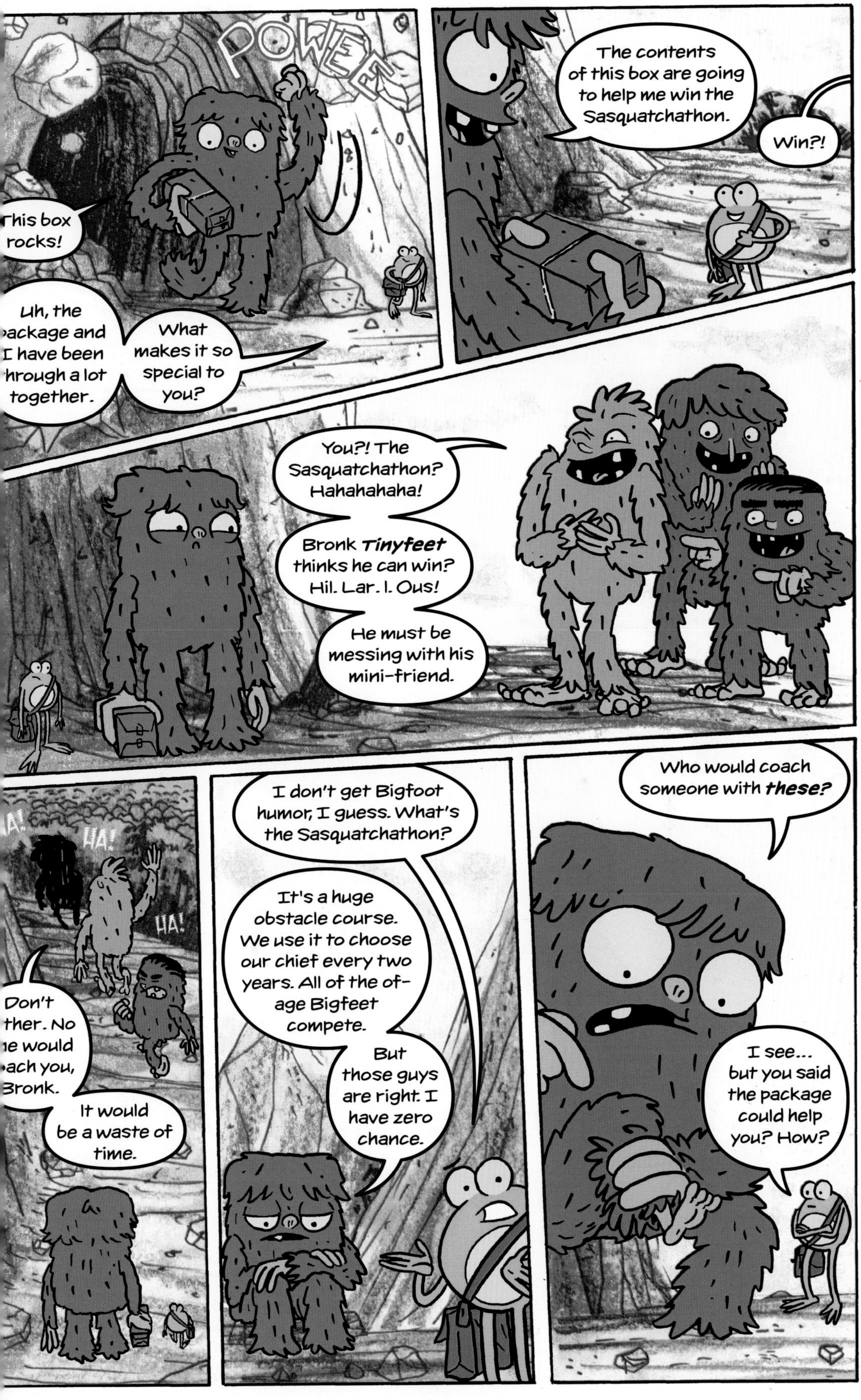
POWEE
This box rocks!
Uh, the package and I have been through a lot together.
What makes it so special to you?
The contents of this box are going to help me win the Sasquatchathon.
Win?!
You?! The Sasquatchathon? Hahahahaha!
Bronk *Tinyfeet* thinks he can win? Hil. Lar. I. Ous!
He must be messing with his mini-friend.
HA!
HA!
Don't ther. No ne would ach you, Bronk.
It would be a waste of time.
I don't get Bigfoot humor, I guess. What's the Sasquatchathon?
It's a huge obstacle course. We use it to choose our chief every two years. All of the of-age Bigfeet compete.
But those guys are right. I have zero chance.
Who would coach someone with *these?*
I see... but you said the package could help you? How?

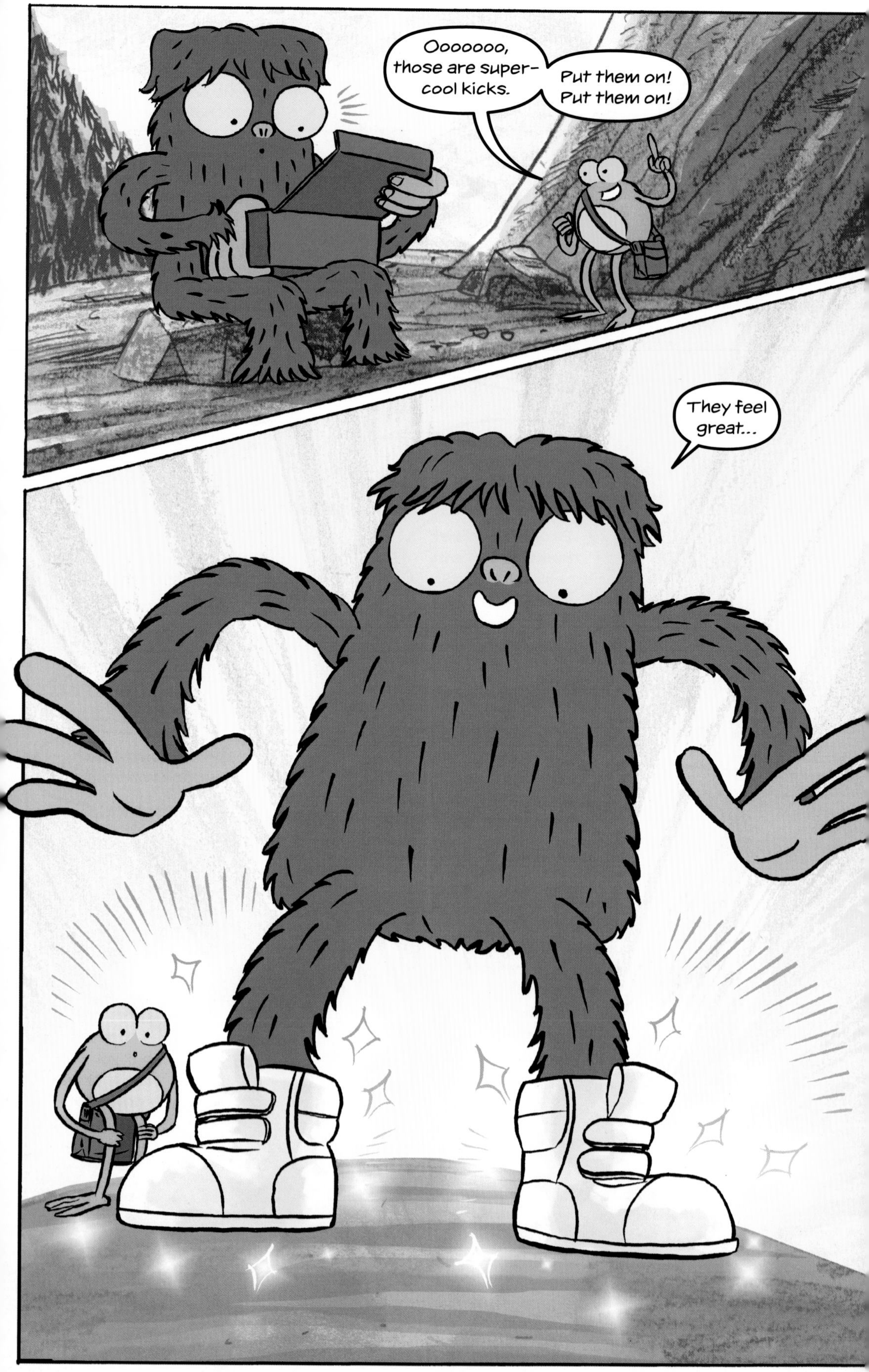
Ooooooo, those are super-cool kicks.
Put them on! Put them on!
They feel great...

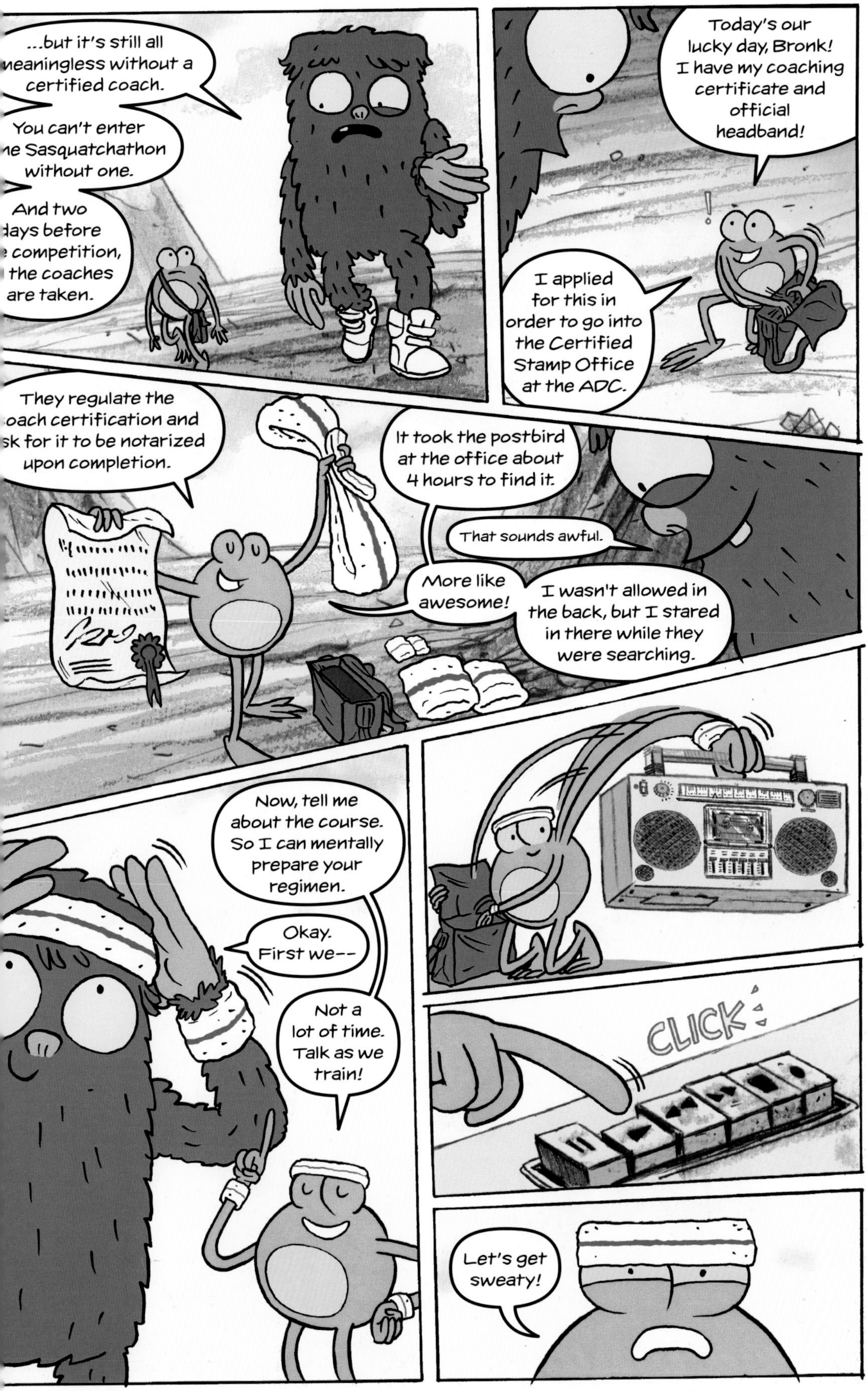
...but it's still all
eaningless without a
certified coach.
You can't enter
e Sasquatchathon
without one.
And two
days before
competition,
the coaches
are taken.
Today's our
lucky day, Bronk!
I have my coaching
certificate and
official
headband!
I applied
for this in
order to go into
the Certified
Stamp Office
at the ADC.
They regulate the
oach certification and
sk for it to be notarized
upon completion.
It took the postbird
at the office about
4 hours to find it.
That sounds awful.
More like
awesome!
I wasn't allowed in
the back, but I stared
in there while they
were searching.
Now, tell me
about the course.
So I can mentally
prepare your
regimen.
Okay.
First we--
Not a
lot of time.
Talk as we
train!
CLICK
Let's get
sweaty!

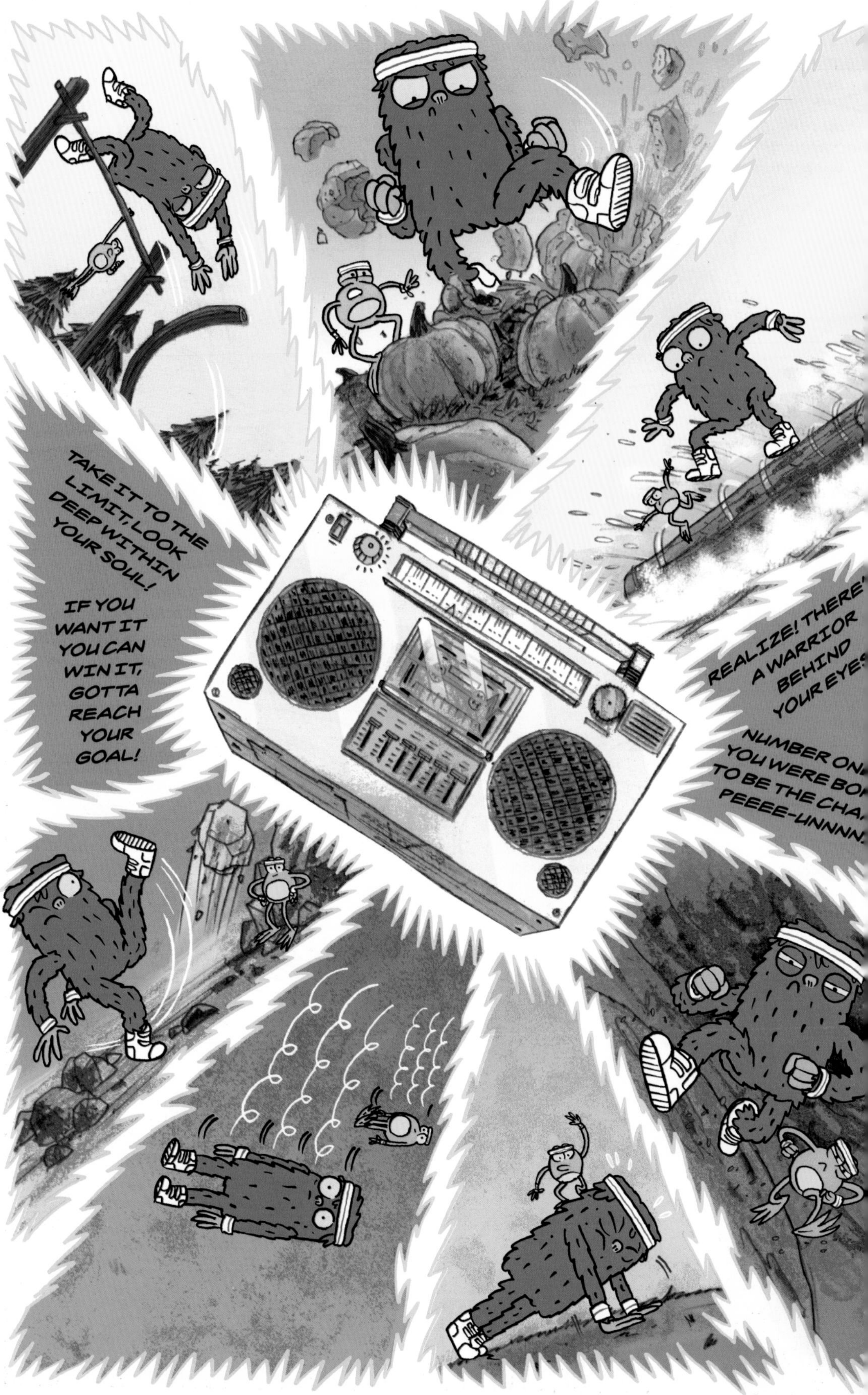
TAKE IT TO THE LIMIT, LOOK DEEP WITHIN YOUR SOUL!
IF YOU WANT IT YOU CAN WIN IT, GOTTA REACH YOUR GOAL!
REALIZE! THERE' A WARRIOR BEHIND YOUR EYES
NUMBER ON YOU WERE BO TO BE THE CHA PEEEE-UNNNN

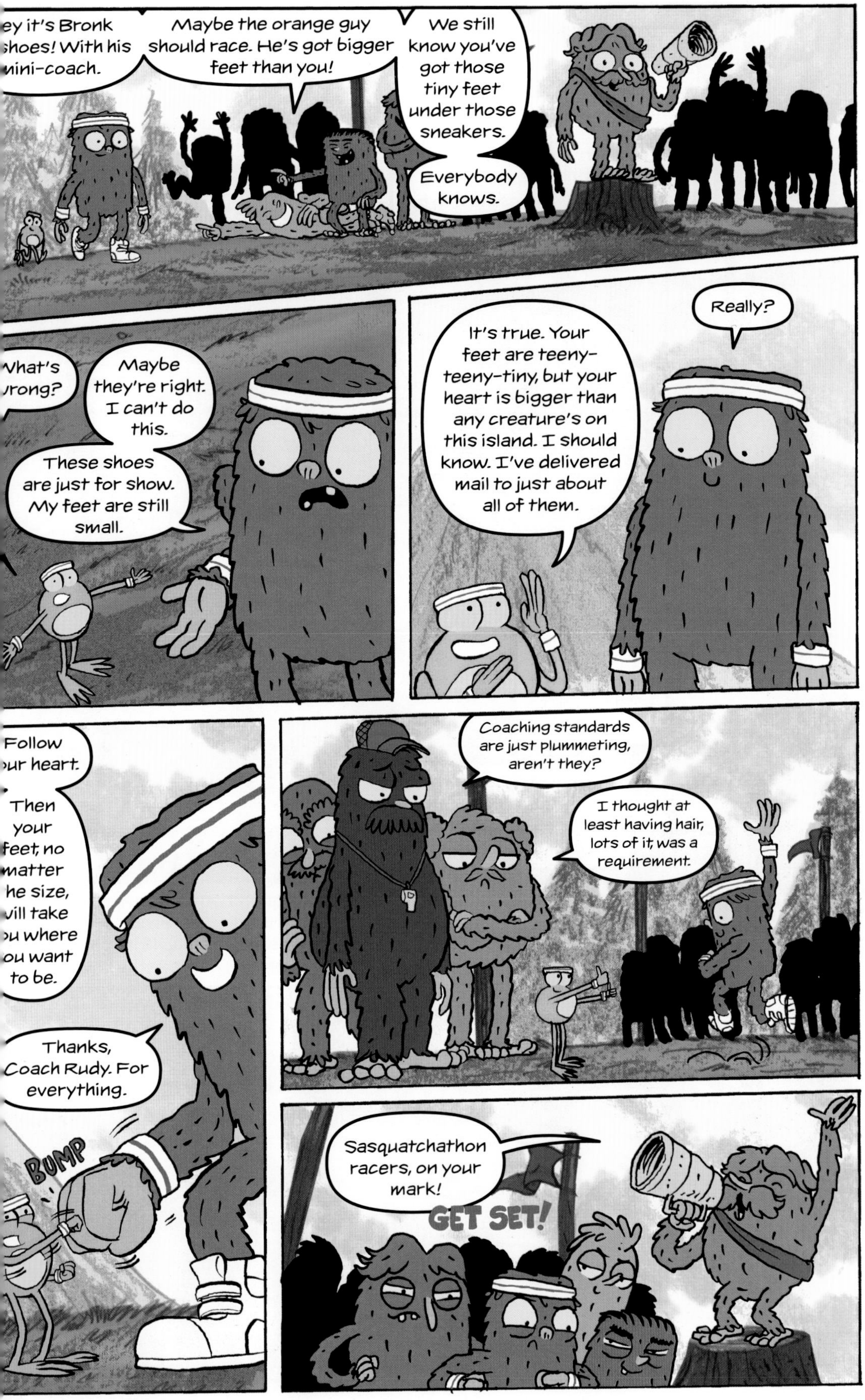

ey it's Bronk
shoes! With his
nini-coach.
Maybe the orange guy should race. He's got bigger feet than you!
We still know you've got those tiny feet under those sneakers.
Everybody knows.
What's
rong?
Maybe they're right. I can't do this.
These shoes are just for show. My feet are still small.
It's true. Your feet are teeny-teeny-tiny, but your heart is bigger than any creature's on this island. I should know. I've delivered mail to just about all of them.
Really?
Follow
ur heart.
Then
your
feet, no
matter
he size,
vill take
u where
ou want
to be.
Thanks, Coach Rudy. For everything.
BUMP
Coaching standards are just plummeting, aren't they?
I thought at least having hair, lots of it, was a requirement.
Sasquatchathon racers, on your mark!
GET SET!

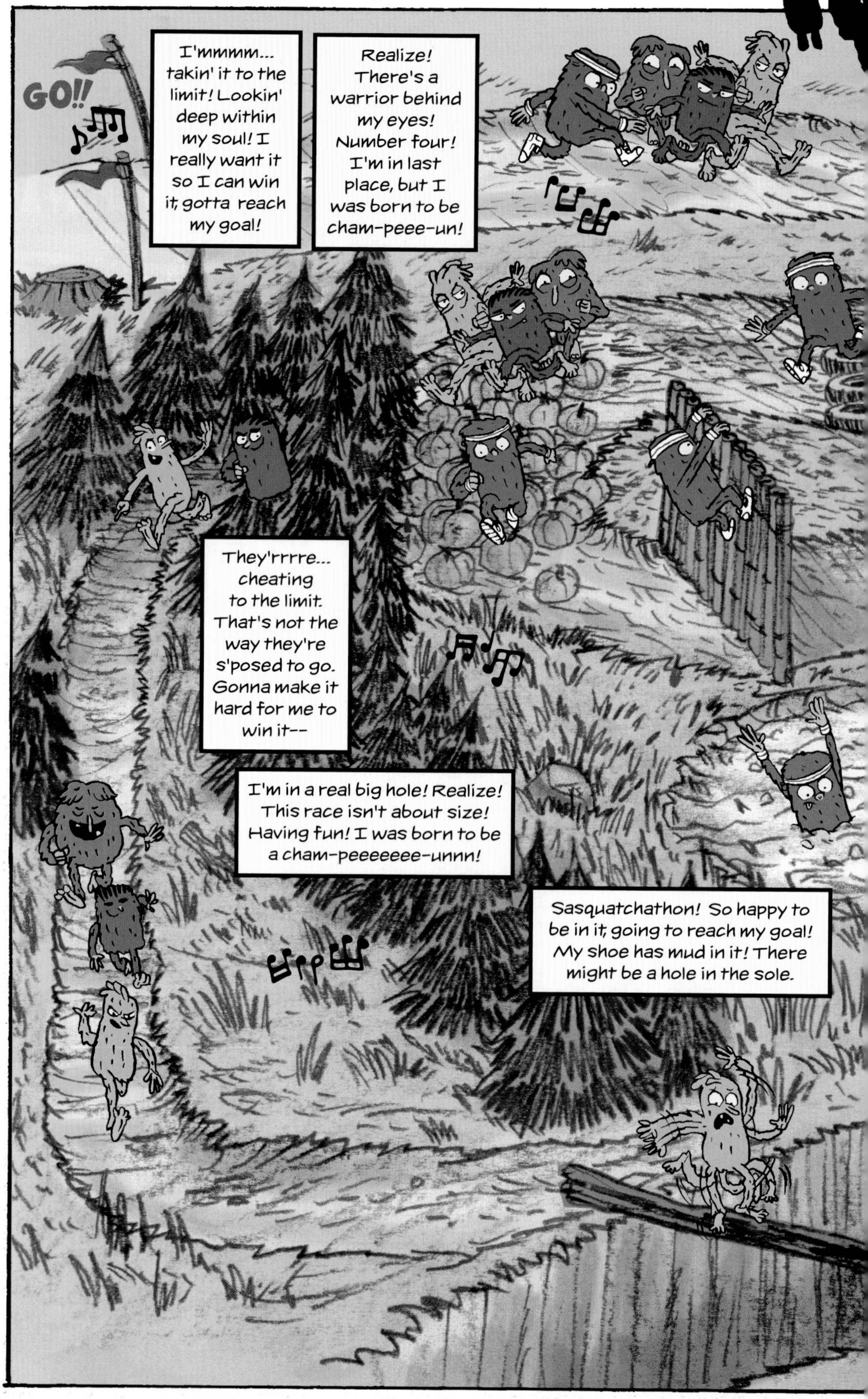
GO!!
I'mmmm... takin' it to the limit! Lookin' deep within my soul! I really want it so I can win it, gotta reach my goal!
Realize! There's a warrior behind my eyes! Number four! I'm in last place, but I was born to be cham-peee-un!
They'rrrre... cheating to the limit. That's not the way they're s'posed to go. Gonna make it hard for me to win it--
I'm in a real big hole! Realize! This race isn't about size! Having fun! I was born to be a cham-peeeeeee-unnn!
Sasquatchathon! So happy to be in it, going to reach my goal! My shoe has mud in it! There might be a hole in the sole.

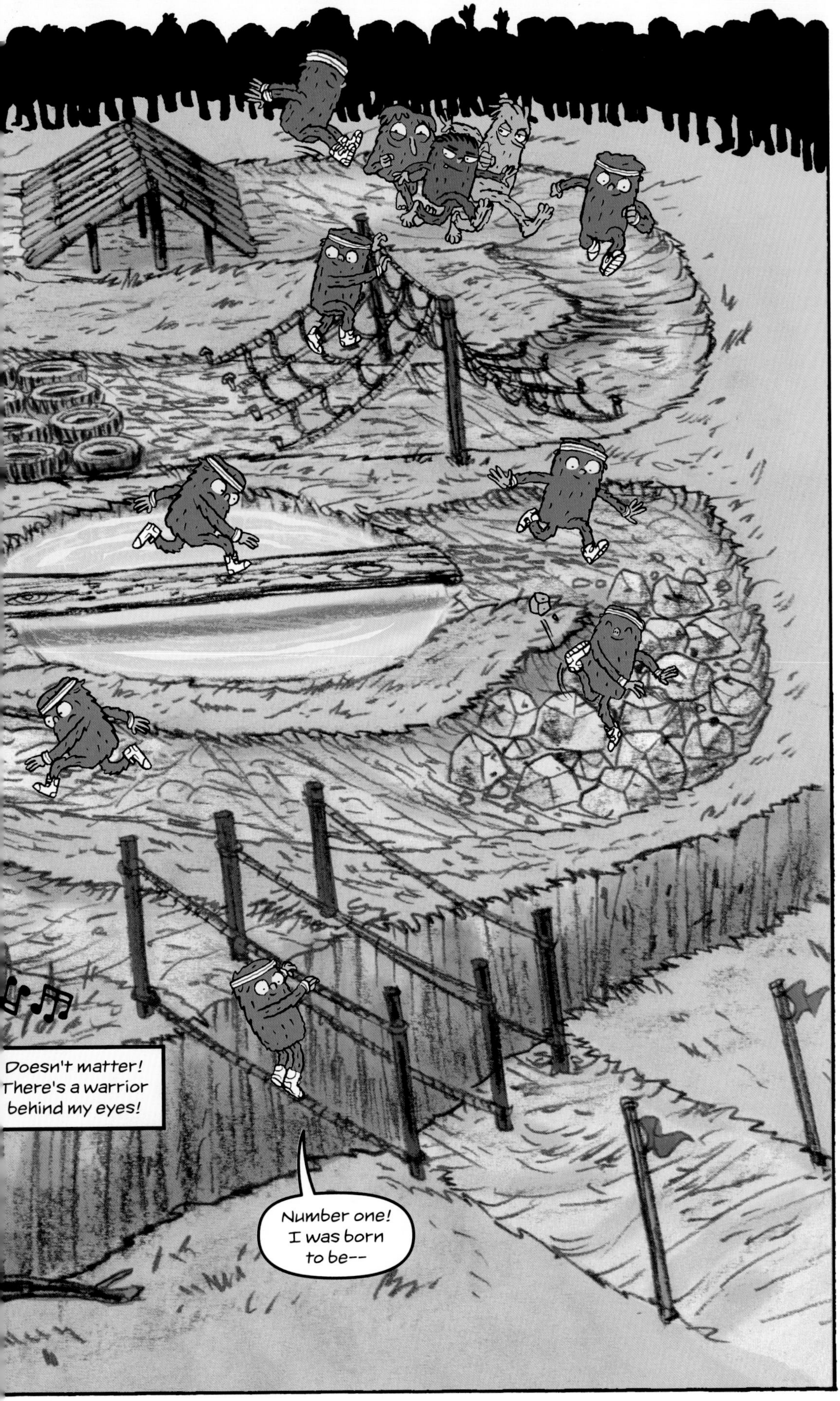
Doesn't matter! There's a warrior behind my eyes!
Number one! I was born to be--

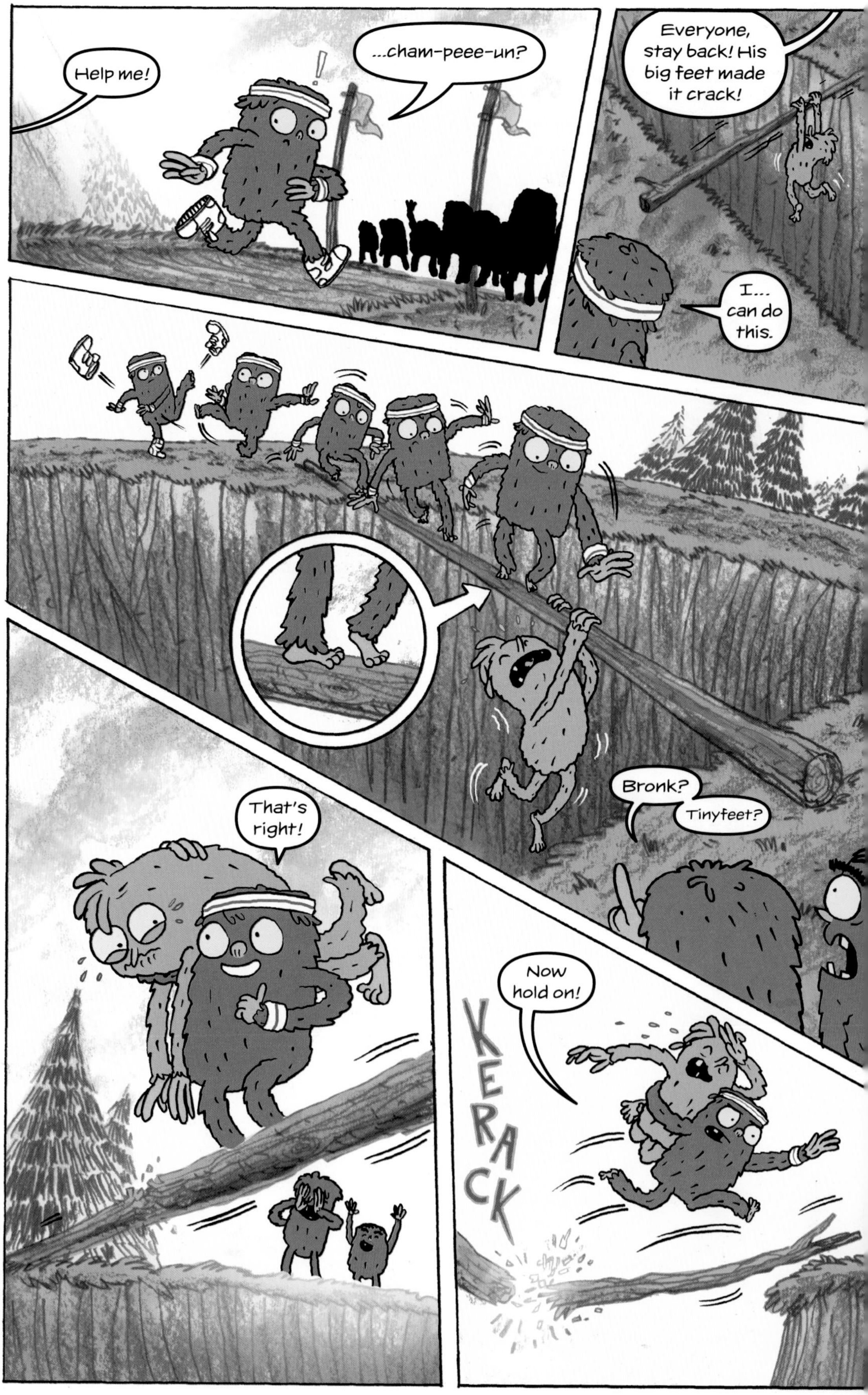

Help me!
...cham-peee-un?
!
Everyone, stay back! His big feet made it crack!
I... can do this.
Bronk?
Tinyfeet?
That's right!
Now hold on!
KERACK

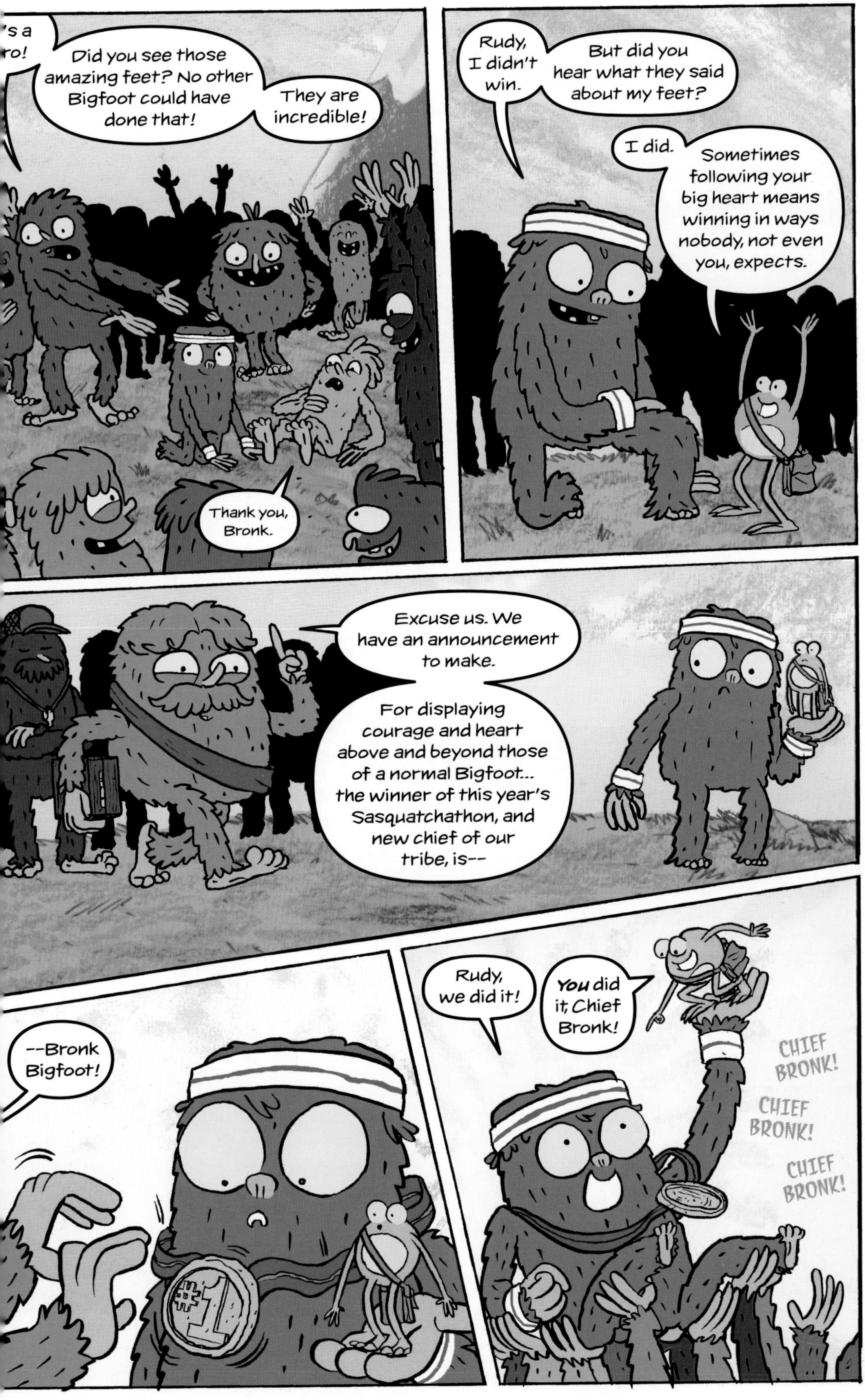
's a
ro!
Did you see those amazing feet? No other Bigfoot could have done that!
They are incredible!
Thank you, Bronk.
Rudy, I didn't win.
But did you hear what they said about my feet?
I did.
Sometimes following your big heart means winning in ways nobody, not even you, expects.
Excuse us. We have an announcement to make.
For displaying courage and heart above and beyond those of a normal Bigfoot... the winner of this year's Sasquatchathon, and new chief of our tribe, is--
--Bronk Bigfoot!
Rudy, we did it!
You did it, Chief Bronk!
CHIEF BRONK!
CHIEF BRONK!
CHIEF BRONK!

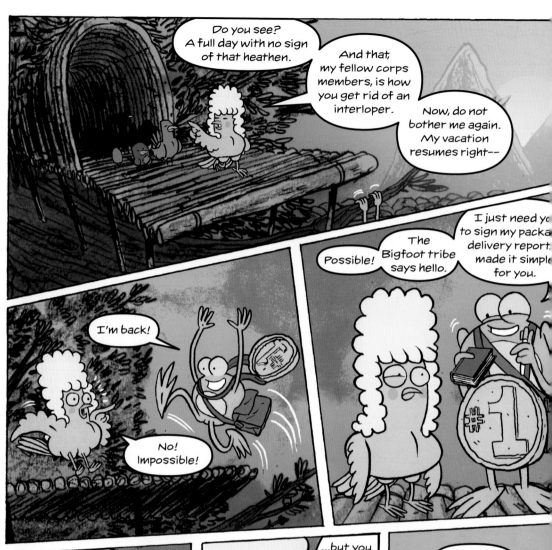

Do you see? A full day with no sign of that heathen.

And that, my fellow corps members, is how you get rid of an interloper.

Now, do not bother me again. My vacation resumes right--

Possible!

The Bigfoot tribe says hello.

I just need yo to sign my packa delivery report made it simple for you.

I'm back!

No! Impossible!

Just sign by the X, please.

Chief Fanny, I just can't thank you enough!

I wasn't sure if you liked me at first...

...but you wouldn't give an important mission like this to someone you don't like, right?

sign by the X

That would be crazy!

I'm so glad we're friends now.

See you in the morning, bestie!

Noooooo!

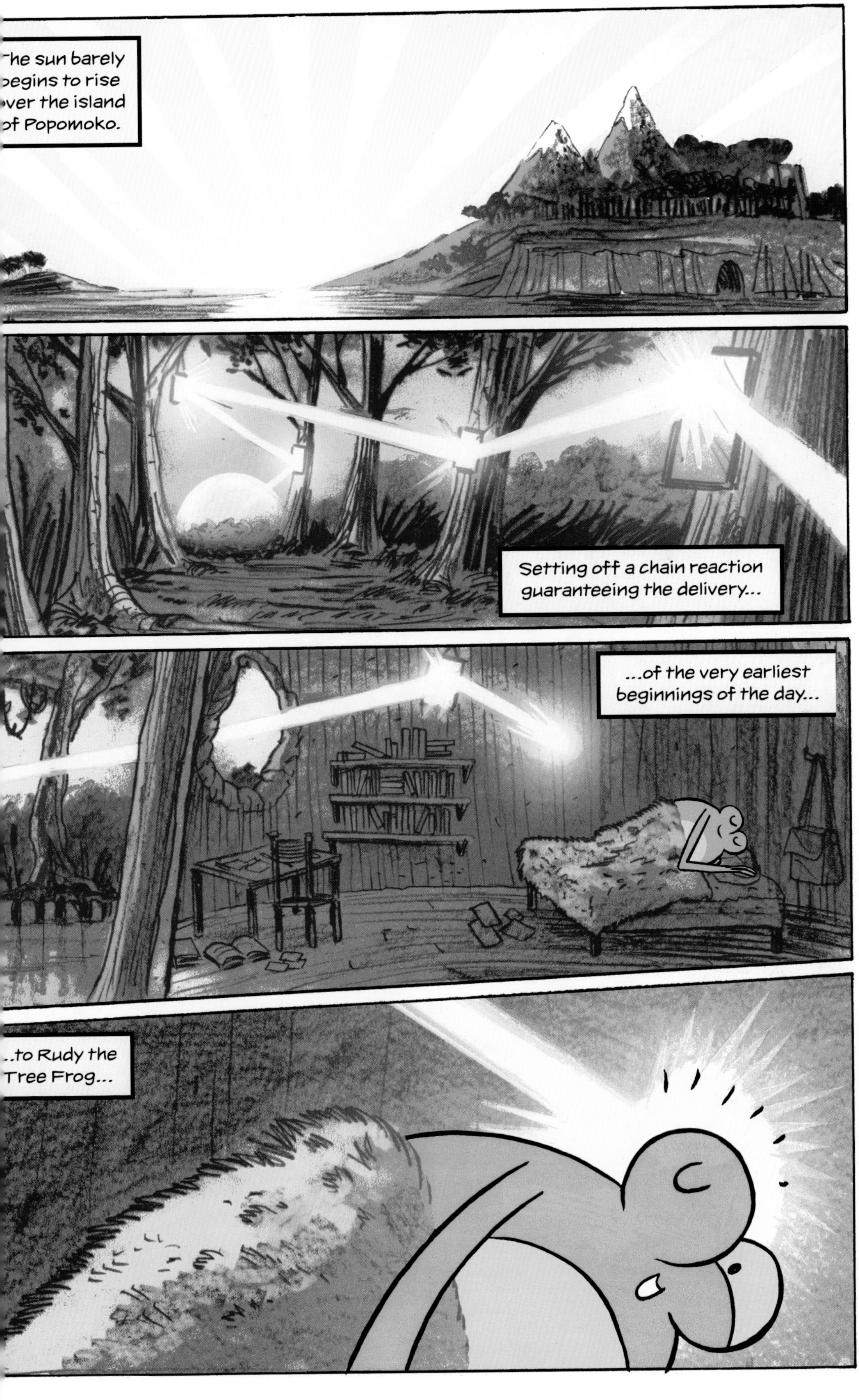

The sun barely begins to rise over the island of Popomoko.
Setting off a chain reaction guaranteeing the delivery...
...of the very earliest beginnings of the day...
..to Rudy the Tree Frog...

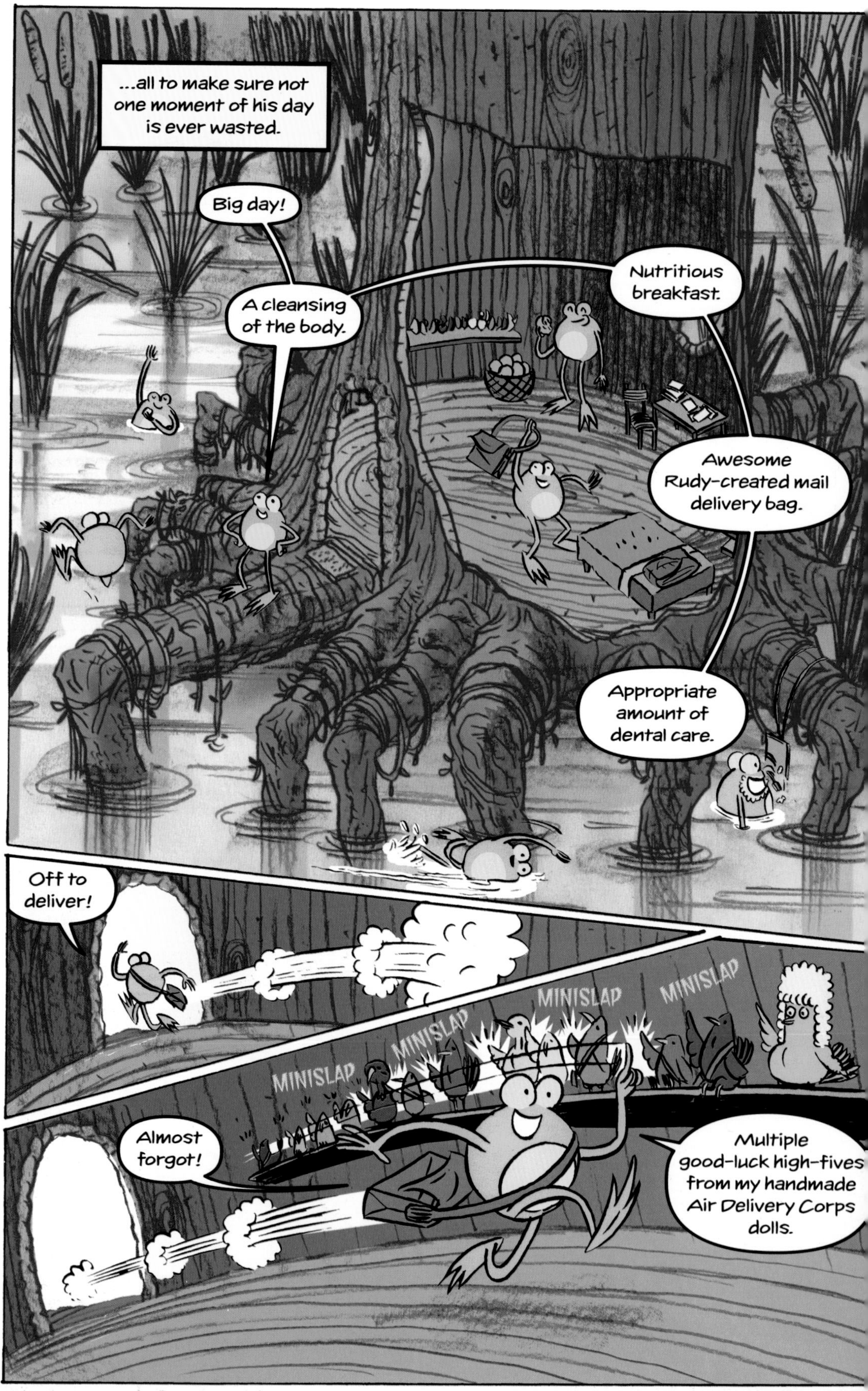

...all to make sure not one moment of his day is ever wasted.
Big day!
A cleansing of the body.
Nutritious breakfast.
Awesome Rudy-created mail delivery bag.
Appropriate amount of dental care.
Off to deliver!
MINISLAP
MINISLAP
MINISLAP
MINISLAP
Almost forgot!
Multiple good-luck high-fives from my handmade Air Delivery Corps dolls.

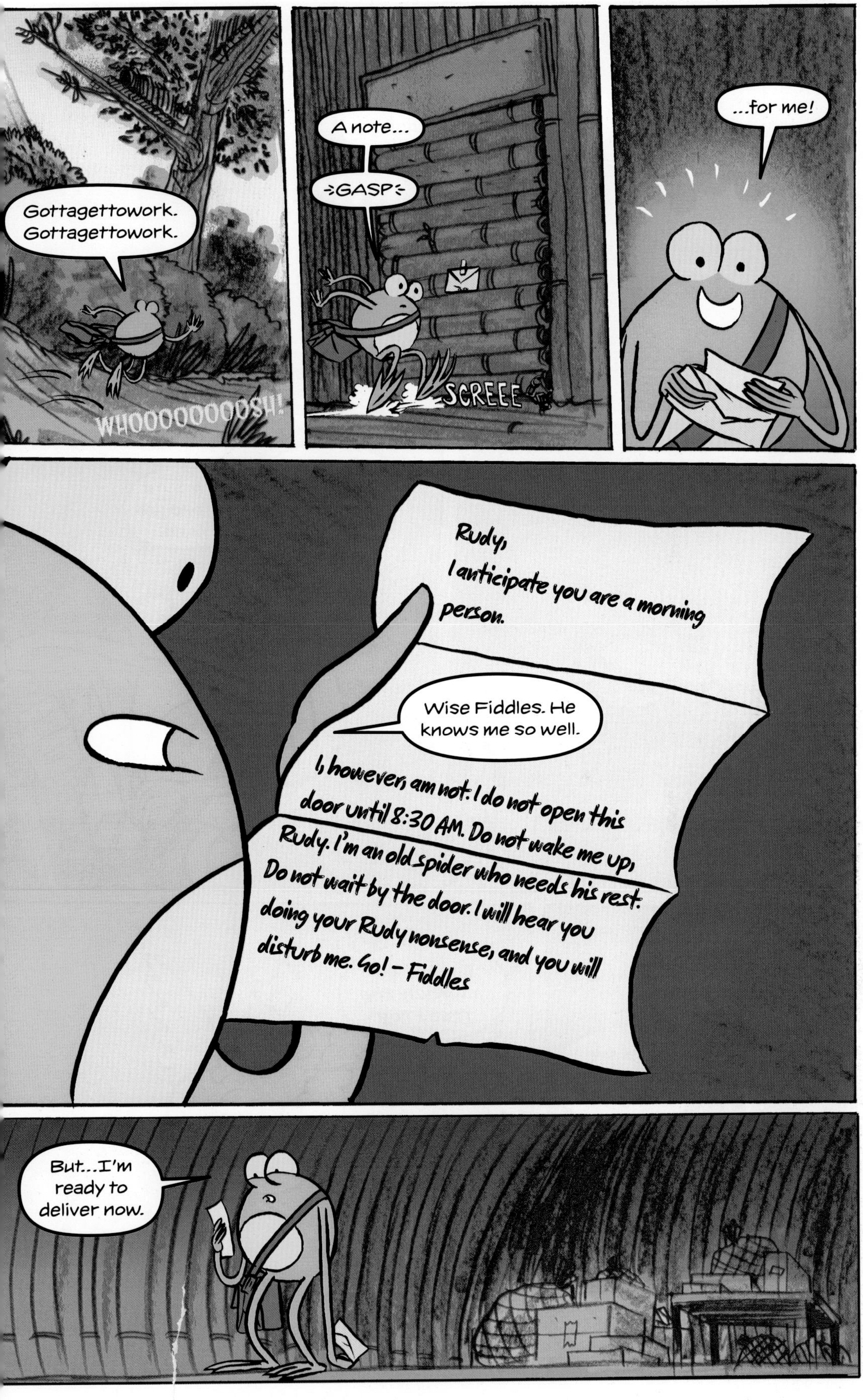
Gottagettowork.
Gottagettowork.
WHOOOOOOOOOSH!
A note...
GASP
SCREEE
...for me!
Rudy,
I anticipate you are a morning person.
Wise Fiddles. He knows me so well.
I, however, am not. I do not open this door until 8:30 AM. Do not wake me up, Rudy. I'm an old spider who needs his rest. Do not wait by the door. I will hear you doing your Rudy nonsense, and you will disturb me. Go! – Fiddles
But...I'm ready to deliver now.

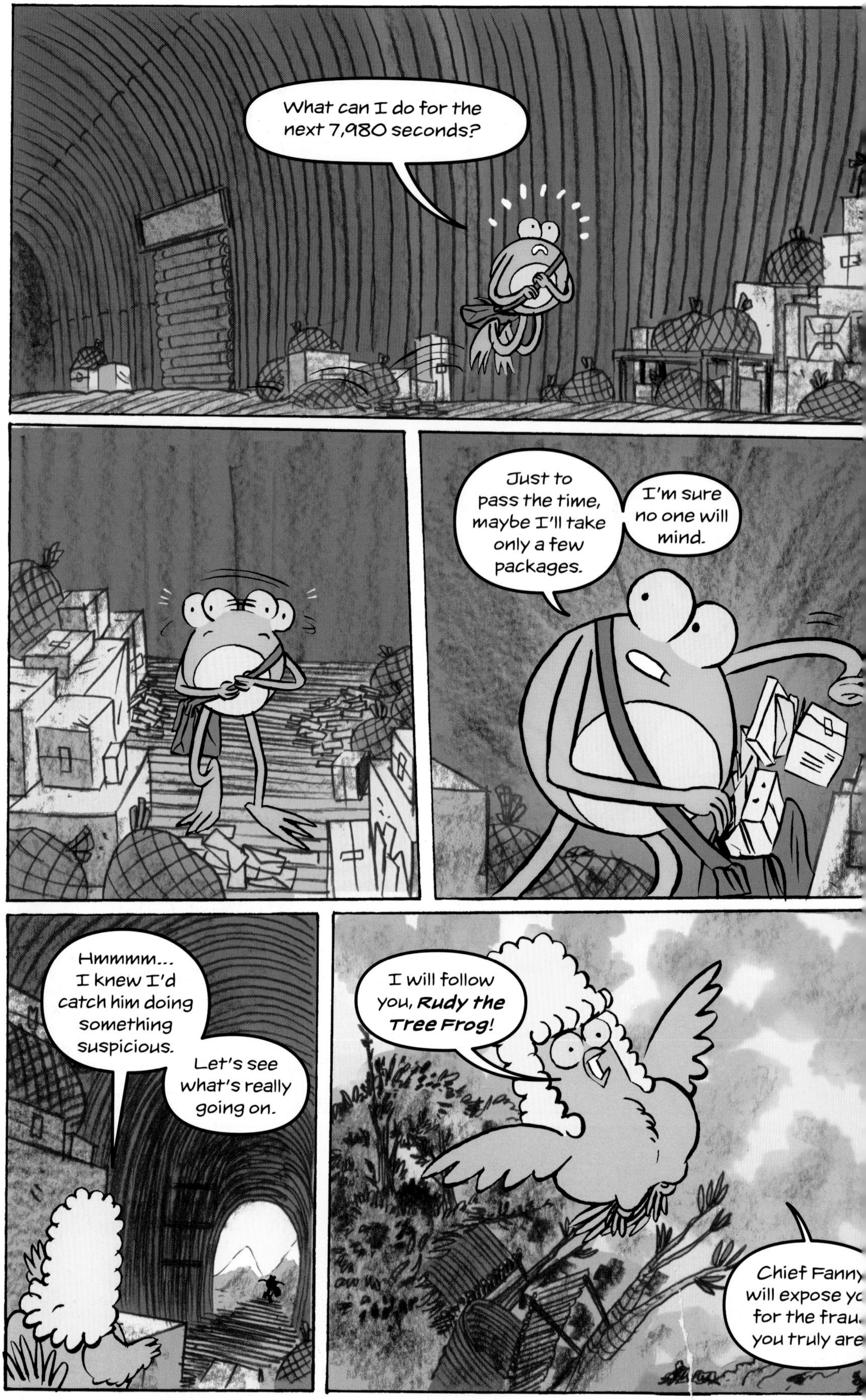
What can I do for the next 7,980 seconds?
Just to pass the time, maybe I'll take only a few packages.
I'm sure no one will mind.
Hmmmm... I knew I'd catch him doing something suspicious.
Let's see what's really going on.
I will follow you, **Rudy the Tree Frog**!
Chief Fanny will expose yo for the frau you truly are

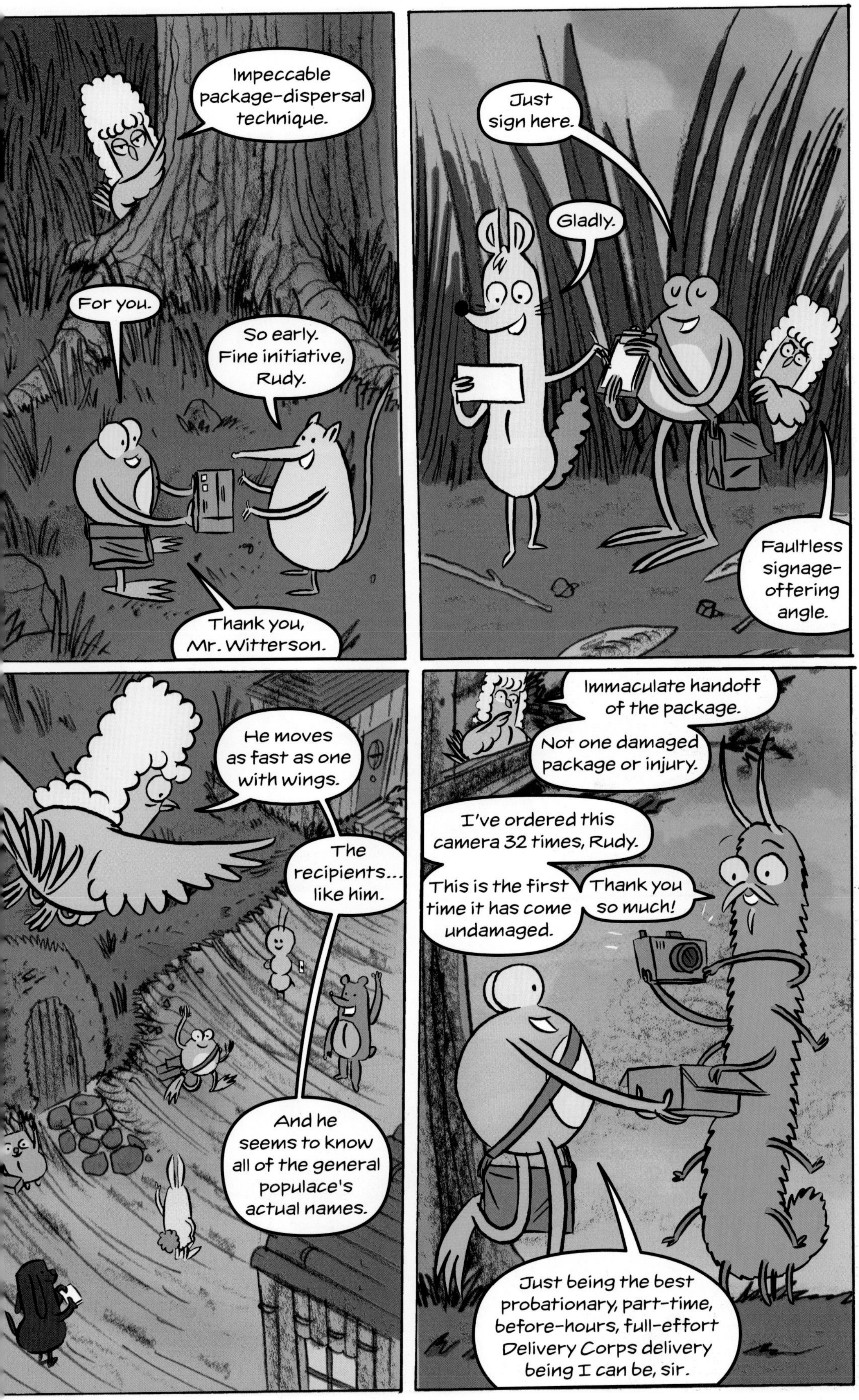
Impeccable package-dispersal technique.
For you.
So early. Fine initiative, Rudy.
Thank you, Mr. Witterson.
Just sign here.
Gladly.
Faultless signage-offering angle.
He moves as fast as one with wings.
The recipients... like him.
And he seems to know all of the general populace's actual names.
Immaculate handoff of the package.
Not one damaged package or injury.
I've ordered this camera 32 times, Rudy.
This is the first time it has come undamaged.
Thank you so much!
Just being the best probationary, part-time, before-hours, full-effort Delivery Corps delivery being I can be, sir.

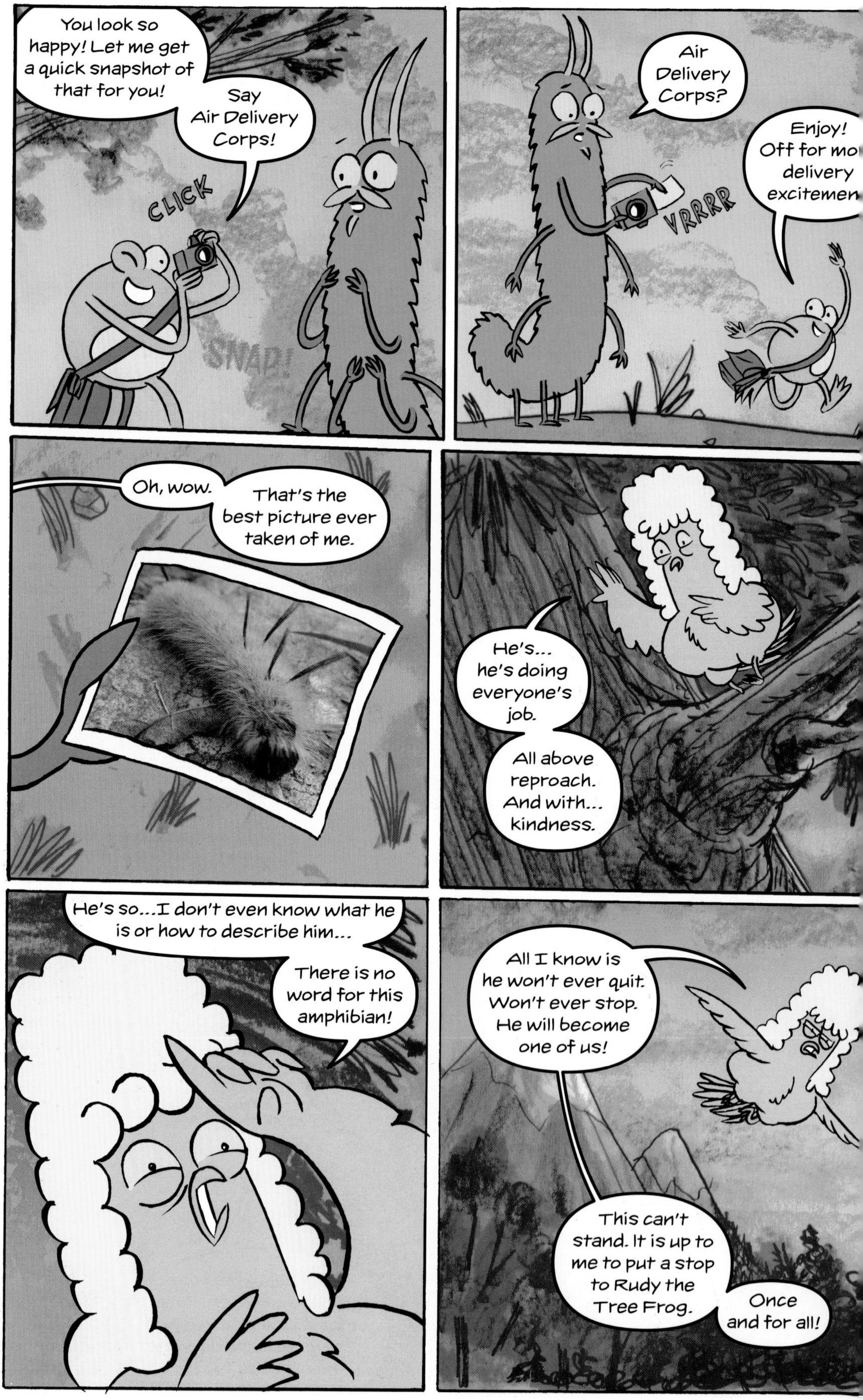
You look so happy! Let me get a quick snapshot of that for you!
Say Air Delivery Corps!
CLICK
SNAP!
Air Delivery Corps?
VRRRR
Enjoy! Off for mo delivery excitemen
Oh, wow.
That's the best picture ever taken of me.
He's... he's doing everyone's job.
All above reproach. And with... kindness.
He's so...I don't even know what he is or how to describe him...
There is no word for this amphibian!
All I know is he won't ever quit. Won't ever stop. He will become one of us!
This can't stand. It is up to me to put a stop to Rudy the Tree Frog.
Once and for all!

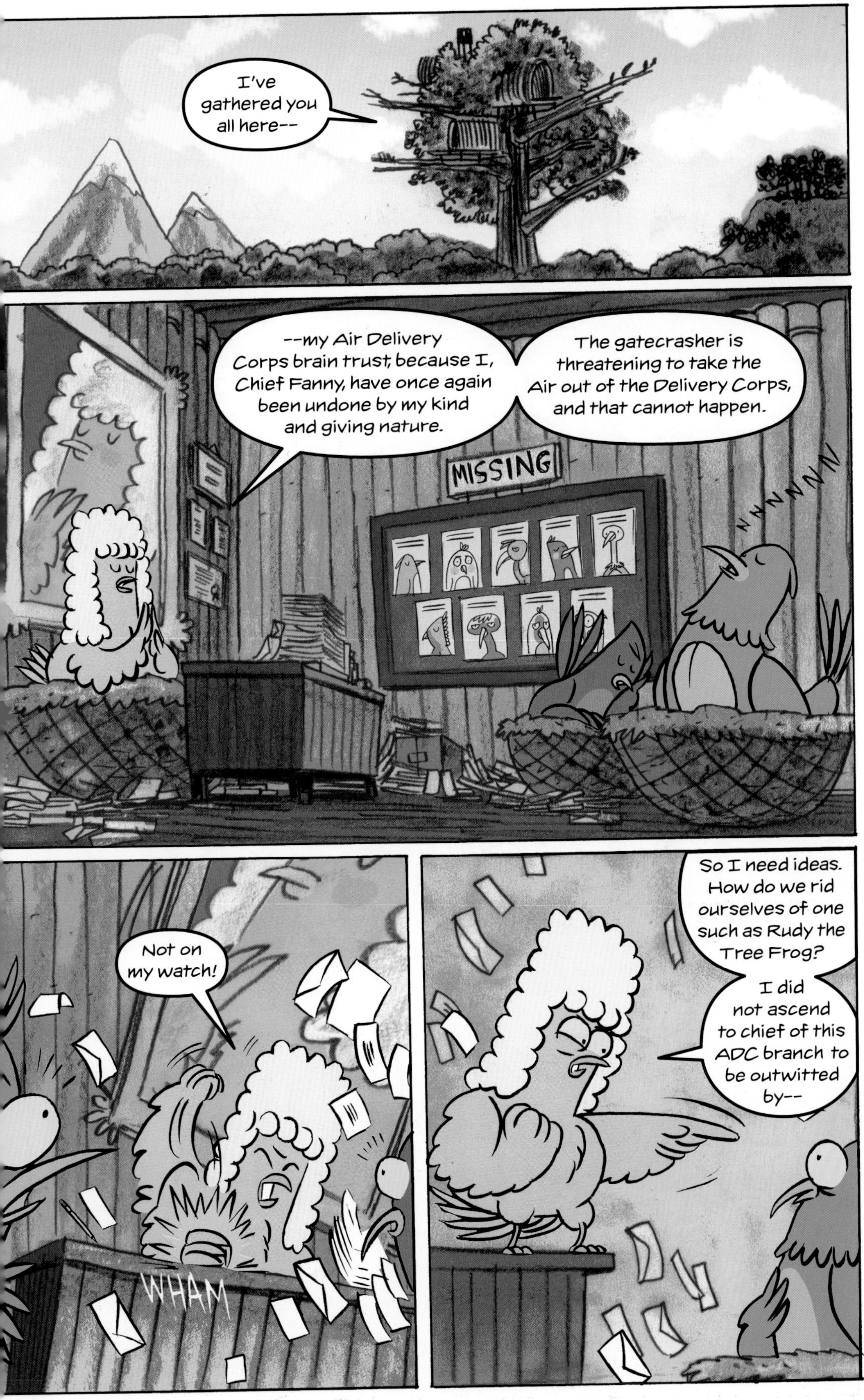
I've gathered you all here--
--my Air Delivery Corps brain trust, because I, Chief Fanny, have once again been undone by my kind and giving nature.
The gatecrasher is threatening to take the Air out of the Delivery Corps, and that cannot happen.
MISSING
NNNNNN
Not on my watch!
WHAM
So I need ideas. How do we rid ourselves of one such as Rudy the Tree Frog?
I did not ascend to chief of this ADC branch to be outwitted by--

--Rudy the Tree Frog.

Package!

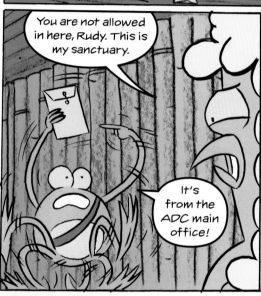

You are not allowed in here, Rudy. This is my sanctuary.

It's from the ADC main office!

And I am sorry to say, since this is a major breach in protocol, you have left me no choice.

You are no longer a Delivery Corps candidate. Goodbye.

Hand must never be washed! Most thrilling day of my life!

Didn't you hear me?! Begone, pest!

I can see your lips moving but I can't hear you! My ears are shaking too much with excitement!

Give me that.

SNATCH

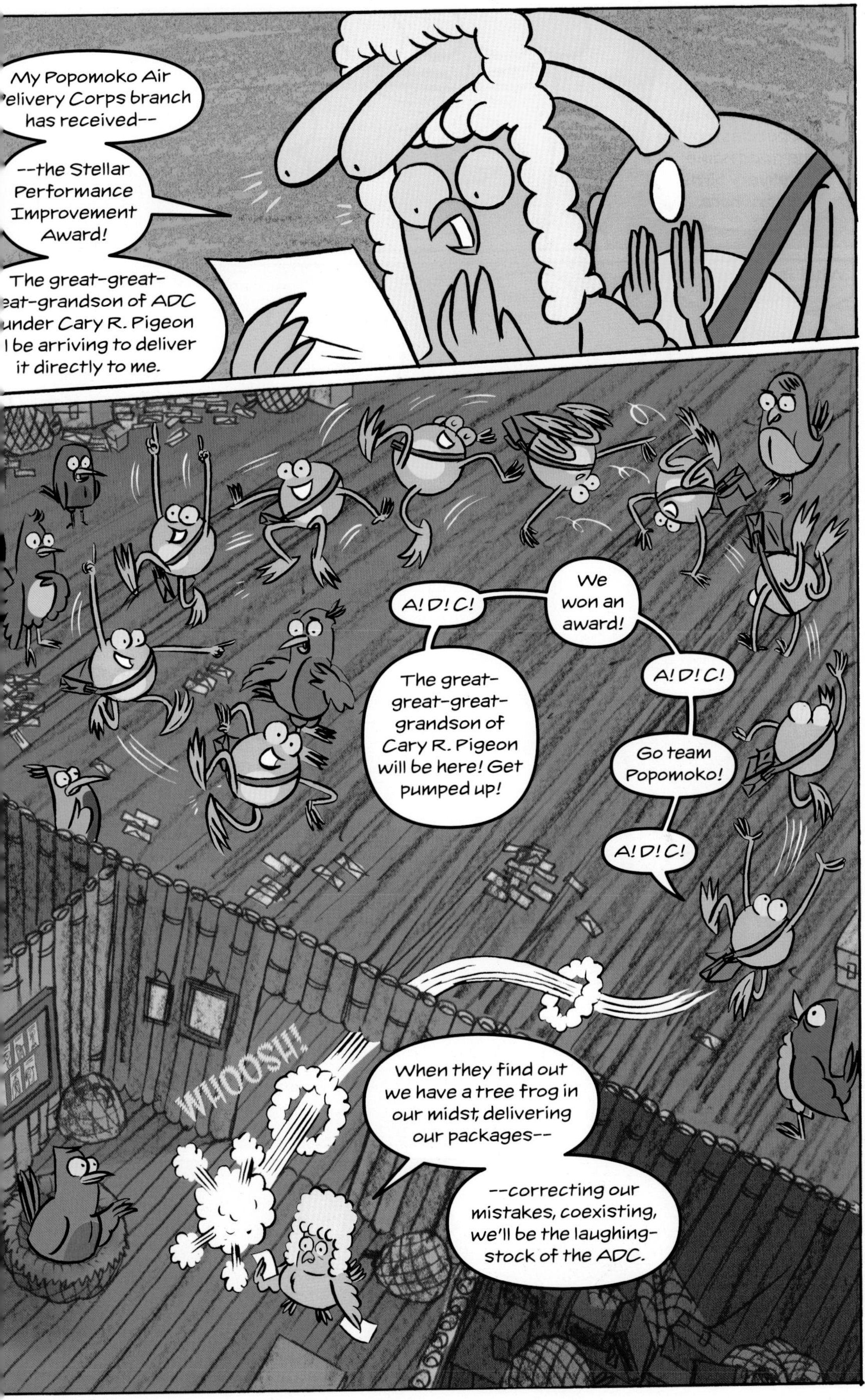
My Popomoko Air
elivery Corps branch
has received--
--the Stellar Performance Improvement Award!
The great-great-
eat-grandson of ADC
under Cary R. Pigeon
l be arriving to deliver
it directly to me.
A! D! C!
We won an award!
The great-great-great-grandson of Cary R. Pigeon will be here! Get pumped up!
A! D! C!
Go team Popomoko!
A! D! C!
WHOOSH!
When they find out we have a tree frog in our midst, delivering our packages--
--correcting our mistakes, coexisting, we'll be the laughing-stock of the ADC.

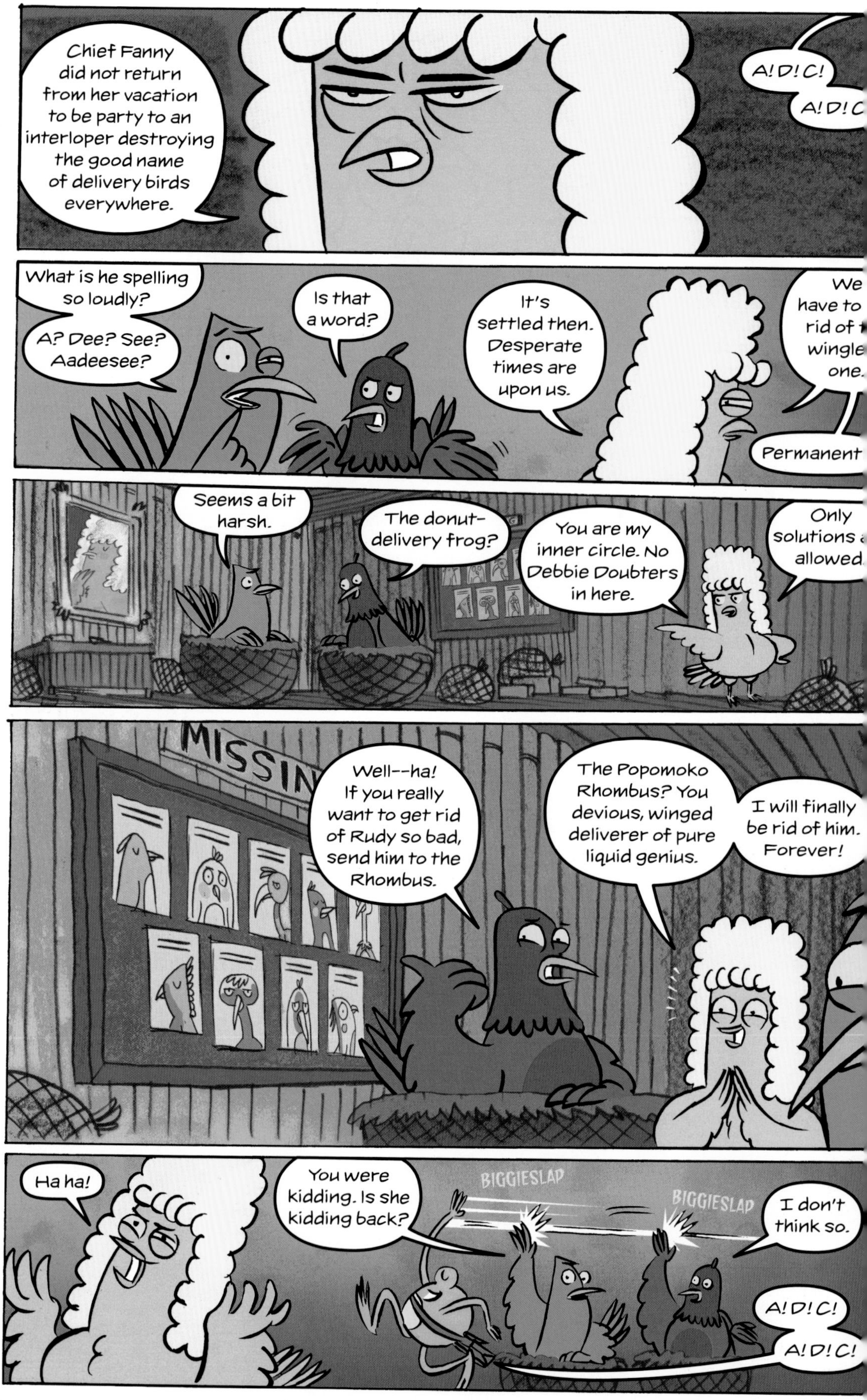

Chief Fanny did not return from her vacation to be party to an interloper destroying the good name of delivery birds everywhere.
A!D!C!
A!D!C
What is he spelling so loudly?
A? Dee? See? Aadeesee?
Is that a word?
It's settled then. Desperate times are upon us.
We have to rid of wingle one.
Permanent
Seems a bit harsh.
The donut-delivery frog?
You are my inner circle. No Debbie Doubters in here.
Only solutions allowed.
MISSIN
Well--ha! If you really want to get rid of Rudy so bad, send him to the Rhombus.
The Popomoko Rhombus? You devious, winged deliverer of pure liquid genius.
I will finally be rid of him. Forever!
Ha ha!
You were kidding. Is she kidding back?
BIGGIESLAP
BIGGIESLAP
I don't think so.
A!D!C!
A!D!C!

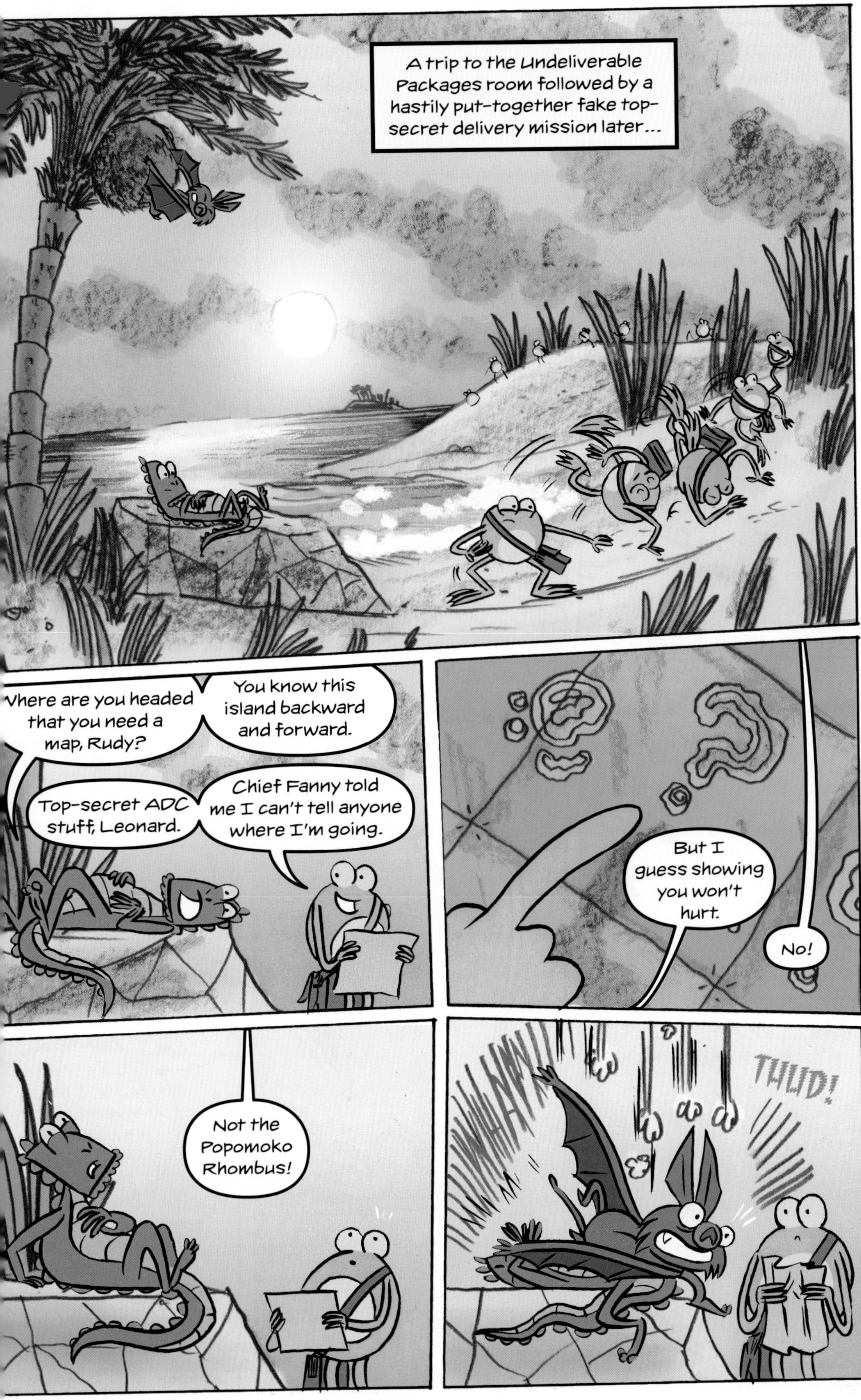
A trip to the Undeliverable Packages room followed by a hastily put-together fake top-secret delivery mission later...
Where are you headed that you need a map, Rudy?
You know this island backward and forward.
Top-secret ADC stuff, Leonard.
Chief Fanny told me I can't tell anyone where I'm going.
But I guess showing you won't hurt.
No!
Not the Popomoko Rhombus!
THUD!

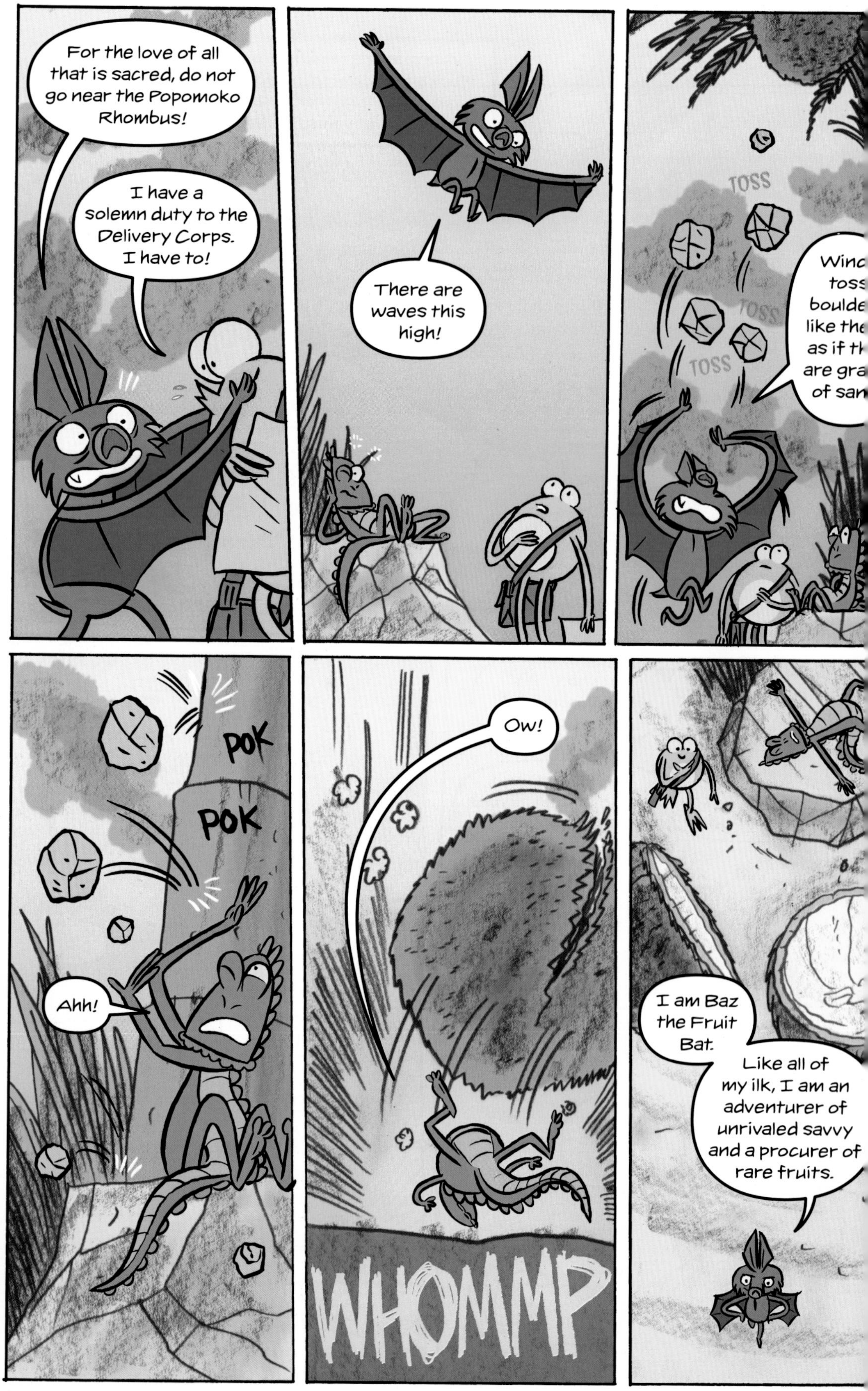
For the love of all that is sacred, do not go near the Popomoko Rhombus!
I have a solemn duty to the Delivery Corps. I have to!
There are waves this high!
TOSS
TOSS
TOSS
Winc toss boulde like the as if th are gra of san
POK
POK
Ahh!
Ow!
WHOMMP
I am Baz the Fruit Bat.
Like all of my ilk, I am an adventurer of unrivaled savvy and a procurer of rare fruits.

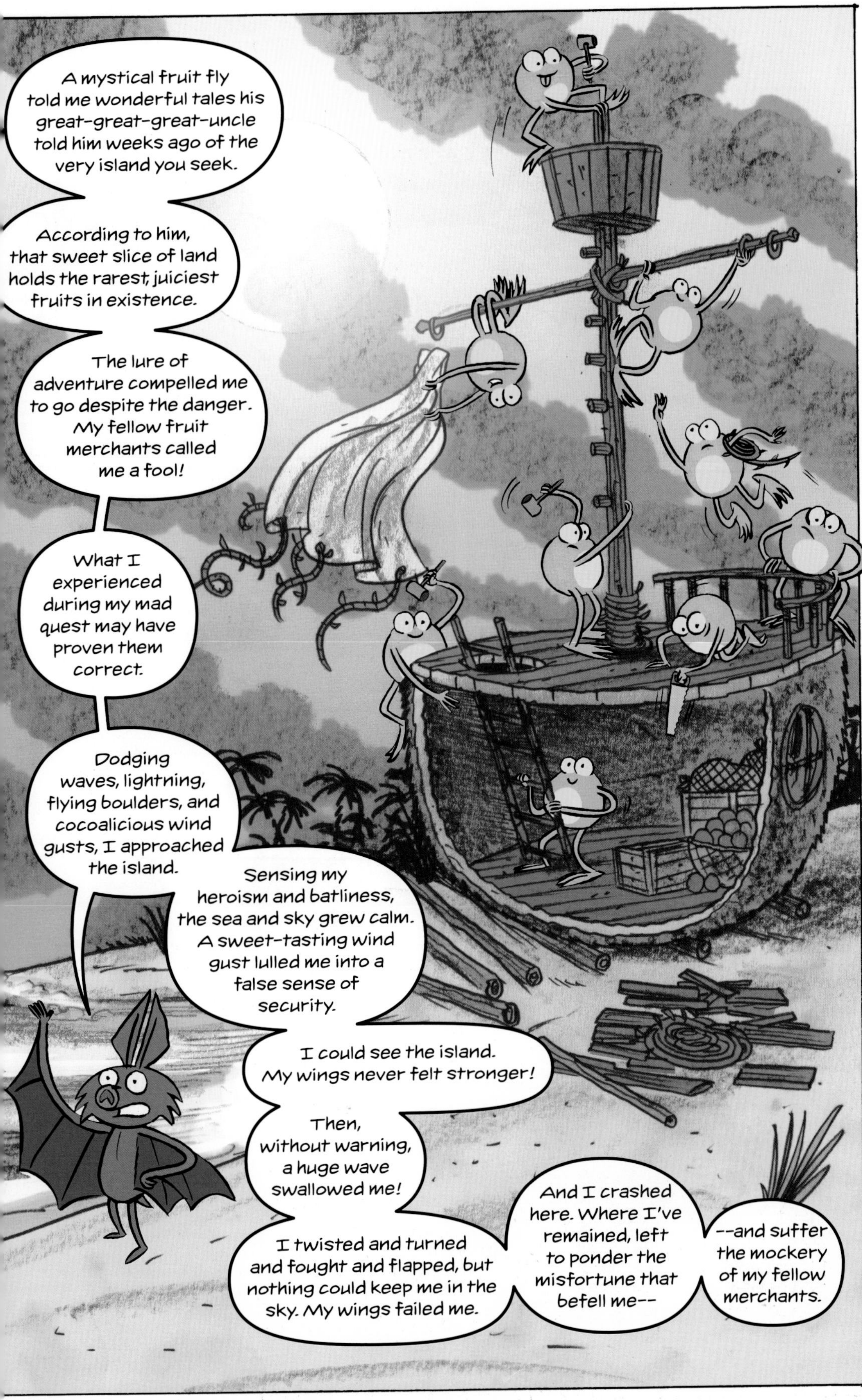
A mystical fruit fly told me wonderful tales his great-great-great-uncle told him weeks ago of the very island you seek.
According to him, that sweet slice of land holds the rarest, juiciest fruits in existence.
The lure of adventure compelled me to go despite the danger. My fellow fruit merchants called me a fool!
What I experienced during my mad quest may have proven them correct.
Dodging waves, lightning, flying boulders, and cocoalicious wind gusts, I approached the island.
Sensing my heroism and batliness, the sea and sky grew calm. A sweet-tasting wind gust lulled me into a false sense of security.
I could see the island. My wings never felt stronger!
Then, without warning, a huge wave swallowed me!
I twisted and turned and fought and flapped, but nothing could keep me in the sky. My wings failed me.
And I crashed here. Where I've remained, left to ponder the misfortune that befell me--
--and suffer the mockery of my fellow merchants.

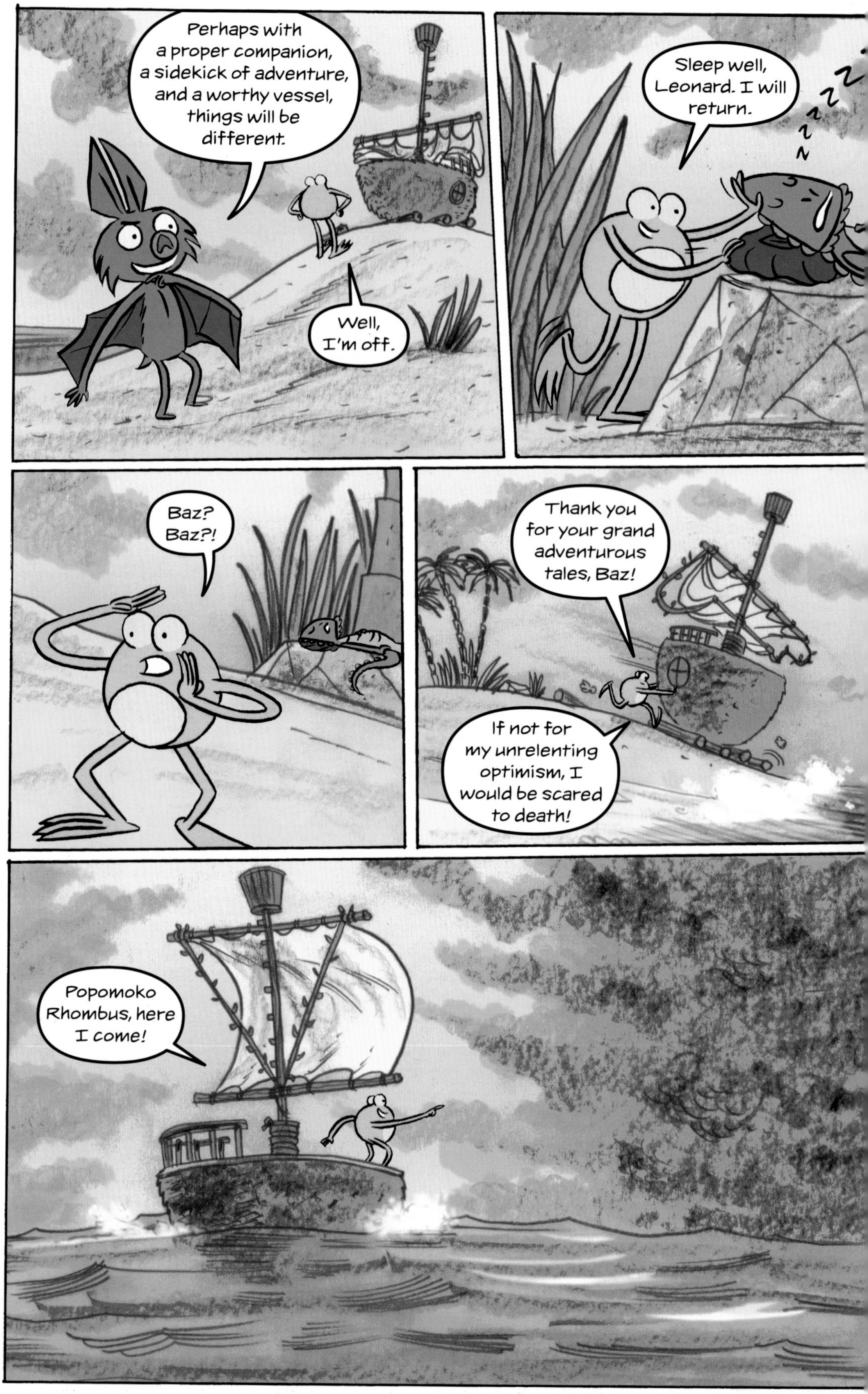
Perhaps with a proper companion, a sidekick of adventure, and a worthy vessel, things will be different.
Well, I'm off.
Sleep well, Leonard. I will return.
ZZZZZ
Baz? Baz?!
Thank you for your grand adventurous tales, Baz!
If not for my unrelenting optimism, I would be scared to death!
Popomoko Rhombus, here I come!

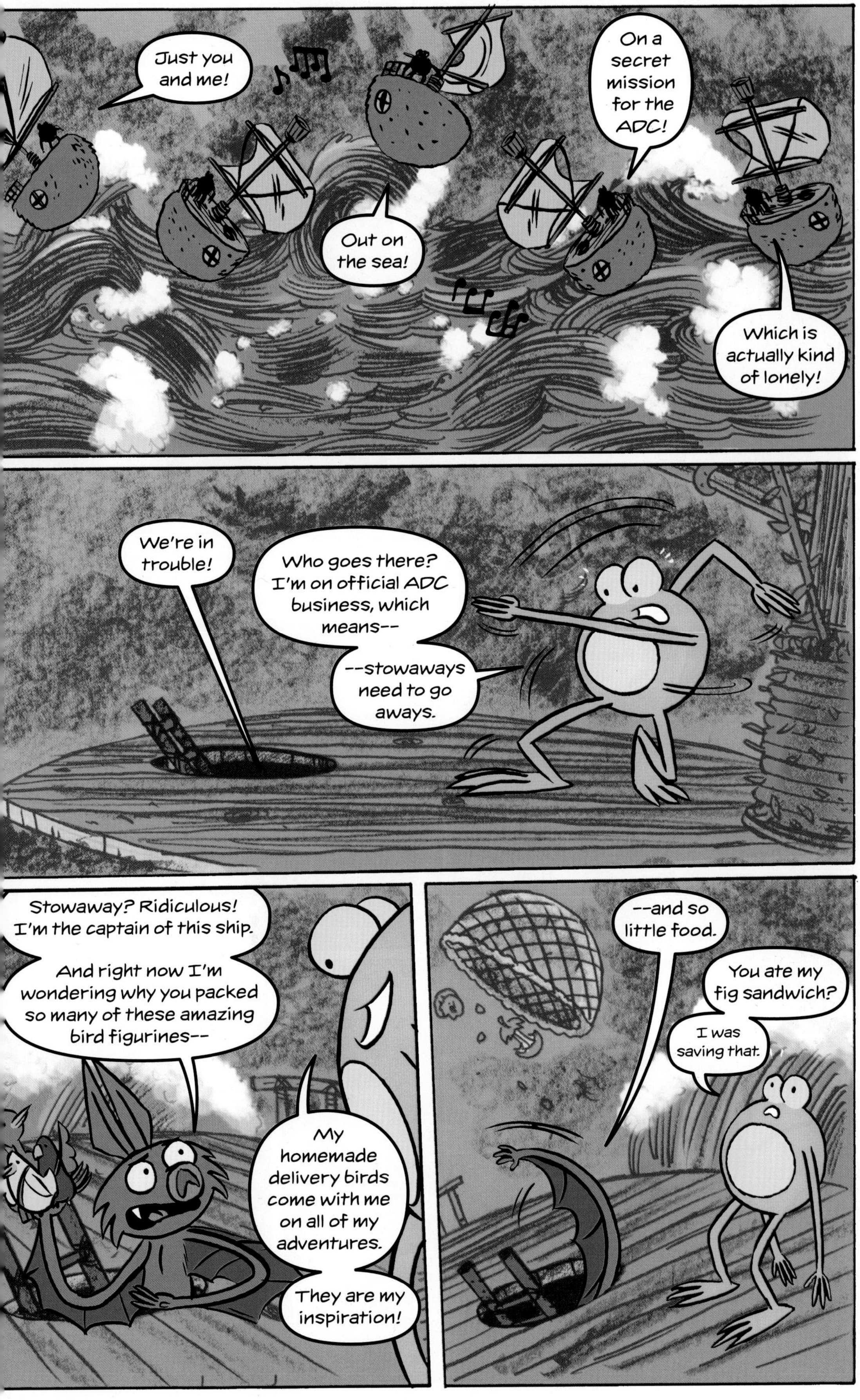
Just you and me!
Out on the sea!
On a secret mission for the ADC!
Which is actually kind of lonely!
We're in trouble!
Who goes there? I'm on official ADC business, which means--
--stowaways need to go aways.
Stowaway? Ridiculous! I'm the captain of this ship.
And right now I'm wondering why you packed so many of these amazing bird figurines--
My homemade delivery birds come with me on all of my adventures.
They are my inspiration!
--and so little food.
You ate my fig sandwich?
I was saving that.

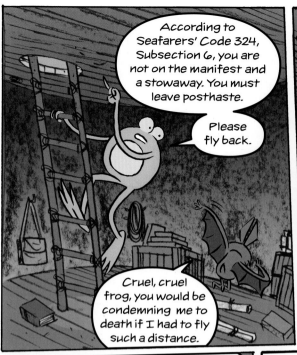

According to Seafarers' Code 324, Subsection 6, you are not on the manifest and a stowaway. You must leave posthaste.

Please fly back.

Cruel, cruel frog, you would be condemning me to death if I had to fly such a distance.

Heh heh! I kind of prefer my adventures a bit more grounded. Less chance of crashing that way.

I appreciate your adventuring savvy, Captain Baz, and deep down I actually want you to come along...

...but if Chief Fanny sees you, I'll be in trouble.

She handed me the oldest package from the Undeliverable room.

"Air Delivery Corps candidate Rudy, you are to te no one of your journey into the Popomoko Rhomb and you are to take no one with you.

"Most importantly, do not ever come back And then she paused f dramatic effect.

And then I said, "Until the job is done?" And Chief Fanny said, "Whatever."

So... you have to go. Begone!

A bit of a rule follower, huh?

Yes. That's what rules are for.

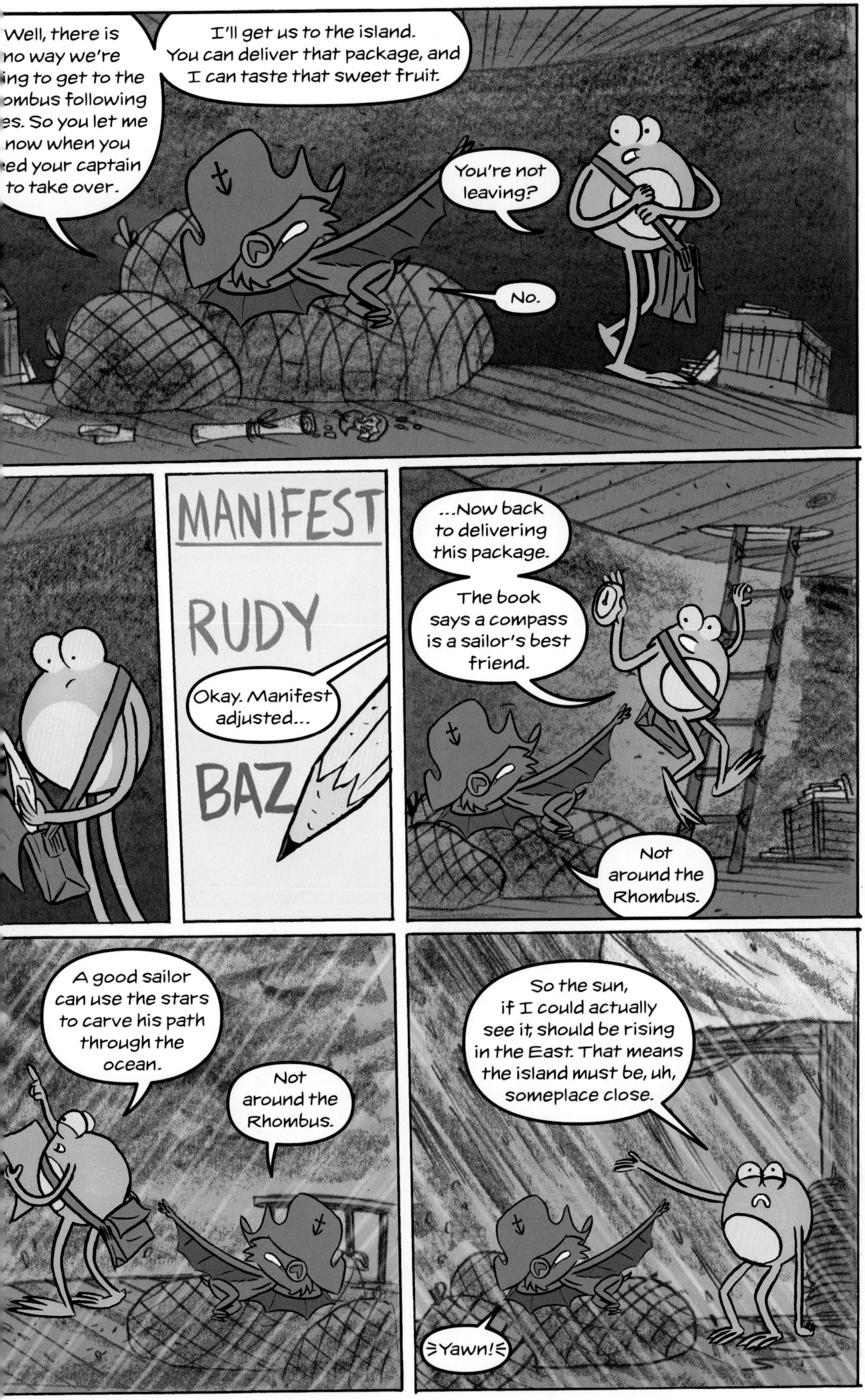
Well, there is
no way we're
ing to get to the
ombus following
es. So you let me
now when you
ed your captain
to take over.
I'll get us to the island. You can deliver that package, and I can taste that sweet fruit.
You're not leaving?
No.
MANIFEST
RUDY
Okay. Manifest adjusted...
BAZ
...Now back to delivering this package.
The book says a compass is a sailor's best friend.
Not around the Rhombus.
A good sailor can use the stars to carve his path through the ocean.
Not around the Rhombus.
So the sun, if I could actually see it, should be rising in the East. That means the island must be, uh, someplace close.
Yawn!

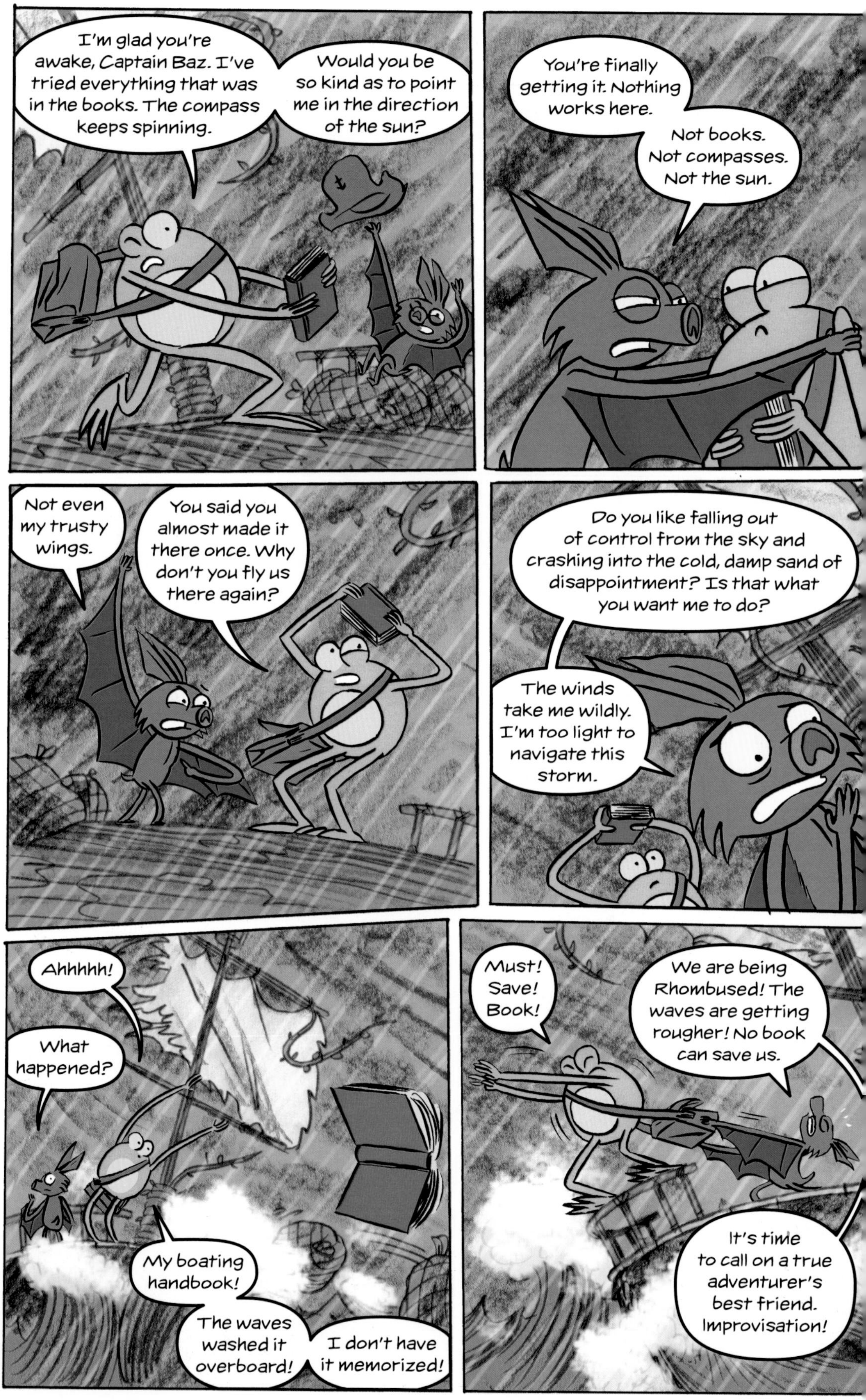
I'm glad you're awake, Captain Baz. I've tried everything that was in the books. The compass keeps spinning.
Would you be so kind as to point me in the direction of the sun?
You're finally getting it. Nothing works here.
Not books. Not compasses. Not the sun.
Not even my trusty wings.
You said you almost made it there once. Why don't you fly us there again?
Do you like falling out of control from the sky and crashing into the cold, damp sand of disappointment? Is that what you want me to do?
The winds take me wildly. I'm too light to navigate this storm.
Ahhhhh!
What happened?
My boating handbook!
The waves washed it overboard!
I don't have it memorized!
Must! Save! Book!
We are being Rhombused! The waves are getting rougher! No book can save us.
It's time to call on a true adventurer's best friend. Improvisation!

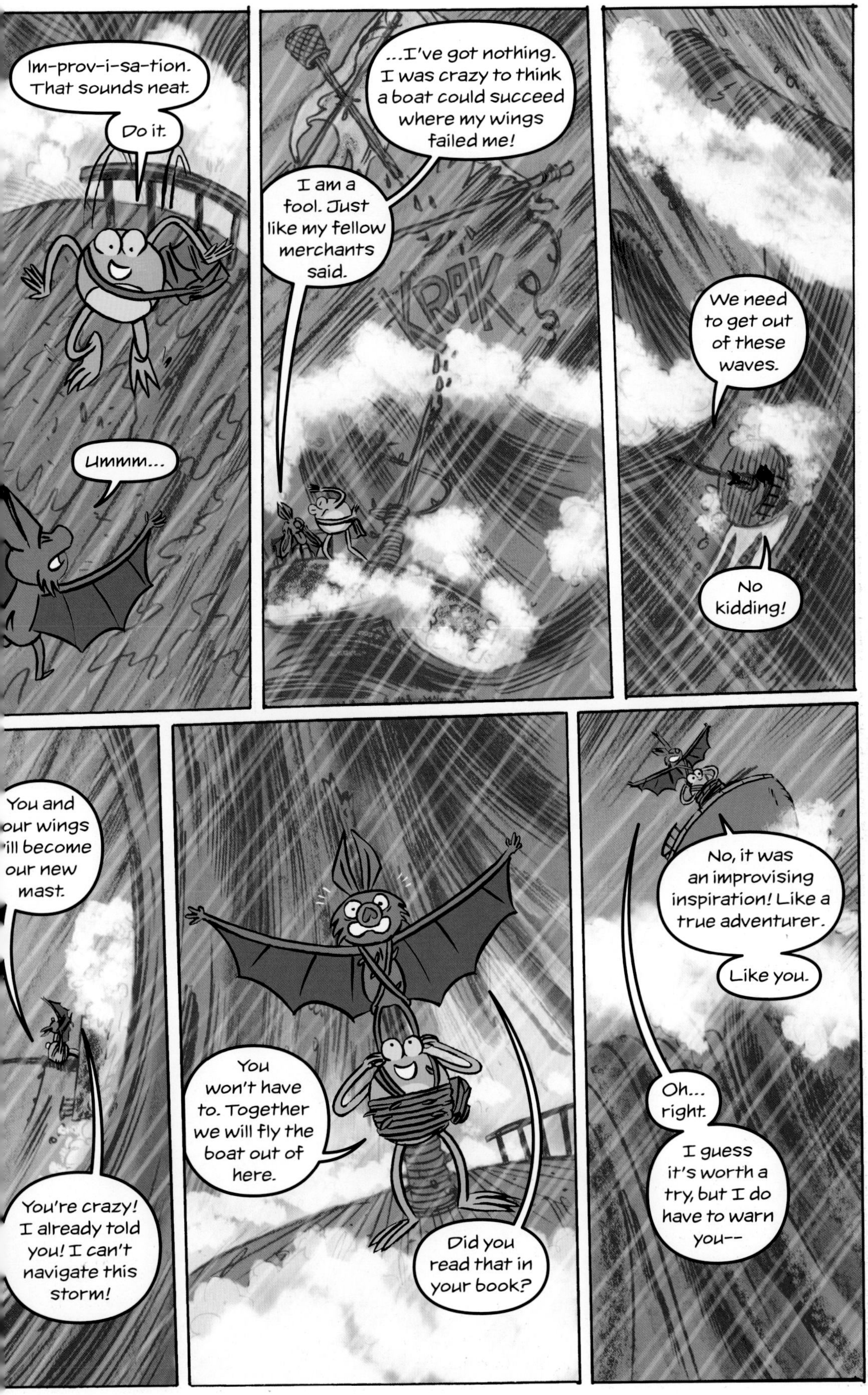
Im-prov-i-sa-tion. That sounds neat.
Do it.
Ummm...
...I've got nothing. I was crazy to think a boat could succeed where my wings failed me!
I am a fool. Just like my fellow merchants said.
KRAK
We need to get out of these waves.
No kidding!
You and our wings ill become our new mast.
You're crazy! I already told you! I can't navigate this storm!
You won't have to. Together we will fly the boat out of here.
Did you read that in your book?
No, it was an improvising inspiration! Like a true adventurer.
Like you.
Oh... right.
I guess it's worth a try, but I do have to warn you--

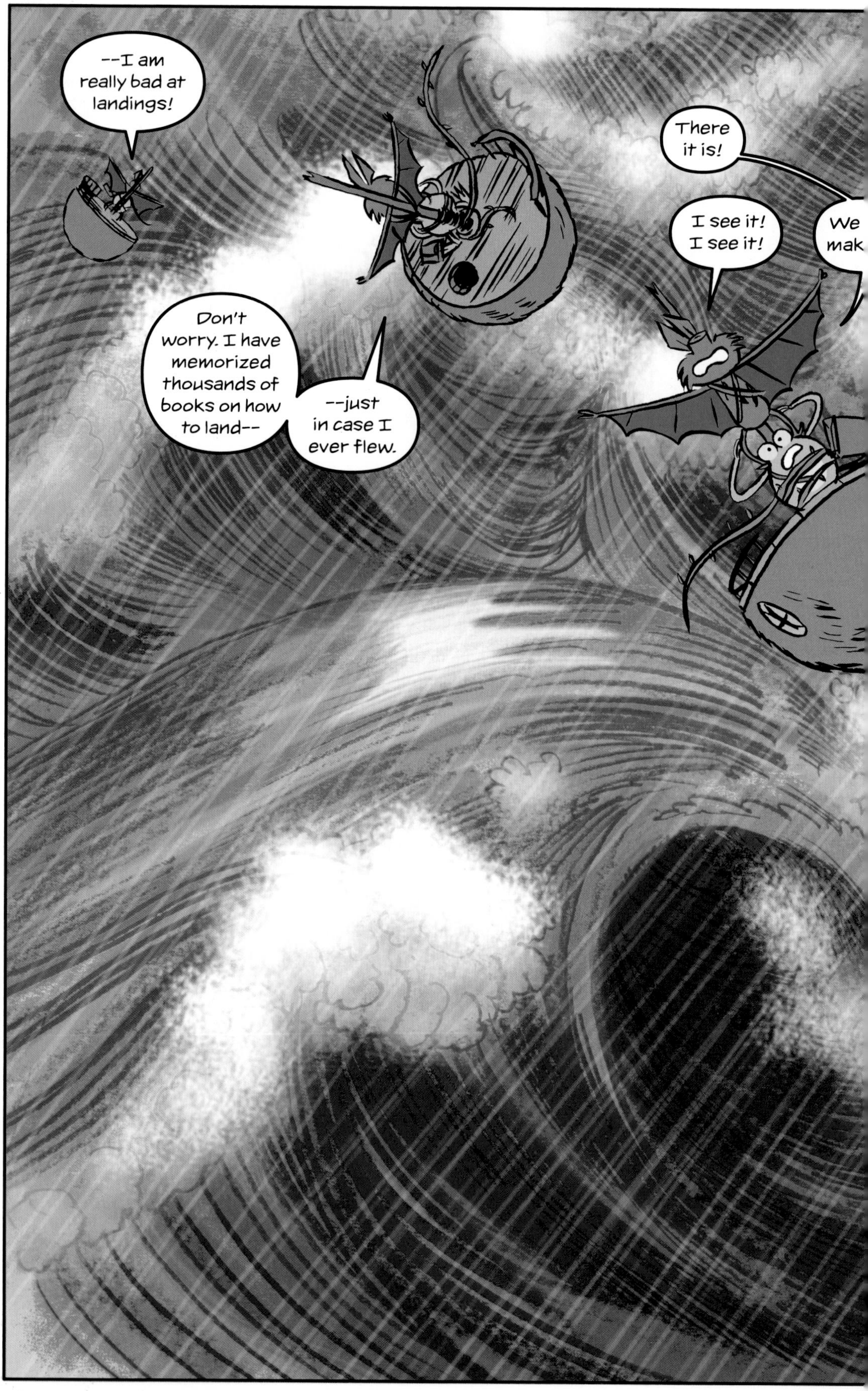

--I am really bad at landings!
Don't worry. I have memorized thousands of books on how to land--
--just in case I ever flew.
There it is!
I see it! I see it!

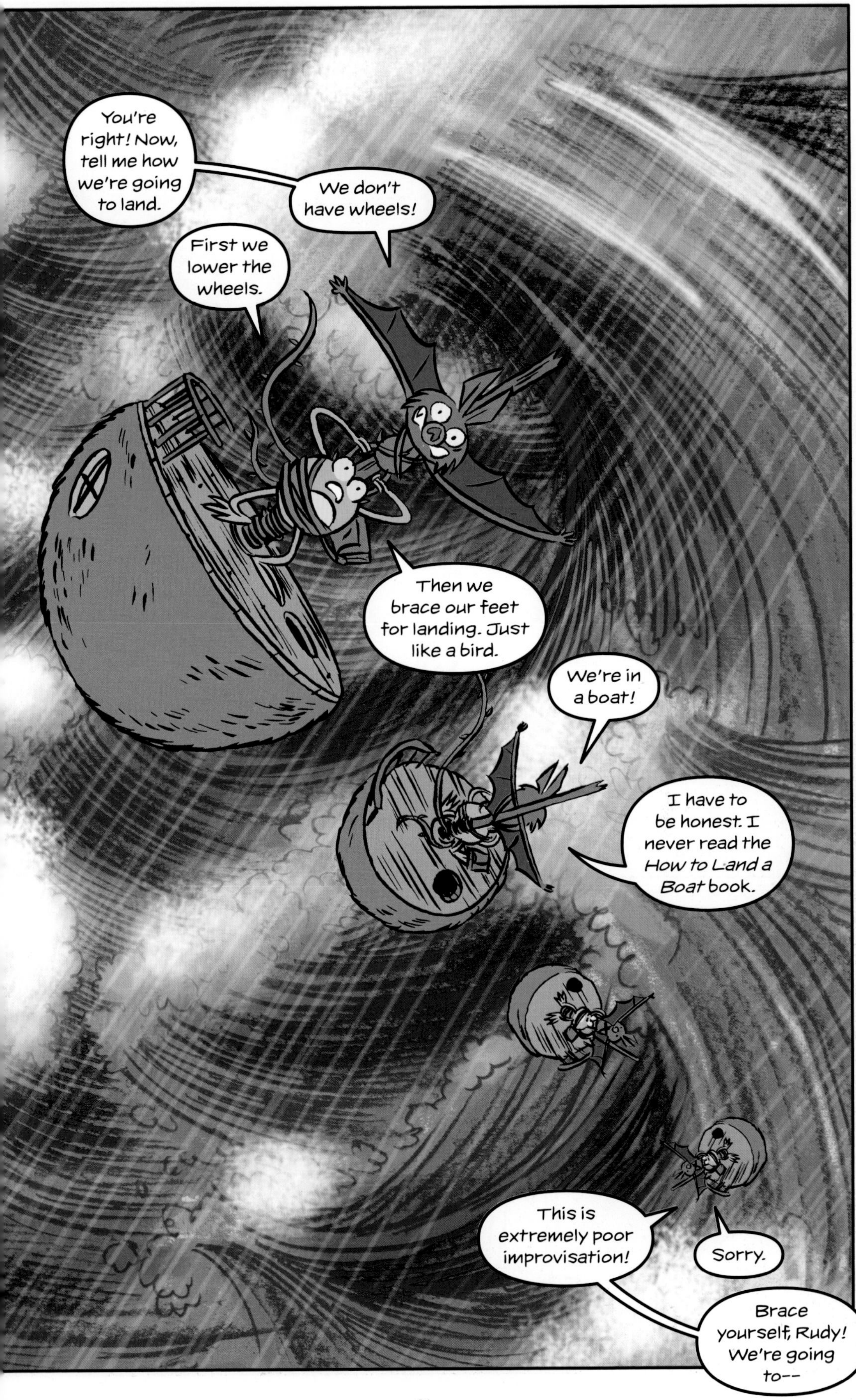
You're right! Now, tell me how we're going to land.
We don't have wheels!
First we lower the wheels.
Then we brace our feet for landing. Just like a bird.
We're in a boat!
I have to be honest. I never read the *How to Land a Boat* book.
This is extremely poor improvisation!
Sorry.
Brace yourself, Rudy! We're going to--

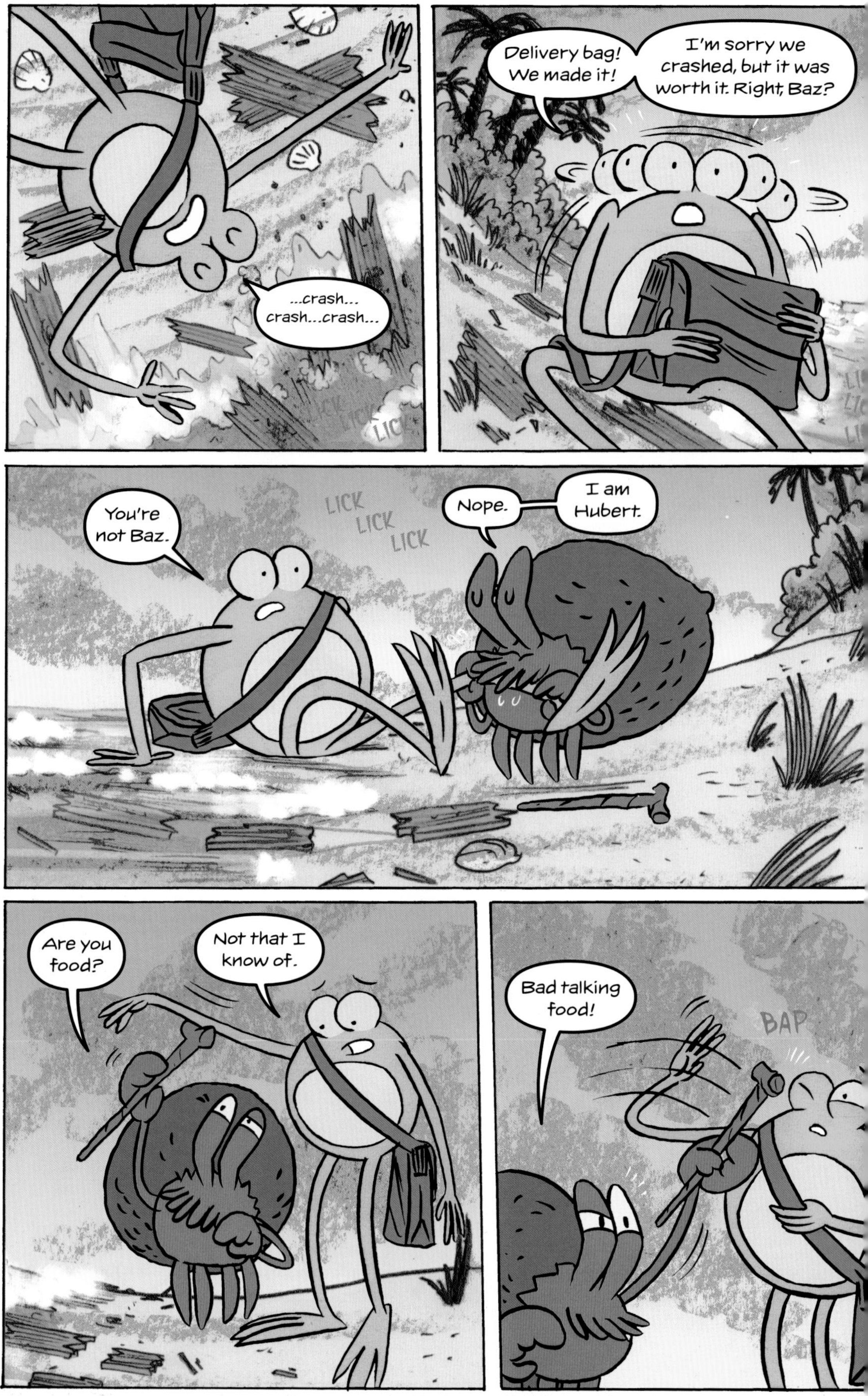

...crash... crash...crash...
Delivery bag! We made it!
I'm sorry we crashed, but it was worth it. Right, Baz?
You're not Baz.
LICK LICK LICK
Nope.
I am Hubert.
Are you food?
Not that I know of.
Bad talking food!
BAP

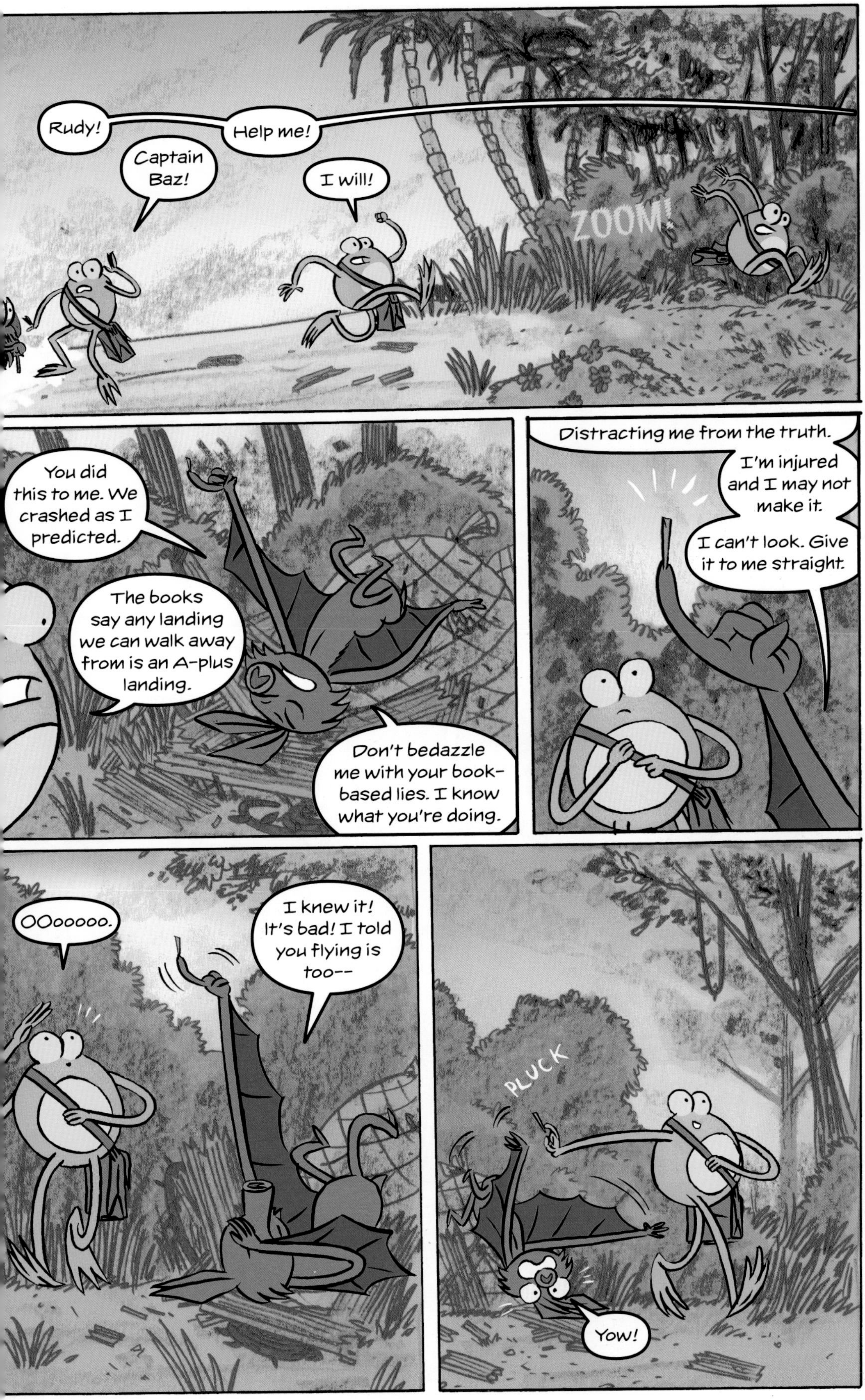
Rudy!
Help me!
Captain Baz!
I will!
ZOOM!
You did this to me. We crashed as I predicted.
The books say any landing we can walk away from is an A-plus landing.
Don't bedazzle me with your book-based lies. I know what you're doing.
Distracting me from the truth.
I'm injured and I may not make it.
I can't look. Give it to me straight.
OOooooo.
I knew it! It's bad! I told you flying is too--
PLUCK
Yow!

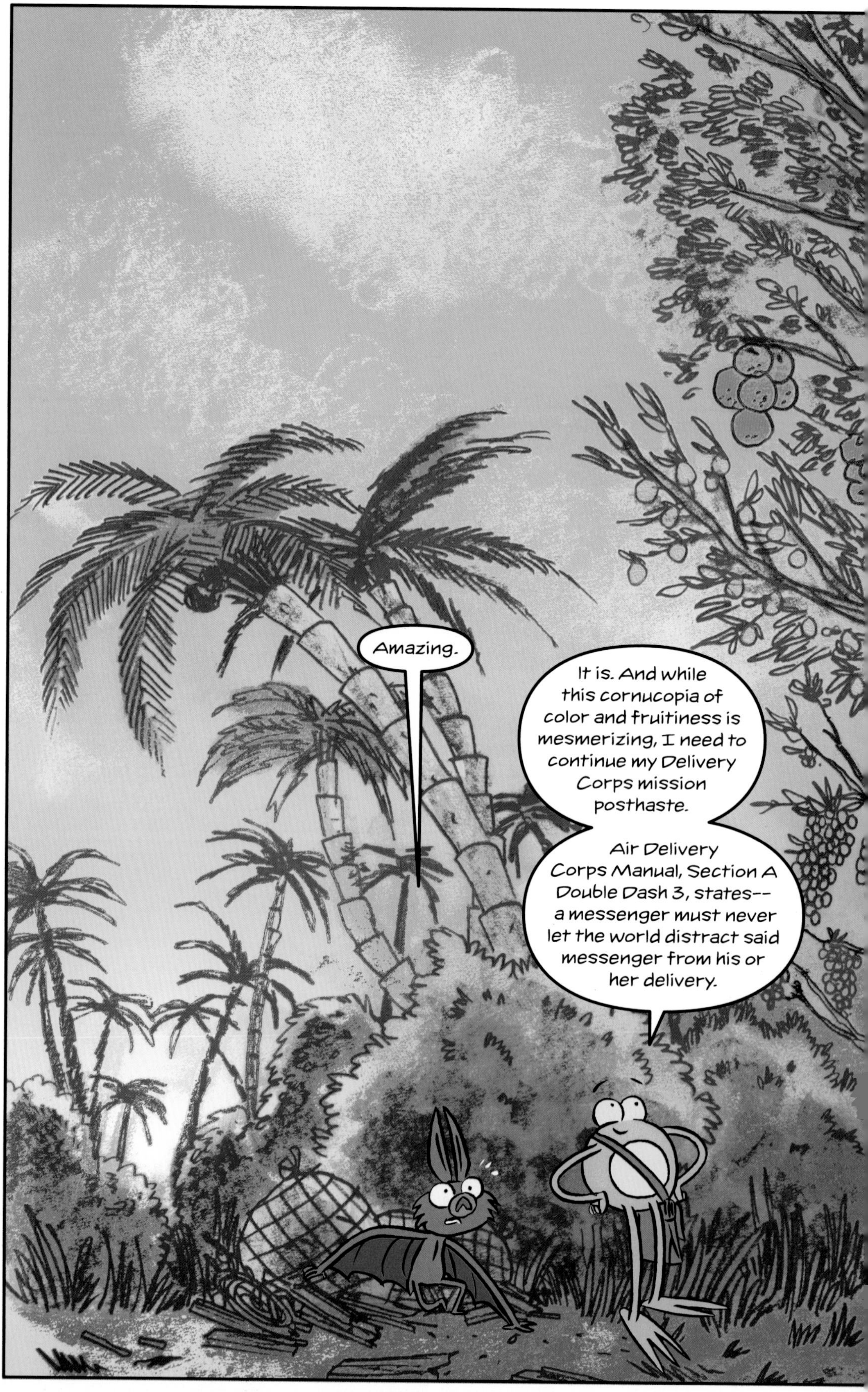
Amazing.
It is. And while this cornucopia of color and fruitiness is mesmerizing, I need to continue my Delivery Corps mission posthaste.
Air Delivery Corps Manual, Section A Double Dash 3, states-- a messenger must never let the world distract said messenger from his or her delivery.

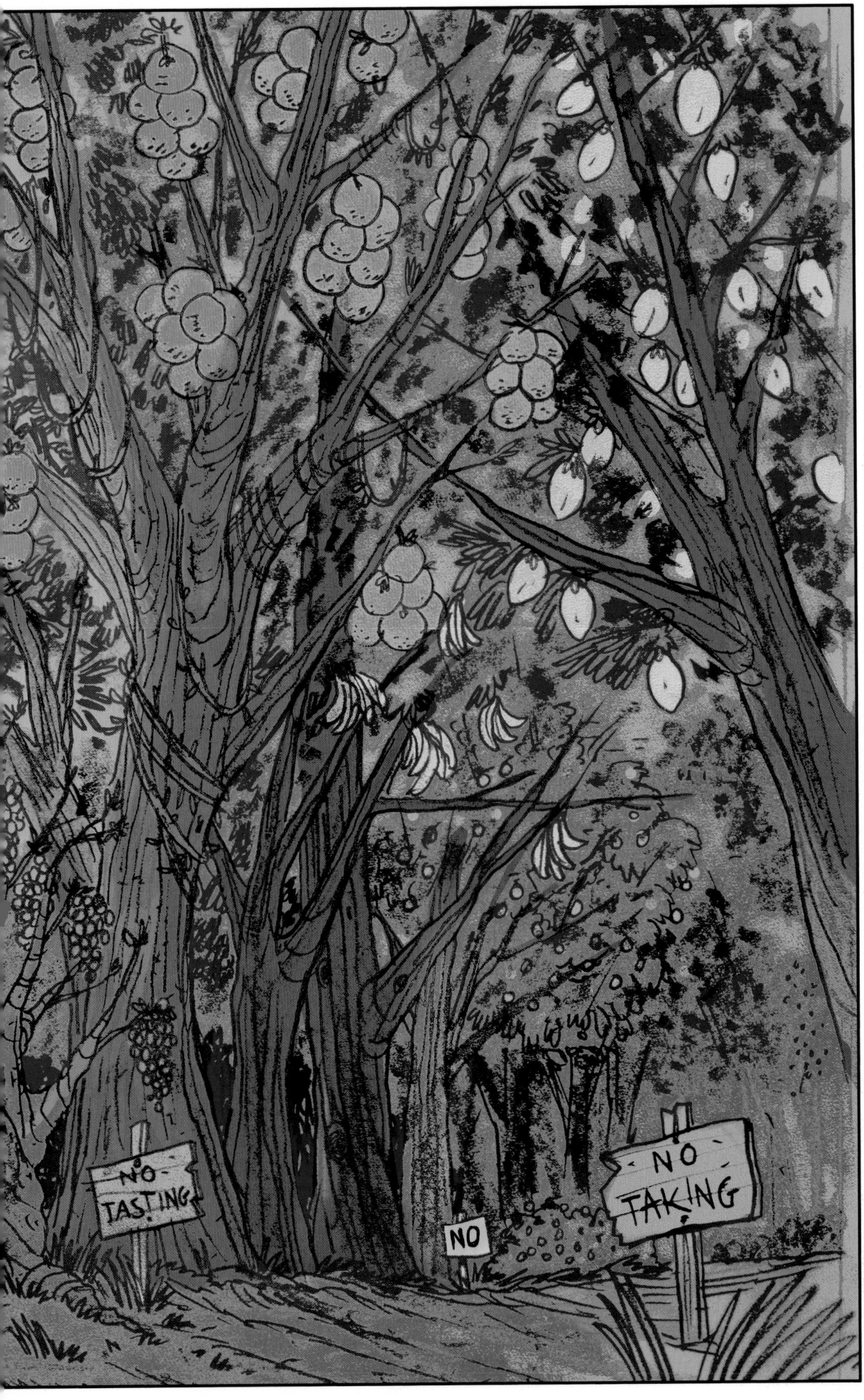
NO TASTING
NO
NO TAKING

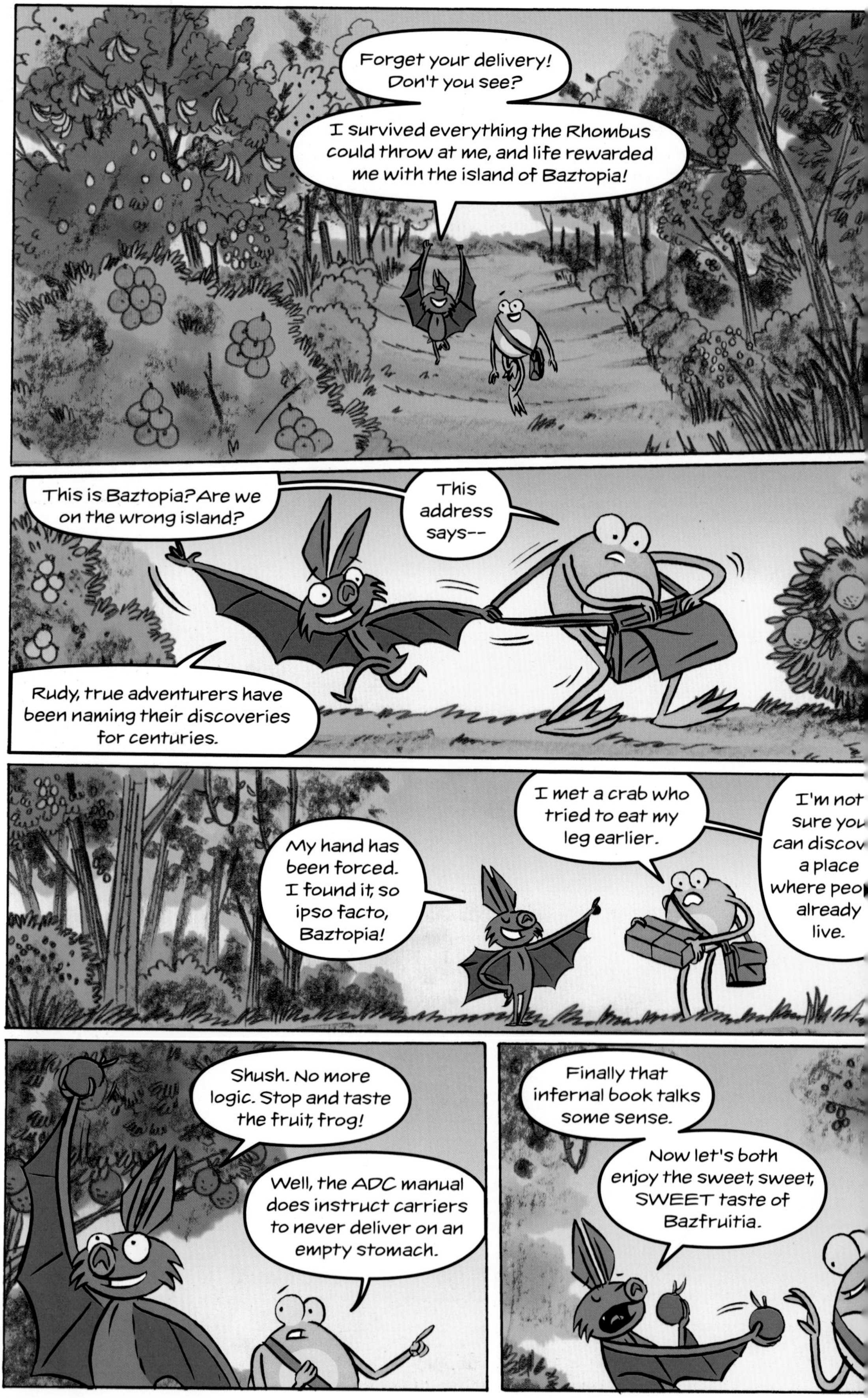
Forget your delivery! Don't you see?
I survived everything the Rhombus could throw at me, and life rewarded me with the island of Baztopia!
This is Baztopia? Are we on the wrong island?
This address says--
Rudy, true adventurers have been naming their discoveries for centuries.
I met a crab who tried to eat my leg earlier.
I'm not sure you can discov a place where peo already live.
My hand has been forced. I found it, so ipso facto, Baztopia!
Shush. No more logic. Stop and taste the fruit, frog!
Well, the ADC manual does instruct carriers to never deliver on an empty stomach.
Finally that infernal book talks some sense.
Now let's both enjoy the sweet, sweet, SWEET taste of Bazfruitia.

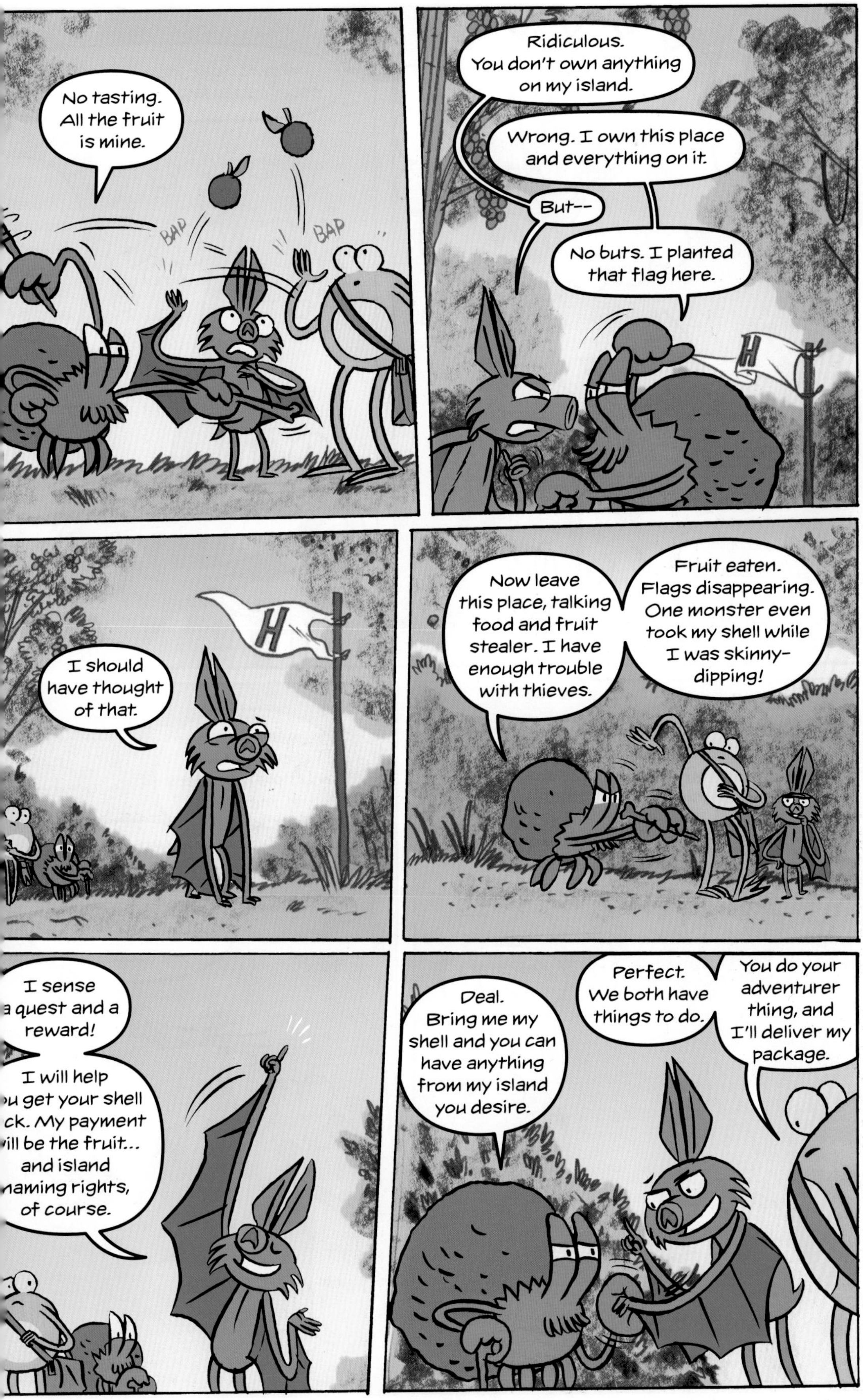

No tasting. All the fruit is mine.
BAP
BAP
Ridiculous. You don't own anything on my island.
Wrong. I own this place and everything on it.
But--
No buts. I planted that flag here.
H
H
I should have thought of that.
Now leave this place, talking food and fruit stealer. I have enough trouble with thieves.
Fruit eaten. Flags disappearing. One monster even took my shell while I was skinny-dipping!
I sense a quest and a reward!
I will help ou get your shell ck. My payment ill be the fruit... and island naming rights, of course.
Deal. Bring me my shell and you can have anything from my island you desire.
Perfect. We both have things to do.
You do your adventurer thing, and I'll deliver my package.

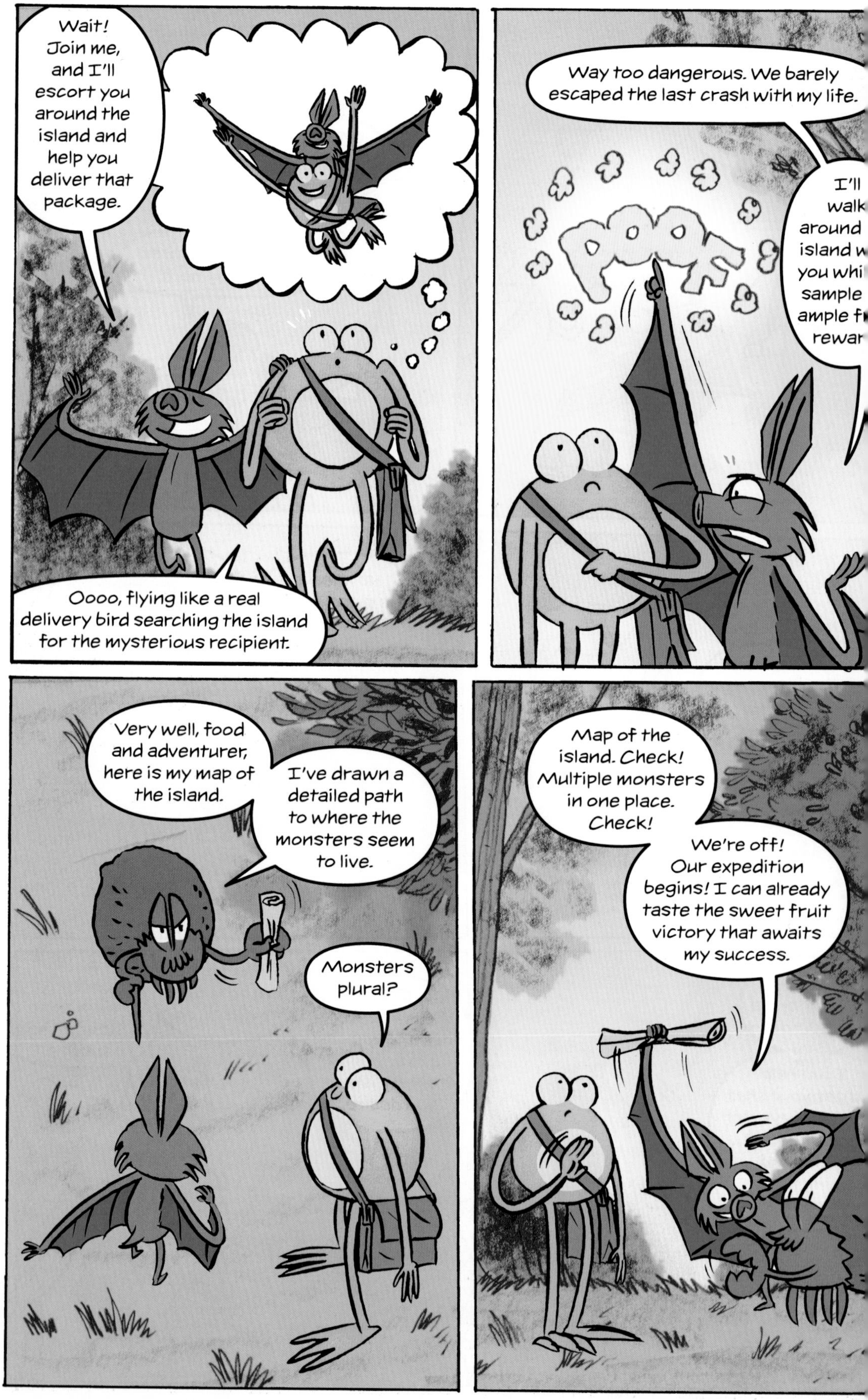
Wait! Join me, and I'll escort you around the island and help you deliver that package.
Oooo, flying like a real delivery bird searching the island for the mysterious recipient.
Way too dangerous. We barely escaped the last crash with my life.
POOF
I'll walk around island w you whi sample ample f rewar
Very well, food and adventurer, here is my map of the island.
I've drawn a detailed path to where the monsters seem to live.
Monsters plural?
Map of the island. Check! Multiple monsters in one place. Check!
We're off! Our expedition begins! I can already taste the sweet fruit victory that awaits my success.

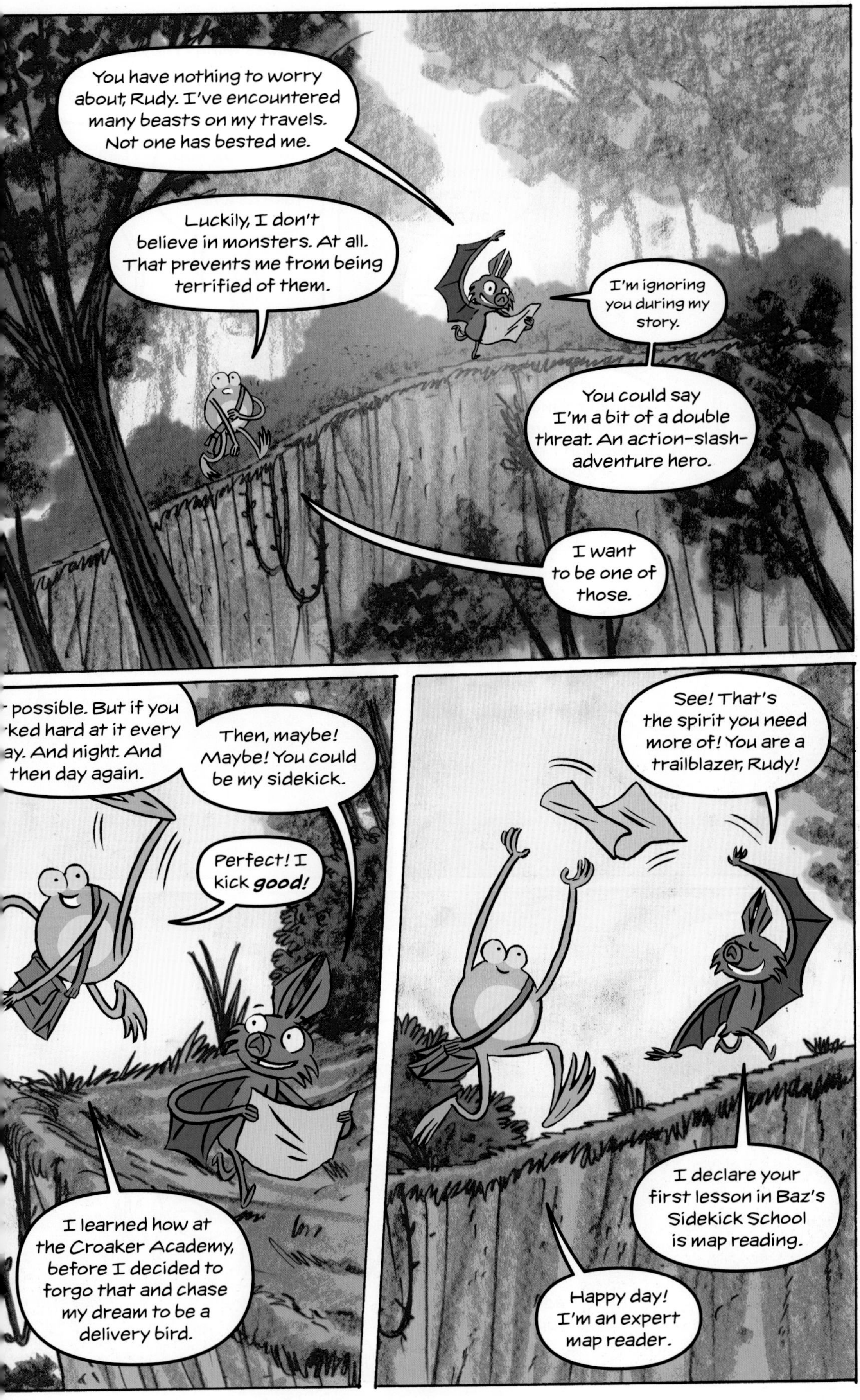
You have nothing to worry about, Rudy. I've encountered many beasts on my travels. Not one has bested me.
Luckily, I don't believe in monsters. At all. That prevents me from being terrified of them.
I'm ignoring you during my story.
You could say I'm a bit of a double threat. An action-slash-adventure hero.
I want to be one of those.
possible. But if you ked hard at it every ay. And night. And then day again.
Then, maybe! Maybe! You could be my sidekick.
Perfect! I kick **good!**
I learned how at the Croaker Academy, before I decided to forgo that and chase my dream to be a delivery bird.
See! That's the spirit you need more of! You are a trailblazer, Rudy!
I declare your first lesson in Baz's Sidekick School is map reading.
Happy day! I'm an expert map reader.

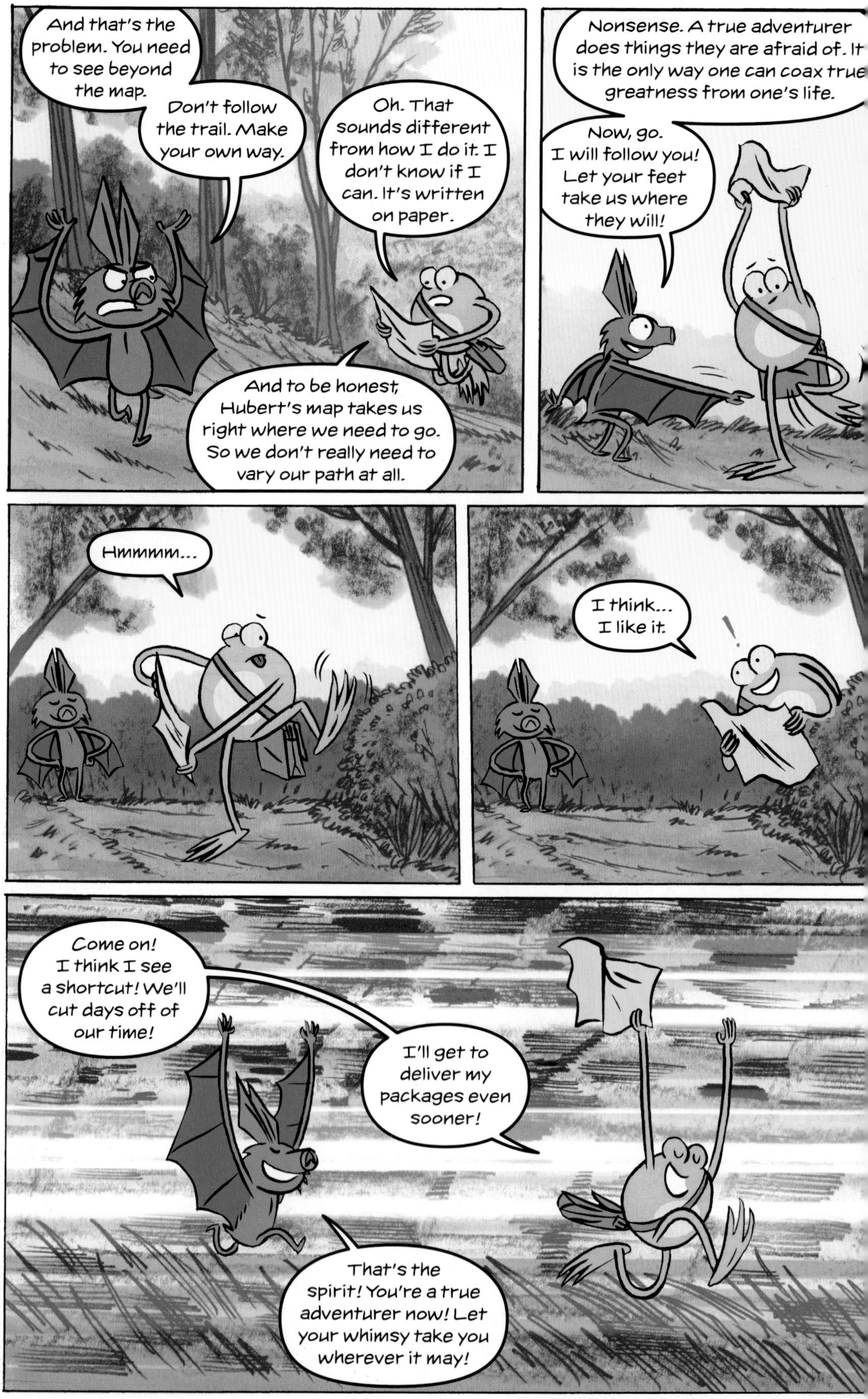
And that's the problem. You need to see beyond the map.
Don't follow the trail. Make your own way.
Oh. That sounds different from how I do it. I don't know if I can. It's written on paper.
And to be honest, Hubert's map takes us right where we need to go. So we don't really need to vary our path at all.
Nonsense. A true adventurer does things they are afraid of. It is the only way one can coax true greatness from one's life.
Now, go. I will follow you! Let your feet take us where they will!
Hmmmm...
I think... I like it.
Come on! I think I see a shortcut! We'll cut days off of our time!
I'll get to deliver my packages even sooner!
That's the spirit! You're a true adventurer now! Let your whimsy take you wherever it may!

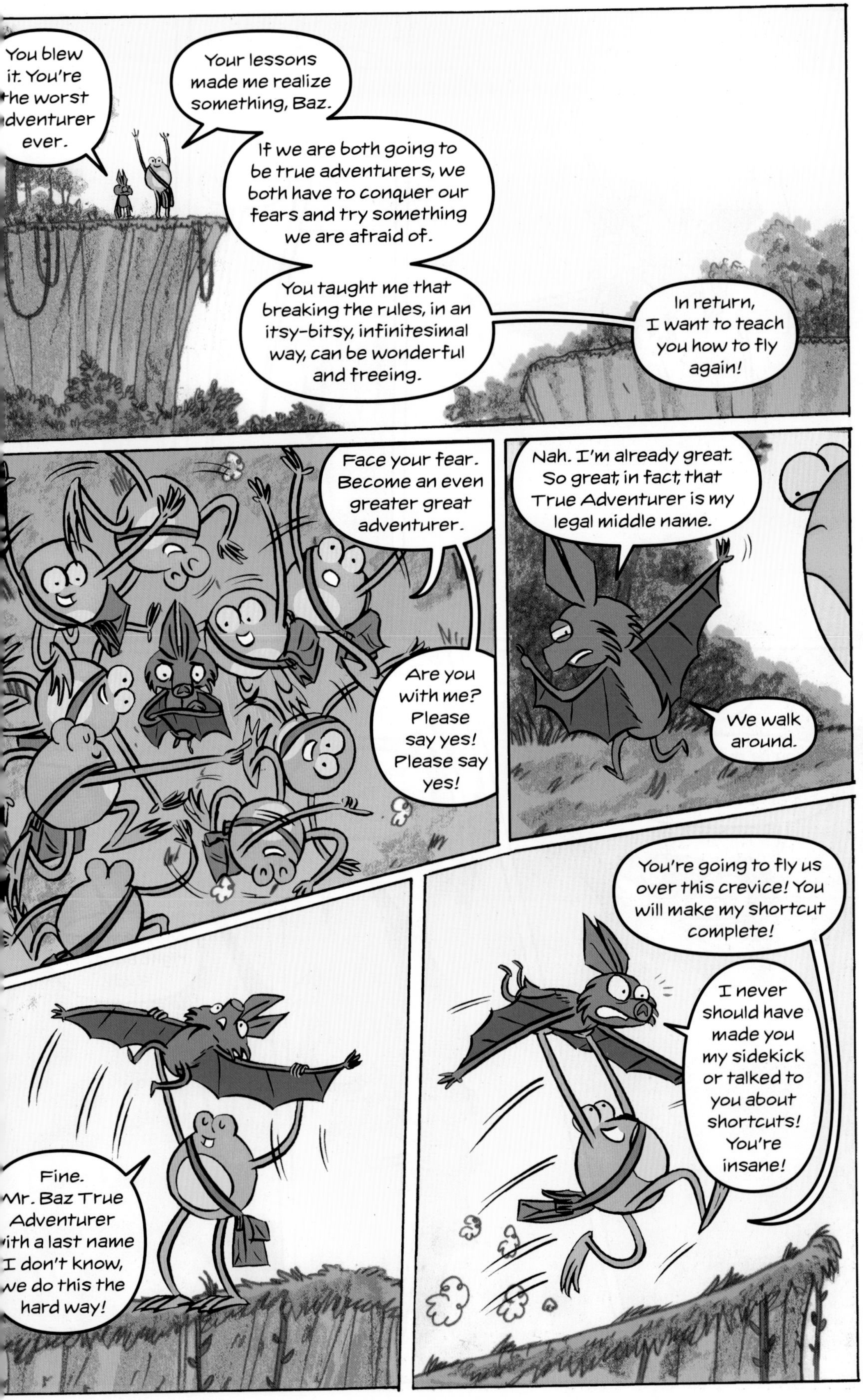
You blew it. You're the worst dventurer ever.
Your lessons made me realize something, Baz.
If we are both going to be true adventurers, we both have to conquer our fears and try something we are afraid of.
You taught me that breaking the rules, in an itsy-bitsy, infinitesimal way, can be wonderful and freeing.
In return, I want to teach you how to fly again!
Face your fear. Become an even greater great adventurer.
Are you with me? Please say yes! Please say yes!
Nah. I'm already great. So great, in fact, that True Adventurer is my legal middle name.
We walk around.
Fine. Mr. Baz True Adventurer ith a last name I don't know, we do this the hard way!
You're going to fly us over this crevice! You will make my shortcut complete!
I never should have made you my sidekick or talked to you about shortcuts! You're insane!

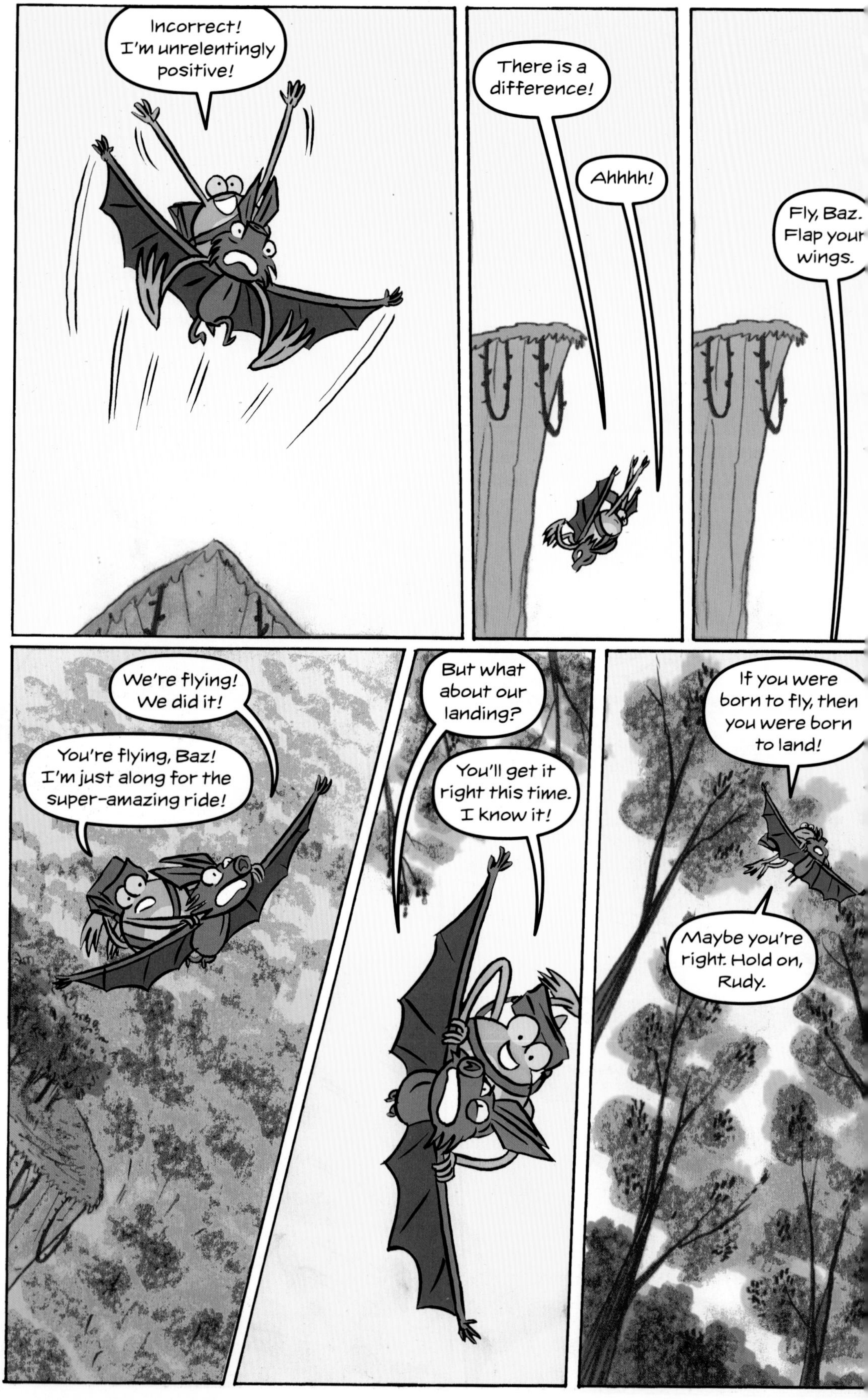

Incorrect! I'm unrelentingly positive!
There is a difference!
Ahhhh!
Fly, Baz. Flap your wings.
We're flying! We did it!
You're flying, Baz! I'm just along for the super-amazing ride!
But what about our landing?
You'll get it right this time. I know it!
If you were born to fly, then you were born to land!
Maybe you're right. Hold on, Rudy.

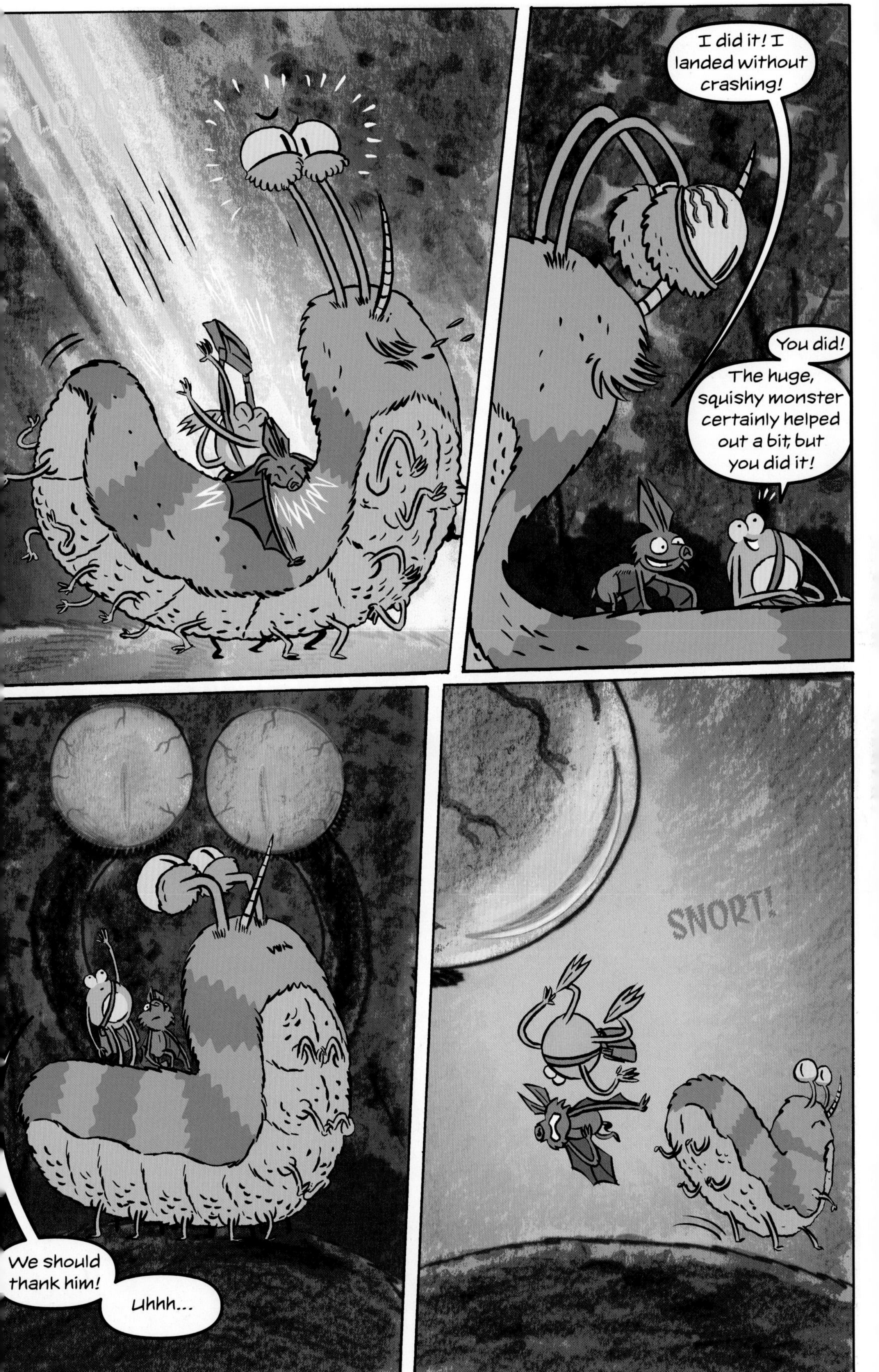
I did it! I landed without crashing!
You did!
The huge, squishy monster certainly helped out a bit, but you did it!
We should thank him!
Uhhh...
SNORT!

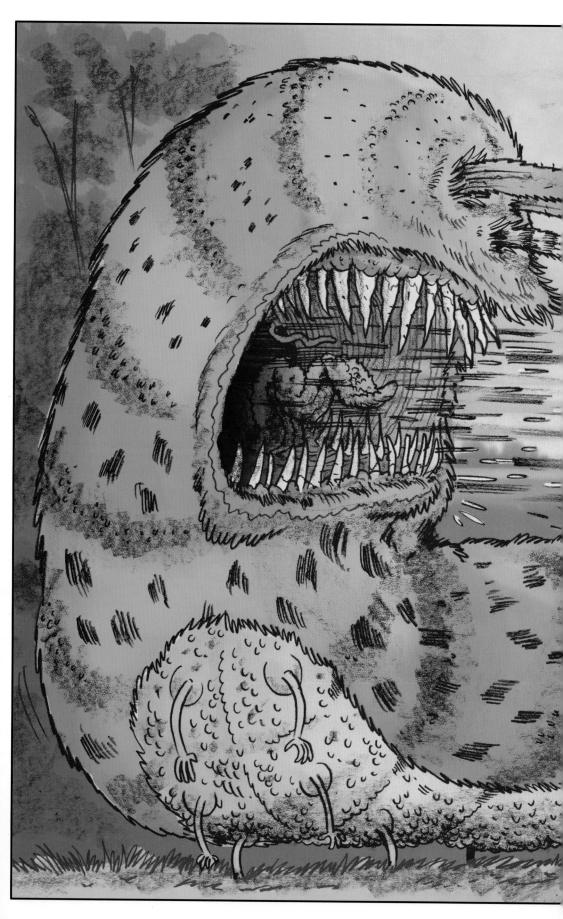

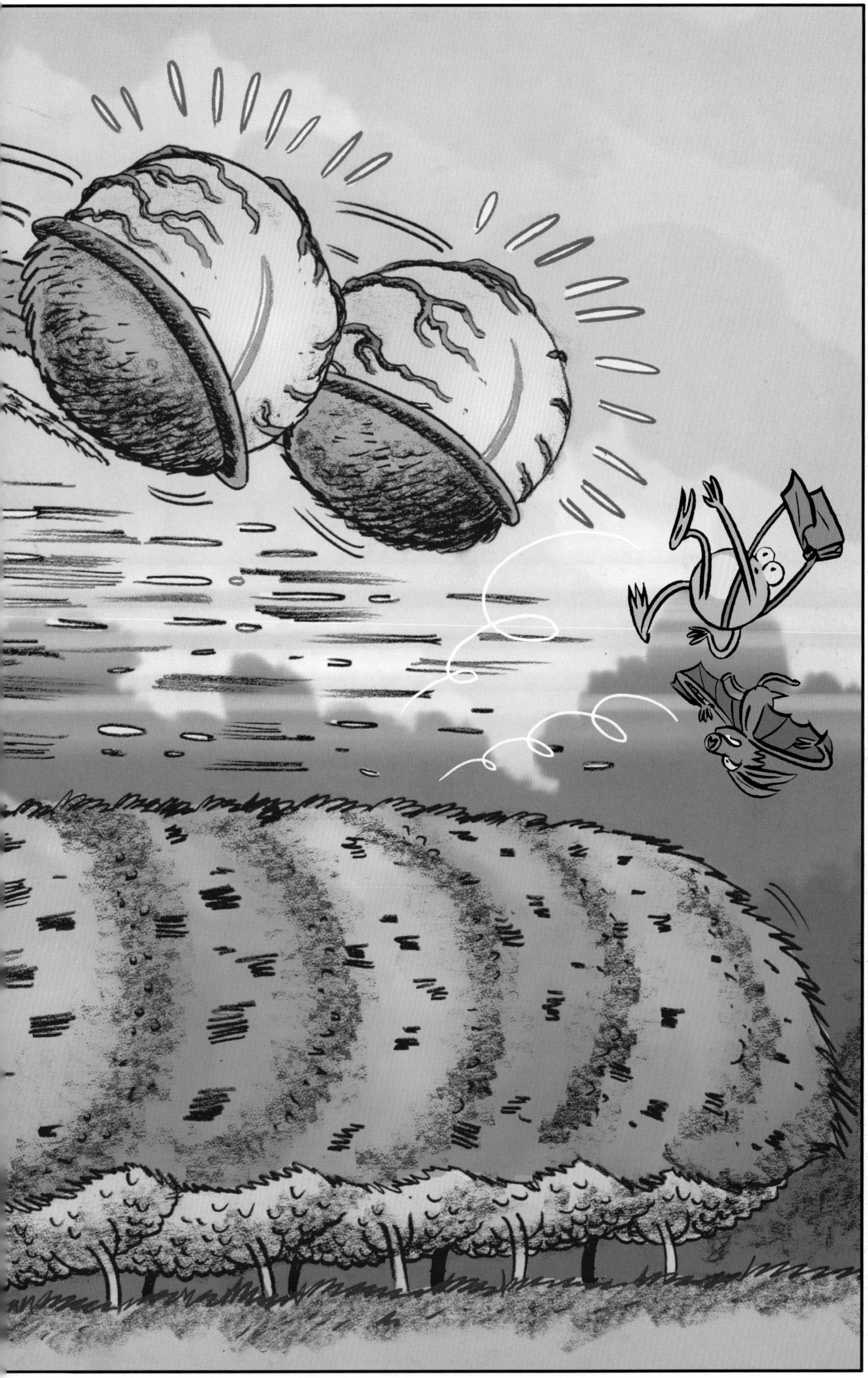

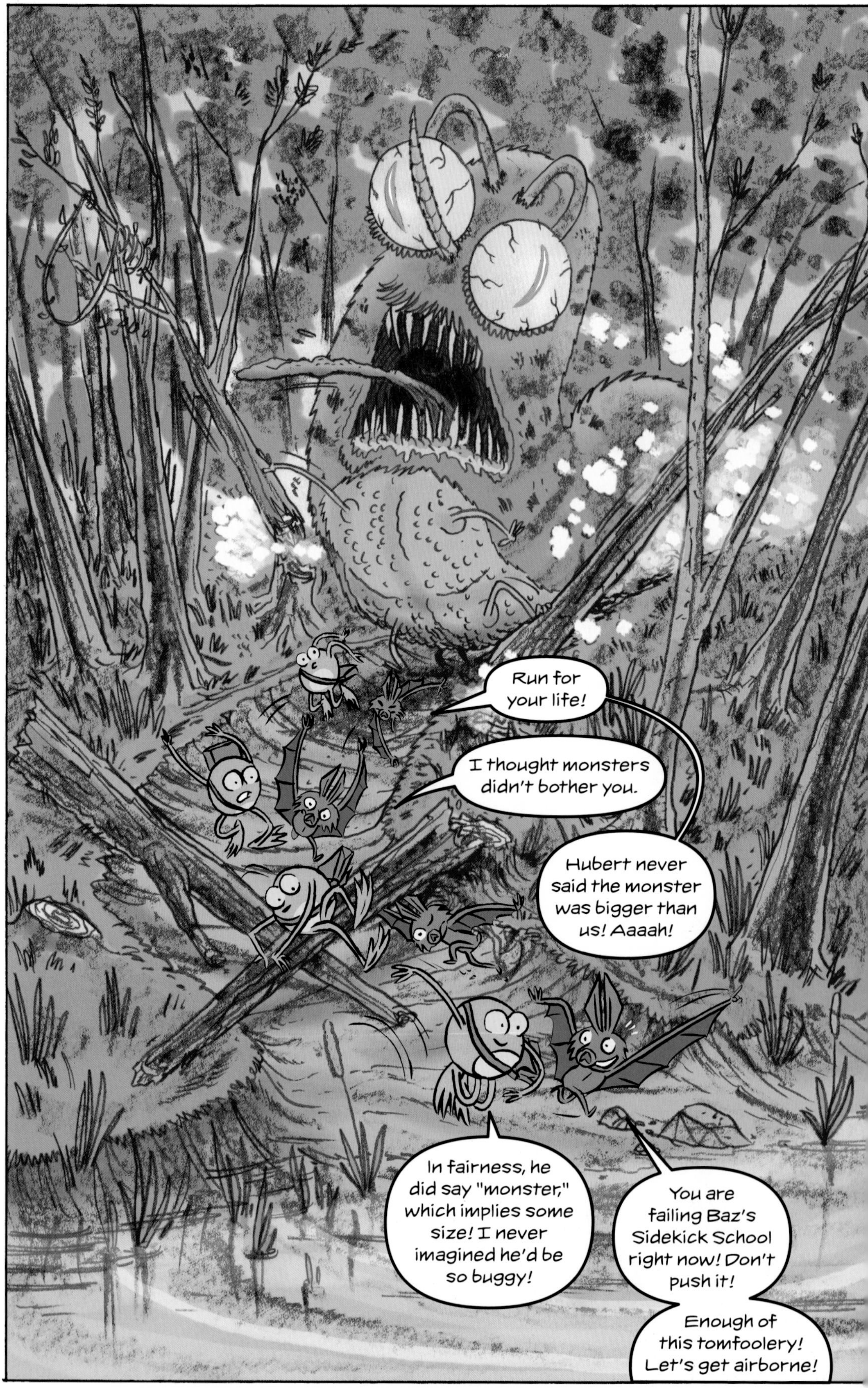
Run for your life!
I thought monsters didn't bother you.
Hubert never said the monster was bigger than us! Aaaah!
In fairness, he did say "monster," which implies some size! I never imagined he'd be so buggy!
You are failing Baz's Sidekick School right now! Don't push it!
Enough of this tomfoolery! Let's get airborne!

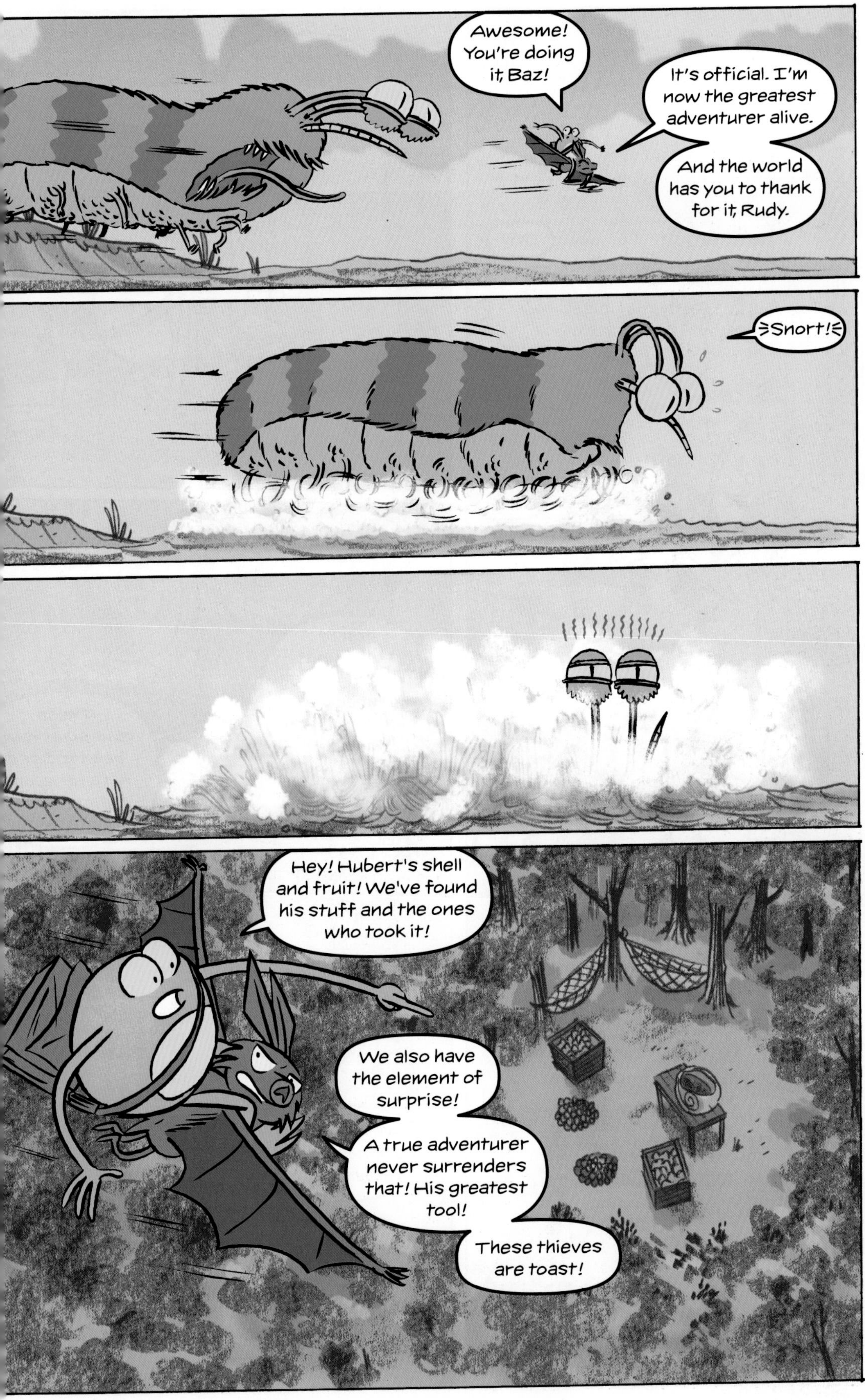
Awesome! You're doing it, Baz!
It's official. I'm now the greatest adventurer alive.
And the world has you to thank for it, Rudy.
Snort!
Hey! Hubert's shell and fruit! We've found his stuff and the ones who took it!
We also have the element of surprise!
A true adventurer never surrenders that! His greatest tool!
These thieves are toast!

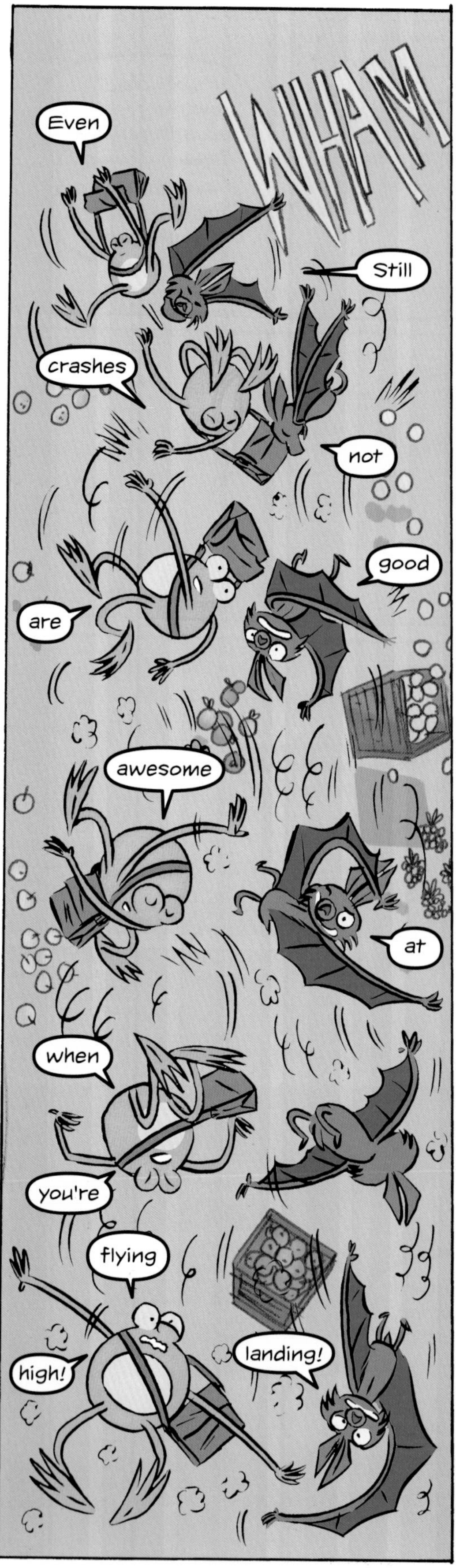
Even
WHAM
Still
crashes
not
good
are
awesome
at
when
you're
flying
high!
landing!

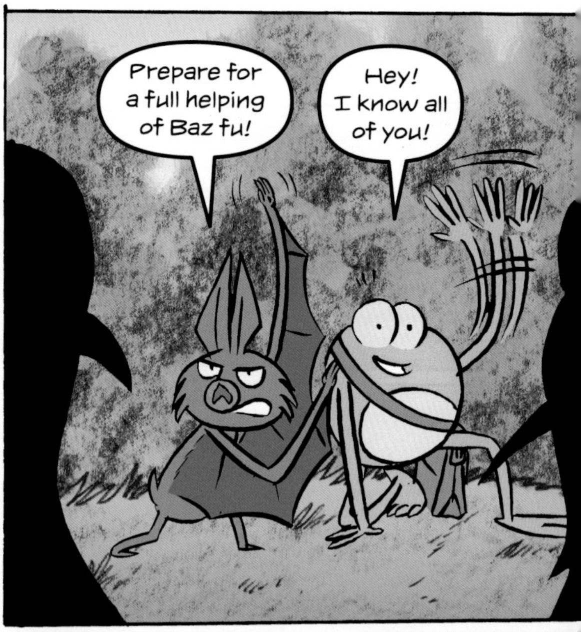
Prepare for a full helping of Baz fu!
Hey! I know all of you!

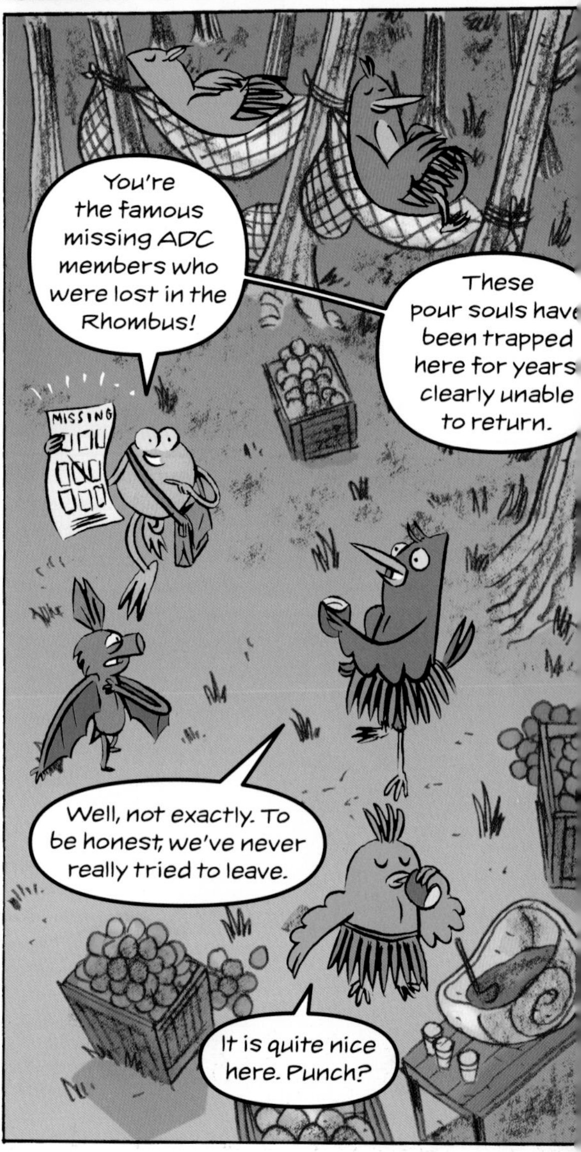
You're the famous missing ADC members who were lost in the Rhombus!
MISSING
These pour souls have been trapped here for years clearly unable to return.
Well, not exactly. To be honest, we've never really tried to leave.
It is quite nice here. Punch?

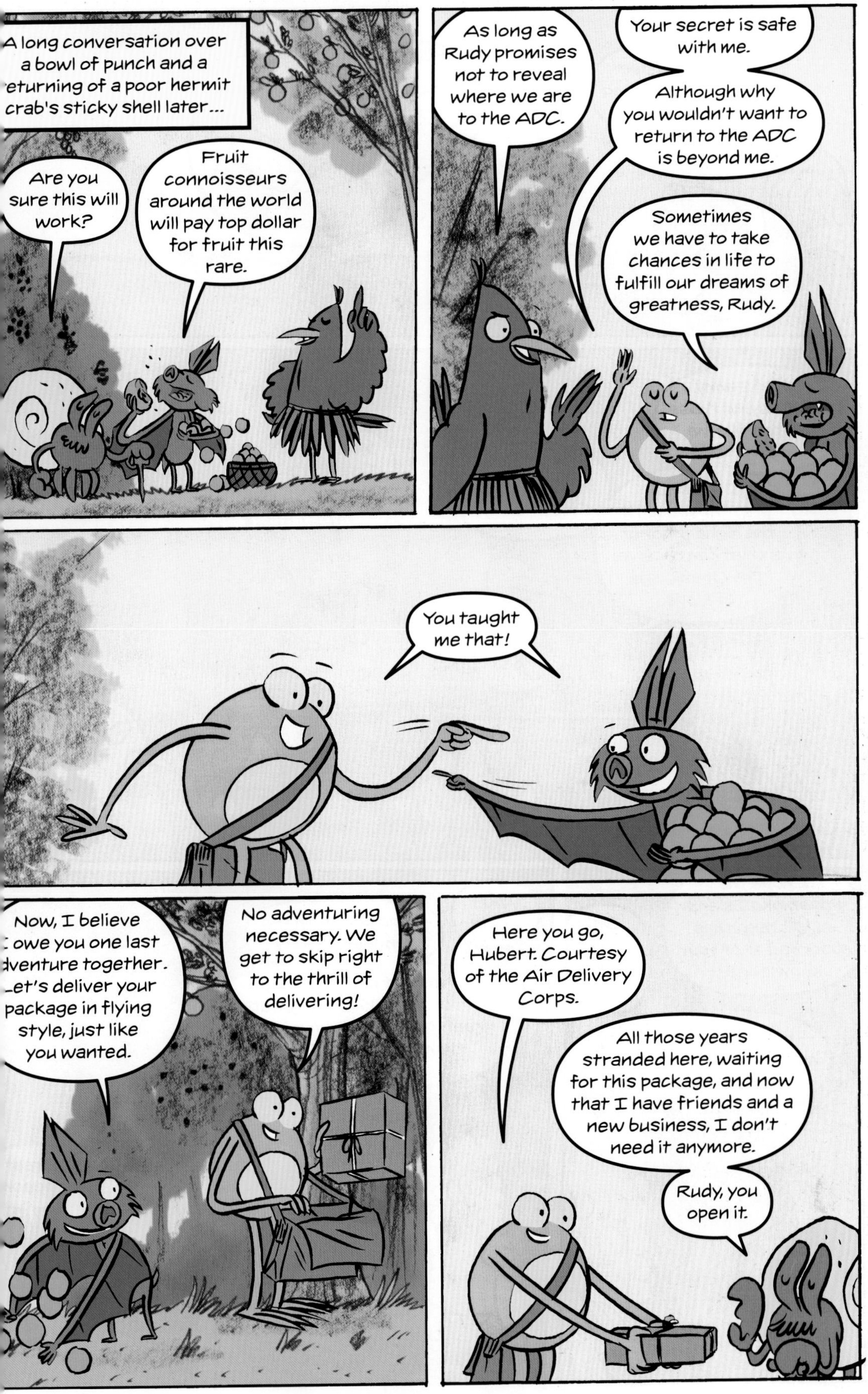
A long conversation over a bowl of punch and a returning of a poor hermit crab's sticky shell later...
Are you sure this will work?
Fruit connoisseurs around the world will pay top dollar for fruit this rare.
As long as Rudy promises not to reveal where we are to the ADC.
Your secret is safe with me.
Although why you wouldn't want to return to the ADC is beyond me.
Sometimes we have to take chances in life to fulfill our dreams of greatness, Rudy.
You taught me that!
Now, I believe I owe you one last adventure together. Let's deliver your package in flying style, just like you wanted.
No adventuring necessary. We get to skip right to the thrill of delivering!
Here you go, Hubert. Courtesy of the Air Delivery Corps.
All those years stranded here, waiting for this package, and now that I have friends and a new business, I don't need it anymore.
Rudy, you open it.

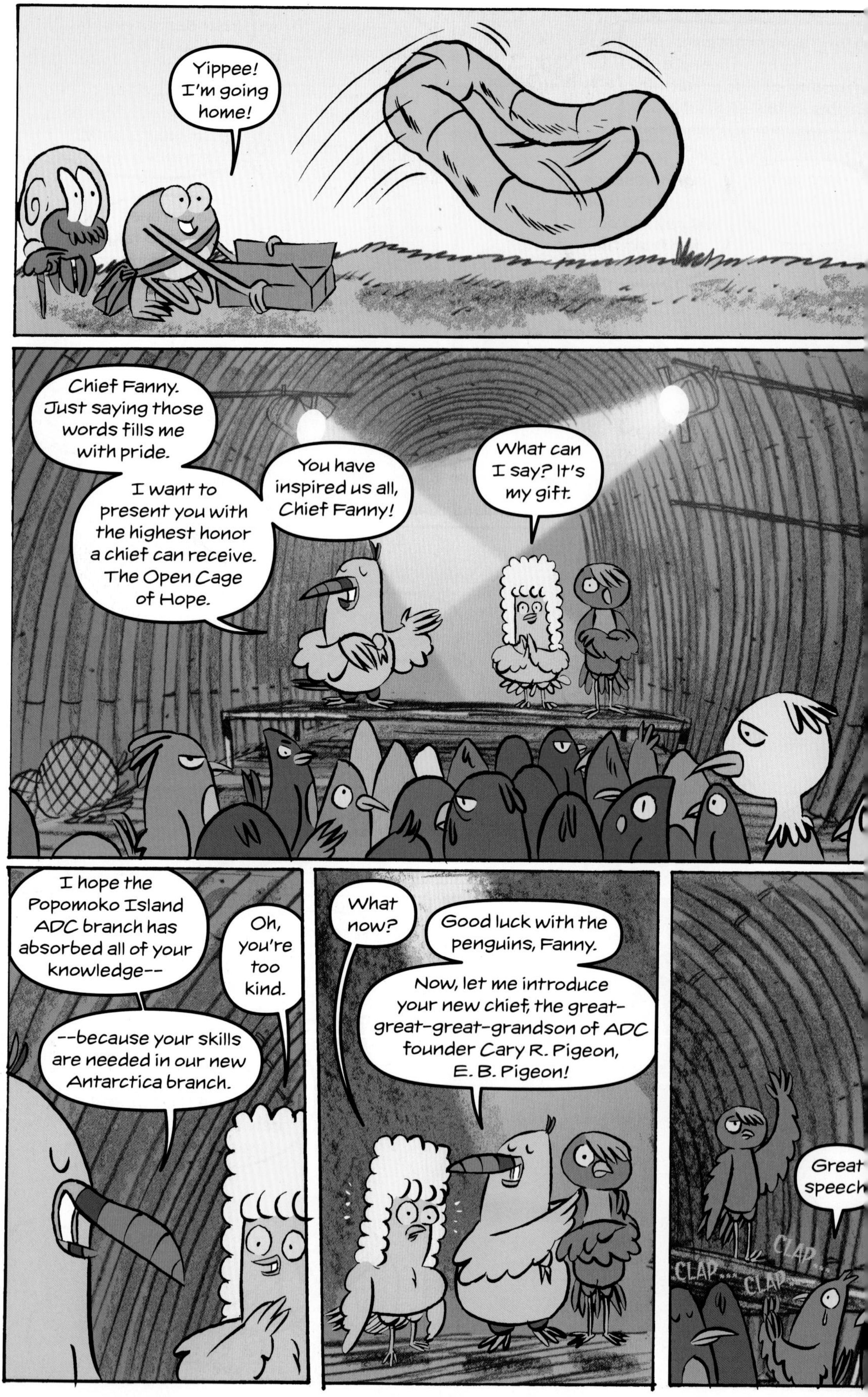
Yippee! I'm going home!
Chief Fanny. Just saying those words fills me with pride.
I want to present you with the highest honor a chief can receive. The Open Cage of Hope.
You have inspired us all, Chief Fanny!
What can I say? It's my gift.
I hope the Popomoko Island ADC branch has absorbed all of your knowledge--
Oh, you're too kind.
--because your skills are needed in our new Antarctica branch.
What now?
Good luck with the penguins, Fanny.
Now, let me introduce your new chief, the great-great-great-grandson of ADC founder Cary R. Pigeon, E. B. Pigeon!
Great speech
CLAP... CLAP... CLAP...

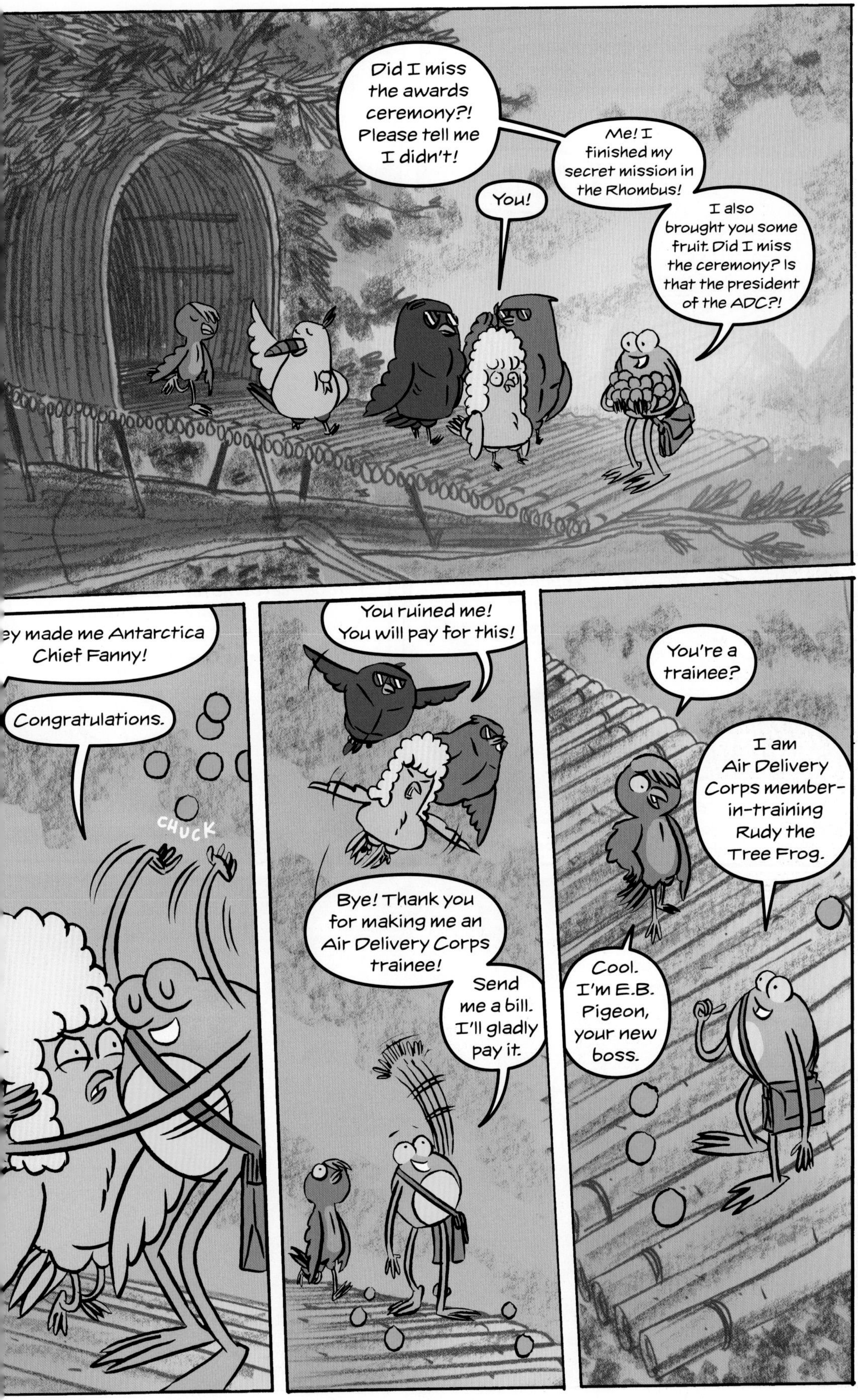

Did I miss the awards ceremony?! Please tell me I didn't!
Me! I finished my secret mission in the Rhombus!
You!
I also brought you some fruit. Did I miss the ceremony? Is that the president of the ADC?!
ey made me Antarctica Chief Fanny!
Congratulations.
CHUCK
You ruined me! You will pay for this!
Bye! Thank you for making me an Air Delivery Corps trainee!
Send me a bill. I'll gladly pay it.
You're a trainee?
I am Air Delivery Corps member-in-training Rudy the Tree Frog.
Cool. I'm E.B. Pigeon, your new boss.

Noway!

You'rethegreatgreatgreat- grandsonofCaryRPigeon.Didyou- knowyourgreatgreatgreatgrandfath- erwasthefirstmailcarrier?

SHAKE SHAKE SHAKE

Uh, yeah. I'd heard that.

ThathecreatedtheADC- inhisbirdcage?

Thathewasthefirstbir tomakeatransatlanticflig withnowingmen?

Do you eve breathe?

CaryRPigeonisaheroof- mine.Iwanttobejustlike- himsomeday.

Thebestofthe- best.FlieroftheYear!

It's been...interesting speaking with you, Delivery Corps member Rudy.

Good day.

Didyouhearthatworld? HecalledmeDeliveryCorpsmember- andthenmyname!

Somemightsaymewanting- tobeFlieroftheYearmakesnosense- becauseIdonthavewingstofly- butIdreambig.

Whatotherwayistheret

...dream?

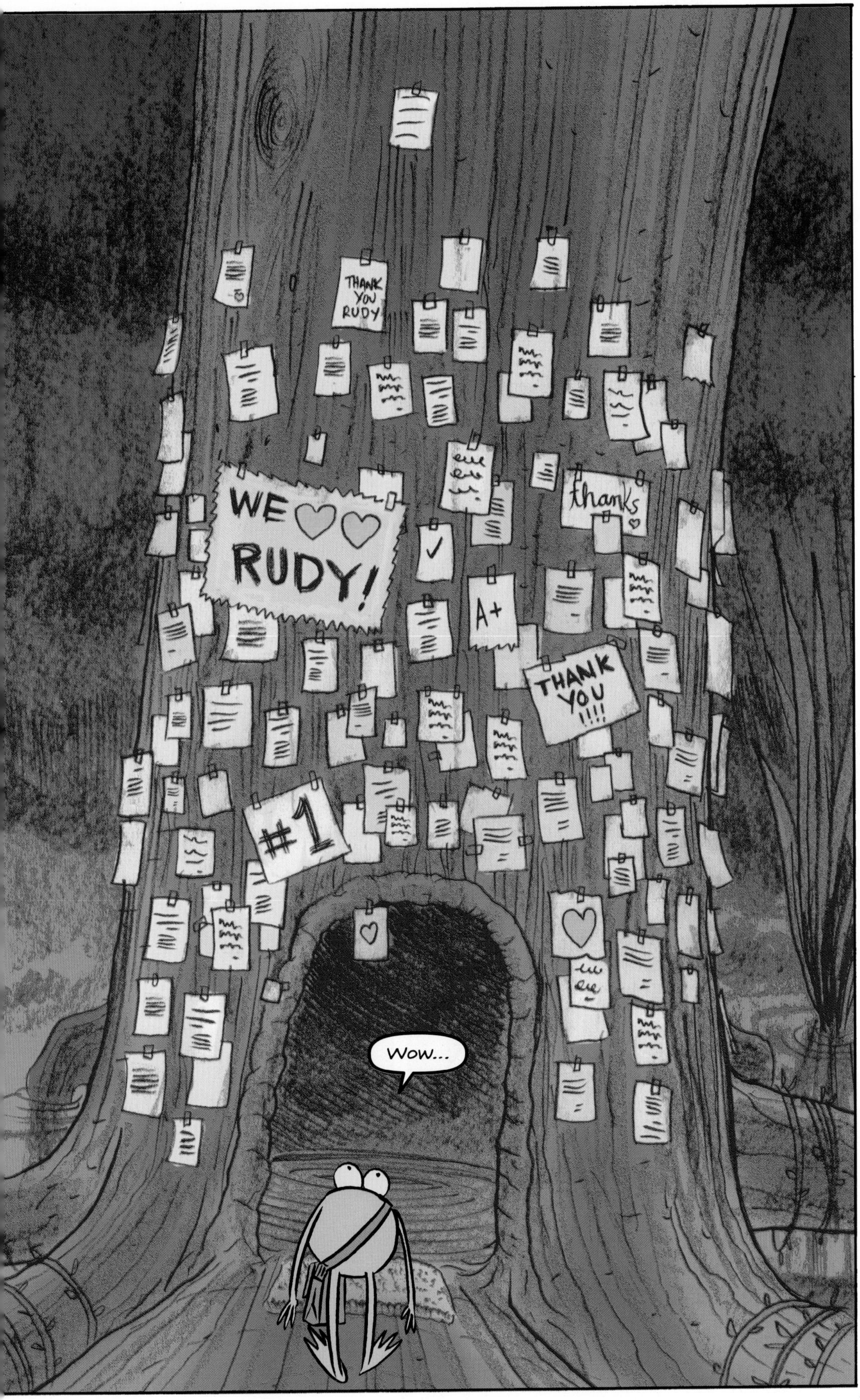
THANK YOU RUDY
WE ♡♡ RUDY!
thanks
A+
THANK YOU !!!!
#1
Wow...

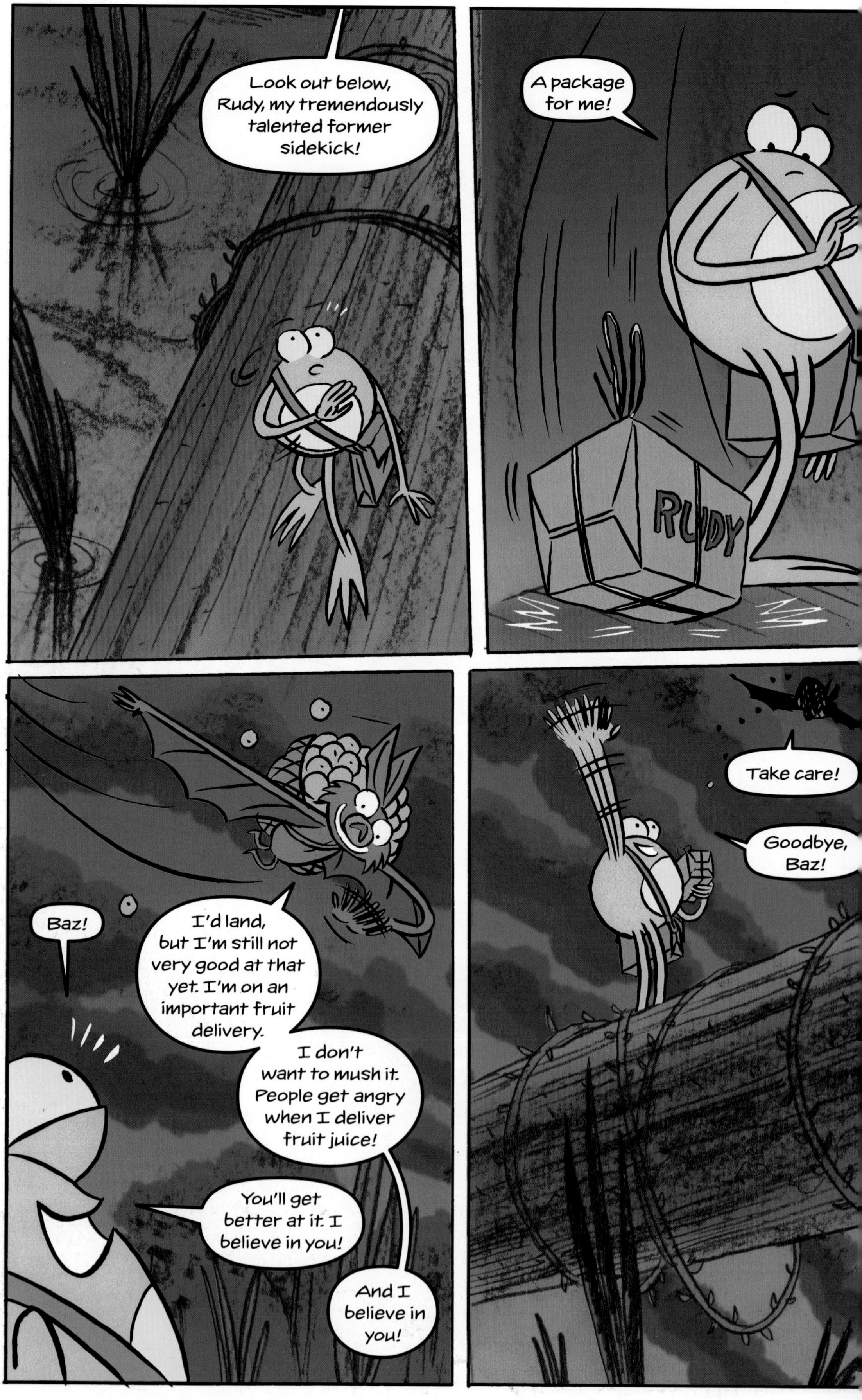
Look out below, Rudy, my tremendously talented former sidekick!
A package for me!
RUDY
I'd land, but I'm still not very good at that yet. I'm on an important fruit delivery.
I don't want to mush it. People get angry when I deliver fruit juice!
Baz!
You'll get better at it. I believe in you!
And I believe in you!
Take care!
Goodbye, Baz!

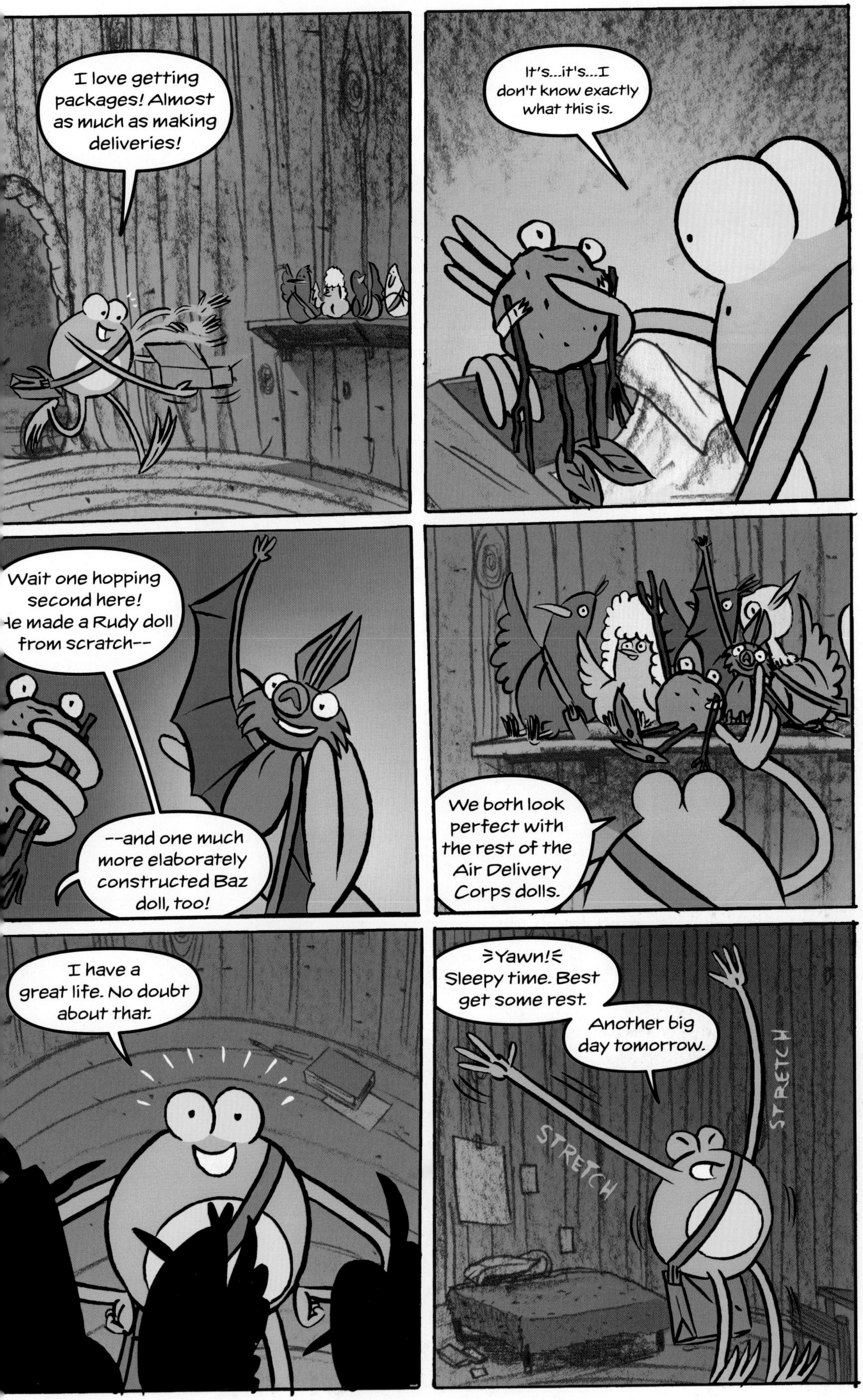
I love getting packages! Almost as much as making deliveries!
It's...it's...I don't know exactly what this is.
Wait one hopping second here! He made a Rudy doll from scratch--
--and one much more elaborately constructed Baz doll, too!
We both look perfect with the rest of the Air Delivery Corps dolls.
I have a great life. No doubt about that.
Yawn!
Sleepy time. Best get some rest.
Another big day tomorrow.
STRETCH
STRETCH

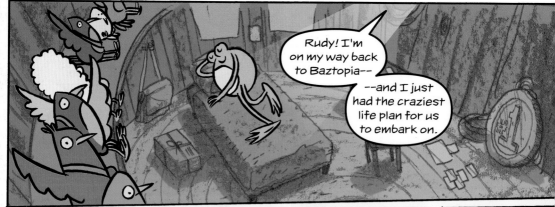

Rudy! I'm on my way back to Baztopia--

--and I just had the craziest life plan for us to embark on.

Oh. Sorry. You've already set down your wheels for the night.

We'll get to it next time, friend.

Sleep tight, Rudy the Tree Frog!

Dream of clear skies, perfectly delivered packages, and pleasant-- uh-oh! Tough wind gust!

Mayday! Mayday!

SMACK!

...False alarm.

I'm all right.

I think.

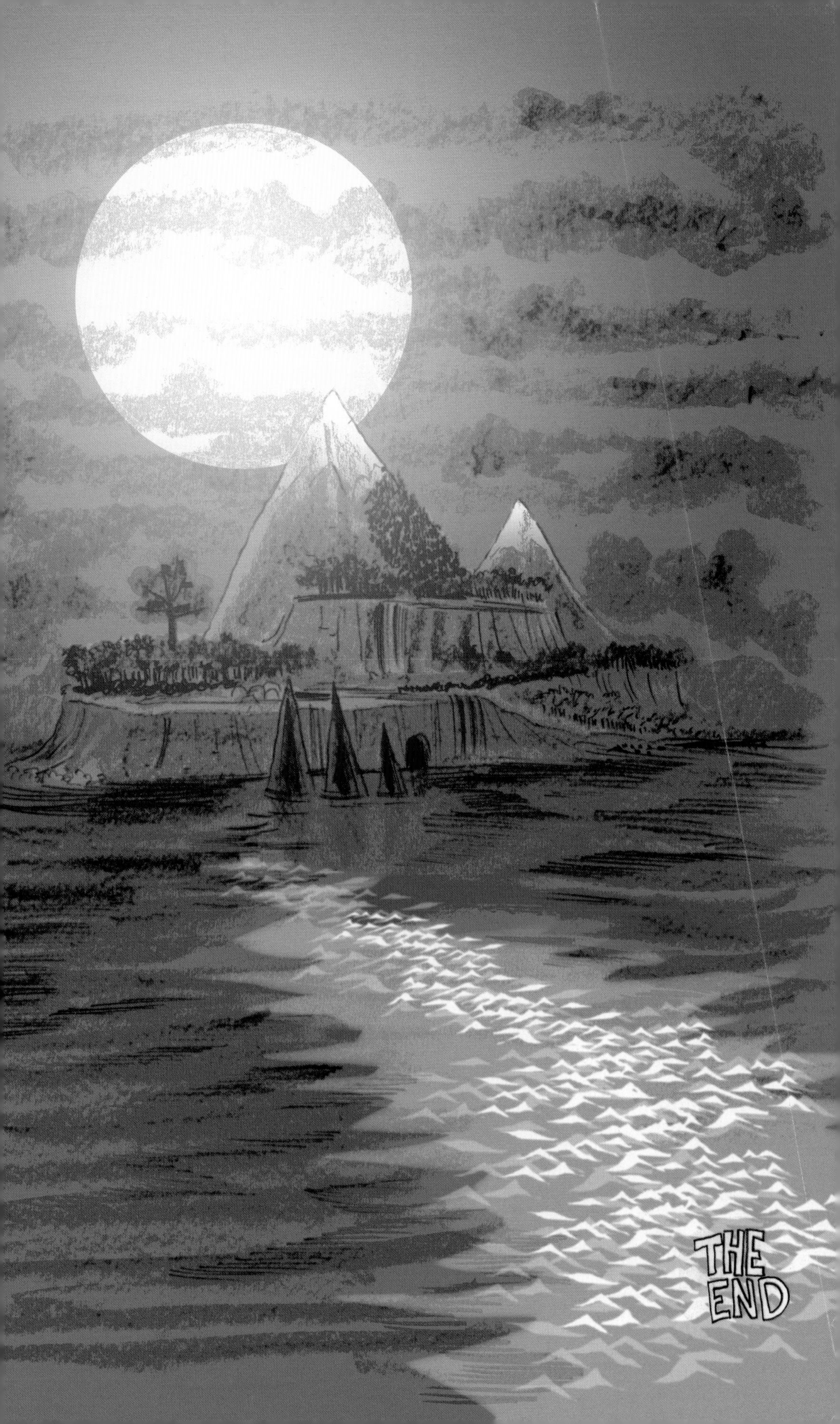
THE END

RUDY'S RADICALLY SNAZZY SKETCHBOOK SECTION!

Sketches, illustrations, and rough layouts by
Tree Mail co-creator Brian Smith

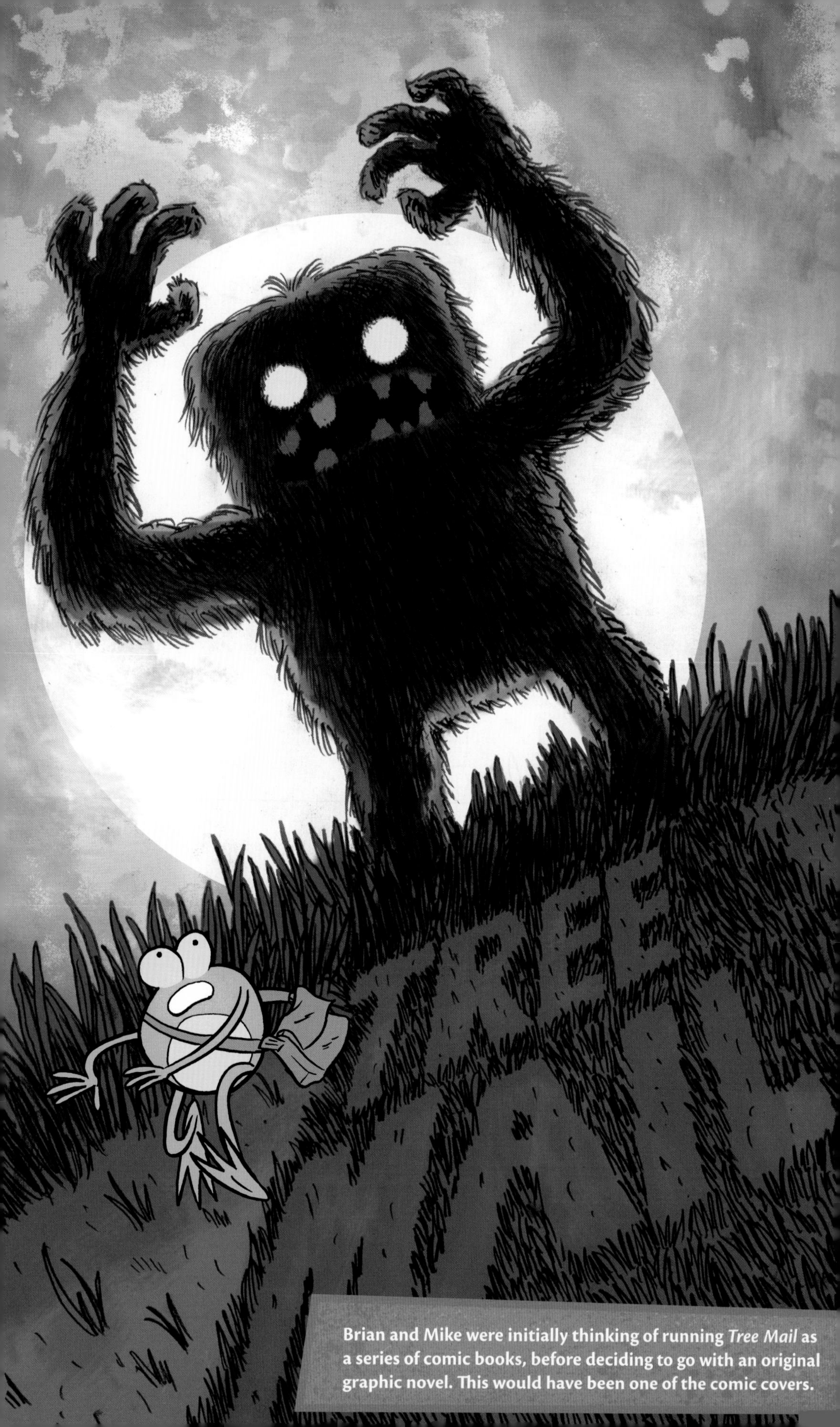

Brian and Mike were initially thinking of running *Tree Mail* as a series of comic books, before deciding to go with an original graphic novel. This would have been one of the comic covers.

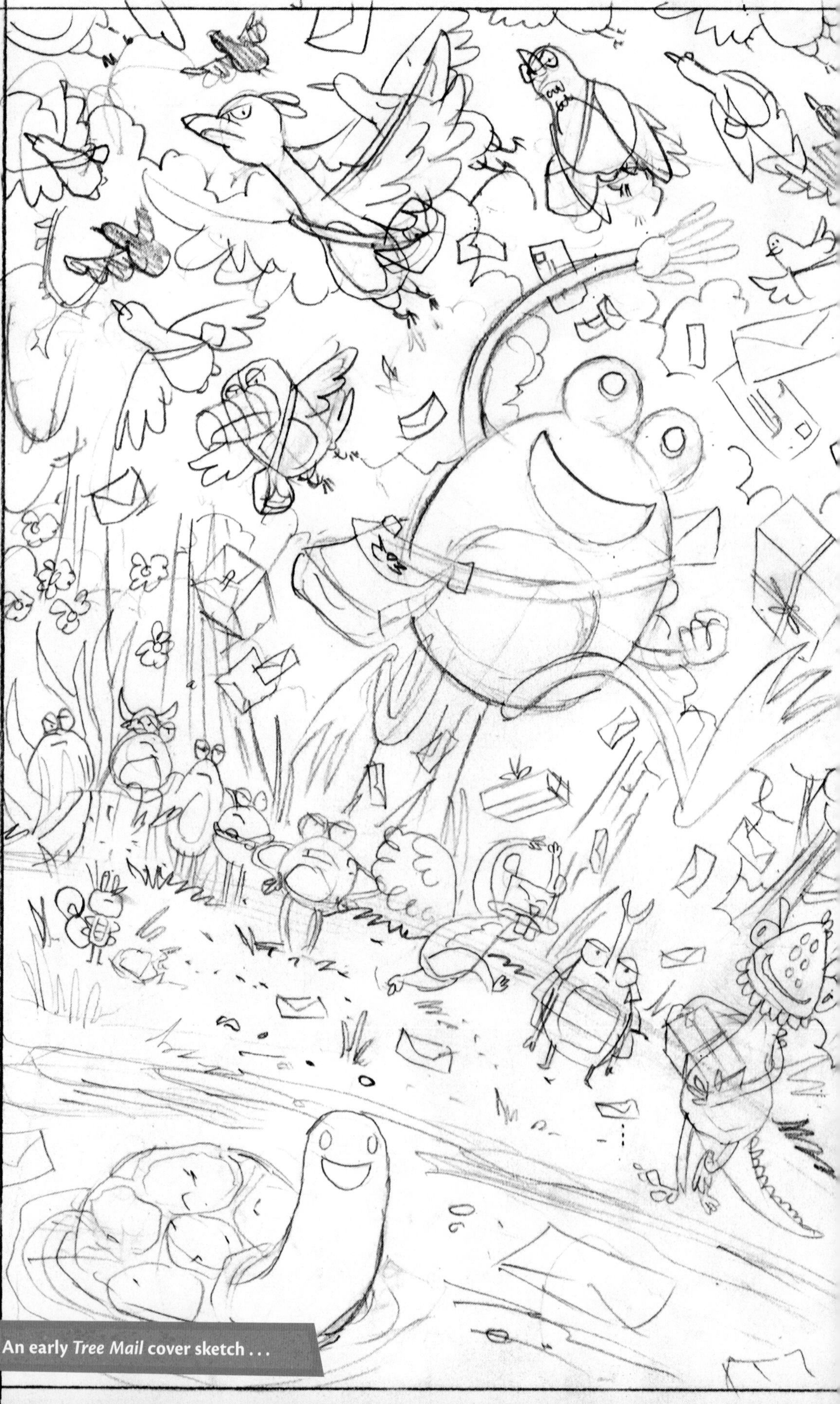

An early *Tree Mail* cover sketch . . .

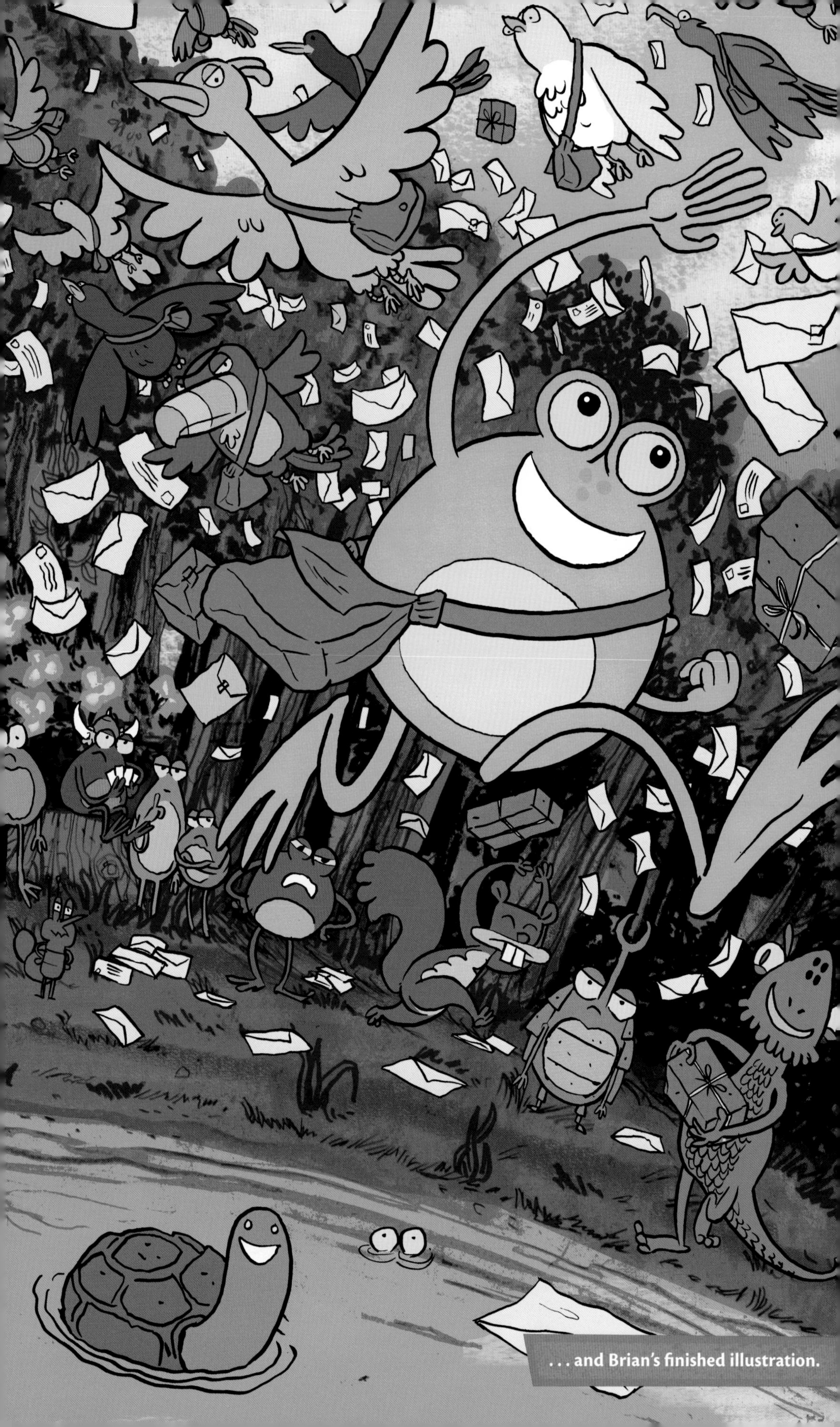

. . . and Brian's finished illustration.

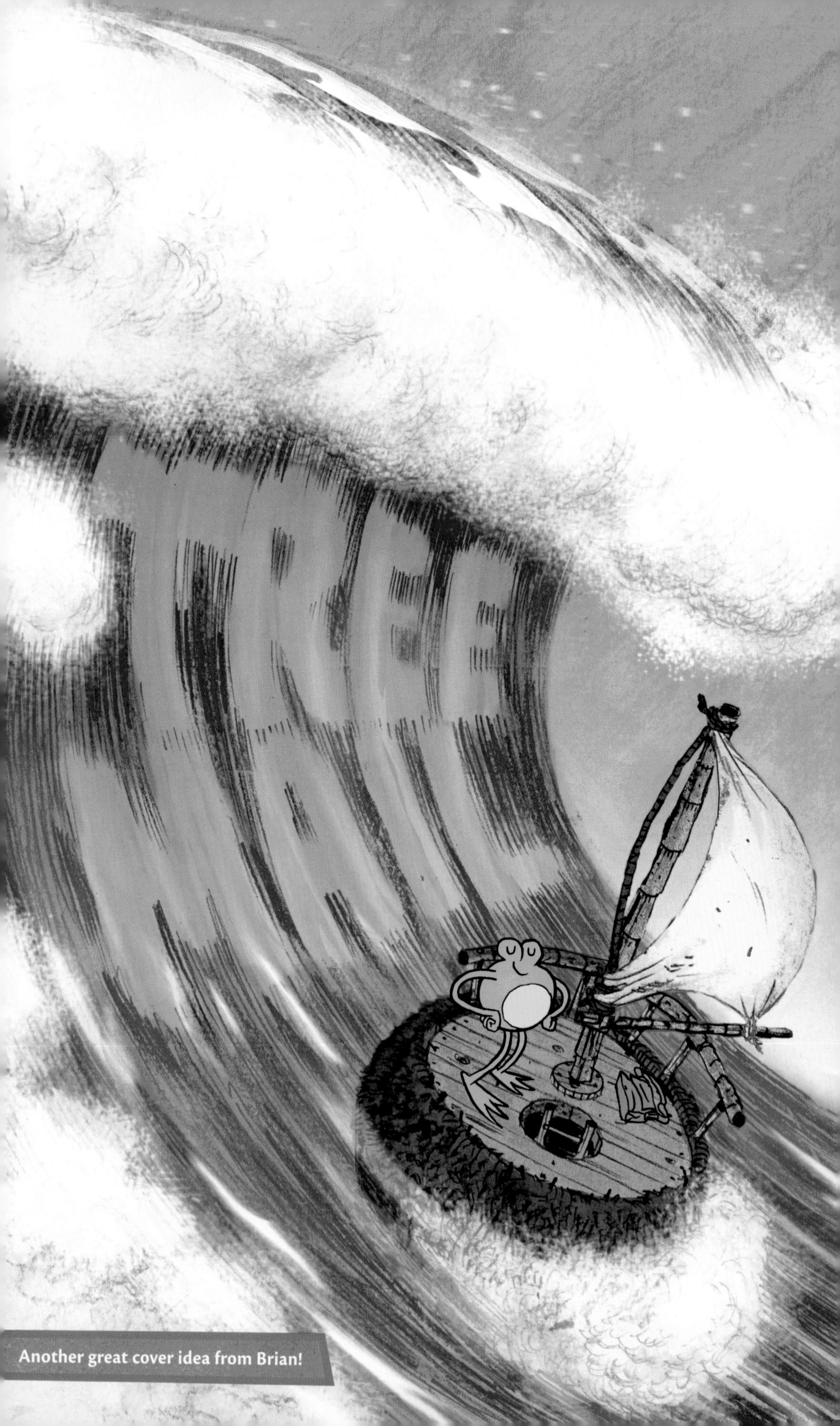

Another great cover idea from Brian!

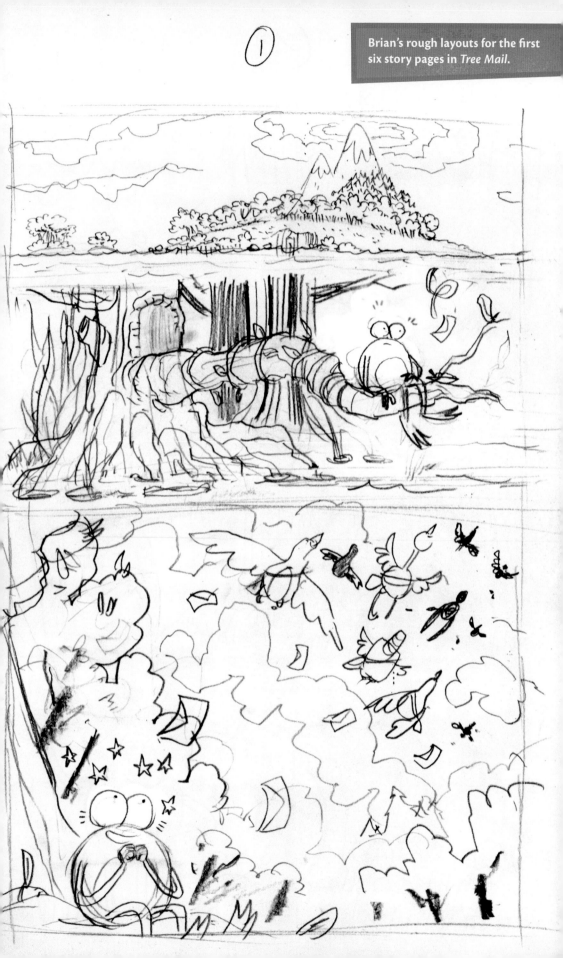

Brian's rough layouts for the first six story pages in *Tree Mail*.

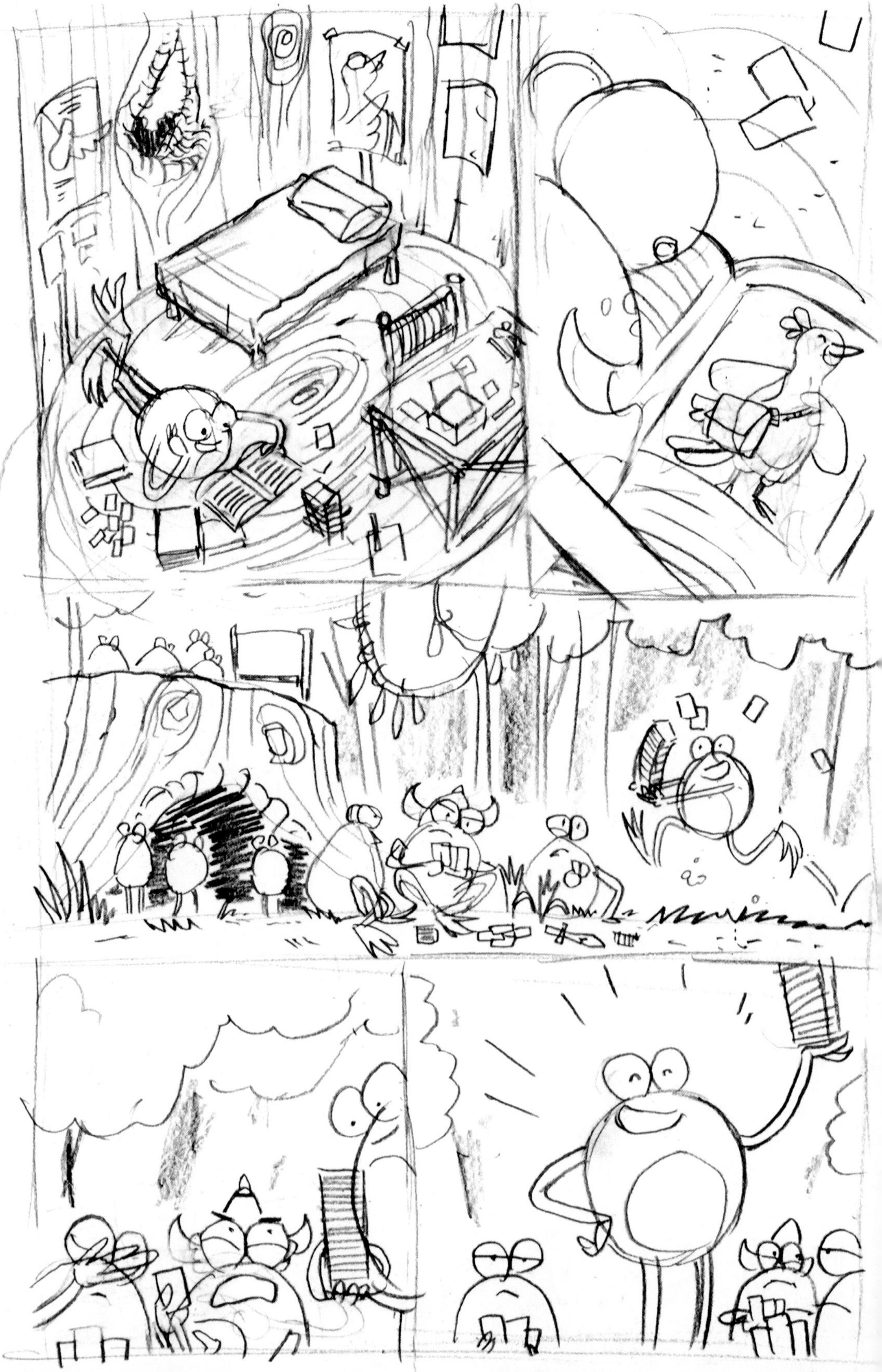

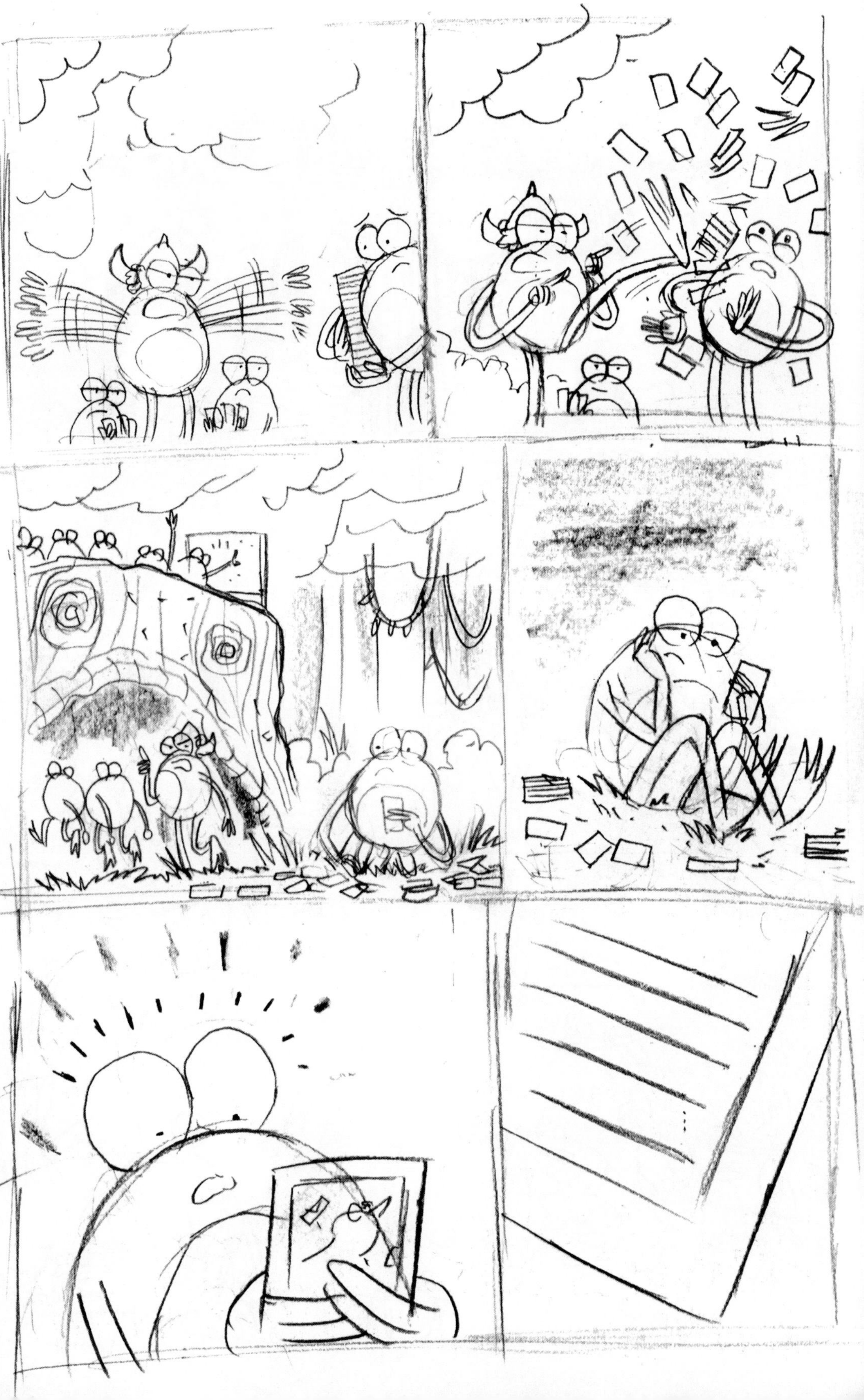

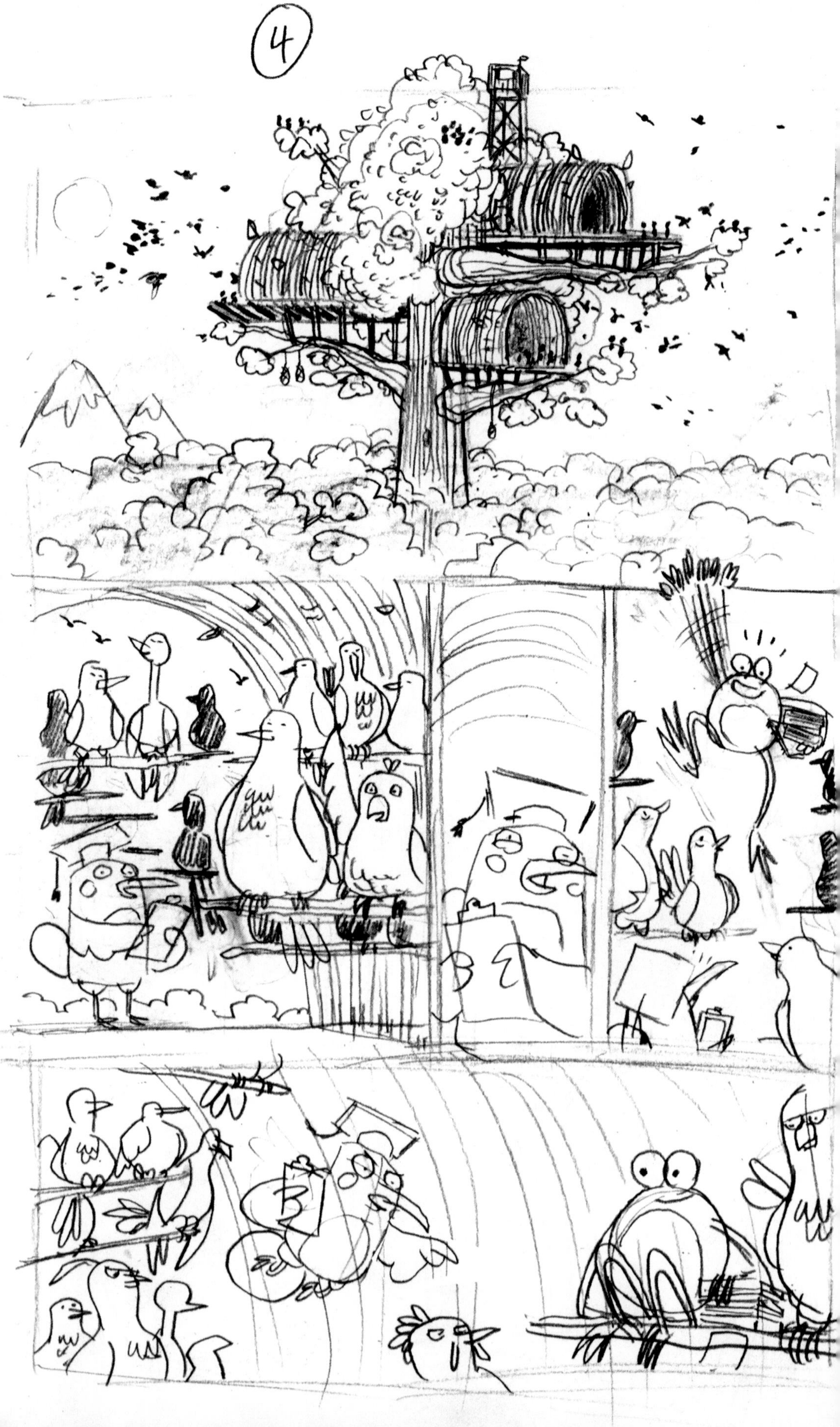
4

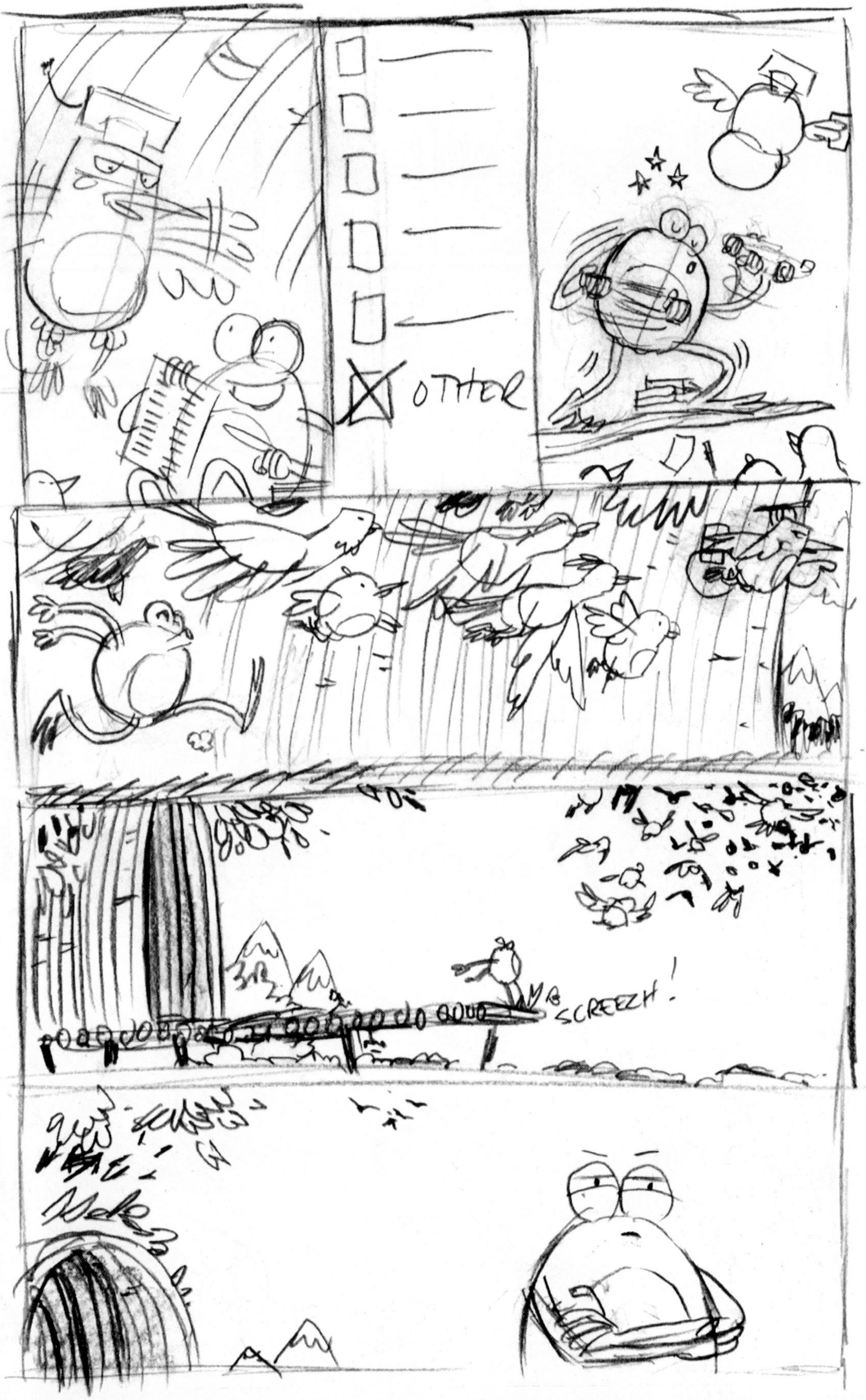
OTHER
SCREEZH!

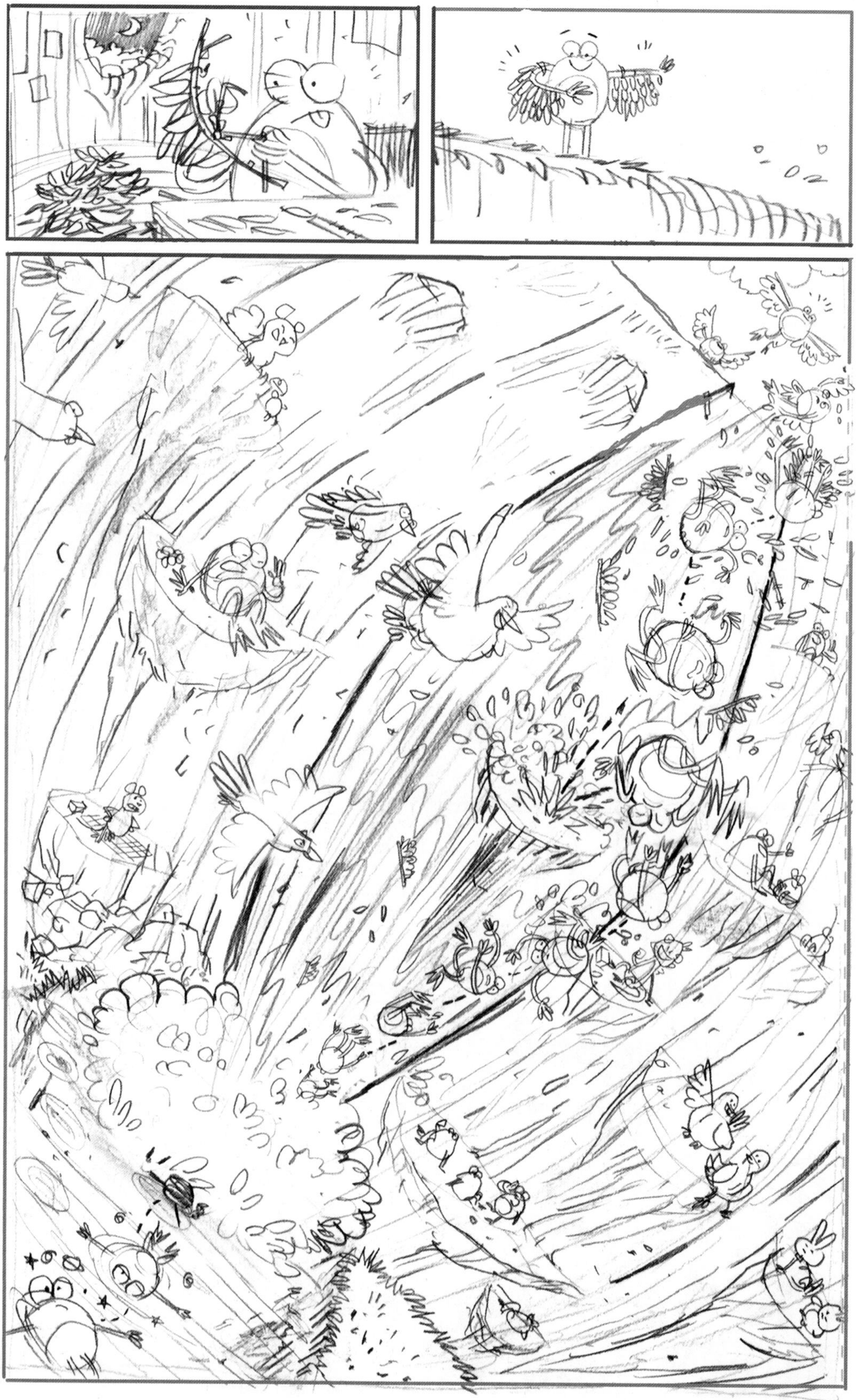

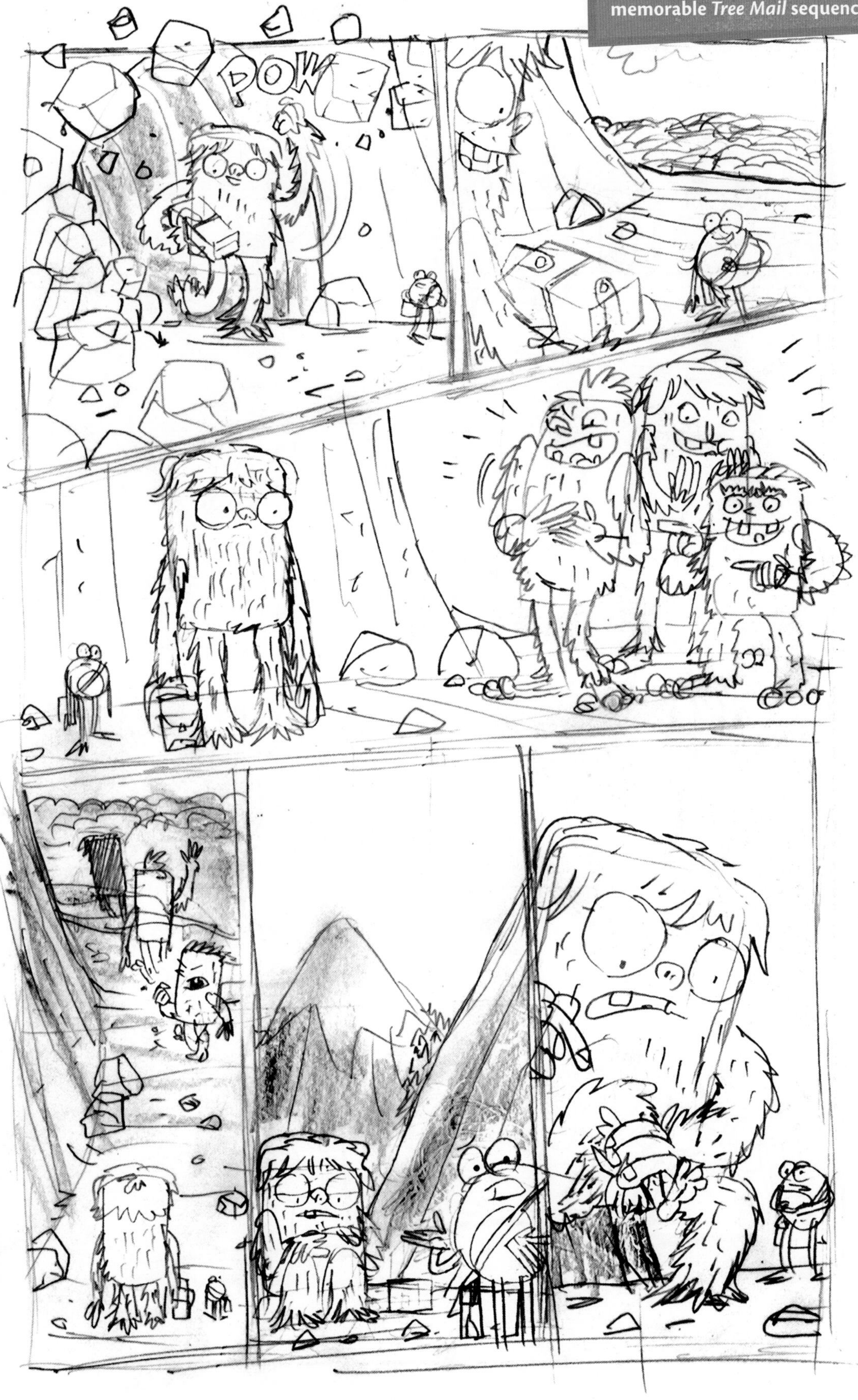
POW

Brian's layouts for another memorable *Tree Mail* sequence.

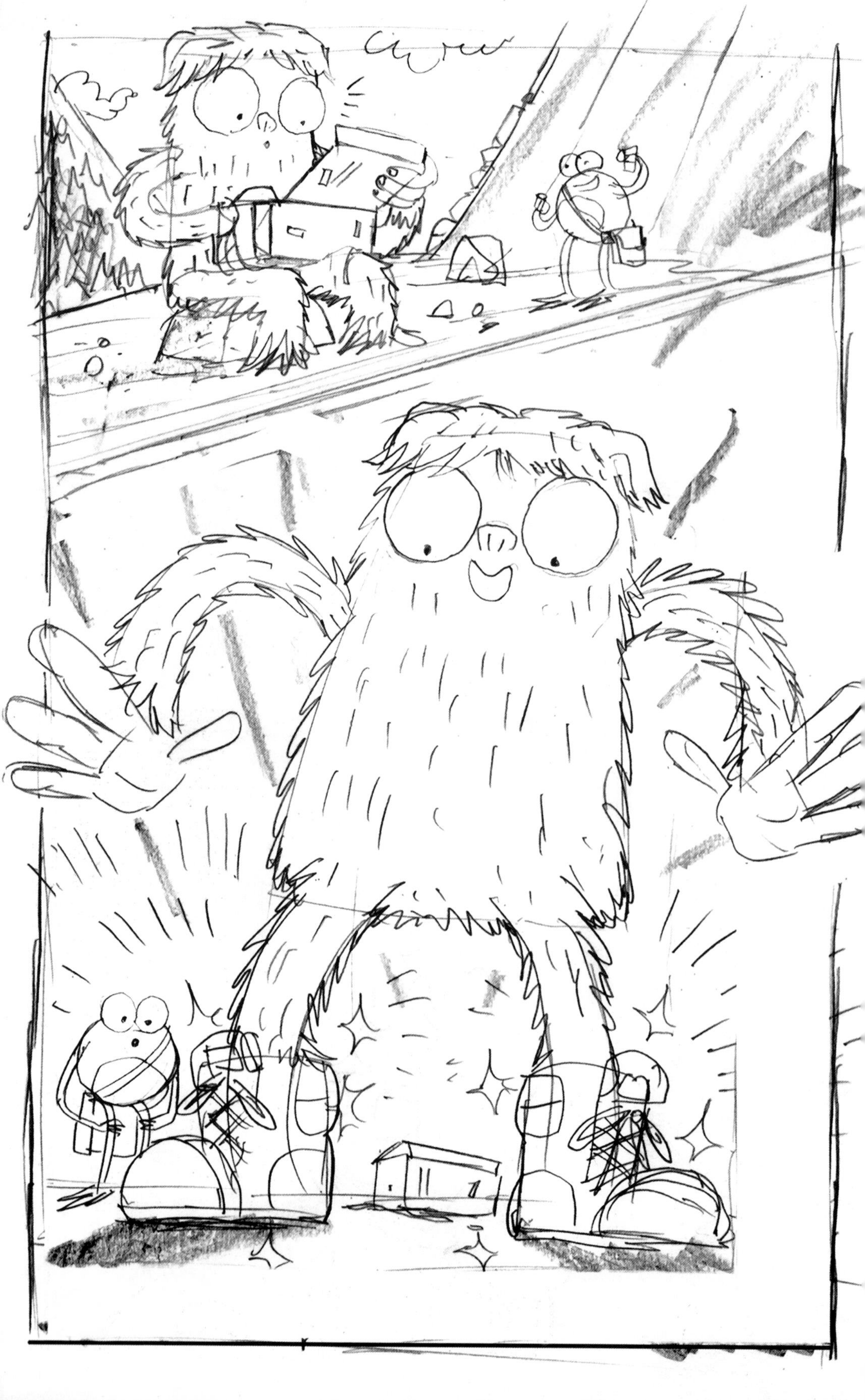

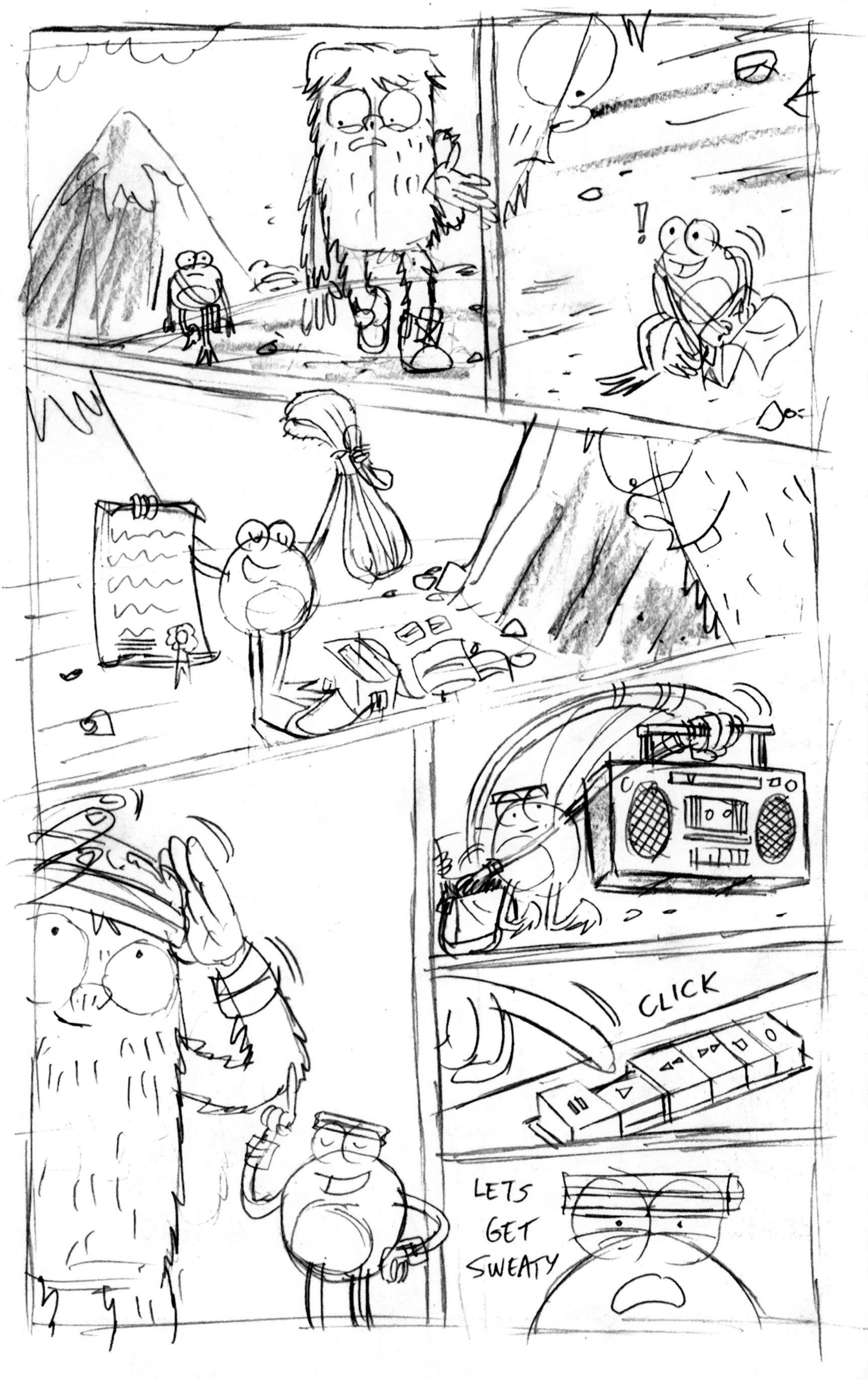
!
CLICK
LETS GET SWEATY

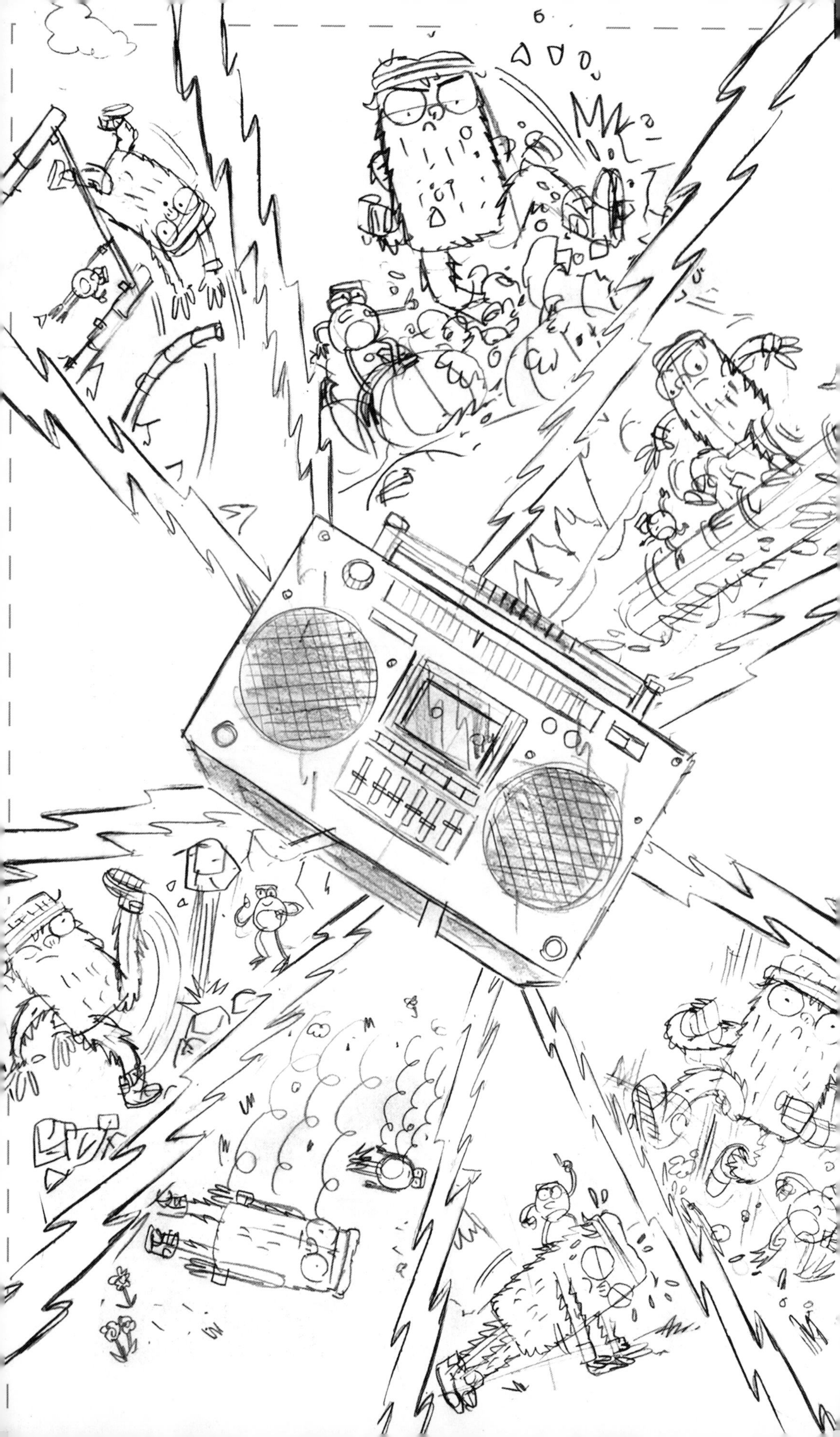

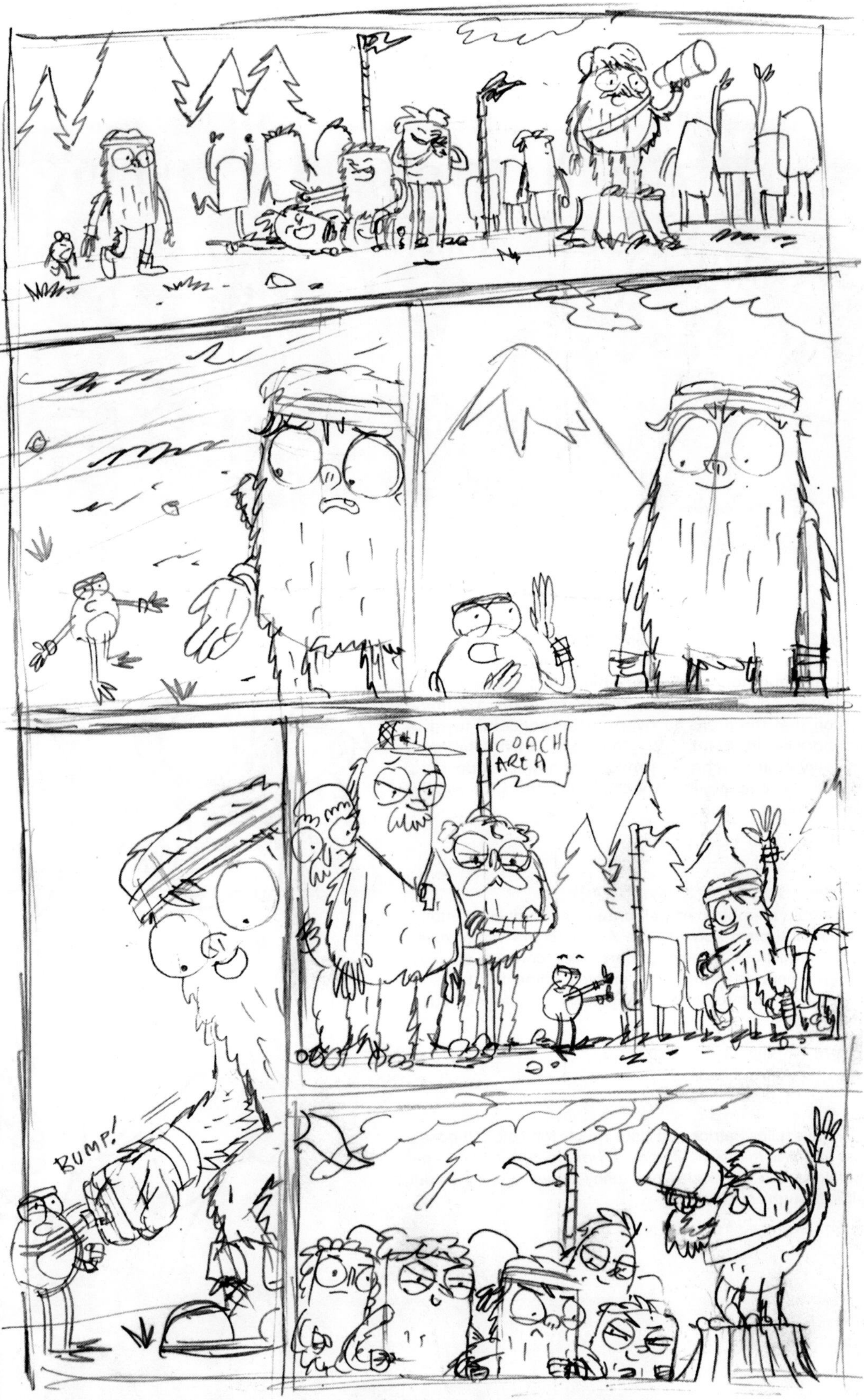
COACH AREA
BUMP!

ALSO AVAILABLE FROM DARK HORSE

THE HIT VIDEO GAME CONTINUES ITS COMIC BOOK INVASION!

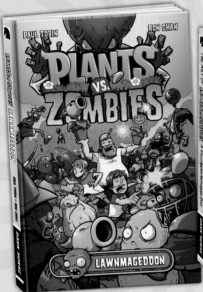  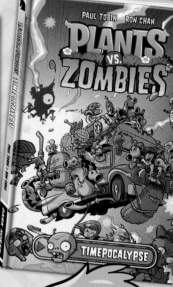

PLANTS VS. ZOMBIES: LAWNMAGEDDON

Crazy Dave—the babbling-yet-brilliant inventor and top-notch neighborhood defender—helps his niece Patrice and young adventurer Nate Timely fend off a zombie invasion that threatens to overrun the peaceful town of Neighborville in *Plants vs. Zombies: Lawnmageddon*! Their only hope is a brave army of chomping, squashing, and pea-shooting plants! A wacky adventure for zombie zappers young and old!

ISBN 978-1-61655-192-6 | $9.99

THE ART OF PLANTS VS. ZOMBIES

Part zombie memoir, part celebration of zombie triumphs, and part anti-plant screed, *The Art of Plants vs. Zombies* is a treasure trove of never-before-seen concept art from PopCap's popular *Plants vs. Zombies* games! A treasure trove of never-before-seen concept art, character sketches, and surprises!

ISBN 978-1-61655-331-9 | $9.99

PLANTS VS. ZOMBIES: TIMEPOCALYPSE

Crazy Dave helps Patrice and Nate Timely fend off Zomboss's latest attack in *Plants vs. Zombies: Timepocalypse*! This new standalone tale will tickle your funny bones and thrill your brains through any timeline!

ISBN 978-1-61655-621-1 | $9.99

AVAILABLE AT YOUR LOCAL COMICS SHOP OR BOOKSTORE
To find a comics shop in your area, call 1-888-266-4226
For more information or to order direct visit **DarkHorse.com** or call 1-800-862-0052

Plants vs. Zombies © Electronic Arts Inc. Plants vs. Zombies, PopCap, EA, and the EA logo are trademarks of Electronic Arts Inc. Dark Horse Books® and the Dark Horse logo are registered trademarks of Dark Horse Comics, Inc. All rights reserved. (BL 6012)

DISCOVER THE ADVENTURE!

Explore these beloved books for the entire family.

AVAILABLE AT YOUR LOCAL COMICS SHOP OR BOOKSTORE

To find a comics shop in your area, call 1-888-266-4226. For more information or to order direct visit DarkHorse.com or call 1-800-862-0052.

DARK HORSE COMICS

kHorse.com

Bird Boy™ © Anne Szabla. Chimichanga™ © Eric Powell. Plants vs. Zombies © Electronic Arts Inc. Plants vs. Zombies, PopCap, EA, and the EA logo are trademarks of Electronic Arts Inc. Scary Godmother™ © Jill Thompson. Usagi Yojimbo™ © Stan Sakai. Dark Horse Comics® and the Dark Horse logo are trademarks of Dark Horse Comics, Inc., registered in various categories and countries. All rights reserved. (BL 6011)

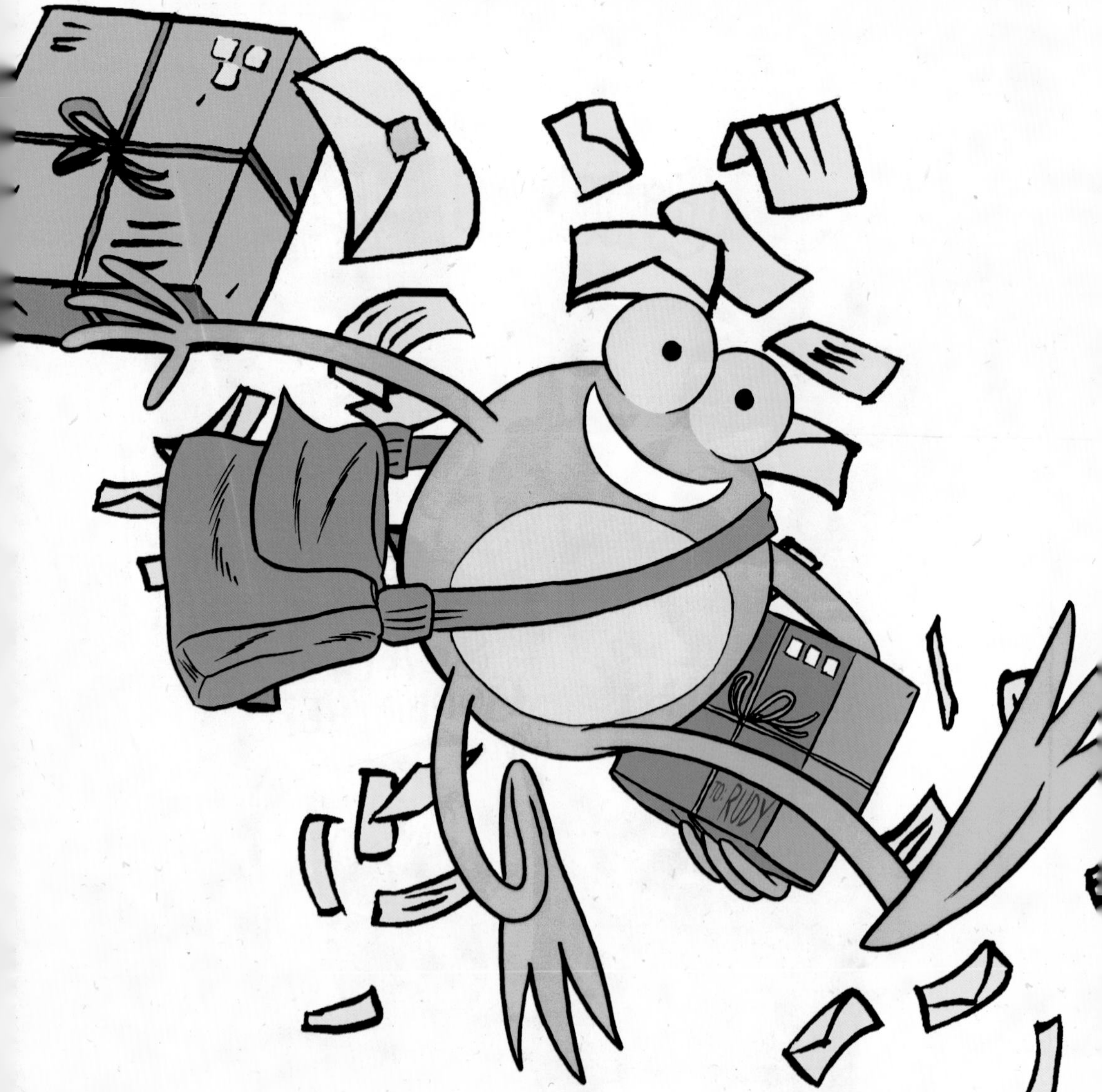
TO: RUDY